"Nan Ryan writes some of the most unique love scenes I have ever read.... She is one of passion's leading ladies."
—*Romantic Times*

ENNIS

Wanted

His hands moved up to cup her shoulders, then slipped down her arms. He covered her hands with his own. Trusting him completely, Mollie simply sighed when he drew her arms behind her and held both her hands in one of his.

Lew reached into his saddlebags.

The steel handcuffs gleamed in the moonlight.

The sound reverberated throughout the steep-sided canyon when he swiftly snapped the handcuffs around her fragile wrists, saying, "Sorry, Mollie."

By Nan Ryan

You Belong to My Heart
Burning Love
Desert Storm
Outlaw's Kiss

Published by HarperPaperbacks

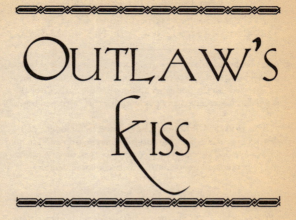

OUTLAW'S KISS

NAN RYAN

HarperPaperbacks
A Division of HarperCollinsPublishers

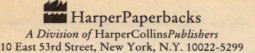
HarperPaperbacks

A Division of HarperCollins*Publishers*
10 East 53rd Street, New York, N.Y. 10022-5299

This is a work of fiction. The characters, incidents, and dialogues are products of the author's imagination and are not to be construed as real. Any resemblance to actual events or persons, living or dead, is entirely coincidental.

ISBN 0-06-108515-4

HarperCollins®, 🔥®, and HarperPaperbacks™ are trademarks of HarperCollins*Publishers,* Inc.

Cover illustration by John Ennis

First printing: August 1997

Printed in the United States of America

Visit HarperPaperbacks on the World Wide Web at
http://www.harpercollins.com

❖ 10 9 8 7 6 5 4 3 2 1

In loving memory of my mother
ROXY BOST HENDERSON
September 8, 1915–November 15, 1995

1

San Carlos, Arizona Territory
September 1872

The bride was crying.

She allowed the tears to slip down her pale cheeks unchecked. With only moments left until noon, she had given up all hope. There was no way out. No one was coming to save her, to sweep her away to freedom.

To deliver her from evil.

It was a high price to pay, but she would, just as promised, walk down the aisle of this old adobe mission at high noon to become the bride of a man she did not love. Would never love. A man she despised and feared.

A violent chill surged through Mollie's slender frame although the day was still and hot, the tiny back room where she waited stifling. She lifted cold fingers to her aching throat, swallowed with difficulty, and moved once more to the vestry's one small window.

Anxiously blinking back the tears to clear her blurred vision, Mollie looked expectantly down the street as she had one thousand times before.

Just as before, all was quiet in San Carlos. No clouds of dust stirred on the northern horizon; no sounds of hoofbeats heralded a last minute arrival. The street was silent and empty. That long, straight road leading out of San Carlos—distorted by rising heat thermals—shimmered and swayed and took on a dreamlike quality.

Much like her own life.

None of this was real. It couldn't be real. Not the white lace dress nor the old mission nor the waiting bridegroom. This couldn't possibly be happening to her. Not to Mollie Rogers. Surely it was all a dreadful nightmare. Soon she'd awaken and *he* would still be alive. She would turn and see beside her on the pillow, that dark, handsome face she adored. His beautiful eyes would be open and focused on her. Seeing she had roused, he would wrap his long arms around her and draw her close against his lean, bare body. He would kiss her tenderly with those sexy, sulky lips and make warm, lazy love to her while both remained half-asleep.

Mollie shut her eyes tightly and shook her head forcefully, willing this time, this place, this bad, bad dream to go away.

She opened her eyes.

All was just as it had been. The silent streets of San Carlos. The white lace wedding gown. The hopelessness and despair. In seconds the mission bells would begin their dooming toll and her fate would be sealed. She would be forever tied to a man whom she hated to the depths of her soul.

Mollie shook her head again, this time wistfully, sadly, and thought back to the summer when she was just a girl, not quite fifteen years old. To that hot, hot July night in 1865 when the sound of hoofbeats had awakened her from a peaceful slumber. On that long-ago summer night in Texas her destiny had been determined because a man she did not even know had killed another man she did not know.

2

Marshall, Texas
July 1865

  At the first faint echo of hoofbeats, Mollie Rogers's violet eyes flew open and she came instantly awake. Heart hammering beneath the worn cotton nightgown, she crept nimbly from the tall four-poster, pushing her tumbled golden hair back from her face. Her slim body tensed, she strained to hear as she crossed the darkened bedroom, slipped out into the hall, and hurried to the stairs.

  Feeling her way in midnight darkness, Mollie clung to the polished banister and stole swiftly down the threadbare carpeted stairs. With single-minded determination she headed for the heavy Henry .44 rifle leaning against the front doorjamb. She jerked up the rifle, dashed to a tall front window, eased back the tattered lace curtain, and peered cautiously outside.

  The lone nighttime intruder was galloping up the oblong front drive. In seconds he would reach the weed-choked front yard.

  Jaw set, eyes squinting in the darkness, Mollie raised

the rifle. She poked the long steel barrel through the open window and waited, gun poised, finger curled around the trigger.

At the front gate the trespasser pulled up on his horse, dismounted, and started toward the house. He was now close enough for Mollie to determine his size, but nothing more. He was a gigantic man, tall and strapping and wide-shouldered. He was, she thought fleetingly, almost as big as her papa. Without hesitation Mollie raised the rifle, sighted, and fired a warning shot directly over the head of the approaching stranger.

Cordell Rogers heard the bullet whip over his head, the echoing slam of the rifle fire, and the scream of a woman all at the same time.

"Mollie, child! It's your papa!" he shouted in a loud, booming voice and threw his big hands high into the air.

"Papa?" Mollie blinked and lowered the heavy gun. "That really you, Papa?"

"Yes, it's me! Mollie, Sarah, it's Cordell. I'm home."

Sarah Rogers stood on the landing above her fourteen-year-old daughter, her screams of fright instantly turning to sobs of joy and relief. With shaking hands she lifted the globe of a coal-oil lamp, lighted it anxiously, and started down the stairs. Midway down she saw her deliriously happy daughter being swallowed up in the powerful arms of her long-absent husband.

"Cordell," Sarah Rogers silently murmured, lifting the lamp high so that she might gaze on the dear familiar face, the thick curly red hair and beard, the twinkling green eyes. "Cordell," she repeated, this time audibly.

At the sound of her cultured voice Cordell Rogers

looked up, and Sarah suddenly felt shy in the compelling presence of the handsome, massive man she'd not seen for two long years.

"Papa, I almost shot you," Mollie declared, her slim arms wrapped around her father's neck as she hugged him tightly. "Why, I might have killed you. I might have . . . oh, Papa."

Eyes only for the frail blond woman slowly descending the stairs, Cordell Rogers said, "You did right, Mollie. Like I taught you." Then he lowered his only child back to her bare feet and stepped onto the stairs.

"Sarah, my love," he said when he reached his wife.

He took the flickering lamp from her shaking fingers, held it away in one big hand while his arm came around his wife's narrow waist and he pulled her into his embrace.

He held her so close Sarah could feel the tarnished buttons of her husband's worn Confederate gray tunic biting into her flesh. But she hugged him even tighter, elated to be safely enclosed once more in his sheltering arms.

"Thank God you're home, Cord," she whispered breathlessly. "At last. Oh, my dear, you've finally come home to us."

Pressing her head to his shoulder, Cordell Rogers gently stroked his wife's golden hair, wondering miserably how he could tell her that he would not be staying home, nor could she. How could he possibly tell this woman he worshiped that they must flee before the morning sun rose?

How could he tell her that he was a wanted man, hunted by both civilian and military law? That his men, riding from the Confederacy's last capital in Shreveport, had shot and killed a Union officer escort guarding a Yankee gold shipment moving through Louisiana? That she must leave this East Texas cotton plantation where he had brought her as his starry-eyed eighteen-year-old bride? That she could take nothing with her, not furniture or paintings or silver or trunks filled with dresses?

How could he possibly tell this gentle soul that they must leave for Mexico with only the clothes on their backs and that they could *never* return to Texas—or to anywhere else in the United States and its territories?

Dreading the moment, Cordell Rogers waited until Mollie had gone back to bed and he was alone with his wife in the privacy of their room. There he held her in his arms and broke the bad news as gently as possible.

Devastated, Sarah Rogers argued, "But, Cord, if you were not the one who shot the Yankee colonel, then surely you could be pardoned." Her eyes misted with tears.

"My dear, it doesn't work that way. *I* am responsible. I was the commanding officer and I led my men on the raid." He paused, shook his head, sighed wearily. "There's more. The man who was killed, the late Colonel Hatton, was the nephew of the secretary of war, Stanton."

"No," gasped Sarah, a hand lifting to her throat.

Cordell nodded. "Yes. We've no choice. We must flee to Mexico."

Sarah stared at him and swallowed hard. "Mexico? Couldn't Mollie and I stay here? Then when all this blows over you could—"

"Jesus, Sarah, look what Stanton did to Mary Surratt." Cordell reached out, drew her again into his arms. "He had the poor woman hanged because of the rumor that she helped Booth with the Lincoln assassination." His chin resting atop his wife's golden head, Cordell Rogers closed his eyes and said, "Sarah, Stanton's placed a ten thousand–dollar gold bounty on all our heads. Mine, yours, and Mollie's."

"Dear God, this can't be happening," she choked. "The world's gone mad."

"Oh, my love, I'm so sorry. I'll make it up to you one day, but we must go now, tonight. This is the first place they'll come looking for us."

Sarah raised her head and began to wipe her eyes. "I'll get dressed and start packing."

He nodded. "I'll wake Mollie and tell her we're leaving."

"What reason will you give her?"

"The truth," he said, turned, and was gone.

Within the hour, Mollie, alert and excited, was outside waiting impatiently with her father, her hand stroking the velvet muzzle of her prized Appaloosa mare, Queenie. Cordell Rogers was strapping valises and carpetbags to a couple of pack horses. Only Sarah Rogers remained inside the mansion.

Sarah paused in the center hallway and slowly looked about. The once rose-and-gold pattern of the expensive wall covering imported from Europe was faded and peeling. The tapestry-covered French sofa and matching chairs were worn and threadbare. Overhead, the tarnished doré chandelier, where once indigo-colored candles had lighted the way for arriving guests, sagged and tilted at an angle.

Still, it was beautiful to the sad woman who was leaving it. Sarah Rogers placed a hand on the mahogany banister and looked one last time up the darkened stairs. In that moment she knew that she would never again sleep in her soft four-poster or stand in the main floor foyer while sunlight streamed in through the fanlighted windows.

Sarah drew a shallow breath and moved toward those doors. She placed the lamp she carried on the hallway table, leaned over, and blew it out. She squared her slender shoulders and stepped out into the early-morning darkness.

But when she turned and carefully closed the massive front doors of her beloved home, she left a part of her heart inside.

3

*They left in the dead of night. Heading south-*west, they rode through the piney woods of East Texas and across the timbered prairies of central Texas. Through the lush green hill country around Austin and on past San Antone and into far South Texas.

The summer heat was fierce and unrelenting, and Cordell Rogers watched helplessly as his fragile wife became pale and hollow-cheeked. Her beautiful violet eyes grew duller with the passing of each hot, tiring day on the long journey.

He knew that her heart was broken, and that he was responsible. For that he would never forgive himself. It was cold comfort that he was not the one who had actually pulled the trigger. He *was* the one who had vowed never to stop fighting. It had been he who planned and led a half dozen loyal rebels in the daring daytime raid on the Yankee gold shipment, he who had declared they would take the gold and rendezvous with General Joe Shelby to fight on forever in the name of the Confederate States of America.

Cordell Rogers's wide shoulders slumped, and he shifted wearily in the saddle.

It was his fault, every bit of it. Lieutenant Jeffrey Battles had been the one who shot and killed the Yankee colonel, but he, Rogers, was the commanding officer. Lieutenant Battles was a good, loyal soldier who had saved his life at Fredericksburg. He couldn't fault Battles for what had happened.

"Look, Mother, Daddy, the Rio Grande!" Mollie shouted, pulling up on her Appaloosa mare and pointing excitedly.

"The Rio Grande, darlin'," Cordell Rogers said to his wan wife, hoping to see her smile.

Sarah Rogers drew rein, turned in the saddle, and smiled, but her dulled violet eyes did not light, and her voice broke when she said forlornly, "When we cross that river, we leave Texas behind forever."

"Oh, sweetheart, we'll have a good life in Mexico! You'll see. Maximilian needs trained officers for his French Empire." He drew his mount alongside Sarah's. "They say that the Empress Carlotta is a lovely, intelligent woman. The two of you might soon become good friends. Why, in a matter of weeks you could be spending time at the peaceful Chapultepec palace."

"Yes, of course," she said, attempting to sound enthusiastic for his sake. She wasn't too successful. Her back was aching and her face was afire and she felt as if she couldn't possibly ride all the way to Mexico City. But she said only, "Cord, could we rest here for a while? I'm feeling a little faint."

"Yes, my love," he quickly assured her. "We'll cross the river, camp on the other side. How does that sound?"

"Good," Sarah replied, knowing her husband was worried about her, not wanting him to be.

She loved him. She loved him so much she hadn't berated him for the foolhardy actions that had made it necessary for her to leave her home—the place where she had been born, where as a girl she had spent long summer afternoons reading poetry with her good friend Napier Dixon under the backyard oak on her father's farm. Where, at age seventeen, she had met a young, handsome, red-haired officer at a summertime ball and had fallen madly in love the first time he touched her hand.

"Sounds wonderful, Cord." She brightened and her smile widened when she saw her husband's sun-bronzed face fill with relief.

Mollie Rogers's mood was the opposite of her mother's. A curious, thrill-seeking child who was more rash tomboy than prim young lady, Mollie viewed the move to Mexico from their war-ruined cotton planta-tion as high adventure, and she couldn't understand her mother's lingering melancholy. Why, already—in the five weeks they'd been traveling—she'd had more fun than in her entire fourteen years.

They had ridden more than four hundred fifty miles, and they weren't yet halfway to Mexico City! It was all too exciting for words, and Mollie hoped it took months to reach their final destination. A rebel at heart, she loved being on the trail. She was free and happy and could ride her mare fast and shoot wild game and watch for savage Indians and hide from the U.S. authorities and do a hundred other exciting things that would surely make her friends back home pea green with envy.

The devil with the palace at Chapultepec or some fine hacienda in Mexico City! She liked it out in the open where she could breathe. She liked sleeping under the stars.

The summer sun was setting as Mollie eagerly swam her Appaloosa across the muddy Rio Grande and up onto the grassy banks on the far side of the river. She let a out a great whoop of joy. Not only was she safe from the pursuing Yankee devils but tonight she, Mollie Louise Rogers, would be sleeping in a foreign country!

It was just too exciting. She couldn't possibly sleep. Not on her very first night in Mexico. Why, she might never sleep again!

"Lieutenant, you must get some sleep."

The motherly, uniformed nurse stepped close to the bed as she spoke. The lamp in her hand gave off the only light in the long, narrow ward where rows of beds lined the white walls. Every bed in the army hospital was filled. In each lay a badly wounded Union soldier.

The nurse set the lamp on the bedside table. She spread the white sheet up over the wide, bare shoulders of the dark-haired, slender man. "It's past midnight, Lieutenant. You need sleep."

"Yes, ma'am," said Lieutenant Lew Hatton.

But he couldn't sleep. Didn't want to sleep until he found the lawless Southern rebels responsible for the murder of his father.

"I'll give you something for the pain, Lieutenant," the nurse said, smiling down at him as she pushed a perspiration-soaked lock of coal black hair back off his shiny forehead.

"No. I don't need anything. I'm fine," Lew Hatton said.

"Sleep then, son," she said, knowing very well that he was not fine,—that in all likelihood, the twenty-six-year-old man lying helpless in this stuffy army hospital ward might never be fine.

The wounds the young Union soldier had suffered in the war's last hours had nearly been fatal. For days he had lain near death, weeks more he had spent confined to this narrow army-issue bed in this crowded Richmond federal hospital. His badly shattered right leg had still not healed properly. It wouldn't surprise her if he lost it yet. And even if he kept the leg, she doubted he would ever walk again.

Feeling sorry for the handsome young man, the nurse walked away shaking her head sadly. Bless his heart, he had been improving until a well-meaning fellow officer had stopped by and brought the upsetting news that his father, Colonel William P. Hatton, while escorting a shipment of gold through Louisiana to Hooker's occupying troops in New Orleans, had been shot and killed by Confederate rebels three months after the war's end.

The nurse was worried about Lieutenant Hatton. Not only was the young veteran badly wounded, his heart was now filled with unforgiving hatred. If he mended, he would go looking for more trouble. She'd been near the wounded soldier's bed when he had received word of his father's death. She couldn't forget the look that had crossed his pain-etched face nor the vow Lew Hatton had made.

"If ever I leave this bed, I'll go after the men who murdered my father. I will *never* rest until they are all brought to justice."

4

Sarah Rogers didn't sleep that night. Her husband snored softly beside her, and a few feet away Mollie slept soundly. But Sarah couldn't sleep. She told herself she suffered from only a minor fever caused by the heat. It would be gone by morning.

At dawn Cordell Rogers awakened, took one look at his wife's flushed face and too-bright eyes, and shouted, "Mollie, your mother's very sick! I'm going for a doctor!"

He rode back across the river and headed straight to Laredo, Texas, where Dr. Tio Sanchez stood idly studying a wanted poster tacked to the wall of the telegraph office. Dr. Sanchez had just returned to his office when a wild-eyed horseman dismounted and stormed through the front door.

Dr. Tio Sanchez immediately recognized the man from the wanted poster—the man beneath whose likeness were the words, WANTED DEAD OR ALIVE.

"Doctor, you must come with me!" Cordell Rogers ordered.

"No," said the doctor. "You are a fugitive from the law, a killer. I must report you to the—"

Before he could finish the sentence, Cordell Rogers drew his Colt .44 and pointed it directly at the doctor's chest. "I'll kill you where you stand if you don't grab your bag and come with me."

Stunned, Dr. Sanchez threw his hands in the air. "Do not shoot me. I have a family!"

"So do I, and you have to save my wife!"

The young doctor knew, the minute he saw Sarah Rogers, that she had scarlet fever. He knew as well that she wouldn't live to see another sunrise. He did what he could to make her comfortable, then examined Mollie for any signs of the contagious disease.

His stethoscope on Mollie's slender back, he noticed the perfectly shaped butterfly birthmark below her waist. "*Mariposa,*" he murmured absently.

"What?" Mollie said over her shoulder.

"Ah, I was thinking aloud, Miss Rogers. Your birthmark, it's a *mariposa*. A butterfly."

"I know that!" she said, jerked her loosened pants up and her shirt down, and hurried back to her mother.

Dr. Sanchez took Cordell Rogers aside and told him the truth—that for Sarah, the end was near. Nervously he waited for the big red-haired man's reaction. But Cordell just nodded sadly and told the young doctor he was free to go.

Sanchez looked Rogers in the eye. "It will be on my conscience if I do not tell the authorities of seeing you."

"Tell them any damned thing you like. Without Sarah, none of it matters."

At noon Sarah rallied a little. She opened her eyes and saw her haggard husband leaning over her. She smiled up at him and in a voice so low he had to lean close to hear, she said, "Look after Mollie and promise you'll not bury me in Mexico. Take me back to Texas, Cord." A lone tear pooled in the corner of her eye.

"Such nonsense," he said, he voice soft, soothing. "You'll be buried nowhere for another thirty or forty years."

She gripped his big hand. "I love you," she said. "Where's Mollie?"

"Right here, Mama," whispered Mollie, leaning closer, dashing at the tears streaming down her cheeks.

"I love you so much, darling," Sarah said to her only child. "You're such a lively, intelligent girl. And so pretty. I wanted to see you grow up."

"You will, Mama."

Sarah smiled at her, turned her eyes back on her husband's grave face, gave a soft sigh of resignation, and drew her last breath.

They buried her that same afternoon. Honoring her wish, they carried her back across the muddy Rio Grande into Texas. They chose for her final resting place a smooth, high spot near the river where the rushing water would sing to her after the summer rains and the tall cottonwoods would drip shade and whisper to her in the winds and scatter their cottony catkins across her grave.

With Sarah gone, Cordell Rogers no longer had any desire to go to Mexico City. It was for her he had wanted to build a new life of respectability. Now he saw no reason to join Maximilian's army. He'd had all the soldiering he wanted.

As they mounted to leave, he said, "It was for your mother I was going to Mexico City. We'll join Lieutenant Battles instead. Jeffrey was heading down to Hermosillo and the gold mines. That all right with you, Mollie?"

Despite her grief, Mollie experienced a mild rush of excitement at the mention of gold mines. What an adventure that would be! Hunting for gold in the wilds of Mexico!

"That would be fine, Papa."

Weeks later, in mid-October, the tired pair finally reached Hermosillo. As they rode down the dusty main street, Mollie felt a terrible letdown. She had expected noise and laughter and gaiety and excitement—a rip-roaring gold town like the ones in California she'd heard so much about.

Instead she saw a somnolent little village with only a handful of Mexican men with sombreros pulled low over their faces, sleeping in the sun outside adobe buildings.

Mollie frowned when her father ordered her to stay outside while he went into the one open cantina. "A cantina is no place for a girl," he said when she protested.

"But no one will know," she reasoned, hastily shoving her thick golden hair up under her hat. "I'm wearing breeches; they'll think I'm boy."

"Come on, then," he said, shaking his head, "but keep quiet inside."

Mollie eagerly followed her father out of the blinding sunshine and into the dim, cool cantina. Blinking, she looked about, curious as only a fourteen-year-old girl can be.

A mustachioed man stepped out of the shadows and up to the long rough hewn plank bar. *"Sí, señor?"*

"Whiskey," said Cordell Rogers.

The barkeep nodded. "And for the *señorita?*"

Disappointed, Mollie made a face. "How did you know I'm a girl?"

The Mexican barkeep just threw back his head and laughed. "You want a nice lemonade, *sí*?"

"I suppose," Mollie said and jerked off her hat, allowing the rebellious golden hair to spill down around her shoulders, wishing, as she had a thousand times before, that she weren't a girl.

The helpful barkeep told them they would find Jeffrey Battles at the Bonita Hoy mine seven miles north of Hermosillo. Mollie immediately felt her sagging spirits rise.

"Let's go, Papa," she tugged on his shirtsleeve. "We could be at the mine by sunset."

"A few minutes more, then we'll go," he said. He downed his glass of whiskey in one swallow and passed the empty shot glass across the plank bar. "Fill it up, barkeep."

Mollie frowned. She didn't recall her papa having such a thirst for whiskey before the war.

On that same October day, Lew Hatton sat in the chilly waiting room of the Overland stage station in Albuquerque, New Mexico. His walking cane resting between his bent knees and his dark head laid back against the wall, he shut his eyes and plotted how he would go about catching up with Cordell Rogers and Jeffrey Battles and the others who had been on the raid that had cost Colonel William Hatton his life.

Lew reasoned that when he finally reached his home in Santa Fe, he would rest and recuperate fully within a few months. When he was again able to ride, he would set out after all five murderers. He had no intention of killing them. He would bring them in and let them hang for their crimes, or else rot away in prison for the rest of their lives.

The thought brought a slight smile to Lew's lips.

Without opening his eyes, he shifted uncomfortably on the hard bench and stretched his stiff, wounded leg out before him.

"*Señor,* excuse me, *por favor,*" came a soft, feminine voice a fraction of a second after Lew felt something bump his foot.

He opened his eyes on the most beautiful young woman he had ever seen. Her hair, as jet black as his own, was parted down the middle and drawn to the back of her head. Her skin was as white and fine as alabaster, and her dark eyes, large and luminous, were shaded with sweeping black lashes. Her nose was small and straight, her lips full and red.

And those lovely lips were smiling at him.

Lew rose so rapidly on his injured leg that he almost fell. The young woman instinctively reached out to steady him. Her fingertips touched his chest for a fleeting moment and Lew knew, in that moment, that he wanted her to touch him there—and all over—for the rest of his life.

Young Teresa Castillo looked up and felt her heart beat erratically. Before her stood a tall, wide-shouldered man in a pearl gray frock coat of fine wool. His shirt was of snowy white silk and his trousers, elegantly cut, had obviously been tailored specifically for him.

An abundance of unruly coal black hair tumbled rebelliously over his high forehead. Thick black brows slashed almost menacingly above eyes as blue as the wool dress she wore. His nose was well shaped, and his lips were full and sensual. There was about him a natural arrogance that Teresa Castillo found appealing.

Suddenly she realized that her hand was still on his chest, and she yanked it away as though she had done something unspeakable.

When Lew had gained his equilibrium, he said, "No, *señorita,* it is I who must be excused. My feet were in the way and I humbly apologize for almost tripping you. Allow me to introduce myself, I'm—"

"*Señor,* we do not care who you are!" A short, stocky woman stepped forward and took Teresa's arm. To Teresa she said, "What would your brother say? Talking with strange gentlemen! Come, we will choose a place to sit."

"But how will I ever be properly introduced if—" Lew tried, but the scolding duenna glared at him and ushered the pretty young woman away.

Lew sighed and sank back down on the bench. But short minutes later he was smiling again. The beautiful young woman and her clucking chaperon were boarding the stage to Santa Fe! Purposely, Lew waited until the last minute. When the driver climbed on the box and took up the reins, Lew stepped up into the coach, took a seat opposite the two women and smiled with delight at the reactions written plainly on each face.

The aging duenna's lips were compressed, and her dark eyes were snapping with annoyance. But the beautiful young woman's face wore an expression of embarrassed pleasure. And when Lew impudently winked at her, she blushed prettily and averted her dark, flashing eyes.

Lew made several attempts at conversation. Each time the duenna looked daggers at him and forbade her charge to respond. He gave up at last, leaned his head back, and closed his eyes. But he didn't sleep. He couldn't. How could he sleep when the most desirable woman God had ever created sat just across from him, so near he could smell the sweet scent of her perfume?

There was only one kind of woman for whom Lew Hatton had a great weakness—the dainty, feminine, innocent ones. Soft, lovely creatures who were as help-less and dependant as newborn babes. Exquisite, fragile females who wore their vulnerability like a mantle around their lovely, luscious bodies.

Not that he hadn't had plenty of the other kind. He had. Wild and reckless in his youth, he had spent more than one night in the arms of women who were less than ladies—bold divorcées and wild, spoiled rich men's daughters and dance hall girls and brothel cuties, even a squaw or two in his days among the Apaches.

But seated directly across from him now was the kind of young lady a man dreamed of. A beautiful, refined, innocent woman whom no man had ever pos-sessed. She was as pure as the Virgin Mary, of that he felt certain. In the depths of her dark, flashing eyes was an unmistakable naïveté.

Hours passed.

The clattering, lurching coach rumbled steadily northward. The sun set. Its afterglow was fading quickly. Lew tore his eyes from the young beauty long enough to notice that the woman guarding her had fallen asleep. To make sure she was really sleeping, he softly addressed her. Her head lolled to one side, her mouth open slightly, and she did not respond.

He looked back at the young beauty. She smiled and shrugged her slender shoulders. Lew grinned and patted the seat beside him. Teresa's dark eyes blinked and she shook her head. Lew again patted the seat.

"Sit by me?" It was an invitation, not a command.

Still she looked skeptical. She glanced nervously at the sleeping duenna. Then Lew's heart skipped several beats when she gracefully rose and moved over to sit beside him.

Longing to touch her slender white hand, not daring to do so, Lew said quietly, "Don't be afraid. I won't hurt you. Ever. I am Lew Hatton and my home is Santa Fe. Tell me how I may meet you properly."

She smiled enchantingly. "My name is Teresa Castillo. My brother is Don Pascual Castillo of Santa Fe. My father has sent me north to live with Pascual until the trouble in Mexico has ended."

"I will speak with your brother as soon as we reach Santa Fe," Lew said. "I will ask his permission to call on you. May I do that?"

"Yes, Lew," she said, and the sound of her voice saying his name made his pulse quicken, "I would like that. But I must tell you that although I attended school in New York City, I still follow the customs of my country." She lowered her thick lashes and admitted, "If you wish to see me, it must be in the presence of my duenna."

Impulsively Lew reached out and gently cupped her chin, lifting her face so that he could look into her beautiful eyes. He said, "I don't mind, Teresa. It will be worth it."

5

Mollie sighed wearily.

They had been in Hermosillo for more than a year, and what she had hoped would be high adventure had turned out to be unending monotony.

Her papa worked from sunup to sundown in the Bonita Hoy mine and made only a pittance. He came home of an evening exhausted, beaten, and uncommunicative while she spent each long, tedious day trapped in their small clapboard shack. She was miserable.

She hated Hermosillo and having nothing to do all day and seeing her papa come home so tired he could hardly eat his supper.

Poor Papa. He had not been the same since her mother died. He never would be again. The vitality, the zest for living was gone. His once-brilliant green eyes rarely disappeared into laugh lines, and his massive shoulders slumped noticeably.

Men's voices carrying on still twilight air pulled Mollie from her painful reverie. She recognized her papa's deep voice, smiled, then frowned when she heard Jeffrey Battles.

Mollie didn't like Jeffrey Battles. Hadn't from the start.

Her papa had told her that women found Battles attractive, and Mollie supposed that he was in a rugged, unconventional way. Not yet twenty-two, he looked much older. Muscular and of medium height, he had thick wavy dark hair and a curly beard that wasn't neatly trimmed like her papa's. But in his eyes of slate gray there was a hint of something that frightened Mollie. He was forever teasing her, telling her she was his sweetheart. She didn't want to be any man's sweetheart, certainly not his!

For her papa's sake, Mollie put a smile on her face as the two men entered the shack. Cordell Rogers's blackened, sweat-streaked face broke into a grin when he caught sight of his daughter. He came directly to the table and proudly laid out the few small coins he had collected for the week's wages.

"Payday already," Mollie said cheerfully. "Seems like it rolls around pretty often, Papa."

"Not nearly often enough," came the flat, insolent voice from behind Cordell Rogers, and Jeffrey Battles, moving into the lamplight, said, "Mind if I stay for supper?"

She did, but said nothing.

After the meager meal Cordell Rogers said, "Mollie, honey, get me that bottle of whiskey from the top shelf."

"Sorry, Papa, the bottle's empty. You finished the last of the whiskey two nights ago."

"So I did," he said, remembering. He glanced at the coins resting on the table. "I don't suppose . . . no, there's not enough money to buy whiskey, and—" All at once he slammed his big fist down on the table, setting the plates to rattling. "Damn it to hell!" he roared. "I work seven days a week and still can't provide my daughter with a decent place to live. All I ask out of life is a good cigar and a drink of whiskey and I can't even have that."

Mollie's violet eyes were round with shock. They widened more when Jeffrey Battles said calmly, "You sick of being broke? Why not do something about it?"

"He's doing all he can," Mollie quickly protested. "We have plenty."

But Jeff Battles pressed on. "Colonel, you're absolutely right. It isn't fair for Mollie to do without nice things. She deserves better. We all do." He leaned forward, scooped up the coins lying on the table. Then let them slowly spill through his fingers. "There's a small bank just across the border in Nogales. An old lady with a riding crop could knock it over." His gray eyes gleamed in the lamplight. "We don't make any money here, yet we can't go home. We are fugitives. They can't hang you but once."

"I need a drink," said Cordell Rogers while the wide-eyed Mollie looked from one man to the other.

"By this time next week you could buy all the whiskey you want." Battles pushed back his chair and rose. "Do what you will. I'm riding to Nogales tomorrow." He smiled at Mollie and was gone.

Jeff Battles didn't show up at the mine the next morning. Days passed and Mollie hoped he was gone for good. But one rainy night he showed up at the shack. He walked inside like he owned the place, lowered the heavy rain-splattered saddlebags from his left shoulder, poured out the contents. Gold, silver, and paper money spilled across the table while Mollie and Cordell Rogers stared, transfixed.

Battles opened the other side of the worn saddlebags and drew out a full bottle of Old Crow whiskey and a half dozen Cuban cigars.

"Nobody got hurt. There's more money there than you'll make in a decade in the Bonita Hoy." He grinned broadly and said, "Have a drink and a cigar, Colonel. We're Southern gentlemen again."

The next time Jeff Battles rode north of the border, Cordell Rogers was with him. Mollie didn't blame her father. She wasn't angry that he had chosen to go on the planned holdup of the El Paso-to-Yuma stage.

But she *was* angry.

She was mad as a hornet that she was a girl and couldn't ride with him.

Cordell Rogers became the gang's leader on that very first trip north. He was the boss. All answered to him: Jeffrey Battles and the others from his war days—the quiet, aging Will Hurdman and the constantly bickering Steven Andrews and W. C. Petty. They willingly followed wherever he led.

The gang made a good living from robbing trains and banks and stagecoaches. Cordell Rogers's conscience bothered him for only a short time. When he'd walked into the tar-paper shack and poured thousands of dollars onto the table before his awed daughter, that had gone a long way toward easing his guilt.

Now, three years later, he never gave it a second thought. For the past two years he and Mollie had lived in a huge hacienda nestled in the broken butte country of northern Mexico, not fifteen miles from the U.S. border. Rumor had it that the thirty-room palace had been built in the days of the conquistadores with gold from the Spanish throne.

So Cordell Rogers lived in total luxury in the isolated mansion with a full staff of servants, his old trusted friends at his side, a trio of loyal Mexican lieutenants, his beautiful young daughter safe in guarded seclusion, and more money than they could hope to spend in five lifetimes.

And whiskey whenever he wanted it.

And he wanted it often.

Rogers and his men were as adept at their profession as they had been at soldiering. Their reputation had quickly spread across Texas and the Southwest. Wanted posters boasted large rewards for the capture of any or all of the Rogers Renegades. Especially Jeffrey Battles. The San Antonio native, known now as "the Texas Kid," had become something of a legend. People spoke of "the Kid" in hushed tones, and Battles enjoyed the notoriety.

Cordell Rogers—his supply of bourbon assured— and Jeffrey Battles had few complaints with life.

But on her eighteenth birthday, Mollie, pacing restlessly inside the opulent hacienda, was almost as unhappy as she had been back in the Hermosillo shack. She had less freedom than ever. Her father's men lived in the compound that surrounded the main house. She couldn't take a step without tripping over one of them.

Especially the Kid.

Now, as the summer dusk descended over the desert, Mollie bristled at the sight of Jeff approaching the hacienda alongside her papa. She had so wanted to celebrate her eighteenth birthday alone with her papa, but he'd insisted on inviting Jeff.

Mollie was further upset when she saw that her papa had been drinking. Heavily. She didn't scold him, but her eyes snapped with annoyance when Jeff, slyly looking her up and down, said, "So you're eighteen and all grown up."

She was about to make a cutting reply when a mannerly Mexican servant appeared to announce that dinner was ready. Her healthy appetite overcoming her displeasure, Mollie grabbed her papa's arm and guided him into the dining room.

"May I propose a toast," said the Kid when they were seated. He lifted his goblet of Madeira to Mollie.

She gave him a withering look, but smiled when her papa unexpectedly poured a splash of Madeira into her glass.

"A toast is definitely in order," agreed Cordell Rogers, slurring his words a little.

"To the most beautiful eighteen-year-old woman in the world," said the Kid.

"Hear, hear," said her papa, and they all drank.

Before Mollie could swallow the wine, the Kid slid a wrapped present before her.

"I've told you not to give me gifts," Mollie snapped.

"Mollie, honey, where are your manners?" chided her papa. "You could behave a little more like a lady."

Mollie snorted. "I'm no lady, and I don't want to be a lady." She ripped the paper open, stared frowning at the matched pair of ruby-encrusted gold combs resting on a bed of velvet.

"Your hair is the prettiest thing about you," said the Kid. "Wear the combs in it . . . for me."

Mollie glanced at her papa. He was smiling, totally approving of the Kid's giving her such an expensive, personal, utterly feminine gift, as if she were his sweetheart. The thought made the wispy hair rise on the nape of her neck. She didn't want to be the Kid's sweetheart. She didn't want to be pretty for him. She didn't want combs and fans and frilly, feminine dresses. She didn't want compliments or teasing or stolen kisses. Not from him. Not from any man!

"I won't be needing the combs, Jeffrey," Mollie announced, shoved back her chair and rose. She dashed out of the room with the two startled men staring after her.

"I'm sorry, Jeff," Cordell Rogers apologized. "Mollie's a stubborn girl."

"She is," said the Kid, grinning. "I had hoped she'd be grown up by now, start acting like a woman."

Cordell Rogers shook his head. "She may never start behaving like a woman. I've bought her countless dresses and she's never put one on." He sighed heavily. "It's my fault. My wife used to berate me for the way I raised Mollie. Said I was responsible for our daughter being as wild as a savage. I guess Sarah was right; I wanted a son, so I taught Mollie to ride and shoot a gun and . . . and . . ." He shrugged, fell silent.

Jeff Battles's smile remained solidly in place. "She'll grow up in time." He turned serious then, said, "Promise me, Colonel, as her father, that I can have her one day."

His eyes suddenly clouding, Cordell Rogers said, "Who else would want Mollie, thanks to her *bandito* father. Jesus God, Sarah would turn over in her grave if she knew. . . ."

"I'll marry Mollie," said the Kid. "We'll move down to Mexico City where she can be a fine lady like your wife would have wanted."

Cordell Rogers nodded. "She's yours, Kid. But it's up to you to convince Mollie."

"I will," said the Kid with total confidence. "Count on it." He reached out, touched the open velvet box. "She'll change her mind about the combs, you'll see. They'll sure look pretty in her hair."

Upstairs in her bedroom, Mollie anxiously bolted the heavy carved door. She then hurried across the room to close the rows of slatted shutters opening to the balcony. All portals secured, she went about blowing out all the lamps, leaving only the one atop her dressing table aglow.

Standing before the dresser, Mollie carefully studied herself in the gilt-trimmed mirror. Running her slender fingers through the long golden hair cascading around her shoulders, she thought about the ruby-encrusted combs. And of the presumptuous man who had given them to her.

Temper rising, Mollie impulsively unbuttoned her tight breeches. Muttering to herself that she would "fix the Kid," she pulled off her boots, assuring her reflection, "I'll show him how much I need hair combs!"

She removed her tight buckskins and, kicking them aside, began unbuttoning her blouse. She stripped it off, tossed it to the floor. She stood there in the lamplight in her underwear. She drew a deep long breath and, from the clutter atop her dressing table, picked up a pair of embroidery scissors.

Taking a seat before the mirror, Mollie lifted a thick lock of gleaming gold hair. Without the slightest hesitation, she snipped it off two inches from her scalp. The pink tip of her tongue caught between her teeth, her violet eyes narrowed in fierce concentration, Mollie sat there in the blistering August heat and clipped and cut and snipped until all her glorious hair lay in discarded golden ringlets at her bare feet.

She stared at herself in the mirror and was pleased. Without her hair she felt certain she was plain, almost ugly. Good! She ran her fingers through the spiky, blunt-cut locks and began to laugh, imagining the reaction of her papa and the Kid. She laughed harder.

She had an even bigger surprise than the haircut in store for them both!

6

⬥

*At dawn the Rogers Renegades assembled out-*side the hacienda. Cordell Rogers stood on the broad flagstone patio and told them where they were going. Only he and the Kid knew. It was they who planned each robbery, they who chose the bank, the stage, the train, the paymaster that would be hit.

"It's the First National Bank in Tucson, boys," said Rogers. "The bank has some of the richest depositors in the state, and I expect to come away with at least two hundred thousand dollars. No need wasting any more time. Let's go."

Spurs jangling, cigar smoke swirling around their heads, the men headed for the stables and their saddled mounts. In high spirits, Cordell Rogers swung up into the saddle, wheeled his roan about, and saw a lone horseman approaching from the east. Backlit by the rising sun, the rider galloped directly toward the mounted men.

"Who the hell is . . ." Cordell Rogers's words trailed away and he stared, puzzled. "Who goes there?" he shouted, squinting. "Identify yourself!"

Face concealed beneath a low-pulled hat brim, the rider galloped straight at Cordell Rogers. Waiting until the big bay drew up alongside Rogers's roan, the silent rider yanked firmly up on the reins. The stallion reared up on its hind legs and whinnied, but the rider easily stayed in the saddle.

When the beast's front hooves again struck the ground, Mollie laughed and shouted gleefully, "Papa, you thought I was a man!"

"Mollie?" Rogers eyes widened in disbelief.

"Yes, it's Mollie." She flashed him a mischievous grin. "You didn't know me, did you?"

"Well, no . . . you're not on your Appaloosa, and your hat's covering your—"

"It covers nothing, Papa," Mollie said, whisking off her Stetson.

"God in heaven!" roared Cordell Rogers, dumbstruck. "You've cut off all your hair! You've ruined yourself. You look like a . . . a . . ."

"A man?" She finished for him and laughed. "That's what you were going to say, Papa? You're right. I can ride with the Renegades and no one will know I'm a woman, not even without my hat."

"Ride with the . . . ?" Rogers's face suffused with color and his eyes flashed green fire. "You get up to the hacienda this minute, young lady! I forbid you to—"

Interrupting, Mollie said, "I can outride and outshoot any of your men."

"That has nothing to do with it, damn it! You're a woman, and—"

"It has everything to do with it, damn it!" Mollie argued. "I am eighteen and I refuse to be punished any longer for being born a female!" Her violet eyes sparkled, and her stubby blond hair gleamed in the rising sun as she reined her bay about and laid her big roweled Mexican spurs to him. The stallion shot away as Mollie shouted over her shoulder, "What are you waiting for, Renegades? Let's ride!"

"Damn it to hell, Mollie Louise Rogers, I've a good mind to turn you over my knee and—come back here! I'll be a son of a . . ." Cordell Rogers cursed and hollered and threatened.

It did no good. Mollie couldn't hear him. She was too far away and she was laughing too loudly.

His shock and anger quickly subsiding, Rogers looked after the slender mounted figure with the butchered blond hair and began to smile. His beautiful, headstrong daughter possessed the same eruptible passions that he had in his youth. Her violet eyes were lusty with life, and from the time she was old enough to think for herself, she had tolerated forced rules, but never fully submitted to anyone. Not to him. Not to her mother. To nobody. "Hell, Kid," he said, grinning as he turned to the younger man, "I can't do anything with her. I don't believe any man can."

"True," said the Kid, nodding, thinking he knew exactly what to do with Mollie Rogers.

Battles kicked his gelding into a gallop and rode after the free-spirited Mollie, his heart drumming with admiration. Her latest show of rebellion—the cutting of her long hair and the firm-chinned resolve to ride with the Renegades—added to her appeal. He had always wanted Mollie. Now he wanted her more than ever and he meant to have her. One way or the other. Knowing she would be in on the Tucson bank robbery made the blood surge through his veins.

Jeffrey Battles enjoyed robbing banks and stages. It was more than a means of acquiring fast money. For him it was like a stimulating sexual experience. Each time he unholstered his twin .44s and pointed them at a frightened man's chest, he felt his belly tighten and found himself half-aroused. More than once he had felt the strong desire to make love just prior to a robbery. Or while the robbery was under way. Or as soon as it was completed. That feeling was sure to increase tenfold with the temptingly defiant Mollie at his side when he burst into a bank, guns drawn. Lips stretched into a wicked grin, the Kid raced after Mollie, envisioning thrilling days and nights ahead. Soon Cordell Rogers could be shunted to the background, left behind at the hacienda, and *he* would lead the gang. He and the tempestuous, daredevil Mollie.

The Kid overtook Mollie, reined his gelding alongside her speeding bay, and shouted, "I don't much like that short hair, but I sure like you riding with me."

Mollie's head swung around. "I'm not riding with you, Kid. I'm riding with my papa, same as you and the others. *Don't* ever forget that. He's the leader. You can't tell me what to do."

"Seems to me he can't either," said the Kid.

Mollie glared at him, leaned low over the bay's sleek neck and urged him on, leaving the Kid in her dust.

Half past noon and furnace-hot.

The baked streets of Tucson, Arizona, were nearly deserted when a gang of mounted bandits thundered into town, guns drawn, their lower faces covered with bandannas. Before the drowsy town knew what was happening, the robbers were at the First National Bank and a trio of gun-toting outlaws stormed through the bank's doors.

"Hands in the air, everybody," shouted the biggest of the three, while a tall, slim youth in tight black charro pants nimbly scaled the counter, swung through a teller's window, and dropped to the floor, empty sack in hand.

"Put all the money in the bag," ordered a muscular, dark-haired man standing just beyond the wire cage. The frightened teller nearest him noticed that the drawstring of his black hat hung over an ear whose lobe was missing.

Mollie moved rapidly from teller to teller, filling the bag with gold and paper money while the Kid covered the employees and her father covered the door. In less than sixty seconds the bag was filled, Mollie was back out into the lobby and rushing for the door, while behind her the Kid and Cordell Rogers held their ground, waiting for Mollie to mount her horse.

But as she stepped on the wooden sidewalk, a cowboy, smelling trouble, rushed around the corner from the barbershop, his face covered with lather. He grabbed Mollie and held her body in front of him as a shield.

"If you fire you'll hit the boy!" the cowboy shouted to the mounted Renegades.

He began backing down the street toward the sheriff's office, dragging the masked outlaw with him. His chin bumped the struggling bandit's Stetson, knocking it to the ground. Chopped blond hair gleamed in the sun as the cowboy's hand, seeking a firmer hold on the robber's shirtfront, grabbed a handful of soft, feminine flesh. Mollie heard his sharp intake of breath. Thunderstruck, the cowboy automatically released her, muttering in disbelief, "Why, you're a girl!"

"And you're a fool," was her reply as she shoved the gaping cowboy from her and ran for her horse.

She swung up into the saddle, wheeled the bay about, and galloped away. She was rounding the corner when she heard the first shots. Her head snapped around. She started to turn back, but the aging Will Hurdman shouted, "No! Keep going!"

She did, galloping ahead of the others as men poured into streets, gunfire erupted, and pandemonium broke out. Riding hell-for-leather, Mollie and the Renegades raced out of Tucson, quickly losing their pursuers.

But leaving behind the trapped Cordell Rogers and the Texas Kid.

By twilight that day, the talk on every street corner and in every gambling den, saloon, dance hall, and bordello in Tucson was of the daring daytime robbery. It was the most exciting thing that had happened in months, and the fact that two of the infamous Rogers Renegades were cooling their heels in the city jail was cause for celebration. Townspeople were delighted that two of the West's most notorious outlaws had fallen into their hands. They spoke loudly of a lynching, theorizing that it was their duty to rid the frontier of outlaws like the pair of animals incarcerated in their jail.

A holiday spirit prevailed, and men drank and shouted and laughed and hurried in and out of the freestanding jail, rushing back to the rear of the building to point and jeer at the captured criminals. One loudmouthed drunk bragged how he would lift the Kid's other earlobe for a souvenir.

No one was having more fun than the lanky cowboy who had discovered, first hand, that one of the Renegades was not a man. Repeating the story over and over, he said, ". . . so I held this here young boy before me, shielding myself from all them mounted bandits. I was pulling the boy along with me when I knocked off his hat and I seen a lot of shiny short blond hair. I clutched at his shirtfront and danged if I didn't have me handful of soft female breast!" He hooted with laughter and added, "Hell, I should have hung on for dear life!"

By dark there was nobody left in Tucson who hadn't learned that one of the Rogers Renegades was a female, a brave, daring young blond girl. A girl they said was Cordell Rogers's daughter. A girl they speculated to be the Texas Kid's woman.

Inside the close, small cell at the rear of the jail, the Texas Kid, his left hand throbbing, paced back and forth, his thin lips pulled tight over clamped teeth, his sunburned face etched in lines of pain.

The marshal's bullet had caught the flesh between his knuckles before he could squeeze the trigger of his .44. Both of his guns had crashed to the wooden sidewalk as he had instinctively grabbed his wounded left hand and shouted, "Get him, Colonel!"

But, strangely, Cordell Rogers had refused to shoot the lawman, although he clearly had the drop on him, a fact that sorely rankled the Kid. He turned now and looked at the big red-haired man lying relaxed on one of the cots.

"You know, don't you," said the Kid, "that they are as apt to hang us as not."

Rogers looked up. His green eyes were calm, pensive. "You knew that going in, Kid. Did you suppose we could spend our lives robbing banks and not court death?"

A muscle twitched in the Kid's jaw. "Why the hell didn't you shoot that marshal?"

"I'm no killer. We've been over this before." Cordell Rogers rolled into a sitting position and swung his legs to the floor. "Since the Hatton shooting, no one's been hurt. I never want another woman to find herself a widow because one of my men killed her husband." He rose to his feet.

"Goddamn it, I don't want to die," was the Kid's angry reply.

"Then you should have chosen another profession. Robbery carries risks." Rogers turned away, called through the bars to the guard, "Jailer, reckon it would be possible for a thirsty prisoner to have one little drink of whiskey?"

As he waited for an answer, his troubled thoughts turned to his daughter. What would become of Mollie if they hanged him? What would happen to his young, defenseless daughter? Who would take care of her if he was six feet under?

He shook his head.

He had meant, so many times, to tell Mollie that if anything ever happened to him, she was go to his and Sarah's dear old friend, Napier Dixon. But he'd never gotten around to telling her. Now it was too late.

Mollie was still wandering in and out of his liquor-clouded thoughts as midnight approached. He had persuaded the jailer to leave him a half-full bottle of good Kentucky bourbon and he lay on his cot half dozing, half daydreaming of happier times.

"Listen!" The Kid snapped him out of his pleasant reverie. "It's the fire wagon! I thought I smelled smoke!" He anxiously sniffed the air.

Cordell Rogers blinked in confusion and tumbled from his bunk as the clang-clang of the fire wagon grew closer. Men shouted, horses whinnied, and the strong smell of smoke permeated the still night air.

"Jailer!" the Kid called out frantically, his hands gripping the bars. "Let us out! The jail's on fire! Open this door!" But his pleas fell on deaf ears as the frightened night jailer dashed for the front of the building and safety. "Jesus God," hollered the Kid, "we'll burn to death!"

At that moment, a heavy chain came snaking through the small back barred window and an unmistakable feminine voice said calmly, "Okay, boy, now!"

Cordell Rogers and the Kid whirled about and watched as the window exploded from the back wall leaving a hole large enough for a man to crawl through.

They looked at each other. They looked at the gaping hole before them. They looked at the mounted horseman outside in the alley.

"Well, what in blazes are you waiting for?" shouted an exasperated Mollie.

Laughing now, the Kid quickly wiggled through the opening and turned to help Rogers get out as thick smoke swirled in and filled the tiny jail cell. Astride her bay, Mollie held the reins of two saddled mounts.

Asking no questions, her father and the Kid climbed atop the horses. The trio headed for the open desert, swiftly disappearing over the horizon while behind them excited, perspiring men pumped water into the brightly blazing, fully engulfed jail shouting to one another, "My God, the prisoners will burn to death!" "How did it happen?" "Somebody must have set the fire!"

The two grateful men making tracks for the border behind a fearless young woman didn't wonder for a second who had set the fire.

7

Santa Fe Sun, August 18, 1868
ROGERS RENEGADES STRIKE AGAIN!

The infamous Rogers Renegades rode into Tucson last noon and made off with $247,638 in gold and paper money. Riding with them was a bold young female believed to be Rogers's only daughter.

It looked as though the gang had finally overplayed their hand when Rogers and the Texas Kid were apprehended and thrown into the Tucson jail. But at midnight a mysterious fire broke out and when it was doused, authorities discovered the outlaws had escaped through a forcefully opened back window. So the city comes up empty-handed, losing the money, the red-haired Rogers, the blond female, and the man with the missing earlobe known as the Texas Kid.

Lew Hatton slowly lowered the newspaper to his desktop. His jaw was clenched, his blue eyes clouded.

"My friend, you do not look like a man who is to celebrate his engagement this very evening."

Dan Nighthorse, the trusted *segundo* of Lew Hatton's huge New Mexico ranch known as Plano Pacifica and his closest friend, had entered the mansion's study so quietly that Lew hadn't heard him. The tall half-breed stood in the doorway, hands in the pockets of his tight black trousers.

Lew held up the paper. "The bastards are at it again, Dan. Thumbing their nose at the law and at me."

Dan Nighthorse didn't need to ask who Lew was talking about. He crossed the room, saying, "What have they done now?"

"Read this," Lew rose and shoved the newspaper at him.

Dan Nighthorse read the article, lowered the paper, shook his head. "I know how you feel, but—"

"Do you, Dan? It's them. It's him, the Texas Kid. Jeffrey Battles, the murdering bastard who killed Dad!"

"You can't be certain." Nighthorse's flat black eyes flickered.

"I am certain. I've told you I learned long ago that dad's murderer was a young, muscular Texan with wavy dark hair, gray eyes, and a left earlobe that had been partially shot away. How many men fit that description? It's Battles, and I'm going—"

"Don't do it, Lew," Dan Nighthorse interrupted him. "It's suicide. Let the lawmen handle it."

"You see how well they've handled it," said Lew. "Had Rogers and Battles locked up and let them escape. They've been riding and robbing for more than three years, for God's sake. Now they're so sure of themselves they've got Rogers's kid riding with them.

That sound like they're afraid of getting caught or killed?"

Ben Nighthorse admitted that Lew had a point. He said, "Says in the paper she's the Kid's woman."

"A charming couple, I'm sure," said Lew. "Imagine what she must look like."

Dan nodded. "And smells like. And acts like. She lives, rides, eats, and sleeps with a bunch of hardened outlaws. I doubt she's much different from them." He smiled, hoping to soften Lew's mood.

Lew's face remained rigid. "I'm going after them. All of them, including the woman who shares Battles's bed."

"His is probably not the only bed she shares," said Dan, still attempting to defuse Lew's anger. Seeing it was no use, he said resolutely, "If you go, then I go with you. If you will not listen to reason, then we ride together."

Lew's gaze met the somber black eyes of the man who to him was a brother. Intelligent, loyal, Dan Nighthorse had been a member of the family from birth.

Fondly Lew recalled the exact day his own life had merged with Dan's. He had been no more than five years old when he had ridden alone out into the rocky, broken country north of the ranch one hot summer's day. He came upon a young Indian woman beneath a massive ledge of volcanic rock. Stoic and silent in her agony, she had been badly beaten and her belly was very fat. Lew brought her home to Plano Pacifica.

That very night the woman gave birth to Dan Nighthorse, with Lew's mother and a half dozen servants in attendance, while a big-eyed Lew waited just beyond the closed door. He was allowed inside for a peek at the squalling, dark-haired infant and all these years later he remembered the exhausted, bruised Indian mother saying proudly, "My son will be called Dan Nighthorse."

It wasn't until much later that Lew learned Dan's father had been a white miner named Daniel McCall and that McCall had left the pregnant Apache girl and returned to his wife in California. Dan's proud mother refused to tell who had beaten her, but Lew suspected it was the white man who had fathered Dan. Apaches would have cut off her nose or an ear had they wished to punish her.

From Dan's birth, Lew had looked on Dan as a brother and had spent as much time down at the Nighthorse adobe at the back edge of the ranch as he had in the big hacienda. When Dan's mother died shortly after his fourteenth birthday, Lew had tried to persuade Dan to move into the hacienda, but Dan had politely refused.

The only time the two of them had ever been apart was when Lew had followed his father, William Hatton, into the war. When he'd left, Lew had said to Nighthorse, "I am leaving the ranch and my mother in your care, Dan."

Seventeen-year-old Dan Nighthorse had gripped his hand and said solemnly, "I will protect both with my life."

And he had meant it. Loyal, trustworthy, and proud. That was Dan Nighthorse.

Now, as Lew looked at Dan, remembering, he said, "No. You must remain here, just as you did in the war."

Dan Nighthorse shook his head. "Then I will not let

you go. Have you forgotten the vow you made to Teresa? You promised you would let the past stay buried."

Lew shrugged, sighed. He hadn't forgotten his promise to the beautiful Spanish girl who was to be his wife. Love for Teresa Castillo had cooled his hot-burning need for revenge. When he'd first returned from the war, limping and thin, his heart had been filled with hatred. He had planned to stay home only long enough to recuperate from his wounds, then go after the men who had killed his father.

But Teresa had changed all that. He had fallen in love with her, and while her protective older brother, Pascual, had made him promise he would wait to marry her until she turned twenty, Teresa had made him promise that he would not put his life in danger. A gentle hand on his arm and he had agreed.

"You promised Teresa," Dan Nighthorse gently repeated.

"I know, but—"

"Need I remind you what a lucky man you are? Tonight you will be officially engaged to Teresa and next year she'll become your bride. Let it go, my friend. Forget about the Rogers Renegades. Focus on the future."

Lew drew a long breath. "Maybe you're right. Nothing can bring Dad back, and I did promise Teresa."

8

Mollie was worried about her papa.

Once so sharp-witted and knowledgeable, he had grown increasingly slow and forgetful. At times he appeared to be totally bewildered and lost, and it frightened Mollie.

Worse, the Kid had criticized her father in front of her and the Renegades. More than once in the past six months, she and the Kid had fought over her father's ability to lead. Their last heated discussion on the subject had taken place earlier this evening and had turned into something frightening.

Now, as Mollie restlessly wandered her darkened bedroom, her thoughts remained on the unpleasant clash with the Kid.

Directly after dinner her father had excused himself, saying he was tired from their last raid. Mollie had teased him about getting old. He had replied that he was indeed growing old, and Mollie was immediately sorry she had said anything.

Sadly she had watched him go, knowing his intent. He would go up and drink himself to sleep as he had done far too many nights of late.

Concerned, Mollie had nervously prowled the big hacienda before finally stepping out onto the back brick patio. A big Mexican moon was rising directly behind the distant mountains, and Mollie inhaled deeply of the bougainvillea-scented air, wishing that her papa would come outside and join her. Wishing they could have one of their long talks like they did when she was a little girl and went to him with her troubles. Wishing he would stop drinking so much whiskey and again be the strong, commanding figure he once had been.

Feeling as if she'd scream if she didn't do something to take her mind off her worries, Mollie crossed the flagstone patio and headed down to the stables.

When she stepped inside the adobe stable, young Raul, one of the three Mexicans who rode with the Renegades, looked up, smiled, and greeted her politely.

"Hello, Raul," Mollie said, returning the smile. "I'm glad you're here. I thought I'd work on my saddle and—"

"You wish to borrow Raul's tin of saddle soap, *sí*?"

"Yes, if you don't mind."

Raul laughed heartily. "My soap is your soap, *Señorita* Mollie." He was handing her the open tin when the Kid sauntered in, thumbs hooked under his low-riding gun belt. Raul nodded to him. "Evening, Kid, I was about to help—"

"Leave us, Raul," the Kid interrupted him.

"Stay, Raul," said Mollie, glaring at the Kid.

Nervously Raul looked at Jeffrey Battles, smiled apologetically at Mollie, and said, "I am going, Kid. I go!" And he hurried out of the stables.

"That was rude," said Mollie. "He was going to help polish my saddle."

"Help you? He can do it for you. Tomorrow."

"I don't want him doing it for me, I want to do it myself. Now if you'll kindly go on about your—"

"Mollie, we need to talk. About your father."

Mollie knew what was coming and she didn't want to hear it. "Some other time, Kid. Suddenly I'm tired. Think I'll go in."

The Kid, thumbs still stuck in his gun belt, stood between her and the door. "We *must* talk, Mollie. It's important."

Mollie decided she'd take the offensive. "Fine, Kid, let's talk. I've been riding with the Renegades for the past eighteen months now. We've hit banks and stages and trains and nobody's been hurt. Eight of us in the gang and not one has ever suffered so much as a hangnail. The Rogers Renegades have an excellent record. So what's there to talk about?"

The Kid grinned and his gray eyes had begun to shine with that hint of madness she'd seen in them when they stood side by side in a bank with their guns drawn.

"We've been real lucky," he said. "Luck doesn't last forever."

"Make your point, Kid. I need to get back to the hacienda."

"No you don't. It's early and you have nothing to do." His tone grew knowing, disrespectful when he added, "I'm sure the colonel has already retired."

"The hour at which my father retires is none of your business."

"When he takes a bottle to bed with him it becomes my business."

Mollie suffered a twinge of guilt. The Kid was right.

Her father's heavy drinking was jeopardizing all their lives. But she lifted her chin and said, "For pete's sake, we just got back from the raid yesterday. He deserves a little time to relax."

"As far as I'm concerned, the colonel deserves a great deal of time to relax. Say for the rest of his life."

"Don't you dare say that about my papa!"

"The old man's had it, Mollie, and it's time you and he faced it. He's going to get us all killed."

"I . . . I'll speak to him about the drinking, but he will continue to lead the Renegades. Understand?"

The Kid took a couple of steps forward. "I'm only thinking of you."

Mollie automatically took a step backward. "Your concern is misplaced. In case you've failed to notice, I never show fear on our raids."

"I have noticed," he said, his eyes gleaming demonically, "and I like that. I like that a lot. I like *you* a lot, Mollie."

"I don't care what you like," she said, the wispy hair on her nape rising.

As if she hadn't spoken, he said, "I especially like it when we knock over a bank together. I like you standing there beside me in those tight charro pants with your gun raised and your breath coming so fast your breasts push against your shirtfront."

"I'm going to bed," snapped Mollie and started past him.

He grabbed her arm, stopped her. "I'll like you in bed too, I know I will."

"Let me go!" Mollie warned, clawing at the strong fingers encircling her upper arm.

The Kid pulled her up against his big, solid frame. "I

will if you'll kiss me." His free hand went into her hair, his blunt fingers tangling in the short blond locks. "Kiss me, Mollie."

"Never!"

"No kiss?" He grinned. "Then show me your birthmark. The colonel says it's a perfect butterfly. Let me see it."

"Certainly not!" she said angrily. "Neither you nor any man will ever see my birthmark!"

"Oh, I will," he assured her. "I'll see it and all the rest when we're married."

"Marriage, the devil!" she shouted, pushing on his broad chest. "You take too much for granted!"

The Kid continued to hold her. Her anger and struggling excited him. The press of her soft body against his brought on instant arousal. He wedged his knee between her legs and wrapped his powerful arms around her in a viselike grip.

Both furious and frightened, Mollie beat on his back and cursed him, turning her head aside so that his questing mouth couldn't capture hers. He bent his head, pressed his bearded face into the open collar of her shirt. When she felt his open lips sucking on the sensitive flesh at the curve of her neck and shoulder, she said the only thing she could think of that might make him stop.

"Let me go or I swear I'll never marry you!"

Reluctantly he raised his head. He looked into her angry, flashing eyes and desire warred with restraint. He wanted her now, but if he took her, it would mean the end. The first and last time. If he waited, she'd be his for a lifetime.

"I'm sorry, Mollie," he said, releasing her. "I was way out of line. Forgive me, it won't happen again."

"You want my forgiveness? Here's how you get it. *Never* touch me again and swear you will never question my father's leadership. Promise me!"

"I promise," said the Kid, thinking how desirable she was, looking forward to the day when this fiery, tempting package would be his to unwrap and enjoy.

"Fine! Now get the hell out of my way!"

Mollie shoved him aside and stormed out of the stables, her heart pounding with fear and anger. She hurried back to the hacienda and rushed up the stairs. Once inside her room she paced angrily, muttering under her breath, wondering why her papa couldn't see the Kid for the kind of man he was.

Jeffrey Battles was dangerous. Deadly dangerous. And he wanted *her*.

Mollie again felt the fine hair rise on the nape of her neck. She crossed the room and threw the heavy bolt on the bedroom door.

As Mollie was anxiously locking her door against him, the Kid was slipping silently through a door downstairs. A door that had been purposely left unlocked. Inside, the Kid's latest conquest, a young pretty kitchen maid, trembled at the sight of him. Guadalupe waited expectantly as the big, bearded man blew out the lone lamp and crossed to her.

Aroused from his encounter with Mollie, the Kid was eager as he pushed the girl's dress up over her brown thighs. In seconds he had stripped her naked and she dutifully crawled atop the bed while he shed his clothes. As soon as he was bare, he was on her, pressing her onto her back, pushing her thighs apart, taking her roughly with a wild hunger spurred by Mollie.

9

◆

"We'll hit the stage right here." The Kid tapped a spread map of New Mexico. "One of the biggest payrolls ever bound for Fort Whipple is coming out of Santa Fe, and . . ."

He explained to Mollie and her father that since the Fort Whipple payroll usually came out of Phoenix, there would be only the driver and one soldier riding shotgun with the Santa Fe shipment.

"On the first leg of the journey—from Santa Fe to Albuquerque—there will be no extra guards," the Kid concluded.

"When?" asked Cordell Rogers.

"The shipment leaves Santa Fe on the Overland stage the morning of October twentieth."

"Only eight days," said Rogers and downed a large swallow of whiskey. "We better leave tomorrow," he said, hoping he'd feel better by then. Hoping that the persistent weakness he hadn't mentioned to Mollie or the Kid would be gone.

"You're the boss, Colonel," said the Kid pointedly.

By morning, Cordell Rogers was feeling worse. Much worse. He was too sick to go on the raid, and

Mollie refused to go without him. She summoned a doctor, remained at the hacienda, and cared for her ailing father.

The doctor confirmed that Cordell Rogers was suffering from a bad case of influenza. He was a very sick man—so sick he told Mollie that if anything happened to him, she was to go directly to his old friend, Napier Dixon, in Maya, Arizona.

"Nothing's going to happen to you," scoffed Mollie.

"Promise me, child. If you're ever in trouble, ever need help, you'll go to Napier," said her father. "Ask anybody in town and they'll know where to find him. He owns half of Maya."

The morning of October twentieth dawned cold and clear in the high deserts of northern New Mexico. At the opulent Castillo mansion two miles east of Santa Fe, an excited Teresa Castillo hurried about her bedroom, checking to make sure her duenna, Conchita, had packed everything for their journey.

Satisfied that all was ready, Teresa took one last quick look in the mirror, smiled, and lifted the cherished gold cross from her full bosom. The cross had been her engagement present from Lew, and she would never forget the look in his eyes when he had given it to her.

"Teresa, my treasure," he'd said softly, and showed her that *Mi tesoro*—"my treasure"—was etched on the cross's smooth back. He had kissed her tenderly, then put the cross around her neck. She hadn't taken it off since. The cross would, she had told her handsome fiancé, rest on her heart for as long as her heart should beat.

Dropping the cross back in place, Teresa offered silent thanks that Lew had finally agreed to let her take this morning's stage to Paso del Norte. He hadn't wanted her to make the trip. He had cautioned that it wasn't safe for a young lady to be traveling alone. She had assured him that she wouldn't be alone, Conchita would be with her. Besides, the short sixty miles between Santa Fe and Albuquerque was to be the only part of the journey without an extra escort. At Albuquerque her cousins, Sergio and Ramon Chagra, would meet her and see her safely across the border and beyond.

"If you must go," he had said, continuing to look worried, "I'm sending Dan Nighthorse with you to Albuquerque."

Teresa grabbed up her warm fox traveling cape and felt bonnet, and hurried downstairs.

Her brother Pascual, a look of apology on his face, met her at the base of the stairs. "I am so sorry, Teresa. You cannot go. Conchita has sprained her ankle badly this morning, and—"

"No! But I must go, I must. Oh, Pascual, you know how I've looked forward to this visit with our parents." Her lips began to tremble and tears filled her dark eyes. "Please let me go. I . . . I haven't seen my mother in more than three years, and I—" She began to choke, stopped speaking.

It was Pascual's undoing. "Ah, little Teresa," he said, drawing her to him, "Sometimes I forget that you are still a child. Not yet twenty years old. Of course you need to see your mother."

Against her brother's shoulder, Teresa said, "Please let me go. Dan Nighthorse is riding with us, and—"

"But there will be no woman with you. No chaperon."

Teresa pulled back, looked up at him. "Just this once couldn't we deviate from the old customs?"

Pascual finally smiled. "I suppose it wouldn't hurt if—"

"Oh, *gracias, gracias,*" she said, hugged him tightly, and confided, "I am so glad I said good-bye to Lew last night. If he knew Conchita was not coming with me . . ." She shrugged slender shoulders, kissed her brother's jaw, and flew happily to the front door.

It was just past noon when the southbound stage reached the flatlands above Bernalillo. Inside the dusty Concord coach, Teresa Castillo yawned sleepily and daydreamed. Atop the box, the white-whiskered stage driver held the lead and swing team lines, skillfully guiding six galloping horses across the flat tablelands. Beside him on the wooden seat, a young army lieutenant in uniform dozed peacefully, his loaded carbine on the floorboard at his feet. Directly behind the coach, Dan Nighthorse, his obsidian eyes keenly alert, loped along on his big chestnut gelding, a walnut-stocked Colt Dragoon riding his hip and a long-barreled Henry rifle in the scabbard on his saddle.

Suddenly his black eyes blinked in stunned surprise as six masked mounted bandits exploded out of a stand of cottonwoods. With lightning speed Dan drew his Dragoon. But the Texas Kid was even quicker. Jeff Battles shot the gun from Dan's hand and shouted as Dan reached for the scabbarded rifle, "Don't try it!"

The startled stage driver shouted to the lead horses and furiously pumped the reins up and down. But two nimble, daring young Mexican bandits, agile as acrobats, leaped from their speeding mounts onto the backs of the stage's leads and within seconds the six powerful beasts slowed. The terrified young lieutenant, hands held high, never even reached for his carbine.

Inside the coach, Teresa Castillo pressed herself back against the leather seat and prayed as the stage rattled to a halt. One of the Mexican bandits rapidly scaled the coach and withdrew from the luggage boot a canvas bag marked U.S. ARMY. He tossed the bag to W. C. Petty while Steven Andrews kept his Spencer trained on the lieutenant. Will Hurdman covered the cursing, red-faced stage driver. The Kid's twin ivory-handled guns were aimed directly at the broad chest of Dan Nighthorse.

"That's it, we have the payroll," shouted Will Hurdman, "let's get out of here."

"Hold on a minute," said the Kid and, reholstering one Colt .44, climbed down off his horse. "The passengers might have money and jewels."

Dan Nighthorse immediately swung out of the saddle and dropped to the ground. "Stay right where you are, Indian," warned the Kid, jerked the Concord's door open, and looked inside. "Well, well, what have we here?"

A muscle jumping in his jaw, his black eyes fierce, Dan Nighthorse shouted, "She has no money, no jewels!"

"Maybe I should find out for myself," said the Kid, lifting a booted foot up into the coach. He looked at the trembling Teresa and liked what he saw. "Keep 'em covered, boys. This won't take long."

"Damn it, Kid," grumbled Will Hurdman, "grab the jewelry and let's go."

"I'll do that," said the Kid and started to climb inside.

Dan Nighthorse moved with pantherlike speed. Unarmed, he reflexively came after the Kid, determined to protect Lew Hatton's fiancée.

The Texas Kid squeezed the trigger of his .44 and shot Dan Nighthorse squarely in the chest. Dan slumped to the dirt, clutching at a white shirtfront that was swiftly turning scarlet. A high, piercing scream came from inside the coach.

"That crazy son of a bitch was trying to kill me," said the Kid, kicking at Dan's limp body.

The grim-faced Renegades exchanged disapproving looks, and Steven Andrews and W. C. Petty said in unison, "That does it. Let's go!"

"No," said the Kid, "*I* am the leader here. I'll tell you when we leave."

He climbed into the coach, shutting the door behind him. He smiled with pleasure and took the seat opposite the softly sobbing Teresa Castillo.

"You . . . you can ha-have my diamond ring," she stammered, stripping her engagement ring from her finger. "It's the only jewelry I have." She thrust it toward the masked bandit, her heart racing.

The Kid's heart was racing just as rapidly as Teresa's. It always beat fast during a robbery, and the excitement of shooting the Indian had increased its acceleration. And, just as always, that old familiar sexual excitement made his blood heat and surge. The arousal he felt was stronger than usual—almost as powerful as that first time Mollie had stood beside him in a Tucson bank demanding money.

Jeffrey Battles realized this was the one time he

could get total release when he most needed it. Unlike the spirited Mollie, this girl was defenseless and frightened. He had always fantasized about making love during a robbery. Here, finally, was his chance.

His groin rapidly swelling, the Kid took the diamond from Teresa's outstretched hand, shoved it into his shirt pocket, and moved across the coach to sit beside her. He snatched the lap robe from her knees and dropped it to the floor. Waving his revolver in his hand, he ordered, "Take off that wrap."

"No, please, it is cold, and—"

"Open it."

Teresa dutifully unfastened the lush fox wrap, supposing he meant to steal it. But when she started to shrug out of it, he stopped her. "That's fine. Leave it around your shoulders."

Sniffing, she gave him a questioning look, and cringed when he pointedly lowered his smoky gaze to her bosom. Her breasts rose and fell rapidly beneath the tight-fitting jacket of her traveling suit, and her heartbeat doubled when she saw the evil gleam in the outlaw's eyes as he methodically lowered the shades over the coach's windows.

Her furiously pounding heart stopped beating completely when, allowing the cold steel barrel of his pistol to gently graze the side of her throat, the bandit said, "Make one sound, *chica,* and I'll blow your pretty head off."

He jerked the bandanna from his bearded face and Teresa watched, horrified, as a huge, black-gloved hand went to the tiny silver buttons at her throat. With amazing dexterity for a man wearing a glove, he managed, in a few short seconds, to flip open the entire row of buttons from throat to waist.

Teresa never made a sound. She didn't dare. The gun's steel cylinder rested just below her jaw. So she remained totally still and mute while the Kid, licking his thin lips, jerked at the tiny pink bow bordering her camisole. He eagerly swept the gauzy fabric aside, exposing her full, quivering breasts. And still Teresa did not make a sound.

Her dark eyes closed in shame and fear when a gloved hand cupped her left breast and his mouth took quick possession of her trembling lips. The unwanted contact shocked her into action and sound, but her cries of outrage were swallowed up in the devouring mouth clamped firmly over hers.

In a nightmarish blur she felt his wet, slick tongue plunging deep into her throat, repelling her, choking her, while strong, gloved fingers plucked cruelly at her naked nipples.

The worst was yet to come.

His lips left hers and he again warned her to stay quiet or die. Then, with his teeth, he tugged the glove from his fingers and lowered his hand to her skirts. In seconds the skirts were shoved up around her waist, and when she heard the ripping of fabric, Teresa knew her silky underwear was being torn away. Chill air rushed in to nip at her exposed flesh, and then hot fingers were on her icy skin, pushing her legs apart.

Again she closed her eyes. He ordered her to open them. She obeyed. And was forced to watch him unbutton his trousers and release his huge, pulsing erection. The shocking sight of the enormous male member jerking on his hairy belly made her whimper pitifully, despite her best efforts to remain silent.

Ignoring her whimpers, he climbed atop her. The

quick stab of pain she felt was excruciating. Tears washed down her flushed cheeks, and she bit the back of her hand to keep from screaming as he callously took her virginity. Blood stained her pale thighs as he pierced the taut feminine barrier of her innocence. Immediately he began to thrust deeply, painfully into her dry tightness, battering her, brutalizing her with his huge, pulsing tumescence.

In a minute his release began. His revolver still held to her throat and his hot gray eyes on her bare bouncing breasts, the Texas Kid spilled himself into the weeping Teresa Castillo, then fell away, panting and gasping.

Frantically lowering her skirts and pulling the dress together over her breasts, Teresa fought the nausea churning inside her and silently endured the pain that was sending fingers of fire throughout her lower belly.

"Hey, what's this?" the Kid asked, pushing her jacket apart again, reaching for the cross of gold resting between her trembling breasts. He lifted the cross, turned it over and saw the inscription. *Mi tesoro*. He grinned. "My treasure. Well, you sure were a treasure, darlin', so I'll take this cross to remember you by." Finally reholstering his revolver, the Kid took the cross from her, draped it around his neck and fastened it behind his head. The heartsick Teresa could do nothing but look at him with sad, dark eyes.

Dropping the gold cross into his thick chest hair, the Texas Kid reached out, took Teresa's chin firmly in his hand, gave her bruised mouth a rough parting kiss, and said, *"Gracias, mi tesoro."*

10

◈

"The Lord is my light and my salvation; whom shall I fear? The Lord is the strength of my life; of whom shall . . ." The minister's strong, clear voice carried on the cold afternoon winds.

Lew Hatton, the collar of his dark chesterfield coat turned up around his ears, stood in the weak winter sunlight before the newly dug grave, his hands folded before him, eyes dry.

Dan's was the second funeral Lew had attended that day. He preferred this simple graveside service to the pageantry of the morning's lengthy ceremony at Saint Mary's.

He looked down at the closed pine coffin.

And saw again that other one, that heavy bronze coffin, open and draped in white lace. He was again lifting that delicate lace to look one final time on her angelic face, so beautiful, so peaceful in death.

Teresa. *Mi tesoro*.

". . . as the soul returneth to God." The minister concluded and closed his Bible. The short service ended with a prayer.

"Won't you come home with us, Lew," said Pascual Castillo. "We will share our grief."

Shaking his dark head, Lew turned and walked away as the first few flakes of snow swirled down out of the wintry New Mexico sky.

Back in his quiet, lonely mansion, Lew shed his coat, poured himself a stiff drink, and stood staring sightlessly into the leaping flames burning brightly in the stone fireplace.

He had lost them both. His brother and his sweetheart.

Dan Nighthorse had lived for ten days before infection had set in. Long enough to tell Lew who had shot him.

"It was him, Lew. The Texas Kid," Dan had said. "Big dark bearded man with gray eyes and no left earlobe. Teresa? Is she . . . ?"

"Teresa is fine, Dan," Lew had lied. "Badly frightened, but unharmed."

In the beginning Lew had believed that it was true. Teresa had weepingly told him that nothing had happened other than the robbery. The bandits had taken her diamond engagement ring and her cross. He had consoled her, assuring her that the jewelry was not important. There would be plenty of diamond rings and gold crosses.

He had felt sure she would be fine when the shock of her ordeal had worn off and she felt safe and secure again at home. But it hadn't happened. She was never herself again. She was nervous and distraught and cold and withdrawn. She shrank from his caresses, found excuses to stay away from him.

When she abruptly called off their engagement and entered Saint Mary's convent, Lew finally forced himself to consider the real reason Teresa had changed so much since the holdup. The hot water that poured into his mouth as fast as he could swallow it was his body's way of telling him he had guessed the horrible truth.

Two short days after entering the convent, Teresa was dead.

They told him that she had died of natural causes, but he knew that a healthy twenty-year-old woman did not die of natural causes. It was whispered that she had taken her own life, but that wasn't true either, as far as he was concerned.

His beautiful Teresa had been murdered by the Texas Kid, the same as his brother Dan. The Kid had killed them both. Murdered them in cold blood. Ended their lives before they had ever really lived.

Slowly Lew sagged to his knees before the fireplace. He bowed his head. A sob of anguish—too long denied—broke from his aching throat. His wide shoulders began to shake uncontrollably, and his body jerked. He fell over onto his stomach and cried heartbrokenly, pounding his fists on the floor until his knuckles were red and raw.

Lew stayed there through the long sleepless night while the fire burned out in the stone fireplace and the desert winds howled outside the frosty windows and the room turned as cold as his shattered world.

At dawn he rose from the hard floor. His dreams, his tears, his regrets, had vanished in the night. Only the need for revenge remained.

Lew Hatton strapped on his gun belt.

Mollie shivered and wondered who would be next.

The past year had been a very bad one for the Renegades. Some unknown, overly diligent bounty hunter seemed to have a blood vendetta against the gang. One by one the men who rode with the Rogers Renegades had disappeared.

The Mexican cousins, Jesus and Arto, who shared the same birthday, were the first to be captured. The story came back that when they rode up to Tillie Howard's Parlour House in Paso del Norte to celebrate, they were greeted by a cold-eyed bounty hunter who had leveled his loaded pistols at them and said, "Happy birthday, *amigos.*"

Next it was N. C. Petty. He had gotten so homesick he had ridden all the way back to El Dorado, Arkansas. He'd no more than sat down at a faro table than the dealer grinned at N.C. and flipped—not a card—but a pair of handcuffs on him, and said coolly, "Welcome home, N.C."

Mollie found it uncanny that the lone bounty chaser had so easily succeeded where dozens of lawmen had failed. For three years the Renegades had lived in the same grand hacienda fifteen miles south of the border without fear of apprehension. They had raided at will in the U.S. territories and had seldom even come close to being captured.

But for the past year, the danger of crossing the border had made only the most lucrative of scores worth the risk. Even in Mexico, Mollie no longer felt safe. Gone was the big hacienda with its luxuries and servants. They now lived in a never-ending succession of Mexican hotels, moving often from village to village, trusting no one. And still Steven Andrews had been captured in broad daylight from a south-of-the-border cantino.

That last incident had happened a couple of weeks

ago, and with the springtime death of Will Hurdman from consumption and the flight of young Raul Rodriguez to Guadalajara, there were now only three Renegades. Her papa. The Kid. And herself.

Mollie felt it was time to give up this dangerous profession. She had argued her point often lately, and to her surprise, the Kid agreed. But only after one last big raid.

Gold mine money was pouring into the Douglas, Arizona, bank. They could grab it and be back across the border in no time.

Mollie was dead set against it, and as soon as she could get her father off alone, she told him so.

"I am ready to give up this kind of life," said Cordell Rogers. "I'm old and I'm tired and the money doesn't mean anything to me. I just want peace. I wish that we could . . ."

"What, Papa? Tell me," Mollie prompted.

"Nothing. Tell you what, if you'll stay here, I'll go with the Kid to Douglas and make it my last holdup."

"No, I'm coming with you,"

"Mollie, honey, just this once, could you please obey your old papa and stay here?"

"I'll stay," she said, "but as soon as you get back, we're clearing out. You and me, without the Kid."

Cordell Rogers nodded. "That might not be such a bad idea."

Cordell Rogers and the Texas Kid, their saddlebags filled with stolen money, galloped out of Douglas, Arizona. A deputy sheriff and a half dozen townsmen chased them for a couple of miles, then turned back.

Relieved that the robbery and lawmen and danger

were behind him, Cordell Rogers spurred his mount ahead of the Kid's. He felt lighthearted for the first time in years. In half an hour they would be back across the border and by nightfall he'd be at their hotel pouring himself a whiskey while Mollie smiled and counted the money.

"Colonel," called the Kid, "hold up a minute."

Rogers reined in his mount, turned and squinted at the Kid. "Something wrong?"

"Not a thing," said the Kid as he drew one of his ivory-handled Colts. "See that mine shack off to your left. Ride to it."

"What the hell's gotten into you?" asked Rogers. "Put that gun away."

"Ride to the shack, Colonel," the Kid repeated, his gun aimed at Rogers.

At the abandoned wooden shack both men dismounted. The Kid hung his sombrero on the saddle horn and, indicating the shack's open door, said, "After you, Colonel."

Inside they stood facing each other, Cordell Rogers with his hands raised, the Kid with both pistols pointed at him.

"Why, Jeff?" Rogers asked. "You've been like a son to me."

"Sorry, Colonel, sentimentality doesn't do a lot for me."

"The question is still why?"

"Necessity. No other reason. Alive, you're in my way. Dead, you have great value."

"Your reasoning escapes me."

"No doubt. There was a time you were sharp and I admired your intelligence. Now you're nothing but a whiskey-soaked old fool and you're standing in my way." He laughed at the hurt expression on Rogers's ruddy face. "All these years you've called the shots when it should have been me. I've been the brains behind the outfit, yet every time we pull a heist, every damned newspaper credits the Rogers Renegades."

"Is that what this is about? Because the gang went by my name and you didn't get your share of notoriety?"

"That's not it," the Kid scoffed. "I want Mollie and I want her now."

"Mollie is not going to—"

"Shut up! I'll tell you what Mollie is going to do. She's going to marry me. I'll console her over her father's death and she'll fall right into my arms."

"Jesus Christ, after all these years you still don't know a thing about my daughter. Mollie will *never* marry you."

The Kid's eyes narrowed. "I know how to handle women like Mollie. She's spirited and needs a firm hand. I'll tame her."

He fired one of his drawn revolvers.

Cordell Rogers didn't flinch when the bullet stung his left ear lobe, tearing it away. Blood dripped down onto his shoulder.

"Now I understand," he said with no emotion.

"Do you?"

"You figure that when the authorities find my body, they will think I'm you."

"So the liquor hasn't completely pickled your brain, eh, Colonel?" said the Kid. "You're right. When your body is found, word will spread that the Texas Kid has been killed. Meanwhile I'll have Mollie and the money."

"I like the scheme. Only problem is, if they find me

too soon, they'll wonder when the Texas Kid's hair turned red."

The Kid grinned. "I'm told that when a man is burned, his hair is the first thing to go."

"I see," said Cordell Rogers.

"Good for you." One-handed, the Kid unfastened the clasp of the gold cross he wore around his neck. Handing it to Rogers, he commanded, "Put this on."

Puzzled, Cordell Rogers took the cross, turned it over, and read the inscription: *Mi tesoro.* "Is this added identification?"

"You talk too much." The Kid aimed, squeezed the trigger again, and watched in fascination as the bullet slammed into Rogers's chest. Rogers swayed, but stayed on his feet.

"Touch Mollie," he warned, "and I'll come back from hell for you, Kid."

Two more bullets struck his chest in quick succession. He sagged to his knees, clutched his throat, which was rapidly filling with blood, and fell forward.

The fire caught and blazed as soon as the Kid put the match to the rotting wood. He felt the heat on his face as tongues of flame shot up the plank walls. He looked one last time at the dead man on the floor.

"It was nothing personal, Colonel," he said. Then he grinned, pivoted, and hurried out of the burning building.

Outside he climbed atop Rogers's mount, leaving his own tied to a nearby cottonwood with his black sombrero hooked on the saddle horn. Laughing, he laid the spurs to Rogers's big steed and headed for Mexico.

And Mollie.

11

Mollie was devastated.

Despite her father's weaknesses, she had always thought him indestructible. Now he was gone—killed by a lawman's bullet—and she was alone.

Head aching, eyes red-rimmed, Mollie was ushered away from the brief late afternoon memorial service by the solicitous Kid. Back at the hotel, he ordered a meal sent up to her suite.

When the food arrived, he poured Madeira into two glasses and handed one to Mollie. "Drink it," he urged. "It will help you relax."

Mollie sipped the wine and almost instantly began to feel its calming affects. When she had drained the glass, she said, "Thank you, Jeff, for taking care of everything. Now, if you don't mind, I'm awfully tired."

"Have another glass of Madeira and you'll sleep like a baby."

"It would be nice to sleep," said Mollie wearily. "I am tired, so very tired."

"Of course you are," he said sympathetically, pouring her another glass of wine.

Then Mollie found herself seated on the sofa with

the Kid beside her, his comforting arm around her. With her thoughts jumbled, her reflexes slowed, it seemed normal to lean her aching head on his shoulder. She finished the second glass of wine.

"I'll stay with you tonight," the Kid said, and warning bells began to ring in Mollie's fuzzy brain.

"No, no, that isn't necessary," she said, slipped from his arm, and stood up.

The Kid rose. "Mollie, honey, your daddy's gone and now it's up to me to take care of you. Tomorrow we'll marry, and—"

"Marry? You?" She was incredulous. "I'm not about to marry you, Kid, and I want you to go. Get out of my room."

"You don't know what you want. You're a child. A spoiled child who has no idea what it is to be woman." He loomed big and close before her. "High time I showed you. Don't want marriage? Fine with me, but you're *my* woman, Mollie, and I'm not waiting any longer to have you."

Mollie automatically reached for the pistol on her hip, then remembered she had respectfully left it behind when she'd gone to her father's memorial service. The gun was in the other room.

Backing away, Mollie said, "You're talking crazy, Kid. I'm not yours, I'll never be yours."

"Sure you will, honey," he drawled, advancing on her, spurs clanking, eyes gleaming.

Fighting to keep the terror from her voice, she warned, "I'll scream. I'll scream so loud—"

"Scream your head off," he said, grinning wolfishly, "no one will pay any attention."

He was right. In this second-rate *posada,* screams

and shouts were heard round the clock. Nobody ever bothered to investigate.

Knowing her only hope was to show no fear, Mollie kept her tone level when she said, "I forbid you to—"

"First lesson," he cut her off, "you'll forbid me nothing. You might have bossed your drunken old daddy around, but I won't hold still for it."

He grabbed her arm then and roughly pulled her to him. Mollie was crushed to his solid length, and before she could protest, his thin, hard mouth came down on hers, pressing her lips painfully against her teeth. She squirmed and groaned and twisted her head.

He released her. She backed away, wiping her mouth on her shirtsleeve. Unruffled, the Kid began to unbutton his shirt.

"You can make this easy or hard on yourself," he said conversationally. "I planned on being gentle with you, but I prefer it the other way." His gray eyes glittered with sexual excitement. "I always figured you'd be the fighting kind. Bet you'll put up one hell of a battle, won't you, darlin'? Scratch and claw and make me work hard to get it?" The grin growing wider on his bearded face, he took off his shirt, tossed it aside.

"You are insane!" Mollie said, repulsed by his words and by the sight of his bare torso. Hair—thick, dark animal hair—covered his entire chest and belly and crawled up over his shoulders and down his back. "You're crazy!"

"Crazy about you," he said. "Have been since the first time I saw you when you were just a skinny fifteen-year-old kid. I wanted you then. Couldn't sleep for thinking about how it would feel to have those long, coltish legs wrapped around my back."

"Shut up, you filthy beast," Mollie shouted, her violet eyes flashing with anger and disgust.

"Now you're no longer a skinny kid. There's soft, lush breasts beneath that blouse. Are your nipples big, Mollie? Are they the size of silver dollars?" He chuckled merrily and continued, "And that pretty little ass of yours. I've watched you wiggle it in those tight pants and dreamed of the day I would bare it and let it fill my hands while I—"

"Dear God!" Mollie choked and ran for the door.

She never made it. He beat her there, blocked her way, and again pulled her into his arms. Sickened, Mollie did exactly what the Kid wanted her to do. She fought him like a tigress. She screamed and cursed and hit at him. She sank sharp teeth into a sweat-slick, hairy shoulder and bit him as hard as she could. He loved it. His erection was already fully formed and Mollie, struggling impotently, could feel the hard length of him straining against her trembling belly.

She fought harder. She shouted louder. She cursed more colorfully.

It was a powerful aphrodisiac to the Kid. He stood, booted feet wide apart, bare arms wrapped around her, and knew this was going to be a night without compare. He raised a hand, gripped Mollie's chin, and bent to kiss her. Catching her with her mouth open, he thrust his tongue deep inside. She frantically tried to pull away. His hand moved around to clasp the back of her head as his plundering mouth stayed fused with hers.

Mollie was panicky. The Kid's thick, bristly beard was covering her nose, his tongue was filling her mouth. She couldn't breathe. Using her sharp nails, she viciously scraped deep furrows down his back.

It worked. He took his mouth from hers and grabbed her arms. "You scratching me up before I even put it in, honey?" A demonic light flashed in his eyes "What *will* you do to me in bed?"

"I am *not* going to bed with you!" she said and spit at him.

He shoved her arms behind her back and held both her wrists in one big hand. He raised his other and rubbed the spittle into the thick mat of hair covering his chest.

Smiling, he said, "That's all right, darlin'. You wet my chest and I'll wet yours." His fingers went to the buttons of her blouse.

Squirming, struggling, Mollie winced when her blouse was pushed apart and he laid a hand on her thin chemise. With one swift jerk he ripped it open, and added heat leapt into his eyes when her bare breasts spilled out.

"Now which one should I lick first?" he said huskily, "the left nipple or the right?"

His fascination with her bared breasts caused him to shift his weight, moving back just a trifle, leaving a bit of space between their bodies. It was enough for Mollie to bring a forceful, punishing knee up to slam into his swollen groin.

The Kid yelped in pain and released her. Mollie flew across the room to the door and had it open before he recovered enough for pursuit. Jerking her blouse together, she bounded down the stairs. Half-crazed, in pain, the Kid came after her. He caught her halfway down. She screamed her outrage when he scooped her up in his arms, turned, and climbed the stairs.

More than a dozen men, loafing in the hotel lobby,

saw and heard them. Some laughed and slapped their knees. Others envied the big, bearded Anglo. None considered the disturbance to be anything out of the ordinary.

Back inside the suite, the Kid kicked the door shut behind them. He walked straight to the bedroom and dumped Mollie on the bed. Before she could rise, he was pinning her to the lumpy mattress with his big body.

They wrestled among the bedcovers and all the while Mollie's fevered brain was churning. While she twisted her head from side to side to avoid his mouth, her eyes fell on the embroidery scissors on a night table where she'd flung them after cutting her hair. The blades were not long, but they were sharp. The scissors were her only hope. No one was going to help her. She had to save herself. She judged the distance to the scissors and inwardly groaned. They were too far away.

There was only one way she would get them within reach.

Mollie abruptly stopped fighting. She made herself go limp and then she said, as if excited, "Kiss me, Kid. Kiss me."

He raised his head and looked at her, an expression of confusion in his eyes. For what seemed an eternity he stared down at her, his big body pinning her, his bearded face looming directly above her own.

"Mollie, darlin'," he said and lowered his mouth to hers.

Fighting her revulsion, Mollie allowed him to kiss her. Acting as though she liked it, she wound her arms around his neck and kissed him back, sighing and moaning to convince him she was enjoying it. Believing that he had subdued her and she was now as aroused as he, the Kid let down his defenses. He rolled over onto his back, bringing Mollie with him.

For a time they stayed like that, kissing, stroking. Then they rolled once more, moving closer and closer to the night table. Mollie was again on her back with the Kid atop her, his mouth ravaging hers, his eyes closed in building ecstasy. Hers were wide open, and her right hand was inching toward the table. When her fingertips touched the scissors, an unconscious gurgle of relief rose in her throat and surfaced. The Kid took it as a sigh of passion.

Mollie snatched up the scissors and immediately raised them over the Kid's broad back. At that second, he raised his head and looked at her with something close to tenderness in his eyes. She gave him one last chance.

"Let me go," she said. "Please. I don't want this. I don't want you."

"Why, you little bitch!" he snarled. "There's no being good to you, is there? There's only one thing you understand and that's force. Well, if it's rape you want, I'm your man." His mouth came cruelly back down on hers while his hand went between them to unbutton his trousers.

With a sigh of resignation, Mollie lifted the scissors high and, with all her strength, brought them down squarely into the middle of Jeff Battles's broad back. It took a second for him to respond, to figure out what had happened.

His face suddenly becoming a mask of shock and pain, he stiffened and collapsed atop her. Crying hysterically now, Mollie managed to roll him off her and scramble to her feet. Trembling and sobbing, she backed away, her hands covering her mouth, her eyes wide with the horror of what she had done.

Was he dead? Had she killed him? Should she run downstairs and ask for help? Go for a doctor? Notify the *federales*?

Mollie hurriedly drew on a fresh chemise and blouse, buckled her gun belt around her hips, took her saddlebags and went directly to the Kid's room. Working quickly, she shoved all the stolen loot into the fancy, blood-red leather saddlebags her papa had given her for her birthday. Gold coins and bars soon weighted down the saddlebags, and when Mollie hung them over her shoulder, she staggered under the weight of the fortune.

She managed to make it down the stairs and out into the dusty street to her horse. It took all her strength to toss the loaded saddlebags over the mount's back. Gasping for breath, she swung up into the saddle and fled.

She had to get out of Mexico. She had a better chance against the authorities in the States than she did in Mexico against the Kid.

Mollie kicked her mount into a gallop and headed north as her papa's words came back to her. "If anything ever happens to me, promise me you'll ride straight to Arizona and my old friend, Napier Dixon."

Lew Hatton didn't hear the knock on the heavy carved door. A servant ushered the nighttime caller into Lew's paneled study. Lew looked up from his desk to see an elegantly gowned woman standing in the shadows cast by the dying fire.

"Mrs. Maxwell," he acknowledged, but did not rise.

"Elizabeth. Call me Elizabeth."

"What is it you want, Mrs. Maxwell?" came the deep, bored voice of the man lounging back in his chair with the buttons of his fine silk shirt open halfway down his dark chest.

"I want you to make love to me," she said, neither embarrassed or ashamed to make such a frank declaration.

Lew gave her a half-scornful smile. "On the very day you buried your beloved husband?"

"Yes," she was quick to reply. "Finally there is nothing standing in our way. You refused me all those years because you had a beautiful young sweetheart. Then even after you lost your sweetheart, you continued to turn me down, saying you didn't make love to another man's wife. I am no longer a wife. I'm a widow. Make love to me, Lew."

Lew slowly pushed back his chair, swung his long legs up onto the desk, and crossed one foot over the other. He raised his arms, laced his fingers loosely behind his dark head and looked at her with amused interest.

Finally he said, "Think you can get out of that dress with no help?"

The brazen woman smiled triumphantly. Then with amazing swiftness she shed her clothes. In a few scant seconds her shimmering satin gown and lace-trimmed underthings were discarded and the petite, ivory-skinned Mrs. Maxwell stood there brazenly before Lew wearing nothing save her black silk stockings, high-heeled slippers, and a glittering diamond necklace with matching diamond earscrews.

She slowly pirouetted for his benefit and when she was again facing him, she asked, "Do you not find me beautiful?" Her hands went to her hips and she moved her satin-slippered feet apart in a provocative pose.

His hooded eyes riveted to her luscious bare body, Lew languidly studied her. The merry widow was exactly the kind of woman with whom he enjoyed making love. Small and soft and fragrant and coquettish. Stunningly beautiful. Fragilely feminine. Endlessly desirable. And shamelessly wanton.

Lew's hands came down from behind his head. His booted feet returned to the floor. He rose and undressed while the naked Mrs. Maxwell watched delightedly. When he was as naked as she, Lew dropped back down onto his leather chair and motioned her to him.

Giggling girlishly, Mrs. Maxwell climbed onto the lap of the dark, handsome man and eagerly began kissing his sulky, sexy mouth. She sighed as his dark, lean hands swept enticingly over her shoulders and back and breasts.

And when, minutes later, Lew easily lifted her, then settled her astride him, she wet her lips excitedly and raised herself up, purposely allowing one of her full, soft breasts to swing into his face. Shivering deliciously as he obligingly kissed the taut nipple, she wrapped slender fingers around his awesome tumescence and eased herself down on his rigid, pulsing maleness. Sounds of wonder and gratitude issued from her open lips.

"Mmm, yes, oh yes," she murmured as she rode him enthusiastically, her hands gripping his muscled chest, her bare breasts bouncing seductively, and her rounded bottom slapping against his hard, hair-dusted thighs.

Lew's strong, sure hands gripped her flaring hips, and he guided her movements as he sat there with his legs apart, rhythmically thrusting his pelvis, driving into her.

Their climaxes came quickly. Too quickly to satisfy either of them completely. Both wanted more. After only a short rest while they regained their lost breath, Lew urged the brunette beauty up off his lap and he too rose.

She said, "Darling, I want more."

"You'll get more," was his quick reply and he swept everything off his cluttered desk, turned her about, and sat her atop it. "As much as you want and more."

Mrs. Maxwell squealed with joy when she lowered her eyes and saw that he was already again erect and able to give her pleasure. She happily looped her arms around his neck as he pushed her legs wide apart and moved into position. His tanned hands went beneath the twin cheeks of her bottom and drew her to him, telling her if she wanted it to take it.

"Yes, yes, I want it. Oh, God, you're so big, so hard," she murmured, reaching for him.

But before she could take him completely a loud knock came on the carved door.

"I'm tied up now, Eduardo," Lew called out as the throbbing tip of his tumescence slid into the hot-as-fire widow.

"It's Chando, *jefe*. There's word on the Kid."

"Be right there," Lew said and quickly pulled out, his desire instantly gone.

Hers, however, was not. Blinking in confusion and frustration, she said, "You can't get me this hot and then leave me like this."

"Sorry, this is important," Lew said, reached for his discarded pants and anxiously hunched into them.

"And I'm not?" she fretted, leaping off the desk.

"Good night, Mrs. Maxwell," Lew said, and left her.

The slender, middle-aged Mexican who had replaced Dan Nighthorse as *segundo* of Plano Pacifica was waiting for Lew in the drawing room.

"The Texas Kid is dead, *jefe*," he came right to the point. "His body was found in a burned building in southern Arizona."

"No!" said Lew. "Damn it, no. I wanted him. I wanted the son of a bitch. Are you sure, Chando? Could it be a mistake?"

"No mistake. His body was found just hours after he and Rogers hit the Douglas bank. The Kid's horse was still outside, his sombrero on the saddle horn. White male fitting the Kid's description. Same height and weight. Missing left earlobe."

"There are surely other men who—"

"They took this from around his neck," Chando said, handing Lew a chain from which swung a half-blackened gold cross.

Lew felt his mouth go dry. The cross lay in his palm; he lifted it, turned it over, and read the words he knew were there.

Mi tesoro.

"What about the others? The old man and the girl?"

Chando shook his head. "Still in Mexico, I guess."

"Keep on it, Chando."

"I will, *jefe*. Good night."

When the *segundo* had gone, Lew, clutching the cross to his bare chest, went back to the study.

"Darling," came Mrs. Maxwell's breathless voice,

"let's make love on this leather sofa before we go up to bed."

"What?" Lew's head snapped around. He had forgotten about her. Still naked, she lolled on the sofa. He said, "Get dressed and I'll have my man drive you home."

She sat up. "Drive me home? You promised me more!"

"I can't be trusted. You deserve better. Get dressed."

The angry Elizabeth Maxwell was still muttering protests when she was ushered out the hacienda's front door.

Lew closed the door behind her as a terrible squeezing sensation started in his chest. He again lifted the gold cross and stared at it for a long moment. Lowering it, he headed for the stairs.

He was relieved that Elizabeth Maxwell was gone. He was in no mood to make love to her. He wasn't interested.

There was only one female who interested him, and it was not the milky skinned, sweet-smelling, dark-haired beauty, Elizabeth Maxwell.

It was a sunburned, foul-mouthed, ugly-as-the-devil blond female gunslinger.

Mollie Rogers.

12

◆

But thy eternal summer shall not fade,
Nor lose possession of that fair . . .

Professor Napier Dixon, mildly annoyed that someone would come calling at this late hour, took off his spectacles, laid his poetry book aside, and went to see who the visitor was.

He opened the heavy door and blinked in disbelief. On the porch stood a tall, slender gunslinger—and a female one at that. A gun belt rode low around her hips, and bulging red saddlebags were slung over her left shoulder. Her clothes, men's breeches and shirt, were filthy, and her dirty blond hair was short and spiky. Her skin was as sun-darkened as an old cowboy's, and her face was streaked with sweat and grime.

But a pair of beautiful, vivid violet eyes flashed in the dirty face, and Napier Dixon's breath caught in his throat.

"Sarah?" he murmured, stunned and overwhelmed. "Sarah?"

"No," Mollie said. "I'm her daughter. I'm Mollie Rogers."

"Oh," he managed. Then, "Yes, yes, of course, Cord

and Sarah's child. Come in, come in," he said, unable to take his eyes off her.

In the foyer he reached for the saddlebags, sensed her reluctance to give them up, and said, "Why don't you put your things here by the door for now."

Nodding, Mollie dropped the heavy saddlebags by the umbrella stand as he closed the door and turned to face her. She saw a silver-haired gentleman who was exactly as her parents had described him—tall, slim, dignified, and immaculate.

Directing her toward his firelit study, Napier Dixon said, "Your mother, Mollie? Sarah? Is Sarah . . . ?"

"Mama's dead," Mollie said flatly.

"Dear God, no!" exclaimed Napier Dixon, stricken. "Not Sarah. Not the beautiful Sarah."

"Yes, and Papa, too." Tears sprang to Mollie's eyes. "They're both dead and I'm alone."

Quickly regaining his composure, Professor Dixon said, "My poor child."

Sniffing, Mollie raised an arm to wipe her nose on her shirtsleeve. Professor Dixon quickly drew a clean white handkerchief from his sweater pocket and presented it to her. Crying quietly now, Mollie took the handkerchief.

"There, there, child. I'm so sorry," Professor Dixon comforted her. "Bless your heart, it's going to be all right."

Knowing she could trust him, Mollie told the professor everything. She left out nothing. She revealed that the heavy saddlebags in the foyer were loaded with a fortune in gold taken on raids. She told him about the robberies and the years in Mexico. She told him about the determined bounty hunter who was bent on capturing all of the Rogers Renegades, including her.

Finally, she told him about the Kid. "I had to do it, Professor," she said honestly. "He was going to . . . to . . ." She shuddered, remembering, and ran her hands up and down her crossed arms. "I stabbed him and maybe killed him, I don't know. If he's alive, he'll come after me. He'll get me and—"

"No, Mollie. You're safe here in Maya." He smiled, and added, "You have a home here with me for as long as you wish."

"But people will see me and they'll know who I am."

"Then you'll have to be someone else," said Professor Dixon calmly. "My two married sisters have a dozen daughters between them. I will announce that one of my nieces is coming in a couple of months to live with me."

"A couple of months? Where will I stay until then?"

"Right here in the house," he said. "But there are rules in this house. I abide by them, and you will too." His words were softly spoken, but Mollie knew he meant what he said.

"I'll get awfully bored cooped up here," she protested.

"No, you won't. You'll be too busy learning how to become a proper young lady." Again he smiled, then said, "Now you must be very tired. There's a big guest room upstairs where you'll be comfortable." He rose.

"Professor," Mollie asked, shooting to her feet, "What about the gold?"

"You went through a lot to get it," he said. "The gold belongs to you."

Upstairs Mollie shed her dirty clothes, climbed into the big soft bed, and was asleep as soon as her head hit the pillow. But a bad dream soon awakened her. The

Kid had caught up with her and was pressing her down on the bed. His hairy chest and bearded face was all she could see.

Bolting upright, her heart pounding, Mollie looked around, frightened and disoriented. Why was there no loud music playing? No shouting and laughing? Then she remembered. She was not in some Mexican hotel room. She was in the big Manzanita Avenue mansion of Professor Napier Dixon. And the Kid was dead.

Or was he?

Professor Dixon took Louise, his housekeeper, into his confidence. Louise didn't like the idea of having an outlaw under their roof, but the professor assured her that Mollie was a harmless child who was in trouble and needed them.

He explained that Mollie hadn't had the advantages and she badly needed the influence and advice of a lady, especially, he added diplomatically, a genteel lady who knew a great deal about breeding and good manners.

Flattered, Louise said, "Well, I'm not sure I can make a silk purse out of a sow's ear, but I shall join you in the effort to do so."

Mollie's metamorphosis began immediately.

On her first morning in the professor's house, she came down to breakfast wearing a girlish pink-and-white checked gingham dress that Louise had supplied. Professor Dixon complimented her on her appearance, carefully hiding his dismay that such a naturally pretty girl would choose to butcher her golden hair and burn her fair skin dark as an Indian's.

Her first lesson began as soon as she was seated. She

reached hungrily for a buttermilk biscuit. Professor Dixon cleared his throat. Mollie looked up. He shook his silver head. She dropped the biscuit.

"We say grace in this house, Mollie." His smile was warm. "Shall we bow our heads?"

Napier Dixon was appalled to learn that Mollie had had no formal schooling after age thirteen. She was very bright, but she was woefully ignorant on a score of subjects. It was almost impossible to believe that she was actually Sarah's daughter.

The professor told Mollie that once, long ago, he had taught young students literature and speech at Tulane in New Orleans. He would be glad to tutor her. Mollie was less than thrilled with the thought of studying, but the persuasive, learned professor soon piqued her interest and had her eager to learn.

It seemed to Mollie that there was no question to which he didn't have an answer, no riddle he couldn't solve. And his expertise was not limited to what could be found in books. Mollie was surprised that a man—a bachelor at that—knew so much about women.

He brought her a big jar of scented cream from the Maya Emporium and told her if she applied it generously—all over—her skin would grow pale and become smooth and soft as a baby's.

"All over?" she'd questioned. "The jar won't last long."

He laughed, enchanted. "Then I'll bring you another. I *own* the Emporium." He continued to laugh.

But he abruptly stopped when Mollie, in a new frilly dress, sank down onto the sofa opposite him. Forgetting she now wore dresses, she thoughtlessly sat with her knees wide apart, hands resting on them.

"Mollie," he said, kindly, "young ladies sit with their ankles together."

Mollie colored, demurely put her feet together and folded her hands in her lap. But it would not be the last time she had to be reminded. The professor and the housekeeper taught and scolded and coached and demonstrated and praised their young student. Mollie read and studied and listened and practiced her manners.

And she brushed her rapidly growing short blond hair and rubbed the expensive creams into her flesh, watching her skin begin to lighten. She did everything she was supposed to do, and she was grateful to the intelligent, good-hearted professor and Louise for all their help.

But sometimes at night when she was in her bed, tears slipped down her cheeks as she thought about her papa. She missed him terribly, and she was sorry that she had never worn any of the pretty dresses he had given her. She wished she had been a more dutiful daughter, had tried harder to please him.

Then she would smile in the darkness. Her papa had loved her just as she was. She was a lot like him, and hadn't they had some great times together?

Remembering, Mollie would put herself to sleep reliving those thrilling days of their bold, daring raids. The close calls. The big hits. The endless excitement.

Would life ever be exciting again?

The big day finally arrived.

Mollie Rogers was to venture forth from the big white house on Manzanita Avenue. But Professor Dixon would not be presenting Mollie Rogers to the citizenry of Maya. The townsfolk would meet a young lady called Fontaine Gayerre.

When Miss Fontaine Gayerre came down the stairs that sunny morning, Professor Dixon looked up and swallowed hard. Twenty-five years fell away and he was again a nervous young man, waiting in the June twilight.

"'A thing of beauty is a joy forever,'" he said softly. "'Its loveliness increases; it will never pass into nothingness.'"

"Lord Byron?" Mollie asked, smiling.

"Keats," corrected the professor. "You are a beautiful young lady."

Mollie laughed. "Thanks, but I'm scared to death this damned false hair will fall off." She patted the sleek blond bun at her nape.

"Mollie Rogers might have talked like that," said the professor. "Fontaine Gayerre would *never* use vulgar language. Now, are you certain you want to work at the Emporium? There's no need, you—"

"Oh, I do, yes. It's ever so nice here and you and Louise are kind, but . . . but . . ."

"But you're restless." She had only smiled in reply. "I understand. But there are other options, since the Emporium isn't all that I own. The livery stables, the barbershop, the First National Bank, the Nueva Sol Hotel, they're all mine."

"Lord, you must be very rich."

"I *am* a wealthy man, Fontaine. When I left Texas and finally teaching as well, I went to the California gold mines. I made a fortune there quickly. Then word got out that gold had been discovered here and I came, along with thousands of others. Overnight the town sprang up, but soon it was clear there was no gold. It was an illusion. The name of the town was changed from Rainbow to Maya. *Maya* means 'world of illusion.' That's all Maya was, all it is."

"Why did you stay?"

He shrugged. "I like it here. I bought up almost the entire town at bargain prices as the gold-seekers fled. Now Maya is a quiet, pleasant town where gentlefolk can live in peace. It's a good place to live."

"And a good place to hide," Mollie said.

He nodded. "We better be going."

Mollie was nervous as she and the professor strolled down Maya's wooden sidewalk on the east side of the plaza. Her throat grew dry when they reached the adobe building with a large sign that read *Maya Emporium*.

At the door, the professor said, "Ready to go inside, Fontaine?" Mollie didn't respond. "Fontaine?"

"What? Oh, yes, I . . ." She leaned up and whispered in his ear, "I forgot my new name. I feel like such a fraud."

He patted the gloved hand resting on his bent arm. "This is Maya, world of illusion. I'd wager you're not the first person—nor will you be the last—to show up in Maya with something to hide. Or appearing to be whom they are not."

Mollie loved her work at the Emporium.

Quick-witted and curious, she wasted no time acquainting herself with the merchandise. If a customer came in looking for hat or hammer, salt or saddle, crackers or cradle, bustle or Bible, Mollie knew right where to find it.

The manager, Mr. Stanfield, was pleased with her work, and Willie, his clerk, a freckle-faced young man of nineteen, followed her around like a puppy. The townspeople commented to Professor Dixon that his lovely niece, Fontaine, was an absolute treasure, so sweet and helpful.

Outgoing and lively, Mollie quickly became friends with the young ladies of Maya, and after only a few days had two very dear girlfriends—Patricia O'Brien and Madeline Summers—with whom she could gossip and visit and sit with at church on Sundays.

When Mollie found out that the professor made weekly treks to a little adobe schoolhouse at the edge of town to teach Indian and Mexican children to read, she insisted on going along. It was a new adventure, and she was full of questions.

"Isn't it hard to teach the Hopis how to read when they can barely speak English?"

"Young minds are like sponges," said the professor. "They quickly soak up knowledge, and I'm always happy to instruct anyone who wishes to learn." He winked at her and added, as the big brougham rounded a corner, "Even grown-up, pretty young ladies."

"Professor Dixon, Professor Dixon," shouted swarms of boisterous children who came running out to meet them.

Several pairs of small hands reached for the professor. He plucked the youngest of the children, a tiny Mexican girl, up into his arms. The others followed him into the old adobe building, clutching at the hem of his suit jacket.

Mollie, lifted down from the carriage by a tall, shy Indian boy, watched the professor with the excited children. That he loved them was all too apparent. That he should have been a parent was evident. Why, she wondered, had he never married and had a family?

"We go in now?" said the tall Indian boy at her elbow.

Mollie looked up into his eager face and nodded. "We go in now . . . ah . . . ah . . . your name?"

"I am John Distant Star."

"John, I'm Fontaine Gayerre," she said, putting out her hand.

His dark eyes widened, and he self-consciously wiped his hand on his trouser leg before taking hers. Mollie smiled warmly and, continuing to cling to his hand, led him inside to join the others.

When spelling and math exercises were completed, the professor called on Mollie to conduct the reading lesson. Flattered, she jumped at the chance. She took up the Brady reader and read in a clear, true voice, adding, with inflection and facial expressions, a dash of drama to the simple story.

She felt happy. Her life had become so full, so busy, she hardly had time to miss the old days with her papa or to worry about the Texas Kid.

Or the mysterious bounty hunter.

13

As the hot Arizona summer turned into a cool, crisp autumn, Mollie became more and more comfortable with her new identity. And she began to enjoy being a woman—a young, lovely, well-dressed woman.

She finally stopped having nightmares, stopped constantly looking over her shoulder, stopped feeling as if she were in constant danger. She was no longer jumpy and anxious. Days passed when she didn't even so much as think of the Kid or the bounty hunter.

She came and went freely from the Manzanita Avenue mansion. She had friends. Life was good. She felt as safe in Maya as the professor had promised.

When the end of October rolled around, bringing with it Maya's annual *El Día de los Muertos* carnival, Mollie could hardly wait to join in the fun. She went to the carnival with her two best friends, Patricia and Madeline.

The eager young girls strolled among the crowds, eating candy apples and checking out the booths. They soon stopped, their interest piqued, before a small blue tent where a pitchman in a striped coat was enticing revelers inside to have their fortunes read by the all-seeing Madame Medina.

". . . Madame can look into her crystal ball and predict your future." The barker's eyes fell on Mollie. "How about you, miss? Want to know what's in store for you? Riches? Marriage? Travel? Danger?" He paused and grinned down at her. "Afraid to find out? Afraid of what Madame Medina might see?"

Challenged, Mollie drew a coin from her reticule, handed it to the flashily dressed barker, told Patricia and Madeline to wait for her, and stepped fearlessly through the blue curtains.

Inside, a woman in a gold satin turban and flowing scarlet robes sat cross-legged on a threadbare Turkish rug. Before her, on a low, square table, was a shiny crystal ball. The woman, whose makeup was garish, motioned Mollie to sit down. Mollie dropped to her knees and sat back on her heels facing the fortune-teller.

Madame Medina looked Mollie in the eye for a long, unsettling time. Then she lifted her hands and spread them over the crystal ball—close, but not touching it. When her hands parted, she leaned directly over the ball and looked into its mysterious depths. When finally she raised her turbaned head and again looked at Mollie, Madame Medina wore a puzzled expression.

"I see very strange things, things that even I do not understand." Her crepey eyelids, painted bright blue, drooped.

Mollie swallowed. "What kind of things, Madame Medina?"

"Weddings. I see weddings." Madame's voice dropped lower. "You in a long white wedding gown and . . . and . . ." She looked up again. Mollie started to speak, but Madame lifted a clawlike hand to stop her. "Two weddings. Two men," Madame Medina continued, her rouged face puckering into a frown. "Two dark-skinned, dark-haired men."

"Well, that makes no sense at all," Mollie blurted out, then laughed nervously. "You just take another look inside that thing," she said, gesturing to the crystal ball.

Madame Medina shook her turbaned head. "It is what I see in the ball. I see you as one person who is at the same time two. You are two women. And there are two men, two weddings." She fixed Mollie with her half-shut eyes. "Two weddings on the same day."

"Impossible!" Mollie declared, her intrepid spirit rising to assert itself. "I've no intention of marrying one man, much less two. You look back into that crystal ball and—"

"No. No more," Madame Medina said, cutting her off. "That is all. It is finished. Go now."

"Go now," the man ordered coldly. "I've had enough of you."

The woman anxiously scrambled from the rumpled bed. She was afraid of him. All the girls in the Las Viguitas bordello were afraid of him. There was something innately evil about this big, dark-bearded man with the missing earlobe.

The woman remembered how she had cringed the first time the cruel gray-eyed man had visited the bordello and his gaze had fallen on her. In the blink of an eye she had found herself upstairs with him, and a frightening bout of fierce lovemaking had begun with him first cutting off her long bleached-blond hair with a dangerously sharp knife. When finally he'd tossed the knife aside, he ran his strong fingers through the butchered hair, squeezing her head painfully.

"That's better, much better," he had muttered, pressing her down on the bed and taking—repeatedly—what he had paid for.

Now, as he lay spread-eagled and naked on the bed, he said, "Your hair needs cutting again. See that you do it before—"

A loud knock on the door interrupted him. He called out, "Come on in, Cuchillo."

A slim Mexican entered and announced without preamble, "There is reason to believe that the *señorita* may be in Arizona."

"Where in Arizona?"

Shoulders lifting, the Mexican replied, "I do not know."

The two men talked, speculating, the Mexican telling what he had learned, the naked man listening with interest. Finally he said, "You and the boys ride on up north and start searching. If she's in Arizona, it's just a matter of time until we find her. That's all, Cuchillo."

The Mexican left. The woman stayed, afraid to leave until she was dismissed. His head filled with pleasant thoughts of what he would do with her once he found his elusive Mollie, the Texas Kid frowned at the blond prostitute and said, "Get out of here. I'm tired of you. Go now!"

"Go now," Lew Hatton said to his *segundo*. "Keep trying. Find new informers. Offer more money."

Chando sighed heavily. "Why don't you let it go? We're almost certain Rogers is dead. That leaves only the girl, and—"

"And what, Chando?"

"She is a woman."

Lew drained his whiskey glass. "That is her misfortune." Lew was determined. He was not going to stop until all of the Rogers Renegades were either dead or had been brought to justice. He had spent great sums of money for information that might lead him to the missing Mollie Rogers.

A long, frustrating winter had passed with no real progress. Then, as an early springtime touched the Sangre de Cristos, the break he'd been hoping for finally came.

Arriving home after a long night of poker, Lew found Chando waiting up for him. He could tell by the look on Chando's face that he had news.

"You've found Mollie Rogers," Lew said by way of greeting.

"There's a great probability that the Rogers girl is in a little town in Arizona. Maya."

"Maya? Never heard of it. How did you find out?"

"The Pinkerton people in Denver got the word, but none of their agents would go after her, even with the big reward on her head."

Lew looked puzzled. "Why not? Afraid of her?"

Chando looked him in the eye. "They don't like the idea of bringing in a woman—a young girl, really—who might spend the rest of her life in prison or . . . or . . . even be hanged."

A muscle jumped in Lew's tanned jaw. "I have no such aversion to bringing in hardened, dangerous criminals, whether they be male or female. In fact, I'll take pleasure in bringing in Mollie Rogers."

"*Sí, señor,*" said Chando.

"Now," Lew motioned Chando to sit down, "tell me everything you know."

"Miss Rogers made one big mistake," said Chando. "She kept some clippings of her days as a Renegade. Apparently after she had been in Maya for a year, she decided it was unsafe to have them, so they were put out to be burned, but part of them survived. A beggar found the half-burned clippings and put two and two together. He informed the Pinkerton people and they told our boys. We paid off the beggar, ordered him to keep his mouth shut and get out of town, and told the Pinks we'd take care of it."

Nodding, Lew asked, "Did the beggar know what name she is using?"

"No. But she is working in an Emporium there in Maya. It's a small town, there can't be many stores."

"There has to be some foolproof way to identify her. I can't just nab some young woman and accuse her of being Mollie Rogers."

Chando cleared his throat. "There is a way, *jefe*, but . . ."

"How? Out with it. We're wasting time."

"It is said that Mollie Rogers has a perfect strawberry-red *mariposa* birthmark."

"A butterfly birthmark?" said Lew, rubbing his hands together. "Perfect. Where is the birthmark? On her cheek? An arm? Where?"

"The *mariposa* is on her back," Chando said, coloring, "well below her waist."

"Below her—" Lew shook his head. "How the hell am I supposed to get a look at it?"

"I guess," said the *segundo,* "you will have to make love to her."

On a perfect May morning in 1872, Mollie rode her spirited gray stallion, Nickel, across the vast reaches of the Arizona desertlands. Her slender body moving in easy grace with the noble beast, she held the reins loosely, trusting the powerful animal as he loped across the cactus and creosote wastelands, heading up into the chaparral country of the Santa Ritas.

Mollie was dressed stylishly in a riding habit of lightweight ebony gabardine, and her golden hair, which now reached to her shoulders, was tucked up under a flat-crowned black hat. Black kid gloves protected her soft hands and in her jacket's lapel, one of the first pinkish red blossoms to appear on the native beaver tail cactus added a splash of color.

Mollie Rogers had been transformed. The wild, rowdy gunslinger was now a sedate young lady—on the outside. Inside, she was very much like she had always been—restless, free-spirited, longing for excitement.

Mollie laughed aloud now, thinking how perplexed the professor would be if he knew she was racing the mighty gray stallion up into the rugged foothills.

The professor had not approved of her choice of a horse. When he had taken her out to the big Willard ranch to buy her a saddlehorse, she had immediately fallen in love with the big gray. The professor and the leathery ranch owner, L. J. Willard, had tried to talk her out of it. Willard cautioned that the big stud was tricky and dangerous. Frowning then, Willard went on to say that he had lost Billy Joe Frazier, his

best horse trainer, and didn't know what he was
going to do.

"Why, I've even placed ads in newspapers as far
away as California and New Mexico," said the big
rancher. "I've got to find—"

Interrupting, Mollie said, "Mr. Willard, although I'm
from back East, I began riding lessons when I was four
years old. I'm an experienced horsewoman." She then
looked hopefully at the professor. "Please say I can have
him."

She got the stallion.

Now, as she rode Nickel into the cool uplands,
Mollie was confident, relaxed, totally in charge. A new
sun was bathing the sandstone cliffs with bright pink
light and creeping down into the grassy canyons.

Mollie and Nickel soon entered the mouth of a narrow arroyo and rode toward the sound of a small creek
that poured down through the U-shaped canyon. Nickel
headed for the gurgling water, snorting and whickering.

Mollie leaned forward, raked her gloved fingers
through the thick shiny mane and murmured into a
pricked ear, "Yes, Nickel, I am going to wade in the
water, but I'll thank you to keep it to yourself."

As Mollie laughingly slipped from the stallion's
back, a lone rider topped an overhang of rock atop the
shallow zigzag canyon walls and abruptly pulled up on
the reins. His lathered black gelding responded
instantly, halting inches from the canyon rim, making
not one sound.

The rider scratched absently at his full, dark beard.
Squinting against the brilliant sunlight, he watched a
willowy woman slide off a big gray stallion and sit
down on a rock. Impatiently she removed her black

gloves, shoving them into the wide waistband of her riding skirt. She then tugged off her tall black boots and stockings and, without using her hands for leverage, sprang to her bare feet.

Eyes narrowed, the rider stared unblinkingly as the woman raised her skirts high above her knees and waded into the icy stream. Squealing from the shock of the cold water, the woman—whose flat-brimmed hat completely concealed her face—surged bravely into the frigid creek, splashing about, playfully kicking up a spritz of water at the gray stallion on the banks.

Mollie played in the water, thinking how outraged the professor and Louise would be if they could see her with her skirts hiked up to her thighs, sloshing about in an icy canyon stream.

Watching every move she made, the rider hunched his wide shoulders, and his dark, bearded face broke into a slow, widening grin.

14

He had put off the unpleasant task as long as possible.

Lew Hatton knew that if he was going to meet—and draw into his trust—the revolting Mollie Rogers, it was time to do it.

It was his third day in Maya, Arizona. The morning he arrived, trail-weary and saddle sore, he had checked into the Nueva Sol Hotel and, using his mother's maiden name, signed the guest register *Lew Taylor*. Then he'd gone upstairs and slept the day away.

The second day, yesterday, he had ridden out to the big Willard ranch where, come next Monday, he would begin work. The prospect brought a groan. It had been a long time since the days when he and Dan Nighthorse had reveled in breaking the wildest broncs on Plano Pacifica. Then it had been great sport. Now he was thirty-one years old, and Lew dreaded the hard, bone-jarring work.

But not as much as he dreaded the prospect of romancing a plain-faced, sunburned tomboy who in all likelihood smelled to high heaven, cursed like a cowboy, and perhaps even smoked cigars. A shudder of distaste rippling through him, Lew envisioned the rough-hewn Rogers woman, and wondered if there wasn't some way he could get her buckskin breeches down to look for the birthmark without ever having to kiss her.

His stomach turning at the thought of making love to such a repulsive creature, Lew shook his dark head and told himself to get on with it. This was as good a time as any to shave off his itchy beard, clean up, and visit the Maya Emporium.

At straight-up noon Lew, freshly shaven and impeccably dressed, stepped off the hotel's broad stone porch, crossed the dusty street, and strolled unhurriedly across the plaza with its splashing fountain, stone benches, shade trees and groups of gentlemen loitering about, talking. Halfway across the square, he met a couple of young, pretty women who stared openly at him, then burst into girlish giggles after he'd passed.

Lew never broke stride. He had a job to do, and the only female in Maya he had any interest in was Mollie Rogers.

After crossing the plaza, he paused. Directly across the street stood the two-story adobe-fronted building on which *Maya Emporium* was painted in bold black letters. Lew saw a young, plainly dressed mother come out of the store, a freckle-faced boy of four or five clinging to her hand and licking a stick of hard candy. On the wooden sidewalk, a portly, bald cowboy removed his sweat-stained Stetson, tipped it to the woman, and went inside. A towheaded youth came out, broom in hand, and looked up the street, then down.

Lew stepped down from the curb and headed for the Emporium. Once inside the cool, dim building, he paused to lounge against a big square table piled high with china dishes. Looking around speculatively, he heard voices at the back of the store. The bald cowboy he'd seen come in was trying on hats. His back was to Lew. He was talking to a clerk who was hidden from Lew's view.

Lew wondered. Was the clerk Mollie Rogers?

Lew moved a little closer, but the pair remained unaware of his presence. The portly cowboy abruptly stepped over to a freestanding mirror to admire the brand-new Stetson on his head.

"The hat looks real nice, Mr. Patterson," came a clear feminine voice and squinting, Lew focused on its owner as a slender young girl stepped out of the shadow and into a shaft of sunlight streaming in through a high back window.

If there had been a chorus of heavenly voices accompanying her emergence, Lew would have known that an angel of the Lord had miraculously descended to earth. She stood there in the shaft of sunlight, a fair-skinned beauty with a face that was perfect in every way. Large, luminous eyes, a small retroussé nose, and soft, luscious lips that were turned up into an incredibly enchanting smile.

Her hair, held back off her flawless face with a wide lilac ribbon, tumbled down her gracefully curved neck, shimmering like spun gold in the sunshine. Tall and long-waisted with gently rounded curves evident beneath her cotton shirtdress, she had that innocent and overpowering beauty that made Lew long to gently enfold her in his arms. He was overcome with the strong desire to hold her and keep her safe and protected and unspoiled.

He felt his heart thump heavily as he stared, transfixed,

at the feminine vision in violet. So compelling, so stirring was the experience it took on a dreamlike quality. He was so moved by the beautiful girl that he shook his head and shut his eyes, as if by doing so the ethereal image would evaporate into mid-air.

It did not.

When he opened his eyes, she still stood there, smiling sweetly, looking angelic, and Lew realized that not since that day so long ago when he had first seen the beautiful Teresa Castillo in the Albuquerque stage station had he been so affected by the mere presence of a woman.

Gripped by an emotion as powerful as it was unfamiliar, Lew watched and listened as she convinced the overweight cowhand that the gray Stetson suited him far better than the black. Carefully avoiding attracting her attention, Lew wondered miserably why his luck was so abominable. Here was the most beautiful woman he'd seen in years, and as fate would have it, not only was she in the tiny town of Maya, Arizona, but she was employed at the very same store where Mollie Rogers worked.

He ground his teeth and muttered oaths under his breath. Damn it to hell! Damn Mollie Rogers to hell!

Lew abruptly turned away, so upset and angry he never knew when the brawny cowboy in his new gray Stetson left the store. Fairly vibrating with frustration, Lew stood, arms crossed over his chest, the long, hard muscles of his thighs brushing the table's edge, praying that the loathsome Mollie Rogers was either in the storeroom or at the boardinghouse eating lunch.

Maybe she wouldn't return for another half hour or more and he'd be allowed to spend a few precious minutes talking to the willowy blond beauty. Lew's dark face hardened, and he cursed himself for being weak and easily distracted. He had come to Maya for Mollie Rogers. He had better get his mind off the angel-faced girl and wait patiently for Mollie Rogers to show up.

While she was helping the cowboy find a hat, Mollie had noticed a customer standing up front beside the dish table. Perhaps he was still there. She'd best see if he needed help. Mollie lifted her skirts and hurried toward the table of the china and glassware and saw him.

His back was to her, but she noticed the shiny blackness of his hair and the way his blue cotton shirt pulled across his wide shoulders. She was a few short steps from him when he slowly turned to face her.

Mollie stopped short.

A pale hand lifted to her racing heart, and she felt she couldn't get a breath. Before her stood a tall, dark, strikingly handsome man with high, slanted cheekbones, a straight, arrogant nose, a chiseled cleft in his strong chin, and a pair of summer blue eyes that were focused solely on her. His sculptured lips were widening into a slow, appealing grin that made her stomach do flipflops and her knees go weak. The tall stranger was handsomer by far than any man she had ever seen. More perfect than any image of virile manhood she'd conjured up in her wildest daydreams.

He was immaculate. A neatly pressed sky blue pullover shirt lay close to the steely muscles of his chest and hugged his wide shoulders. A pair of sharply creased hard-finish dark trousers clung to his slim hips and fell to just the right break atop his polished boots, a detail that bespoke custom tailoring.

His skin was smooth and suntanned, his teeth straight and white. His hair, so black that blue highlights glinted in it, was brushed back from his temples, but a thick unruly lock fell forward over his high forehead.

Transfixed, Mollie stared at him.

Lew stared right back at her.

There was, between them, an immediate heated atmosphere of extraordinary physical attraction and subtle erotic frustration. Lew knew exactly what it was. Mollie Rogers did not. She only knew that her mouth had gone so dry she couldn't swallow and that this tall, good-looking stranger's arresting blue gaze held her so that she couldn't break away.

Her head was tilted back and her eyes were riveted to his ruggedly handsome face. The grin that had been there when he first looked at her was gone, and his mouth, unsmiling, was more appealing than ever. His wide, full lips had a sulky, brooding look that Mollie found heart-stoppingly seductive.

At last he spoke, breaking the spell.

"Are we both customers, or does one of us work here?" he said softly, the slow smile returning, the summer blue of his eyes gleaming with mischief.

Mollie laughed, relieved that the tension had eased. "I work here, sir," she said, moving closer so that Lew caught the faint scent of her freshly shampooed hair. "Is there something special you are looking for?" She tilted her head to one side. Lew found the gesture charming.

"Umm," Lew looked anxiously about, at a loss,

searching for something he could buy. His gaze fell on a shelf of shaving cups. "A shaving mug," he said decisively. "I need a new shaving mug."

"Follow me," said Mollie, turning away, and Lew, exhaling, thought to himself that he would like to follow her for the rest of her life. "We have these," she pointed to the shelf behind a counter where he had spotted the rows of plain and fancy shaving mugs displayed. "See anything you like, sir?" She moved around behind the counter.

Looking only at her, Lew said, "You choose for me."

Accustomed to helping customers make choices, Mollie turned about, looked at the many mugs, reached out and picked up one of robin's-egg blue porcelain, thinking guiltily that it was the exact same shade as the tall stranger's eyes.

"This one suits you," she said, holding it out to him.

"I'll take it," Lew was agreeable.

"You're too easy," Mollie teased and then reddened when he replied, "For a girl like you, you've no idea how easy."

As she carefully wrapped the mug in plain brown paper, he introduced himself, extending a lean brown hand. Mollie placed her palm atop his and said, "I'm Fontaine Gayerre, Mr. Taylor, and I'm very pleased to meet you. Welcome to Maya."

"Fontaine," he repeated, continuing to hold her hand in his, "such a lovely name. It suits you."

"Thank you, Mr. Taylor," she said, smiling. "Now, if you'll kindly let go of my hand, I'll finish wrapping your mug."

"Forgive me, Fontaine—if I may call you Fontaine—and please, call me Lew." Reluctantly releasing her hand, he glanced at the clock above her head. "I suppose you go to lunch when the other girl gets back?"

"Put your finger right there, Mr. Tay . . . Lew," Mollie instructed, thinking that his name fit him too. Lew. She liked it. Lew placed a tapered forefinger directly on the crossed string while Mollie pulled the twine tightly, then tied a perfect knot. "Other girl?" she said, lifting her eyes to meet his.

"Yes," Lew answered casually. "The other female clerk who works here with you. Is she at lunch?"

Mollie handed Lew the neatly wrapped package. "There is no other female clerk, Lew. Just Mr. Stanfield, the proprietor, and Willie, the other clerk who is now out sweeping the sidewalk. And me."

Lew's jaw dropped and his blue eyes widened, then narrowed. Taken aback, Mollie wondered what on earth had gotten into him. For a long, uncomfortable minute he stared at her as though suddenly he disliked her intensely. His handsome face hardened perceptibly and his rich baritone voice took on a sharp edge.

"There's not another woman who works at this Emporium?"

"No. Nor has there ever been," Mollie proudly informed him. "*I* am the first and only female who has ever worked at the Maya Emporium."

"No," Lew muttered aloud, a stricken expression on his face. "No."

"Yes. Are you all right, Lew? You look ill."

15

◆

Lew quickly regained control. He consciously relaxed his tall, tensed body, softened his hard face, and smiled engagingly down at Mollie.

"I'm fine, Fontaine," he said evenly, then proceeded, immediately, with his well-laid plans, forcing himself to remember his one and only purpose for being in Maya: to charm and seduce this violet-eyed, ivory-skinned impostor who looked nothing at all like the outlaw she was. Holding the package with a forefinger curled around the tied twine, Lew idly tapped it against his thigh. "I have never felt better in my life."

Skeptical, her face reflecting her confusion, Mollie asked, "Have you eaten today?"

Lew laughed easily. "As a matter of fact, I haven't. Why don't we walk over to the Nueva Sol and share a meal? I'm told the chef performs magic with leg of mutton."

"Indeed he does," Mollie affirmed, relieved to see his appealing grin return. "The spring duck is even better, but I'll have to decline your kind invitation." She gave him a coquettish smile, just as the professor had coached her to do, letting this attractive man know that she was flattered by the offer, and casually interested, but was, of course, too much of a lady to seriously consider accepting such an invitation from a stranger.

He was instantly apologetic. "No, of course, you can't. How presumptuous of me to suggest it. I've not even inquired . . . you may be a married lady, and—"

"No!" Mollie burst out shrilly, caught herself, and lowered her voice to a soft, cultured pitch. "No, Lew. I have no husband. I've never been married."

He visibly exhaled, as though greatly relieved, and Mollie felt her face flush with joy. She grew uncomfortably warm when, his voice low and oh so enticing, he said, "Since you have no husband and I have no wife, may I come to call on you one evening soon? After I've met your folks and asked their permission?"

Mollie blinked up at him. She wasn't sure what her answer was supposed to be, but she knew what it was going to be. "Yes, Lew, I'd like that. I live with my uncle in a big white house at the northern end of Manzanita Avenue. Why don't you join us for dinner tomorrow night?" Smiling eagerly, she added, "My uncle is Professor Napier Dixon. You can find him almost anytime in his office above the First National Bank."

"I'll go there this afternoon," he said, his blue eyes caressing her face. "I'll be honored to dine with you and your uncle. May I bring wine? Or perhaps you are too young for—"

"I'm twenty-one!" she quickly informed him and then wanted to bite her tongue.

Patricia and Madeline had told her that many men were not interested in a woman who was twenty-one and had never been married. They said that you were considered an old maid in the Territory by the time you turned eighteen. Madeline was almost eighteen. Patricia was twenty, but she had been wed for a few short weeks to a young army lieutenant who had been killed by the Apaches. It was, Patricia said, all right to be a widow, in fact, men found experienced women exciting.

All at once Mollie was terrified that Madeline and Patricia would come sweeping into the emporium and Lew Taylor would lose interest in her and want to court the experienced Patricia.

"I attended a very strict girl's academy back East where I came from and . . . and . . ." She was making it worse, she knew, rattling on, sounding like a pitiful spinster with her first gentleman caller. But she couldn't stop herself. ". . . and so I was not allowed to go out with any of the young gentlemen who took a fancy to me and that's the reason I've reached twenty-one without . . . without . . ."

"Thank the Almighty you're not a child of eighteen," Lew broke in smoothly. "I've passed my thirty-first birthday, Fontaine, and I feel that anything more than ten years between our ages would be too broad a gap. Don't you?"

"Oh, most definitely," she replied with cool authority, delighted now that she was a mature woman.

Mollie stood before a tall window in her spacious upstairs bedroom. Silvery moonlight washed over her, and a chill May breeze lifted tendrils of loose blond hair and pressed the soft batiste of her long white nightgown against the bare, warm curves of her tall, slender body.

It was well past midnight. The professor was sound

asleep in his room at the far end of the hall, as was Louise in her quarters downstairs. Most of Maya was asleep and had been for hours. Mollie could look out over the moonlit valley and see only a few sparsely scattered lights twinkling.

Alternately sighing and smiling, Mollie was tired, but she was not sleepy. She was sure she would never be sleepy again. Besides, her flair for the dramatic, heightened by her newfound appreciation of poetry and literature, told her that on such a momentous night as this it would be nothing short of sacrilege to entertain notions of doing something as mundane as sleeping.

Stretching and purring like a lazy, satisfied cat, Mollie impulsively hiked up her nightgown, climbed up onto the window ledge, and sat down. Resting her back against the sill, she drew her legs up, wrapped her arms around them, and laid her cheek on her knees. She sighed dreamily. Then quickly raised her head, unfolded her arms, turned and swung her legs outside the window. She remained perched there for only a second before she placed her bare feet on the smooth wood of the veranda and crossed to the gallery's railing.

Swinging a long, bare leg over, she climbed up and straddled it as she would have done in days of old. Clutching the railing, she leaned way out and squinted in the moonlight, anxiously searching for the Nueva Sol Hotel. She let out a little whoop of joy when she located the red-roofed, gleaming white adobe building where a handsome, raven-haired stranger was spending the night.

"Lew. Lew Taylor," Mollie murmured his name aloud. "Lew," she said more softly, experiencing that same unfamiliar fluttering in her stomach and dryness in her mouth that she'd felt earlier in the day when she'd walked over to wait on a customer whose back was to her and the handsome Lew Taylor had turned around.

Whether she lived to be ninety and saw Lew every day for the rest of her life or they were never to meet again, Mollie knew she would always remember the thrilling moment when he had slowly turned and smiled down at her.

Naive though she was, Mollie realized that the tall, black-haired stranger had touched something in her that no other ever had. She was unafraid of this new emotion. She had always thrived on risks and excitement, and she had the delicious feeling that she was about to embark on a new, electrifying adventure. She was ready for it! She would meet it the same way she had met every challenge of her life: with unrestrained enthusiasm and eagerness.

She wanted to miss absolutely nothing life had to offer and the strange tingling she felt from just looking at Lew Taylor's mouth had her already wondering what it might be like to feel those sulky, sensual lips pressed to hers. Mollie exhaled with frustration. She would have to wait to find out. She was not Mollie Rogers, who could behave as shockingly as she pleased. She was now Miss Fontaine Gayerre, a highborn, sheltered young lady who wouldn't consider allowing a gentleman to kiss her until she had known him for months.

"Rats!" Mollie muttered irritably into the rising night winds. "Being a lady can sure be a pain in the rump."

She screwed up her face at the thought. But almost immediately she found herself smiling again. Violet eyes flashing with excitement, Mollie sat astride the railing on that windswept balcony and pictured Lew Taylor in his Nueva Sol suite. Was he sleeping? Was his long, lean body stretched out full length and comfortable in one of the hotel's oversize pine beds?

Or was he, like she, too excited to sleep? Was he out on his balcony in the moonlight wondering how he could stand waiting for weeks, maybe months before he could kiss her?

His white shirt open down his dark chest, his black hair disheveled, an edgy Lew Hatton restlessly paced his Nueva Sol suite, a glass of bourbon in one hand, a smoked-down cigar in the other. He had been pacing for the better part of the evening. He was too irritable, too distracted to consider a poker game at one of the saloons or even to go downstairs for a sumptuous meal in the dinning room.

He had ordered a light supper sent up on a tray. It remained untouched on a round piñon table in the sitting room. He had not so much as lifted the white linen cloth to uncover the dishes. He was not hungry. Not at all. Now it was very late and he was not sleepy.

He was angry.

Lew was angry with Mollie Rogers for being so breathtakingly beautiful. Angry because he was helplessly drawn to her. Angry because the repugnant chore he had laid out for himself was not going to be repugnant after all. Damn her for being so pretty!

A vein pulsing on his forehead, Lew drained his liquor glass and slammed it down beside the untouched supper tray. He felt uncomfortably warm. He impatiently crossed to the double doors, pushed them open, and stepped out onto the hotel's stone balcony. He drew in a long, deep breath of the cool desert air.

He stood there in the cold, a chill wind out of the

west lifting locks of his hair and causing orange sparks from his cigar to swirl around his head. He gripped the railing and, squinting, directed his narrow-eyed gaze to the big white mansion located on a natural rise at the north end of Manzanita Avenue.

No lights burned in the mansion. Lew envisioned the young woman claiming to be Fontaine Gayerre sleeping soundly. He pictured her in her girlish bed with her glorious golden hair fanned out on the pillow. He could almost see that angelic face in sweet repose, the soft baby lips partially open, the thick lashes closed over those magnificent violet eyes.

Lew groaned aloud.

He told himself that maybe she wasn't Mollie Rogers. There was always that possibility. He had no proof of her identity. It could be a mistake. She might well be Miss Fontaine Gayerre from back East, come to live with her uncle, just as she said.

Lew took the cigar from between his teeth, dropped it, and ground it out with his bootheel. He exhaled heavily. There was only one way to find out if the golden-haired beauty was Fontaine Gayerre or Mollie Rogers.

Make love to her.

If the butterfly birthmark was there on her creamy buttocks, he would take her in, turn her over to the authorities. If there was no birthmark . . .

One thing was certain. Whoever she was, making love to her was going to be anything but distasteful. So why the hell was he so angry? Why in God's name should he be disappointed that the thieving, murdering female renegade he had come here to capture was so gorgeous it would make his job easy?

Too easy.

16

Professor Napier Dixon was smiling.

He had smiled often in the past year, more than he had smiled since the carefree days of his youth back in Texas. Just as it had been then, a pretty woman was responsible for the frequency of his smiles. She was, in fact, responsible for his newfound joy in living.

The spirited charmer who now shared his home never ceased to amaze and amuse the reserved professor. From the night he had opened his front door to find an ill-kempt, sunburned young face looking up at him, his quiet, orderly life had been turned upside down by the most exasperating, adorable, stubborn, changeable, shocking, impressionable, engrossing creature he had ever known. His role as her teacher was for a him a delight, although there were times he had the distinct feeling that it was she who was teaching him.

He now saw life and the living of it afresh through her inquiring, eager eyes. The desert sun seemed a bit brighter because its splendor so overwhelmed the intense, appreciative Mollie. Food, plain ordinary food, took on added flavor with her at his table rolling her violet eyes and exclaiming how delicious everything tasted. Poetry and literature, his grand passions, had deeper meaning and afforded extra enjoyment with her listening, enraptured, her ever-changing emotions marching across her pretty face, as he read aloud.

Like her father before her, Mollie was open and outgoing, lusty for life and its pleasures. Daring and unpredictable—exactly like the young, dashing Cordell Rogers—Mollie possessed the same magnetic quality, the same irresistible charm. And she had her mother's fair, blond beauty.

Professor Dixon's smile broadened.

From the kitchen, Mollie's clear, strong voice raised slightly when, as though she had just learned the evening's menu, she complimented Louise on her choices. Obviously Mollie had forgotten that it was she who had rushed in out of breath yesterday afternoon, floating right past him, blowing a kiss, and hurrying into the kitchen. There she had excitedly informed Louise that the most important guest ever to visit would be dining at the mansion in twenty-four hours and she thought it would be appropriate to begin the momentous meal with mock turtle soup. The soup should be followed with filet mignon, asparagus spears, boiled potatoes, stewed parsnips, and green peas. And, oh yes, for dessert those delicate little French pancakes filled with that delicious banana sauce and covered with the mouth-watering chocolate syrup that she, Louise, made like no one else on earth.

Even the formidable Louise Emerson had fallen victim to Mollie's youthful charms. The straitlaced middle-aged widow no longer cast disapproving glances in Mollie's direction. Louise had been won over and was eager to please the lovable, sunny-dispositioned Mollie.

The undemonstrative woman had grown very fond of the uninhibited girl. The professor had caught the look of embarrassed joy in Louise's eyes when Mollie—pleased with a special meal Louise had cooked or a pretty dress she had chosen—impulsively threw her arms around the older woman and gave her a bone-crushing hug.

And he knew, without being able to see her plump, florid face, that Louise was at this very minute beaming happily as Mollie praised her culinary talents.

Napier Dixon's twinkling eyes lifted to the tall grandfather clock standing beside the door. He shook his head. If Mollie didn't soon go upstairs and get dressed, she was not going to be ready for her young man.

The professor was impressed with the courteous Lew Taylor. Yesterday the young horseman had come to the professor's office to introduce himself and ask if he might call on Fontaine. Graciously supplying answers to questions before being asked, Taylor said that he had come from a big ranch in the New Mexico Territory, where he had worked for years. He was in Maya to take the horse trainer's position at L. J. Willard's ranch. The two of them had talked for several minutes, and the professor found Lew to be pleasantly frank and forthcoming. And truthful. He had quietly checked up on Lew Taylor shortly after the young man had registered at the Nueva Sol. He had learned that Taylor had credentials and letters of recommendation from his former employer. Nothing seemed amiss. Permission to call on Fontaine was granted.

Rising from his chair now, the professor hurried into

the kitchen to inform Mollie that the hour was growing late.

"Seven-forty-five?" she squealed, hands flying to her cheeks. "It can't be. Why, Lew will be here by eight, and I'll—"

"Still be in your dressing gown if you don't get on upstairs," cautioned the professor.

Mollie looked down at herself. "Jesus, Joseph, and Mary!" she exclaimed loudly, sailing across the kitchen. At the door she skidded to a stop, whirled and apologized. "There I go, swearing after I promised never to do so again. I am sorry, truly I am." She spun about and was gone while two heads wagged back and forth and two pairs of smiling, forgiving eyes looked after her.

A bottle of Medoc from the hotel's wine cellar in one hand, a fancy wrapped box of bonbons in the other, Lew Hatton stepped onto the broad front porch of the Manzanita Avenue mansion at exactly one minute before eight. Professor Dixon answered the door, took the wine, and shook Lew's hand. He ushered the younger man into the drawing room, explaining that Fontaine was running a little late, but would join them shortly.

Both men rose when, twelve minutes later, Mollie swept into the room looking stunningly beautiful in a new dress of vivid rose silk. Handmade imported Fortaleza lace, delicate as a cloud, edged the shimmering garment's low-cut bodice and tiny puffed sleeves. The fine fabric whispered as the slender blond beauty crossed to the tall, dark man, her hand thrust out, her violet eyes aglow.

"We're so happy you could come, Mr. Taylor," she said calmly, and Professor Dixon, watching, wondered if this could be the same girl who only moments ago had stood in the kitchen in her wrapper with her hair askew.

"It's my pleasure, Miss Gayerre," Lew responded evenly and, taking her hand, held it warmly in his for a long moment.

Mollie, looking into his summer blue eyes, was again struck by the smoothness of his tanned face, the flash of his straight white teeth. Dressed in an elegantly cut suit of dove gray, a starched white shirt, black silk cravat, and gleaming black boots, he was even more handsome than when they had met.

Holding her soft hand in his, Lew looked into Mollie's huge violet eyes, which were ringed with thick lashes as black as his own. He noticed the tiny pinpoint mole near the left corner of her pink-lipped mouth and the shadowed valley between her full, high breasts. Her gleaming golden hair was parted down the middle, brushed back, and held in place with matching oyster-shell combs. She was even more beautiful than he had remembered.

"Shall we all sit down?" The professor suggested and from the way both their heads snapped around, he knew that they had forgotten he was present.

"Yes, Mr. Taylor," Mollie managed, taking her hand from his, "this chair is most comfortable." She indicated one of a matched set of yellow brocade-covered wing chairs.

Lew nodded, but waited until Mollie settled herself on the long navy velvet sofa. Ignoring the suggested chair, he took a seat beside her, handed her the box of bonbons. Thanking him, she swallowed nervously when he smiled and raised a long arm up behind her to rest along the sofa's humped camel back. He sat so close the fabric of his jacket sleeve brushed her bare left shoulder. She shivered. He didn't seem to notice the contact, but she could think of nothing else.

Hardly able to breathe, Mollie turned and placed the box of bonbons on an end table while Lew fell into easy conversation with the professor. Hands folded in her lap, Mollie stole glances at Lew's handsome, harshly planed face as he talked. His thick, dark eyebrows lifted not at all as the professor fired questions at him that Mollie thought bordered on rudeness.

"Tell me again, Lew, what was the name of that *rancho* where you worked in New Mexico? That's right, I remember now. And the owner's name? Yes, yes, the Poyner brothers. You were there how long? I see, I see."

". . . and I wanted to be closer to my sister down in Tucson," Mollie heard Lew calmly explain.

Lew, quietly sizing up the slender, silver-haired man questioning him, correctly suspected that Professor Dixon—whatever his tie to this girl who called herself Fontaine—was going to prove extremely protective of her. There would be no overnight seduction of the blonde beside him. Her aging mentor would have to be won over before a hand could be laid on his beautiful protégée.

So Lew Hatton sat there on the sofa and answered every question, surprised at the ease with which he lied. He told himself he had no choice. He couldn't admit that his name was Hatton and that he had come from Plano Pacifica. If this girl was indeed Mollie Rogers, she would recognize the Hatton name. Nor would it have been safe to pretend he had worked at Pascual Castillo's *rancho*. The Texas Kid might have learned Teresa's name before he . . .

Lew shifted, bringing his arm down from the sofa's back. The movement caused the small cross beneath his white shirt to move and fall onto the flat muscles directly above his heart. Fleetingly he wondered if Mollie's desperado lover had worn the cross around his neck when the two of them made love. Had Mollie, on horseback just outside the coach, been with the Kid while he raped the helpless Teresa? Had she been jealous, or had she laughed at the Kid's playfulness, or had she cared not at all?

Lew made a mental note to leave the cross in his foot locker in the future. If Mollie saw the crucifix, it might well give him away.

Mollie, looking at him from beneath lowered lashes, saw a turbulence in Lew's expressive blue eyes despite his easy banter and relaxed manner. She was wondering what was going through his mind when Louise appeared to announce that dinner was ready.

The meal was a pleasant affair, with Lew eating heartily and offering his compliments to the cook. He was charming and talkative, and the professor found the young horseman from New Mexico to be well-mannered, intelligent, and excellent dinner company. Mollie, reading the professor's approval, felt relieved, happy, and grateful to learn the two men had so much in common.

Her eyes shining in the candle's glow, Mollie sipped Medoc from a sparkling glass and felt the smooth wine warm her right down to her toes. Or was it the warmth caused by the handsome man seated across from her with his long, lean fingers curled caressingly around a wine glass and his fathomless blue eyes holding her in their thrall?

Mollie could hardly believe it when, having after dinner coffee in the library, the clock struck eleven.

Carefully setting his cup aside, Lew said, "I had no idea it was so late. I've overstayed my welcome."

"Nonsense, Lew," said the professor. "We've enjoyed your visit. You must come back."

Mollie held her breath, waiting for Lew's reply. He gave none but smiled and stood up. The professor rose. Lew helped Mollie to her feet and she heard the professor say, "Fontaine will see you to the door." He shook Lew's hand.

"Good night, sir. The evening was most enjoyable."

Lew turned to Mollie. She almost winced when he gently took her elbow and ushered her toward the wide corridor.

She was talking a mile a minute as they neared the front door. She had no idea what she was saying, she was simply trying to delay his departure. She had a terrible sinking feeling that once he said good night he would step right off the porch and out of her life.

"Fontaine," he said, smiling, when they reached the door, "may I interrupt you for a moment?" Blushing, she fell silent. "I want you to have dinner with me tomorrow night. Will you?" Mollie stared at him wide-eyed, and she was momentarily speechless, her heart fluttering wildly. Lew laughed softly. "Does that mean yes?"

"Oh, yes, Lew. Yes, yes, it means yes."

"I'm glad. We will dine at the Nueva Sol around nine tomorrow evening, if that's convenient."

Mollie nodded happily, then said, "I'll have to ask my uncle."

Again Lew laughed. Then he lifted a dark hand and gently guided a wayward lock of golden hair back over a bare, pale shoulder. "Fontaine, I meant for the professor to join us, of course." A slight, barely discernible frown flitted across her fine features and Lew caught it. Lowering his voice, he teased, "Don't you want the professor to join us?" His eyes gleamed, daring her to admit the truth—that she would rather the two of them dine alone.

Mollie surprised him. Lew's heart kicked against his ribs when she smiled demurely, opened the front door, and said, "I want what you want, Lew."

And then it was she who laughed.

17

Mollie thought it fitting that Lew had ridden into Maya—and her life—in the spring. Spring was the best time in the desert. The warm, clear days stretched into fiery, spectacular sunsets and then gave way to cool, breezy, blossom-scented nights.

Her newly discovered romantic's heart told her that all was as it should be. From out of her sweetest dreams had stepped this magnificent man who was as fiery, exciting, and lusty as her dear dead papa. And at the same time as intelligent, kind, and gentle as the professor. Fate had deemed it to be, she was sure.

"Spring, the sweet spring, is the year's pleasant king;
Then blooms each thing,
then maids dance in a ring . . ."

Mollie recited aloud, pleased with herself for remembering the verse and thankful that Professor Dixon had insisted she learn to appreciate poetry. It hadn't seemed terribly important then; now it did.

Now there was Lew, and Lew could hold his own with the learned professor when it came to poetry and literature. And that was saying a lot. Mollie smiled, fondly recalling the second evening Lew had come to call. She, wearing a pastel pink frock, was waiting when the professor ushered Lew into the drawing room.

Lew had looked at her and said, "Would I were a poet, I might offer proper homage to your beauty."

The professor had smiled and quoted,

"Shall I compare thee to a summer's day?
Thou art more lovely and more temperate."

He had paused then and his eyes had widened in surprise when Lew, in that deep-timbered voice, had continued,

"But thy eternal summer shall not fade,
Nor lose possession of that fair thou ow'st . . .
So long as men can breathe, or eyes can see,
So long lives this, and this give life to thee."

Now, as Mollie lay on her bed on this hot June afternoon, she flopped over onto her back and sighed dreamily. A month had passed since then, and Lew had not missed a single night coming to call.

Clean and suntanned and handsome, he arrived each evening at twilight, a ready smile for the professor and a devilish wink for her. Then the three of them either enjoyed a superbly cooked supper at the mansion or they strolled down to the Nueva Sol in the gathering dusk to the hotel's dining room. And as they walked, Lew took her hand possessively in his, lacing his long tapered fingers through hers. It always sent a shiver of excitement up her spine.

On Thursdays, when she and the professor taught the three Rs to the Indian and Mexican children, Lew would meet them at the schoolhouse. He stayed outside, smoking in the twilight, until classes were dismissed.

Suddenly Mollie sat up on the bed, her smile broadening, a satin strap of her chemise slipping down a bare shoulder.

Today was Thursday, but the professor was not going to the little schoolhouse this evening. He had to attend a bank board meeting. She was to teach the children their lessons and afterward . . . afterward . . . Mollie drew in a quick breath and tumbled over backward on the bed. She slid her hands over the silky coverlet beneath her and felt her heart begin to pound and pound.

Lew was to meet her at the schoolhouse and drive her home. It would be the very first time that she had been alone with him! Just the two of them, riding through the summer darkness, arriving back at the mansion well before the professor was due home. She would invite Lew in and the two of them, sitting side by side on the velvet sofa, would share coffee and cake.

Envisioning the romantic ride from the schoolhouse, Mollie tingled with sweet anticipation. Would tonight be the night Lew . . .

"Mollie," came the professor's voice from just beyond the door, "are you ready? I'm due at the bank in half an hour. If I'm to drive you to the schoolhouse, we'd better be on our way."

"Ready!" Mollie called and flew into her dressing room. Scant minutes later she skipped down the stairs to find the professor waiting patiently in the foyer. She smiled and said, "Go on out, Professor. I'll be right behind you."

Before he could respond, Mollie hurried toward the back of the house and Louise's kitchen. She found the housekeeper sitting on a tall stool, beating batter in a crockery bowl. She looked up when Mollie dashed in.

"My goodness, you look pretty this afternoon," Louise said, her spoon pausing in midstroke. Then, "You better go, you're keeping the professor waiting."

"I know, but I had to see if you—"

"Yes," Louise replied, anticipating the question. "The pound cake will be sliced and topped with my best orange glaze. There will be fresh strawberries with warm honey for dipping. I have polished the silver tea service, and I'll—"

"You're wonderful!" Mollie exclaimed, then spontaneously dipped a forefinger into the crockery bowl, licked it, and nodded approvingly. Backing away, she said, "Now, don't feel like you must wait up."

Louise Emerson's eyebrows lifted. "Young lady, I'll be wide awake when you get back and the door to my room with be open. If it gets too quiet in the drawing room . . ." She clicked her tongue against the roof of her mouth. "I guarantee you it'll scare that young broncobuster to death if Louise Emerson storms in with a rolling pin."

Mollie smiled. She knew Louise was teasing. The older woman had warmed to Lew from the beginning and was as pleased as a proud parent that such a mannerly, handsome gentleman came calling every evening.

Out at the big Willard ranch, Lew was an easygoing fellow who took his share of good-natured razzing when he was thrown from a particularly mean bronc or drew costly, second-best hands in the bunkhouse poker games. Or when he dressed up in what the cowhands called his "dandy dudes" and went into Maya each evening.

A certain amount of ragging was standard fare on any big spread where dozens of men lived and worked closely together. Lew had grown up around it and took it in stride. He had never been a man who was easily rankled.

So he smiled when one of the ranch hands, Dusty Caprock, nudging his buddy, big Sonny Bullock, said, "Hey, Lew, how long you gonna be content to hold that pretty blond girl's hand?"

Lew, naked to the waist, a towel draped around his shoulders, stood before a mirror in the crowded bunkhouse with a straight-edged razor in his right hand. Shrugging negligently, he said, "Don't know, Dusty. How you gonna be content just holding onto yourself?"

Big Sonny Bullock exploded with laughter and slapped his buddy on the back. Sonny and Lew laughed even louder when a flustered, red-faced Dusty sputtered and defended himself. "Why, I don't . . . that ain't true! I ain't never done . . . I wouldn't . . . hell, I got me plenty of women!"

"Yeah, well, a hit dog always howls," Sonny accused him.

Then he went into more fits of laughter, as did the dozen or so cowpokes straddling their chairs and lying on bunks in the big room. Dusty, muttering to himself, stalked out of the bunkhouse, his face aflame.

It was the kind of talk and ribbing that went on all the time. So Lew took no offense when one of the cowboys, a leanly built, cat-eyed man they called Puma, said in low, suggestive tones, "Come on, Taylor, ain't you man enough to find out what's under that Fontaine Gayerre's petticoats?"

Lew's razor continued its flashing movement, the sharp blade cleanly sliding down the smooth brown skin of his left jaw. He didn't reward the waiting Puma with a reply. Just kept on shaving. And smiling.

"Puma, just 'cause she would never in a million years let you under 'em," said Sonny, "don't mean Lew won't get there one of these nights. Right, Lew?"

Puma's cat eyes narrowed and he said, "That haughty little piece thinks she's too good for—"

"—any of us," Lew interrupted him, lowering the blade. He turned about, looked directly at Puma, and said, "And you know what? She's probably right."

Puma finally grinned grudgingly and nodded. Continuing to smile, Lew wiped the residue of lather from his face, set his blue shaving mug back on the shelf, and went for a shirt.

At the little adobe schoolhouse, Mollie recruited one of the students to pass out paper and pencils. She chose John Distant Star, the tall, shy Hopi who had become like a younger brother since she'd begun helping the professor teach the children.

In the beginning it had been mostly pity that had so drawn her to the proud seventeen-year-old. John was very poor, but he worked very hard, hammering and sweating his days away at the blacksmith's shop. He received only a pittance for his labor, but was allowed to sleep there on a bed of straw at night.

The blacksmith's shop was the only home John Distant Star had. John was an orphan, and nobody in Maya could recall where he had come from or when. Since Indians were looked down on by the gentry, John had few friends, but he hardly noticed. He had been alone for as long as he could remember. Loneliness was, as far as John was concerned, a condition of living.

John did have a good friend in the professor. And now he had one in Mollie as well.

Mollie liked John Distant Star and no longer felt any pity for him. He was, she had learned, highly intelligent, well-mannered, proud, dependable, and generous. From that first time they had met and she had thrust out her hand and introduced herself, she had sensed how desperately he wanted her to like him. His expressive dark eyes almost begged for her approval and friendship.

She could look right into John's innocent heart, and it made her own swell with affection for him. As the weeks had passed, she had managed to draw him out. Then she had thoroughly shocked him—and the rest of Maya—when one day she walked right into the blacksmith's shop and asked John if he would like to join her for lunch.

His mouth dropping open in surprise, he looked down at his bare, blackened, sweat-slick torso, then at his scowling boss. Unruffled, Mollie had laughed and said, "I didn't mean that we'd go to the Nueva Sol. Louise packed me the most delicious picnic, and there's way too much food for just one person." She looked over at the frowning smithy. "John is allowed a half hour to eat his lunch, is he not, Mr. Bledsoe?"

"Well, yes, but—"

"Good. Why don't you take a quick wash-up, John, and I'll meet you outside."

That day had been the first of many lunches they shared. The fact that the good folk of Maya nodded to one another and whispered when the tall Indian youth and the slender blond girl strolled down the wooden sidewalk to the plaza worried John Distant Star. It bothered Mollie none at all.

She had the professor's blessing. She did not need theirs.

Lew drove the ranch-owned gig into town as the sun was slipping behind the blue-tinted mountains. When he reached the adobe schoolhouse and climbed down, he began to smile. He stood, arms crossed over his chest, leaning back against the gig. He could hear, through the schoolhouse's open windows, young voices responding to questions asked by their beautiful blond teacher.

Lew liked the kids, all of them. But there was one in particular who had quickly captured his attention, a tall, slim youth with soulful eyes and a shy manner. John Distant Star had the firm handshake of a man, the quiet temperament of an Indian, the trusting nature of a child, and a pair of eyes that truly were windows of the soul. In their dark depths, Lew could clearly read John's adolescent worship of the young woman calling herself Fontaine Gayerre.

Giving the devil her due, Lew had to admit that Mollie Rogers did not intentionally encourage the young Hopi. She was naturally outgoing and friendly, and she treated John as though he were a kid brother.

Apparently she had no idea what was really in John's heart.

But Lew knew.

From the time he was five years old, he had spent his days with Dan Nighthorse. He had learned to read the stoic Dan as no one else could. This slender Indian boy reminded Lew of Dan, and he recalled, vividly, the same look in Dan's dark eyes one summer when a pretty blond girl had moved to Santa Fe and stolen Dan's heart. She had flirted, teased, and led him on, then cruelly rebuffed the naive Dan when he asked if he could call on her. She had acidly reminded Dan that he was a savage—barely out of a breechcloth—while she was a highborn young lady.

Lew smiled ruefully.

The roles were reversed in this case, but John didn't know it. He assumed that the beautiful Fontaine Gayerre was far, far above him. Too bad he couldn't be told the truth: that the blond angel he yearned for was actually far beneath him. A desperado in a dress. A hardened, world-wise woman who had ridden, robbed, and slept with a gang of outlaws.

Lew ground his teeth. He couldn't tell John Distant Star about Mollie. But he would do the sensitive Indian lad the favor of getting her out of Maya—and out of John's life—as quickly as possible.

Lew was abruptly shaken from his thoughts when the schoolhouse door burst open and the shouting, laughing children streamed out and ran toward him. He crouched down on his heels and swept a couple of little girls up into his arms as the others swarmed about him like bees around the sweetest blossom.

The children had quickly learned that this tall, laughing man always carried a paper sack filled with the most tempting candies they had ever eaten. They knew that he intended the sweets for them. Polite, even when excitedly anticipating their first taste of the treats, the children hastily lined up, youngest to oldest, to take their turn at reaching into the bag. The two little girls Lew held were the youngest. Giggling happily, one stuck her tiny fingers down into the sack's depths and drew out a tart lemon drop. The other girl asked if she too might have a lemon drop.

"Help yourself, sweetheart," Lew said and watched, smiling, as she searched until she found what she was looking for, then popped it into her mouth.

Lew lowered the little girls to their feet and rose as the other children stepped forward to take a turn. Over their heads he saw Mollie descending the steps. The sun's lingering afterglow made a golden halo of her hair as she looked up at the tall youth beside her.

John Distant Star.

John laughed at whatever it was she had said. Mollie turned back, paused on the step, and looked directly at Lew. Her lovely face immediately broke into a wide, winsome smile meant especially for him. Lew didn't have to force his response. She was, standing there in the fading twilight, a vision to bring a smile to any man's lips, a tightness to his chest.

"Lew." She silently formed his name with those soft, luscious lips, and he felt the troublesome tingling of joy that claimed him every time she spoke his name.

Mentally shaking himself, Lew focused his attention back on the chattering children. When he saw John Distant Star at the end of the line, he grinned at the boy. John had a real sweet tooth. He loved candy even more than the little ones did.

When John reached him, Lew put a hand on his shoulder and said, "Take the rest, John. There are several pieces left, and—"

The Hopi shook his head firmly. "I will take only my share." He chose a licorice stick, thanked Lew, and turned away to herd the younger students into a group for the walk home.

"I'll take more than my share from you, Lew," Mollie teased playfully as she stepped up before him.

Tilting her head to one side she stuck her hand down into the paper bag. Reflexively his long fingers wrapped themselves firmly around her wrist, capturing her hand inside the bag.

His lips thinned, and his eyes narrowed to blue glint. "You won't get the chance."

18

◈

"Lew, what is it?" Alarmed, Mollie looked up into his icy eyes and asked anxiously, "Is something bothering you?"

Instantly he softened his expression. Flashing her a boyish smile, he said, "Yes. You are. You bother me unmercifully, Miss Gayerre. Didn't you know that?" He released her fragile wrist. "Do I bother you? Do you think about me when we're apart?"

Relieved and charmed, Mollie withdrew her hand from the candy sack and said honestly, "I do, Lew, yes I do." Blushing then, her eyes dropped to his mouth and she added, "All day I kept thinking that this would be our first time alone."

"Why do you suppose I cut myself shaving?" He touched a pinpoint nick on the tanned skin just below his right cheekbone.

Mollie screwed her face into a sympathetic frown, impulsively kissed the tip of her forefinger and touched it to the minuscule bloodspot. Lew again captured her wrist, but this time he gently drew her open hand up to his lips. Mollie felt all the air leave her lungs when his thick, dark lashes closed seductively over his blue eyes and his smooth lips brushed a slow, warm kiss to her sensitive palm.

When Lew raised his head, he flattened her open hand on the broad expanse of his chest, then placed his own atop it. Mollie thrilled to the touch. His work-callused hand, with its long, lean fingers, felt good covering hers—almost as good as the hard, flat chest muscles under her spread hand. Awed by the strength and heat beneath her fingertips, she could feel the crisp hair through his silky white shirt. And she wondered, fleetingly, if she would be repulsed—the way she'd been with the Kid—if Lew were to take off his shirt. Her wildly beating heart told her that she wouldn't.

"Would you like to go with me for a ride in the moonlight, Miss Gayerre?" Lew's voice was soft, persuasive.

"Oh, yes, I—no, Lew. We can't. I'm sorry. I promised the professor that I would have you drive me straight home." She gave him a weak smile.

He was annoyed, but he carefully hid it. He said, "I don't blame the professor." His fingers closed around hers and he slowly lowered her hand from his chest. But he continued to hold her hand loosely in his. Then he shook his head and looked worried. "Perhaps the professor doesn't trust me. Maybe he doesn't want me to—"

"Oh, no, that's not it! He trusts you completely, honest he does. It's just that I haven't known you that long, really, and—You understand, don't you?"

"I sure do, sweetheart. Come on, I'll drive you home." Impatient to get on with his plan, Lew thought irritably that seducing this luscious little outlaw was going to take a hell of a lot longer than he'd counted on.

Mollie smiled happily, pleased that he was so agreeable and such a gentleman.

At the gig, Lew's hands went to her waist and he lifted her easily upon to the leather seat. Settling herself comfortably, Mollie fussily arranged her long, billowing skirts, carefully arranging the folds and gathers of the starched organza.

"There," she said, finishing, and looked up.

Lew had not yet climbed into the gig. He stood, one foot on the step, a hand on the seat back, watching her with a devilish smile on his handsome face. "What? What is it?" she asked, suddenly embarrassed by his scrutiny, wondering if he were laughing at her.

"You are a constant delight, Fontaine Gayerre," he said evenly. "Such a well-bred young lady." He leaned very close then and, his foot never leaving the step or his hand the seat back, he toyed with the hem of her frilly dress. "I wonder," he mused aloud, his fingers snaking up under the folds of organza to capture a slender ankle, "are you a woman as well as a lady?"

Mollie couldn't speak. She swallowed. Then swallowed again, but couldn't make a sound because his fingers, those long, warm fingers were wrapped around her ankle and they felt for all the world like a band of fire. His thumb began sliding slowly, tantalizingly up and down her shin bone while his middle finger located and caressed the pulse beating in her foot. He said nothing more, just looked at her with humid blue eyes as if waiting for her to answer.

Her own eyes wide, her bosom rising and falling rapidly, Mollie finally broke the tension-filled silence. Mesmerized by his intense gaze and stirring touch, she said truthfully, "I don't know yet, Lew. I'm not sure."

Biting his tongue to keep from reminding her that she knew all too well, Lew gave her shapely ankle one last intimate squeeze, withdrew his hand from beneath her dress, and swung up into the gig beside her.

Unwinding the long leather reins from around the brake, he said, "I do, sweetheart. I'm sure."

"You are?"

He clucked to the horse and the wheels of the carriage began to roll as the responsive pony pranced away into the deepening darkness.

"Yes," Lew said, turned and smiled at Mollie. "You're a woman, all right." His gaze shifted to her parted lips. "My woman."

"Oh, Lew," she murmured breathlessly.

Mollie was so thrilled and captivated she hardly noticed that on the ride home through the gaslit streets of Maya, Lew asked more questions than he ever had before. Thrown off guard by his masculine charm and compelling closeness, she hemmed and hawed and stumbled over her answers, momentarily forgetting some of the detailed background she and the professor had so carefully made up.

"It's so strange, Fontaine, to hear a beautiful young lady from back East speak with an . . . umm . . . almost a Southern accent. No, no, not Southern." His eyes flashed in the darkness when he said, "I was in the army with a couple of men from Texas. That's it. You sound a lot like them. Ever spend any time down in Texas?"

"I . . . I . . . my mother had some cousins in Texas and I went with her to visit them when I was younger."

"Really? What part of Texas?"

"San Antonio." Mollie said the first place that popped into her head.

"San Antone," echoed Lew. "Good town. Been there myself. Maybe I'd know your cousins. I met a lot of—"

"They moved a long time ago," Mollie anxiously interrupted. "They all came east to be closer to the rest of the family."

Lew nodded and let that subject drop. But the questions continued—tactfully, subtly—and the totally enamored Mollie never became suspicious. The wise interrogator was far too clever and charming to arouse any distrust or suspicion in his cooperative suspect.

Mollie was smiling when the gig rolled into the mansion's graveled driveway. She was flattered that Lew was so interested in her. He wanted to know everything about her. She understood perfectly, since she longed to know everything there was to know about him.

A rising desert moon, full and white, now bathed the Maya valley in silvery brilliance. Lew swung down, turned, and lifted his arms to Mollie. When his hands encircled her waist and he plucked her from the seat, Mollie found herself held high in the air for a moment.

Laughing, she scolded, "Lew Taylor, you put me down this minute!"

"Anything you say, sweetheart," he replied, looking up at her.

Then took his own sweet time.

Before he released her he drew her to him, pressing her against his tall, hard body. His face at the level of her full breasts, he looked unblinkingly into her eyes as he slowly, suggestively, lowered her to her feet. Purposely sliding her down his lean frame, he made sure the soft contours of her slender body met and melded with the harsh planes and hollows of his.

When Mollie felt her toes finally touch the ground,

she was trembling from the unsettling, intimate contact. Staring up into his handsome face—half-shadowed in the darkness, half-lighted by the moon—she became aware of his quick breathing. Or was it her own?

Nervously she freed herself from his arms and hurried toward the yard. In two long strides Lew caught up with her, took her hand in his, and squeezed it reassuringly.

When they climbed the steps to the broad veranda, Mollie said, "We have the drawing room all to ourselves." Halfway to the front door, she asked, "Shall we go inside and talk?"

Lew paused. Mollie, clinging to his hand, stopped, turned back, and looked questioningly up at him. On his dark face was an expression of such intensity Mollie was awed and a little frightened. A tiny muscle spasmed in his jaw, and his eyes gleamed with a strange new light.

"I don't want to hold a conversation," he said, "I want to hold you." Then he quickly backed into the deep shadow of a tall porch column, drawing her to him. Mollie blinked, trying desperately to see the face of the magnetic man speaking to her from out of the darkness while she stood squarely in the bright moonlight. "I only want to hold you, sweetheart," came that low, caressing voice as he pulled her to him until she too was swallowed up in the deep blackness. His arms went around her and he drew her into his embrace.

The seductive darkness, the feel of his lean, muscular frame pressed against hers, made Mollie extremely nervous. Her hands anxiously dancing over the fabric stretching across his biceps, she said, "Louise has fixed a delicious dessert for us."

"That's nice," he responded distractedly, his hands sweeping over Mollie's waist, urging her steadily closer. He stood with his back against the tall porch pillar, his feet apart, his arms wrapped around her. "Kiss me, Fontaine," he whispered, his breath ruffling the wispy hair at her temple. "It's dark and no one can see us. Kiss me. Just one time, kiss me."

Mollie was going to say no. At least she was almost certain that was what she had intended to say. But he never gave her the chance. Before she could say anything his mouth was on hers, smooth and warm and wonderful. It was a proper kiss, a kiss of decorum, lips pliant but closed. A guarded, tender kiss.

When it ended, Mollie was convinced that their first kiss had been exactly as it should be. Pleasant, but restrained, demonstrating that Lew knew she was a proper young lady and he had great respect for her.

However, his muscular arms were like bands of steel as he continued to hold her. She could feel his strong heartbeat against her breasts and the granite hardness of his thighs brushing against her own. His hands, slipping low on her hips, were pressing her dangerously close, and his clean, uniquely masculine scent filled her senses.

The warm June night grew warmer still, and Mollie struggled to free herself, saying uneasily, "Louise has outdone herself, Lew. There's lemonade with ice and a twelve-egg pound cake, and—"

"Sounds delicious," Lew interrupted, but didn't move or release her. "Delicious," he repeated as his lips slowly descended to hers again.

Sighing, Mollie closed her eyes and told herself that one more little good-night kiss could hardly be construed as unseemly by Lew or anyone else. But this time, to her surprise and pleasure, Lew's lips didn't stay completely closed. And the kiss that began as a single one turned into a dozen kisses that made Mollie's face feel uncomfortably hot, her lips become soft and full.

When finally—after several long, heart-stopping kisses—their mouths separated, Mollie, unsteady on her feet, said with a touch of desperation in her voice, "And . . . and there's orange sauce for the cake."

"Mmm," was Lew's reply.

And again his mouth masterfully took hers in a heated, coaxing kiss that caused her to cling to him, her hands anxiously gripping his smooth, clefted back, her sharp nails punishing the flesh through his shirt. His tongue slid provocatively along the seam of Mollie's full lips until they parted to him. Still she kept her teeth tightly shut, so Lew gently chewed on the fleshy inside of her lower lip, pressed wet little kisses to the corners of her mouth, and raked his teeth over her kiss-swollen lips until, half-dazed but determined to stop behaving so improperly, Mollie abruptly pulled away.

"And strawberries," she managed, her breath coming fast, "big, ripe strawberries." Her hands were gliding up and down Lew's shirtfront now, her fingertips exploring the breadth of his chest, the hard sinew, the crisp hair. "With warm honey to dip—"

Lew's lips silenced her. His breath mingling with hers, he said against her trembling mouth, "You've got the warm honey I want to taste." He pressed a kiss to her parted lips, raised his head, and looked down at her. His blue eyes flashed in the darkness when he said, "Give it to me, sweetheart. Let me have all your sweet honey."

Mollie shivered, but gave no answer as his lips brushed back and forth on hers before settling squarely on her mouth. He kissed her so commandingly, so hotly, she felt a new kind of heat envelop her.

When the kiss began, Lew's hands were on her face, his fingers gently cupping her flushed cheeks. His thumbs caressing her temples, his lips toyed and licked and played with hers. As the long, ardent kiss continued, his mouth opened and his tongue slid sensuously between her teeth. His hands left her face, moved down to clasp her shoulders and drew her more intimately to him. Then the kiss deepened as he thrust his tongue into the silky sweetness of her mouth, tasting, stroking, devouring.

A white-hot flash of desire jolted through Lew when Mollie, sweetly molding herself to him, sighed and touched her tongue to his. At once he felt himself surge and harden while his heart hammered wildly in his chest.

Mollie was unaware of what she was doing to him; she was far too swept away by what he was doing to her. Awakened for the first time in her life to her own innate sensuality, she stood there in Lew's embrace, responding totally. His exquisite, experienced lovemaking causing new and wondrous sensations to wash over her, she melted into him.

Her eyes shut, her arms twined around Lew's neck, Mollie stood in the darkness on that hot June night eagerly kissing Lew Hatton, learning quickly, teasing him just as he teased her, purposely pressing her pliant body to the hard, ungiving length of his.

And Mollie blinked, confused and disappointed, when Lew abruptly took his hot mouth from hers, set her back from him, and said, "You said something about lemonade with ice?"

19

Mollie found herself faced with a dilemma.

The raising of the First Methodist Church on a vacant lot two blocks south of the plaza was planned for Saturday, June twenty-first. Less than a week away. All the men of Maya, including the cowboys from the Willard ranch, would be helping with the work. Willing spirits banding together for a common goal—the good of the community.

The ladies of Maya would be there to lend moral support and to bring plenty of tempting foods to feed the hungry volunteers. Her best friends, Madeline and Patricia, had assured Mollie that the day would be most enjoyable and she had better persuade the professor to close the store so she could be there for the fun. If she wasn't, her tall, raven-haired broncbuster might well get snatched away from her. After all, Patricia confided, every lady in town was talking about the handsome New Mexican horseman. And, Madeline put in, she had it on good authority that a certain divorcée, the rich, sophisticated Mary Beth McCalister, had made no secret of the fact that Lew Taylor was her idea of a real man. Gossip had it that Mary Beth had told her maid

144

that if Lew didn't soon make a move on her, she was going to make one on him, even if it meant riding out to the Willard ranch alone some dark night.

So Mollie was worried. The entire town knew that the voluptuous Mary Beth McCalister was fast and loose, yet the men of Maya grinned like dumbstruck fools anytime she passed them on the street, fluttering her eyelashes and swaying her hips. Mollie thought that Mary Beth was downright disgusting with her little-girl voice and her silly simpering and posturing. And she felt sure that Lew was far too clever to be snared by Mary Beth's too-obvious charms. Still, Mary Beth was supposed to be the best dancer in all Maya. And therein lay Mollie's dilemma.

The Saturday church-raising would end with a big celebration dance. Lew had already invited her to go to the dance with him. There was only one little problem. She did not know how to dance! The professor had taught her everything, except how to dance.

Frowning, Mollie exhaled heavily, leaned her elbows on the Emporium's front counter, and rested her chin in her hands. Unsettling images filled her head. Lew whirling about on the dance floor with a smiling, flirting Mary Beth McCalister in his arms while she, Mollie the wallflower, stood at the edge of the crowd as everyone laughed and pointed and pitied her.

"Is business that bad this morning, Fontaine?"

Mollie looked up and gave a loud sigh of relief. "I need to talk to you."

Smiling, the professor took off his hat and crossed to her. "Then why don't you grab your bonnet and come along with me. I'm on my way out to the Willard ranch to take a look at a bay stallion L.J.'s been telling me about."

"Do you think it would be all right?" Her violet eyes immediately lighted.

"I think Mr. Stanfield can spare you for a couple of hours."

Mollie shook her head in impatience. "That isn't what I meant, Professor!" She was already reaching for her bonnet. "We might run into Lew at the ranch, and—"

"Lew's the one who's breaking the bay. I'd like to see him work." His blue eyes twinkled merrily. "Wouldn't you?"

"Would I!"

The flat, endless desert shimmered under a hot morning sun beating down mercilessly from a cloudless blue sky. As Mollie and the professor rode across the barren plain, the carriage wheels churned up loose sand, leaving fine dust hanging in the still air.

"I just know I shall be the object of derision come Saturday night," Mollie was saying, clinging to the seat with one hand, her bonnet with the other. "Professor, I don't know how to dance!"

The professor chuckled. "My dear, would you believe an old man if he were to tell you that young men find it both enjoyable and flattering to be called on to teach their sweethearts to dance?"

"They do? Did you ever teach a young lady to dance?"

"I did," he said, remembering, a warm light shining in his pale eyes. "And it was one of the greatest pleasures of my life."

"Really? Was she lovely? Who was she? Did she . . . ?"

"Mollie, I simply wanted to point out that you needn't worry. If Lew knows how to dance, and I'm sure he does, he'll be more than pleased to teach you."

"I suppose, but won't he think it strange that I don't know how?"

"He believes that you attended an academy for young ladies where you had few opportunities to be around young men. He won't be suspicious. Stop your needless worrying."

Mollie was still troubled. "Suppose Lew sees what a marvelous dancer Mary Beth McCalister is and wishes he was with her instead of me."

Professor Dixon turned and looked directly at her. "What do you know about Mary Beth McCalister?"

Mollie shrugged. "Not much. Patricia and Madeline say she entertains gentlemen in her mansion like some . . . some . . ." Her face colored and she fell silent.

"Patricia and Madeline gossip too much. Mrs. McCalister may 'entertain gentlemen' on occasion, but Lew Taylor is not one of them."

"How do you know?"

"Well, for one thing, he's been with you every night."

Mollie smiled finally, then immediately frowned. "He might go to her house after he leaves me!"

"He doesn't," said the professor with conviction.

He didn't tell her that he had, from Lew's first day in Maya, been having him discreetly watched. Highly protective of Mollie, he was taking no chances that Mr. Lew Taylor was anyone other than a rugged young broncbuster from Bernalillo who was genuinely interested in the sweet girl he knew as Fontaine Gayerre. If it was within his power, he would see to it that the charming child beside him would not be hurt or deceived.

Mollie was satisfied at last. The professor had told her once that he knew just about everything that went on in Maya. She believed him.

"Professor," she said thoughtfully, "would you think me terrible if I told you I love it that every woman in Maya is just green with envy because I have Lew and they haven't?"

He laughed and shook his silver head. "I would think you are quite normal and painfully honest."

Mollie frowned again. "Honest? We both know that I'm anything but." She bowed her head. "What would Lew think if he . . . ?"

"He doesn't and he won't. The past is dead. You're a different girl."

Mollie remained silent, wondering how Lew *would* feel if he learned the sordid truth. The disturbing thought caused a tightness in her chest. Distracted, she missed what the professor was saying. "I . . . I'm sorry, Professor, I didn't . . . what did you say?"

"I said, dear, that I will be going to California the first week of August. I try to get out there and check on my gold mines once or twice a year. I thought you might like to come with me."

"How long will you be gone?"

"Not much over two weeks . . . three at most."

She hesitated, and he could see the wheels turning in her head. She was thinking about being away from Lew Taylor.

She smiled prettily, and said, "I have always wanted to go to California, but I don't think Mr. Stanfield could do without me at the Emporium for so long."

"That's true. I failed to consider that." He grinned and lifted a silver eyebrow, letting her know he was on to her.

She laughed merrily then, pressed her cheek against his shoulder, and said, "Mister, that's my story and I'm sticking to it!"

He threw back his head and laughed. They were both laughing when they drove through the tall ranch gates of L. J. Willard's big upland spread.

Mollie felt her excitement mount as they drove past headquarters, a big, boxlike, two-story frame house painted a dismal shade of brown. Her palms grew moist when she saw—in the near distance—a piñon pole corral with a dozen or so cowboys and *vaqueros* milling around.

"There's L.J.," said the professor, pointing to the stockily built rancher.

Mollie nodded absently and anxiously scanned the rugged male faces, hunting for Lew. He was nowhere in sight. L. J. Willard was bearing down on them, a big grin splitting his leathery brown face.

"My, my," he boomed, "what have we here? Miss Gayerre, we're mighty glad you came out with the professor." He whisked Mollie out of the carriage, took her hand, and pumped it. "Lordy, the boys will all be a-wantin' to show off for you."

While the three of them stood in the morning sunshine making small talk, Lew, carrying his favorite rigging, stepped out of the tack room not forty yards away. He stopped. Squinting from underneath the brim of his low tilted Stetson, he spotted her immediately. He felt his heart kick against his ribs, and a foolish grin lifted the corners of his mouth.

The purely reflexive response was gone in a second, and he swore under his breath. He reminded himself that while the girl standing in the blazing sun was incredibly beautiful and had given him kisses that were so sweet they haunted his dreams, she was a cold, cunning criminal who had given other men a hell of lot more than kisses.

Lew threw his gear up onto the corral fence, forced a smile to his face, and started toward her.

Mollie, only half listening to the professor and L. J. Willard, looked up, saw him coming, and felt her stomach contract. Was it only last night they had kissed? It seemed like a millennium. She wished she could kiss him right now.

Breathlessly she watched him approach. He looked different this morning. She had never seen him in anything other than his dress clothes. While he had been outrageously handsome last night in a dove gray linen suit and snowy white shirt, he was even more appealing—if that were possible—the way he was dressed now.

He wore a collarless pullover shirt of pale lavender. A vest of buttery brown leather stretched across his broad shoulders. A pair of faded denim Levi's were almost indecently tight, revealingly contouring his flat belly and slim hips and long legs. A wide leather belt rode low around his waist, its square silver buckle gleaming in the sunlight. Tied around his tanned throat was a lavender cotton bandanna that matched his shirt. A dark brown Stetson was pulled over his eyes, and thrown carelessly over his left shoulder was a pair of rough chamois shotgun chaps.

He walked with a sure, masculine stride, his long

arms swinging at his sides. In charge. Sure of himself. All man. And he was smiling.

"Morning, everybody," he said as he reached them.

"Good morning, Lew," said the professor, warmly shaking the hand Lew held out to him.

"Lew," said L. J. Willard, "I was a-tellin' them how you don't mind at all if Miss Gayerre watches you ride that mean bay."

"If you do, Lew, I can—" Mollie began.

"Not at all," said Lew evenly. "The more the merrier."

The talk was of breaking horses, and Lew spoke with quiet authority, easily captivating his small audience.

Even the crusty old rancher nodded his head, saying, "Yes, yes, that's right, son." L.J. then told Mollie and the professor, "This boy is the best on the back of a beast I ever did see. Ain't nobody like him."

Mollie was impressed, but too distracted to pay close attention to the conversation. Lew, towering over them at six foot three, stood very close to her. His nearness was unsettling. She inwardly shivered when he casually lifted a hand to toy with the green ribbon that went around the crown of her straw hat and fell midway down her back. He slipped the grosgrain ribbon between two lean fingers, pulled the ends around over her shoulder, and idly fiddled with them as he spoke.

When finally he released the ribbon, allowing it to fall on her left shoulder, then pressed it with his fingers against the exposed flesh of her collarbone, Mollie felt as if she would surely suffocate.

"Well, guess I might as well get to it," she heard him say and was relieved. "Come on, Fontaine. I'll give you a front row seat." He took her arm and propelled her toward the corral fence while L.J. and the professor lagged behind. Glancing over his shoulder to make sure he couldn't be heard, Lew leaned down to Mollie and said, "God, I'd like to kiss you. Right here, right now." He touched her bottom lip with a callused thumb. "Right there."

Her lip trembled and she was momentarily terrified he would bend his head and kiss her in front of everybody. She opened her mouth to protest, but before she could utter a word, Lew said, "You stand right here, sweetheart. And if that mean mustang heads this way, jump back fast." He touched her cheek and was gone.

Mollie stepped closer to the corral fence, went up on tiptoe, and folded her arms over the top rail as Lew opened the gate and went inside. Cowboys seemed to materialize from everywhere. Spurs clanking, their laughter and cigarette smoke filling the air, they hurried from the barns, the bunkhouse, and the cookshack. To a man, they all noticed Mollie immediately. They grinned foolishly and touched their hat brims and elbowed each other like flustered schoolboys.

Mollie paid them no attention. She had eyes only for Lew.

Unhurriedly, as he did all things, Lew stood just inside the piñon corral putting on his shotgun chaps. A newly lighted cigar clamped firmly between his teeth, he shook out the chaps, then spun them around his slim hips like a matador swirling a cap. With an economy of motion, he buckled the chaps behind his trim waist. Mollie felt her throat go dry when he smoothed the chamois fabric around one long leg, buckled it just under his lean buttock and behind his knee, then repeated the action with the other leg.

Chaps in place, he stood, hitching them up, pulling them tight, unconsciously directing Mollie's attention to the only part of his tight Levi's not covered by the chaps—the faded fabric that was stretched taut over his groin.

A horse neighed loudly, and Mollie looked up. A huge, magnificent bay thundered into the corral, his sharp hooves kicking up dust, his big eyes wild with fear and hate.

Lew walked over and plucked his looped lariat from a fence pole. He looked up when the man they called Puma, swinging up onto the fence, softly taunted him.

"Sure hope you don't get thrown on your ass by that big stud 'cause you're tryin' to be a big stud in front of that pretty blond gal."

Lew just smiled, pulled his hat brim lower, took the gloves from his hip pocket, drew them on, and walked away.

All eyes were then riveted on the tall, lean cowboy as he calmly crossed the corral, moving steadily closer to the snorting, bucking bay. Mollie watched, impressed, as Lew deftly raised the lasso and began to twirl it over his head. Then, with perfect aim and lightning speed, he threw it. The rope's big loop sailed out and came down over the sleek, perspiring neck of the stallion.

Terrified, the horse squealed and reared his forelegs high into the air. Lew, cigar still clamped between his teeth, dug his bootheels into the dirt and allowed the frightened bay to pull him around until he got close enough to the snubbing post at the corral's center to get the rope wrapped around his hips.

The rearing, whinnying stallion was choking himself. His big eyes bulged and he fought hard, his slick body quivering from withers to flanks. Lew hung on and finally spit his cigar on the ground.

"It's okay, fella." Lew's voice was low and deep. "Easy, easy now." Slowly, surely, he worked his gloved hands up the taut rope while the horse neighed wildly and shook his great head and pounded the earth with flying hooves.

The crowd of cowpokes watched, shaking their heads appreciatively and shouting as Lew stepped in and touched the horse's muzzle. His hand gently rubbing the sweating face, he crooned soothingly to the stallion.

Mollie watched entranced as Lew skillfully managed to get a bridle, then a blanket, and finally a saddle on the stallion. She held her breath as he reached under the rearing horse and grabbed the cinch ring, pulling it beneath the stallion's heaving belly.

"I won't hurt you, boy. You'll see." Lew's tone of voice never changed; it remained low and soothing.

He continued to patiently gentle the frightened stallion with words as he lifted a booted foot into the stirrup and swung his leg over. Before the horse realized what was happening, both Lew's feet were planted firmly in the stirrups.

The stallion felt the man's weight and discharged a sound of outraged fury that made the hair rise on Mollie's neck. Terrified, mesmerized, she clung to the rail as the huge stallion pitched and grunted and did everything in his power to unseat the rider.

Lew knew he was aboard one of the toughest stallions he'd ever mounted. It was impossible to get the bay's rhythm. He bucked sideways and spun and twisted and leaped and kept his big head low. Lew spurred and quirted and pulled and jerked, trying vainly to get the snorting stallion's head up. He knew if he could get the beast's head up, the bronc couldn't get nearly as much deadly power into his wild bucking.

"Get his head up, Lew! You must get his head up!"

Mollie didn't realize she was shouting until the professor looked sharply at her and shook his head. Realizing what she had done, she glanced anxiously at L. J. Willard. He hadn't heard her. He was shouting too loudly himself. She bit her lip and looked back at Lew and the stallion.

Stubborn and incredibly strong, the stallion bowed his great neck, kept his head down, and continued to spin and plow and grunt and rear. Lew was being pounded to death.

Each time the bay's hooves struck the hard ground, Lew felt the shock waves in every bone and muscle of his body. The battle continued, man against horse, until finally Lew felt that he was winning. The beast was tiring, his breath was growing short, his coat shimmering with sweat, his head lifting. The stallion had obviously run out of fight, because he stopped bucking, began to hop frantically about, and finally to trot around the corral.

The spectators roared their admiration and Lew started to grin, the taste of victory sweet in his mouth. Sweet, but premature.

Abruptly the trotting erupted into a spinning, spiraling fit of bucking that caught Lew off guard. He could feel himself flying high into the air, but impending danger was not what flashed through his mind. He was thinking that the beautiful young woman who had shouted for him to keep the bronc's head up knew a damned sight too much about breaking horses to be an Eastern miss.

Mollie screamed and clasped her hand over her mouth as Lew left the horse's back and flew high into the air. In that moment when Lew was silhouetted against the clear blue Arizona sky with a look of shock on his dark, handsome face, Mollie knew she loved him.

When his body struck the hard ground with a loud thud, she felt the pain jolt through her own. He lay unmoving, a crumpled form in the dirt. The men were already running toward him.

Mollie started climbing the fence. She had to get to him. The professor's firm hand on her arm stopped her.

20

The next few moments were an eternity.

Saying silent prayers and promising God she would never do anything wrong again if he would only let Lew be all right, Mollie clung to the fence with a death grip, her heart pounding with fear.

When a collective shout went up from the cowhands, she drew a much-needed breath. And when she saw Lew's dark head rise above the others, she uttered a soft cry. As if he knew how upset she was, Lew, assuring the boys he was "fine, just fine," walked through them and straight to her. A self-effacing smile on his dirty face, he winked at Mollie and placed a gloved hand over hers.

"Looks like that bay decided to show off for you too, Fontaine," he said. "And he did a better job of it than I did."

"You were wonderful, Lew," she said, and he was shocked to see a mist of tears in her beautiful violet eyes.

"You sure you're unhurt, son?" asked the professor.

"Positive, sir. Thanks."

It wasn't quite true.

The fall that had knocked the wind out of Lew was causing terrific pain in his right side. He hurt so badly he could scarcely breathe, much less talk, but he managed to hide his discomfort until Mollie and the professor left. Waving good-bye, he stood, smiling easily, until the carriage was completely out of sight.

Then, heading straight for the bunkhouse, he ignored Puma's derisive laughter and taunts. Inside he made sure he was alone, then stripped off his leather vest and soiled shirt. He winced when he laid a hand on his broken ribs. Broken or bruised; he wasn't sure which. Embarrassed that he had let the stallion throw him, he told no one about his injury.

But he was relieved when later that morning, L. J. Willard said casually, "Lew, why don't we let Slim work that bay with a rope for a week or so before you climb back on him."

Lew grinned. "You're the boss."

Saturday, the twenty-first of June, 1872, was a near-perfect day in Maya, Arizona. A sudden thunderstorm had rolled down out of the Santa Ritas around dawn, awakening the town's light sleepers with its brilliant lightning flashes and cannonading booms of thunder.

For almost an hour great drops of rain, driven by a hard west wind, pounded the high desert, soaking the dry, dusty earth and splashing great drinks of water over the thirsty cactus and scrub plants dotting the vast expanse of wasteland.

Mollie awakened with the first echo of distant thunder. She leaped from her bed and rushed through the open double doors onto the balcony. Blinking the sleep from her eyes, she inhaled deeply, relishing the sweet scent of rain on desert; a smell like no other on earth. She smiled, feeling the mist kiss her face while the big, wet drops drummed a loud tattoo on the porch railing and steep roof above.

The unexpected rainstorm filled her with joy. She knew that it wouldn't last long enough to spoil the day's activities. But it would cool the hot, dry air, which would make the outing more pleasant and the strenuous labor easier on the men. Especially on Lew.

The prospect of being with Lew from morning until well past midnight made Mollie shiver with anticipation. She considered which dress and shoes she should wear. The decision quickly made, she impulsively lifted her nightgown up past her knees and ventured out to the porch railing. Knowing she would have a hot bath and a shampoo before getting dressed, she decided to first enjoy an impromptu rain bath right there on the porch.

Laughing merrily, Mollie stepped on the windward side of a Doric porch column, leaned back against it, and allowed the driving rains to hit her full in the face. In seconds her hair, face, and nightgown were wet.

It was wonderful.

She opened her mouth and took licking drinks of the limpid rainwater. She lifted her hands and spread the raindrops over her face and throat. Her shoulders pressed against the dripping porch column, she arched her back and angled her slender body forward. Sighing, she welcomed the forceful rain that plastered the thin nightgown to her sensitive flesh.

Mollie wasn't certain when her simple joyous rain bath turned into a new experience in erotic pleasure.

But it did change. As she stood there in the rain while lightning flashed and thunder clattered and needles of wind-driven rain assaulted her, she thought about Lew. And she began to feel like she felt when he kissed her. She had that same funny fluttering in her stomach, was seized with that familiar breathlessness, was plagued with that sweet, torturous yearning.

Mollie sighed softly while the pelting rain teased nerve endings throughout her gently undulating body. Her head back against the porch column, eyes closed, she was caught up in something she didn't fully understand, but guiltily enjoyed. She was vitally aware that the powerful pounding had molded her soft, warm nipples into pebble-hard points of sheer sensation. The flesh of her belly quivered involuntarily, and she instinctively parted her long slender legs to the force of the rhythmic driving rain.

"Lew," she murmured into the storm, picturing him asleep in his bunk at the ranch, his dark head on the pillow, brown chest and shoulders bare above the covering white sheet. And beneath the sheet . . .

Mollie shuddered, shook herself soundly, and hurried back inside.

Lew awakened with the first rolling rumble of thunder. But he didn't rush out into the rain. He gingerly eased himself up onto his left elbow and examined his badly bruised ribs. From two inches below his armpit to just above his waist, the flesh was a dark bluish purple. Beneath the discolored skin, his ribs ached dully. The pain was minor but constant.

Reaching for a cigar, Lew lit up and lay back down,

folding an arm to cradle his head. Around him slumbering cowhands snored loudly, oblivious to the gathering tempest. Lew smoked contemplatively in the storm-lit room and found his thoughts returning—as they too often did—to the lovely young woman who called herself Fontaine Gayerre.

An earsplitting crash of thunder followed a ground flash of near lightning. Lew hardly noticed. *"Get his head up, Lew. You must get his head up."* He could still hear her sweet, frightened voice calling out those words to him. He smiled sardonically. A prim miss from back East wouldn't know a thing about breaking broncos. But Mollie Rogers would.

Damn her! Damn her to eternal hell! Why in God's name did she have to be so pretty? And why, when she was nothing more than a hardened criminal, did he constantly catch himself thinking of her as a warm, desirable woman?

Lew groaned in agony.

Mollie kissed him the same heart-stopping way that his beautiful Teresa had when she'd first kissed him. Like a sweet, trusting innocent whose lips had never been tasted. Like a naive yet passionate young girl who had belonged to no man before him. Soft honeyed mouth trembling and tentative and timid.

Recalling last night's hurried, heated embrace, Lew ground his teeth down on his cigar, almost biting it in two. She had been in his arms for only a moment. But the vivid recollection of her soft, warm lips clinging to his sent a sharp surge of unwelcome longing through Lew's body.

The lightning flashed closer. The thunder grew louder. And Lew Hatton, his body responding to remembered scents and sensations, grew uncomfortably warm in the darkened bunkhouse. Perspiration dotting his face and bare chest, Lew climbed out of his bunk, drew on a pair of Levi's, and went outside.

Walking barefoot on the rain-slicked porch, he tossed his cigar into a stream of swirling water, leaned a muscular shoulder against a post, and drew a deep, slow breath. He stood there in the violent rainstorm allowing the deluge to hit him full in the face. He welcomed the rain that plastered his hair to his head, peppered his upturned face, drenched his bare shoulders, and saturated his Levi's.

And temporarily cooled the heat in his blood.

Two hours later Lew sat polishing his boots. The storm had passed, and bright summer sunshine streamed in the open windows of the bunkhouse. The cowboys, back from a quick breakfast at the cookshack, were busy getting ready for the daylong celebration.

At the table where Lew sat, a young wrangler straddled a chair and bragged how he planned to dance with every girl in Maya and to take the prettiest one home. A bewhiskered old-timer looked up from his game of solitaire, shot the kid a snaggletoothed grin, and taunted, "Reckon that'd be Mary Beth McCalister. Think you'd be man enough for her once you got her home?"

The wrangler's face turned scarlet. "I could handle her all right, if I got the chance." The old cowpoke snorted while Lew smiled. "Well, I could!" Frowning, the boy rose and walked away, muttering, "I sure could."

The old man laughed and laughed. He drew a

handkerchief from his pocket and was wiping his eyes when he heard Puma's distinct voice. Lew heard it too. It came from the porch. Lew's head snapped around when he heard Fontaine Gayerre's name.

"She's a mighty pretty thing," said Puma, "but I don't think Lew's the only one that's getting some of that."

"What do you mean?" asked one of the cowhands.

The snaggletoothed old cowpoke lowered his handkerchief, his eyes on Lew. He saw the muscles tense in Lew's shoulders, saw the hardening of his jaw.

"Hell, she goes around with that tall Indian kid," Puma continued. "Eight to five says she's enjoying some dark cock out behind the blacksmith's shop these hot afternoons."

His face a mask of rage, Lew shot to his feet. Ignoring the old man's admonition to let it alone, he charged out the door like a crazed animal and swung a hard-driving fist into Puma's ugly face. Lew tagged the bigger, heavier man full in the mouth, sending a spray of bright red blood across Puma's face. Stunned, Puma raised a hand to wipe his eyes. Lew gave him a quick one-two punch to the belly, putting all his weight behind the blows.

Puma grunted loudly, sucked for air, and threw a big fist. He missed by inches, and Lew promptly stung him with a swift left cross. Puma's next blow connected with Lew's left eye. It sounded like an explosion inside his head, but Lew felt nothing. He was far too angry to feel any pain. His eyes wild, he stood toe-to-toe with the longer armed man and fought with superhuman strength fueled by a wrath so fierce Puma feared for his life.

For a short time the other cowhands enjoyed the fight, shouting and egging on the participants. But as the hard-fought battle continued, they began to fear someone might get badly hurt or even killed. They stepped in and stopped the fight, pulling the bloodied men apart.

"What the hell's got into you, Taylor?" shouted Puma, as two men pinned his arms behind his back.

Lew, struggling to be freed, was being dragged away by a trio of cowboys. His murderous blue eyes never leaving Puma, he said in a low, deadly voice, "I *ever* hear you say anything like that again, I'll kill you."

"Hell, how was I to know you're loco over the girl?"

Lew spit out a mouthful of blood. "The girl has nothing to do with it."

"No? Then what's eating you?" Puma asked.

"John Distant Star is a fine boy. I won't hold still for you or anybody else insulting him!"

Lew told himself it was the truth. That his anger had flared because Puma had spoken disrespectfully about a decent Indian kid who didn't deserve it. John Distant Star reminded him of the young Dan Nighthorse and of all the fights he had gotten into because ignorant, unfeeling people had insulted Dan. This was the same thing. Nothing more.

He sure as hell didn't care what anybody said about Mollie Rogers.

21

By that afternoon the heat had returned.

At three o'clock the mercury hovered near the one hundred degree mark. Not a breeze stirred as the white-hot sun shone down from a cloudless sky.

Cardboard fans stirring the still dry air before their faces, the young ladies of Maya sat on quilts watching the men labor. Wives and sweethearts beamed proudly as their robust husbands and beaus sawed, hammered, and lifted as the raising of Maya's First Methodist Church steadily progressed.

Laughing, singing, and shouting, the men worked tirelessly, very much aware of the ladies' presence. Knowing that admiring eyes were constantly upon them, the men behaved accordingly. Bare-chested under the broiling Arizona sun, their strong backs and muscled arms glistening with perspiration, the laborers felt as though they were on stage. Performers in some grand pageant, admired by their worshiping audience.

And so they were.

Only the hale and heartiest of the men worked on in the intense heat. The older, less stalwart had given out before noon. They now dozed in the shade of porches or played dominoes, resting, waiting for the evening meal and dance.

It was the same with the ladies. Mothers and grand-mothers, herding young children, slipped away to homes for siestas. Others gathered in the cool lobby of the Nueva Sol to relax and gossip.

Mollie was one of a group of young ladies who braved the punishing sun and heat to watch the men work. A silk parasol shading her face, she sat between Patricia and Madeline, chattering, laughing, looking only at Lew. When Patricia commented on Lew's obvi-ous reluctance to remove his soiled shirt, Mollie said sharply, "Perhaps he is too much a gentleman!"

"Pooh," Patricia exclaimed. "That's silly. He's the only one who isn't bare-chested. And look at his shirt; it's drenched with sweat and sticking to his skin."

Mollie made a face. It *was* curious that Lew had not taken off the shirt. Even the shy John Distant Star, working alongside Lew, had discarded his colorful red shirt hours ago. Why hadn't Lew followed suit? Was he ashamed? Were his chest and shoulders and back covered with thick, ugly animal hair like the Texas Kid's?

Mollie shuddered, then quickly scolded herself. Maybe Lew's black eye wasn't his only injury from the fight he refused to talk about. But surely that couldn't be. He had worked all day, moving agilely, in no appar-ent discomfort.

Mollie was not the only one who was curious as to why Lew Taylor didn't remove his shirt.

Mary Beth McCalister, gorgeously gowned in a fash-ionable summer frock, studied the disturbingly hand-some man with barely disguised lust. Gazing at Lew, she wondered how he would look without his shirt. And without his trousers.

She fully intended to find out.

Loud cheers went up from the swelling crowd when the church's frame was raised shortly after five o'clock. By six, the tired workers had put away their tools and were heading for the Nueva Sol. Professor Dixon had announced that any worker wishing to use one of the hotel's many bathtubs was welcome to do so free of charge.

Lew, his swollen black eye throbbing, his bruised ribs aching, was relieved that the day's hard work was behind him. He wanted nothing more than a hot, restorative bath and a change of clothes. Looking forward to a nice, long soak, he walked tiredly over to where Mollie sat on the grass with her girlfriends. Smiling easily, he crouched down on his heels beside her, nodding to Madeline and Patricia.

"No," he cautioned when Mollie lifted a hand toward his blackened eye. "Don't touch me. I'm too dirty to be touched."

"Yes, of course," said Mollie, longing to touch him.

"I'm on my way to the hotel to clean up," he told her, a forearm draped across his thigh. "Meet me in the dining room in an hour and I'll buy you an iced tea."

"Yes, of course," she said again, her heart misbehaving when he smiled disarmingly and affectionately touched the tip of her nose with his forefinger.

"Patricia, Madeline," he said, but looked only at Mollie.

Slowly he rose to his feet and stood for a long

moment looking down at her. Mollie trembled. This tall, looming specimen of virile masculinity was surely the most beautiful man the Almighty had ever created, and he had eyes only for her!

"One hour," Lew said, turned, and walked away.

Mollie watched him cross the churchyard and step into the street. She was still watching when he paused on the busy sidewalk, turned as if called, and spoke to someone. Someone she couldn't see. Someone hidden by the milling crowds. Mollie sprang to her feet, lifted a hand to shade her eyes, and squinted. The crowd suddenly dispersed, and Mollie's heart stopped beating.

Lew was smiling down at Mary Beth McCalister, who was saying something to him. He shook his dark head and started to walk away. Mary Beth reached out, touched his arm, and moved a step closer. Head tilted back, she said something that made Lew's smile broaden. Then she urged him to bend down as she cupped her hand to his ear and whispered something that made Lew laugh out loud.

"Better watch her, Fontaine," Patricia said. "I'm warning you, she's dangerous."

Icy fear gripping her heart, Mollie responded with a nonchalance she didn't feel. "I'm not afraid of Mary Beth. If Lew wanted her kind of woman, he wouldn't spend every evening with me."

"Just the same, I'd watch her closely," Madeline put in. "You saw that exchange. I'll bet she was reminding Lew to dance with her tonight."

Patricia, the experienced widow, shook her head scornfully. "You two are truly green as children." She crossed her arms over her chest. "I've a notion that Mary Beth has more than dancing planned for Lew."

Jealous, Mollie managed, "Lew is a big boy."

Patricia made it worse. "That's the trouble. Lew *is* a big boy and Mary Beth McCalister knows just how to please big boys."

The hot desert sun had finally slipped below the distant mountains. A slight cooling breeze had come up from out of the east. Couples were making their way toward the open-air dance floor of the First Methodist Church's newly built shell. A string orchestra was in place in the loft meant for a choir.

Lew and Mollie lingered alone in the large dining room of the Nueva Sol. At a table near the cold stone fireplace, they sat across from each other, Lew's square hand covering hers on the white tablecloth.

"You're teasing me," he said when Mollie, eyes downcast, confessed she didn't know how to dance.

"I'm not. I don't know how. I never learned." She lifted her eyes, met his gaze squarely.

His thumb rubbed the back of her hand. "A cultured young lady from back East who never learned to dance?" A heavy eyebrow lifted questioningly.

"I've told you, I attended a very strict girl's school. I . . . we . . . were rarely around boys." She knew her feeble explanation sounded far-fetched.

To her shocked delight, Lew squeezed her hand, and said, "I'm glad, sweetheart."

"You are?"

"Yes. I'm flattered that I'll be the one who teaches you to dance. It will be a pleasure."

Mollie stared at him. The professor had been absolutely right. Relieved, she smiled and said, "I learn quickly, Lew."

He laughed softly. "I know you do, Fontaine, I know."

They remained in the deserted dining room for another half hour, talking, laughing, holding hands. Both looked up, startled, when Professor Dixon said from the wide arched doorway, "May I join you?"

Lew pushed back his chair and rose respectfully. "By all means, sir."

A white-jacketed waiter appeared and placed a tall glass of iced tea before the professor. Then the three sat there and talked of the day's work, of the big supper they'd eaten earlier, of the evening's upcoming dance. The conversation turned to travel, and the professor mentioned that he was going to California the first week of August.

As casually as possible, Lew asked, "Will Fontaine be going with you?" He shot her a sideways glance.

"No, she's needed at the Emporium," said the professor. "Aren't you, dear?" Eyes twinkling, he smiled conspiratorially at Mollie.

"Absolutely. Why, Mr. Stanfield couldn't possibly get by without me for two whole weeks. I'd love to go along, but . . ."

Lew's heart thumped against his ribs. His brain raced. Mollie's watchful protector gone for two whole weeks? With the professor out of his way he could get this distasteful chore over with and go home.

". . . and watch after her for me, won't you, Lew?" the professor was saying.

Lew smiled easily, but felt like a first-rate heel when he said, "Be happy to, Professor."

"I knew I could count on you," said the professor. He drew the hunter-case watch from his vest pocket, flipped it open, and said, "It's after nine. Shall we go to the dance?"

They strolled unhurriedly down the sidewalk toward the sound of music. Walking between them, Mollie felt happy and confident. That confidence remained when Lew led her onto the dance floor and said in that low, soft voice that so enchanted her, "Just follow me, sweetheart."

"Always," said Mollie with meaning and stepped into his arms.

She was the tallest woman Lew had ever danced with. Her height made her remarkably easy to lead. Her slender body fit against his so perfectly it was as if they'd been fashioned for each other. Her temple rested against his jaw, her firm, high breasts against his chest. Her long legs moved against his in a graceful, sensuous way that caused his arm to tighten reflexively around her.

Not once did Mollie look down at her feet.

It wasn't necessary. She could sense Lew's movements before they were made, and her body responded naturally.

She loved dancing!

It was even more fun than she had imagined. She had been foolish to dread this night. There was nothing to dancing. Nothing at all. Nothing but the wonder of being in Lew's arms while they swayed and turned and touched each other more intimately than they ever had before.

Through the gathered bodice of her cool summer dress, Mollie could feel her breasts flattening against Lew's hard chest. The heavy cadence of his heartbeat seemed to become her own. And hers his. Two hearts beating as one.

"You were teasing me, weren't you, sweetheart?" Lew's warmth breath ruffled a blond ringlet beside her ear.

Her hand caressing the night black hair curling down over his shirt collar, she asked dreamily, "About what?"

"Not knowing how to dance." His lips brushed her cheek.

She sighed. "Yes. I was teasing you."

The dance continued, and Mollie and Lew never left the floor. Between numbers they clapped enthusiastically, then stood, holding hands, waiting for the music to resume. It was during one such pause that Mollie caught sight of John Distant Star standing alone at the edge of the crowd. His brooding eyes were locked on her.

"Oh, look, Lew," she said, inclining her head, "John's come to the dance. I'm so glad. Will you excuse me for a minute?"

"Sure," Lew said calmly. But Puma's taunting, dirty slurs leapt into his mind. "Go on. Dance with John, but—"

"Don't be silly," she interrupted him. "I don't want to dance with John. I want John to meet and hopefully dance with a pretty young girl who recently moved to Maya with her family."

"You do?"

"Yes." Her eyes met his. "Lew, I'm so afraid that John has grown too attached to me, and . . ." She shook her head worriedly. "I wouldn't hurt John for the world. He's such a sweet, good boy. He badly needs to meet some friends his own age."

"Yes, he does," Lew agreed.

But he felt unreasonably angry with Mollie for being sensitive to John's growing affection and genuinely concerned about hurting the boy. Robbers and murderers were not supposed to feel and behave like kind-hearted human beings. It rankled him. Frowning, he watched her walk away, stubbornly conceding that there was *some* good in her.

But not enough.

A soft hand on his arm and a throaty voice saying, "You look lost, but I've found you, so now you are mine," drew Lew's attention to the small, dark-haired woman smiling seductively at him.

When the music began, Mary Beth McCalister lifted her arms up around his neck, lacing her fingers together behind his head. "Dance with me." It was more command than invitation.

Lew's hands spanned her small waist and he obligingly spun her about the crowded floor. Mary Beth quickly pressed her small, curvaceous body suggestively to his, standing on tiptoe, undulating her generous hips against him. Urging his head down, she spoke softly into his ear of the extreme heat and of what it was doing to her.

"Since the breeze died at dusk," she murmured huskily, "I've hardly been able to get a breath." She inhaled deeply then, causing her large, soft breasts to swell and push against Lew's white shirt front.

"It is warm," Lew agreed.

"Hot," Mary Beth corrected. "It's hot, Lew. May I call you Lew?" Not waiting for an answer, she said, "Know what I like to do when it's this hot, Lew?" She plucked playfully at the open collar of his shirt.

"I've no idea."

Dark, flirtatious eyes holding his gaze, she confided, "I ice down some French champagne and take it up to the privacy of my bedroom." She giggled naughtily. "Then I strip off *all* my hot, confining clothing and stretch out on my luxurious mink comforter. I sip champagne and . . ." she paused for effect, "I rub tiny chunks of ice all over my nude, feverish body."

She leaned back in the circle of Lew's supporting arms, waiting for him to reply.

He smiled and said, "I'm sure that cools you off."

"Sometimes. Sometimes it does the opposite. Have you ever lain naked on soft, ticklish fur while a beautiful woman rubbed ice over your throat and chest and belly?"

Lew shook his head. "I think I'd remember."

"Oh, you would. You'd remember all your life." She wet her lips and whispered, "Come out to my ranch tonight after the dance. Let's cool off, Lew. Together."

"I don't think so, Mary Beth."

"Why not? Fontaine Gayerre won't cool you off, and we both know it. All she does is make you hot."

"Now, Mary Beth—"

"Don't say no now. Think about it. I'll be waiting, naked, with the champagne chilled and the ice chipped. And I'll be hot, Lew. Soooo hot."

Her brazen suggestion was more than a little appealing to the hot-blooded Lew Hatton. She was exactly the kind of bedtime playmate with whom he'd spent many wonderful nights in his wild youth. Turning down what she offered was not easy. He had considered, more than once, visiting the fun-loving grass widow.

But it was too dangerous. Maya was a small town. And he was here for one purpose only. To take in the renegade, Mollie Rogers.

Mollie stood on the fringes of the crowd, talking distractedly with John Distant Star and pretty Margarita

Rios. Margarita was an outgoing, friendly sixteen-year-old whose dark eyes had stayed locked on the tall, slender John from the moment Mollie introduced them.

Margarita had quickly put John at his ease and Mollie could hardly believe her ears when he shyly agreed to Margarita's suggestion that they walk down to the refreshment table. Smiling and waving the couple away, Mollie turned her attention on another couple. A handsome couple swaying sensuously together on the dance floor. Lew and the glamorous Mary Beth McCalister.

Mollie tried very hard not to be jealous. But it didn't work. She was sick with jealousy and sure that the beautiful, experienced Mary Beth was effortlessly succeeding in doing just what Patricia and Madeline had warned her of—stealing Lew.

It took all her firm resolve to stand idly by, smiling, while a woman she thought far more beautiful than she, and who knew far more about pleasing a man, went shamelessly about seducing Lew while the entire population of Maya looked on.

"What did I tell you?" Patricia stepped up beside Mollie.

"Song's almost over." It was Madeline. "Get over there!"

The music finally ended. Lew's hands dropped to his sides. He looked around. He saw Mollie approaching, her expressive eyes flashing purple fire.

Mary Beth McCalister turned to face her. "I was just telling your handsome beau," she said, smiling at Mollie, "that I was glad the dance was ending. It's so warm on the floor. Too warm." She pointedly looked up at Lew, laughed low in her throat, and said, "It's hot."

22

    "It's warm."

"It's hot."

"Yes," Mollie agreed. "It's hot."

Mollie and Lew sat in the professor's parked brougham on a spit of land up in the foothills overlooking the city of Maya. It was past midnight.

They had left the dance as soon as the professor took Lew aside and told him he could drive Mollie home and take the long way. "But not too long," he had added. "I will, of course, be waiting up."

Anxious to get back in Mollie's good graces after his dance with Mary Beth, Lew had promptly taken the professor up on the offer. He had gone directly to Mollie, whispered in her ear that he wanted to take her for a ride in the moonlight and show her that she was his only sweetheart. There was no other.

Mollie had been immediately agreeable. Naive and desperately in love, she had jumped at the chance to be alone with him. She was determined to make him happier than Mary Beth McCalister ever could. She would kiss him and kiss him until he would never want to kiss anyone but her.

Now, as they sat in the parked brougham, Lew leaned back comfortably and laid his arm along the seat behind Mollie. He looked at her and thought that he had never seen her look quite as beautiful. Her eyes flashed arrestingly, and her mouth was incredibly tempting. Her golden hair—silvered by the moonlight—spilled down around her pale bare shoulders. An errant lock had fallen across the swell of her bosom, and its wispy ends had worked their way down inside her low-cut bodice.

A muscle twitching in his jaw, Lew reached out, wrapped his fingers around the shiny lock of hair and slowly, gently tugged it free. His heated gaze on her décolletage, he didn't release the strand of hair. Holding it between thumb and forefinger as if it were some priceless treasure, he gazed at the pale, luminous flesh exposed above her dipping neckline.

Finally his eyes lifted to meet hers and he told her, "Some night, sweetheart, I am going to kiss the spot where this golden curl was lying."

Mollie's heart tried to beat its way out of her chest and she knew that, as a lady, she should protest such a brazen remark. She started to do just that, but thought better of it. Mary Beth McCalister wouldn't object to such talk—nor even the deed itself—and she had to keep Lew from Mary Beth.

So she smiled seductively, put a hand to his handsome face and, letting her fingertips glide over his smooth, dark jawline, said breathlessly, "It all belongs to you, Lew."

The simple statement gave Lew a quick rush of excitement. Then he reminded himself that this was no sweet maiden. If it belonged to him now, it had belonged to the Texas Kid and so many others in the past. Consciously pushing the unpleasant thought to the back of his mind, he slowly bent his head, and said, "And I want it all, sweetheart. Every precious bit of it."

His warm lips brushed Mollie's while his fingers continued to clasp the lock of hair. There was no mistaking her eagerness. She tilted her face up and leaned into him, her eyes closing. With deliberate slowness, Lew kissed her softly, his lips tenderly molding, tasting, playing.

His arm left the seat back and—her hair still entwined in his fingers—he gently cupped her cheeks in his hands. He nibbled teasingly on her full bottom lip and kissed its fleshy inside, slanting his mouth across hers. His hands left her face and slipped down to the sides of her throat. He took plucking, sucking kisses from her soft, moist mouth, and all the while he was whispering that she was his only sweetheart, his only woman. He wanted to kiss her forever. He wanted to kiss her all over. To make her his completely.

His low, soft-spoken words and his exquisite kisses so excited Mollie that she moved her hands from his shirtfront and wrapped her arms tightly around his trim waist. She heard his quick sharp intake of air as he winced.

She pulled back immediately. "Lew, what is it?"

Teeth clenched, he managed, "Nothing. It's nothing."

"That isn't true. You're hurt. I've hurt you."

"No, sweetheart, you didn't hurt me. I bruised my ribs the day that bay stallion threw me."

"You bruised—why didn't you tell me? Oh, Lew, let me see. I never knew . . . and you worked all day." Already her nimble fingers were at his shirt's buttons.

In seconds she pushed the white cotton fabric apart and, seeing the large area of discolored flesh, she gasped. And then she acted instinctively, a woman in love whose man had been hurt. "My darling," she murmured and bent to him.

Tenderly, lovingly, she began kissing his corded ribs while Lew, stunned and speechless, trembled and felt his heart race as he gazed down on the golden head bent to him.

"Lew, my poor Lew," Mollie murmured, her warm, open lips pressing kisses to the bruised flesh.

Short of breath, Lew leaned back and clung to the carriage seat with both hands. He sat there in the summer moonlight, his knees wide apart, his naked chest expanding, while this beautiful golden-haired woman sweetly aroused him with angel kisses to his aching ribs. Her long eyelashes fluttered against his hot skin, and her silky hair fell in a silvery pool over his bared chest and onto his lap, tickling him, exciting him.

Lew groaned aloud when he felt her tongue licking hot, wet fire over his throbbing heart. His muscles tightened instantly, causing the waistband of his trousers to fall away from his belly. Of their own volition, his hands went to Mollie's head to guide her face down to his contracting stomach. His blue eyes closed in ecstasy, then opened in shock when her warm, soft lips began to follow the vertical line of dark hair marching down his taut abdomen. Holding his breath he watched the blond head move lower and lower until her mouth was nearly to his navel. A large section of her hair had fallen between his legs and lay fanned out over his straining, aching groin.

"Oh, God, baby," he moaned, roughly pulled her up,

and kissed her deeply, hotly. When finally he dragged his heated lips from hers, he pressed her face to his bare heaving chest and fought to regain his equilibrium.

Mollie, inhaling deeply of his heated male scent, thought happily that Lew was nothing short of beautiful without his shirt. The crisp black hair on his chest grew in an appealing fanlike pattern that covered only the flat, hard muscles before narrowing into a heavy, distinct line going down his stomach to disappear into his trousers. His sculpted shoulders and long, deeply clefted back were smooth, dark, and devoid of hair. Glad that it was so, she lifted her head and kissed his dark throat, where a pulse was beating heavily.

"It's time I get you in out of this heat," Lew said hoarsely.

Mollie smiled contentedly. "It is rather warm, isn't it?"

Lew tangled his hand in her hair and pulled her head up. He bent and kissed her urgently, a prolonged, open-mouthed, deep, probing kiss of unrestrained passion.

And with his scorching lips still on her, he said into her mouth, "It's hot."

"It's hot."

"I am sorry."

"Damn you, get off me. It's hot."

The Texas Kid roughly shoved the woman out of bed, turning a deaf ear to her startled cry of pain when she hit the floor with a thud. She crouched, naked beside the rumpled bed, biting her lip to keep from weeping.

Slowly the Kid got up, swung his heavily muscled legs over the bed's edge and sat there, scratching his hairy, sweat-drenched chest and itchy crotch.

It was hot in the little two-room shack. Too hot. Nightfall had brought no relief from the blistering heat that had held the dusty town of Magdalena, Mexico, in its punishing grip ever since he had arrived.

Three days ago the Kid and his men—en route to Arizona—had ridden into Magdalena at sundown. At the community well on the outskirts of the sleepy little village, a woman was filling her water bucket. She was a pretty woman, young and full-figured, and her smooth skin was as shiny as brown satin.

The woman, sensing danger, dropped the water bucket, turned and ran. Laughing, the Kid pursued her. She screamed when he caught her and swept her up into the saddle before him.

It would be the first of many such screams for the terrified young wife and mother. While her family—a hardworking husband and three little boys—waited for her return to their modest home a mile from the well, the Texas Kid carried her away.

With his minions following, the Kid laid the spurs to his mount and headed into the forbidding stillness of the Chihuahuan desert. Darkness had enveloped the land when they reached the remote two-room hideout high atop the Presa Plateau. Motioning his men to pull up, the Kid coaxed his surefooted gelding up a narrow, winding trail to the shack.

Up on the plateau there was no sound save the call of the night birds and strangled sobs of the terrified woman. Down below, on the desert floor, the lights of Magdalena twinkled. The Kid dismounted, pulled the crying woman down off the horse, and dragged her over close to the cliff's edge.

He held her in front of him and said, "Tell me, pretty, can you pick out your home from up here?"

The woman, shaking with sobs, sniffed and nodded her head.

"Which one? Show me," ordered the Kid.

"Th-there," the woman said, pointing, directing his attention to a little house set apart east of the village where each day she cooked and cleaned and lived and loved. "*Por favor, señor*, let me go home."

"Sure, I'll let you go home."

"You . . . you will?"

He laughed, tightened his arms around her, and drew her closer against him. "Tomorrow. You can go home tomorrow." With that he picked her up and carried her into the darkened cabin, leaving the door ajar. Unmoved by her screams of fear, he tore her clothes off while she fought him with all her strength.

"You're a regular little Mexican spitfire," he said admiringly, ripping the blouse from her back. "But damned if you don't look more like a squaw." He cupped a coppery breast, rubbed a callused thumb over the nipple.

The woman knocked his hand away, shouting, "I am Apache! My brother is the powerful Chief Red Sunset."

"No kidding? Big brother sell you to the Mexicans?"

Her tear-filled eyes blazed with indignation. "I marry fine brave Spanish man, Gilberto Lopez. My husband and brother will kill you for this!"

The Kid guffawed. "They'll have to catch me first."

Tired of playing, he grabbed her, tore the remaining clothes from her body, threw her on the bed, and brutally took her there in the stifling hot room.

Now, three days later, the beaten, stoic woman sat

naked on the floor by the bed, bearing her pain in silence. Within sight of her own home, she had lived through a nightmare of agony in this nature-concealed hideout. More than once her cruel captor had dragged her to the plateau's rim and taunted her, allowing her to witness the comings and goings of her husband, sons, and worried friends who were all frantically hunting for her.

Late one blistering hot afternoon, he had forced her, naked, out of the cabin, shoved her up against a large leaning rock, and used her sexually while her husband paced their dusty yard far below. After a few minutes of pounding fiercely into her, he pulled out, spun her around, and pressed her face-first up against the rock.

"Look at this, Gilberto," he shouted to the man pacing below who could not hear him. "See what we're doing?" Laughing, he took the woman from behind then. "Bet you didn't know your little wife liked it like this." He grabbed her hips and started pumping madly. "See how she loves it, Gilberto. Tell him, *chica*. Tell him you love it."

Afterward he took her back inside, where he kept her locked up most of the time. There she was forced to do and endure unspeakable things with him. She had learned, only hours into her captivity, that she had to humor the big, bearded man with the missing earlobe or face even worse degradation. She obeyed him. She did as she was told because he threatened that if she did not, he would turn her over to his men. It was up to her. A little fun and frolicking with him, or servitude to five dirty, lusty men.

Cowering silently on the floor beside the bed, Petra Lopez felt a hand on her shoulder. She raised her head.

The Kid smiled at her. Dutifully, she smiled back, though she despised him. She made no effort to stop him when he jerked her to her feet, then pulled her down astride his lap. Gripping her hips, he bounced her up and down on his knees as though she were a child. He grinned as her soft bottom slapped against his hairy, sweat-slick thighs and he watched the seductive dance of her bare, heavy breasts.

Knowing he should release her, clear out himself, and ride on up north to Arizona to search for Mollie and his money, he decided that another week or so wouldn't make that much difference. This woman was so sweet with her wide, soft mouth and her unwashed flesh and her firm brown thighs. And it was so hot. So damned hot.

The Kid looked into the pretty Apache woman's dark eyes as desire rose again. His bearded face descended to her breasts.

"It's hot."

23

*Professor Dixon, a book on his lap, was doz-*ing in his favorite chair when the sound of girlish laughter awakened him. He lifted his head from the chair's tall back and laid the book aside. He took out his hunter-case watch and checked the time as deep male laughter mingled with the girl's.

Lew and Mollie were climbing the porch steps when the professor rose. He had started toward the door, intending to invite them inside, when he heard Mollie say, "No! Lew Taylor, you can't kiss me on the porch."

"I don't want to kiss you on the porch," came Lew's teasing reply. "I want to kiss you on the mouth."

Laughter from Mollie.

Then silence.

Smiling, the professor returned to his chair. More laughter and whispers and finally Lew saying, "Good night, sweetheart. Sleep well and dream of me."

"I will, Lew, I promise."

Silence once more, then Lew crossing the porch. Seconds later, the sound of drumming hoofbeats as he rode off into the night. Mollie stepped inside, humming, so lost in a world of her own she didn't notice the professor until he called out to her.

"Oh, I'm glad you're still up," she said, hurrying into the lamplit drawing room. "I'm not at all sleepy, are you?"

He smiled. "Did you enjoy the dance, dear?"

"Oh, yes!" Mollie exclaimed dramatically, clasped her hands to her breast, whirled dizzily around in a circle, then dropped to her knees beside his chair, and sat down.

He beamed at her, charmed. She was part child, part woman, part Mollie, part Fontaine; all utterly irresistible.

"Professor, I had the most wonderful time of my life," she said, settling herself cross-legged on the floor, smoothing down the billowing folds of her dress.

"I'm glad, child."

Impulsively, she raised her hands and pushed her hot, heavy hair up off her neck. "Shall I tell you something?" she asked. Nodding, he watched while she twisted the lustrous golden hair into a thick silky rope atop her head. "I am in love with Lew Taylor!" She released the rope of hair, put her hands on the floor behind her and threw her head back, allowing the hair to cascade down her back. "Should I tell him that I love him? I started to tonight when he—" She looked at the professor. "He just *has* to love me. I would surely die if he did not."

"Dear," the professor began diplomatically, "I'm sure that Lew is very fond of you. But you might want to delay declaring your love for him. A young lady generally waits until her suitor has professed his love for her before she admits her own."

Mollie made a face. "I don't see why it must be that way. I love him. I want him to know that I love him. Oh, Lord, he just has to love me back."

"Give him time. I'm sure in time he'll come to realize that he loves you."

Mollie brightened. "Yes, of course! He's probably already in love with me and just doesn't know it. Oh, he is so . . ."

Mollie talked and talked, filling the professor in on all that had happened, including the fact that Mary Beth McCalister had danced with Lew and flirted outrageously. The professor didn't tell her that he already knew. As it happened he had been standing below the platform not a stone's throw away when Lew and Mary Beth danced. He had heard snatches of their unorthodox conversation.

". . . and I just wish everyone could be as happy as I am." Mollie paused to catch her breath. Smiling dreamily, she announced, "Love is truly wonderful." She frowned suddenly and asked bluntly, "Why did you never fall in love?"

"I did," he said evenly.

"You did? Tell me about her. Was she pretty?"

The professor exhaled. He closed his eyes, opened them. "Pretty?" he said. "She was breathtaking."

"Really?" Mollie leaned up closer. "Describe her."

"Well, she was a very cultured young lady and highly intelligent. She loved poetry and literature and she was kind, sensitive, and gentle. She was all that is good and pure in this world." Mollie, listening intently, noticed that the professor's pale fingers were gripping the chair arms as he spoke. "She was a small girl with hair of gold and eyes . . . her eyes"—his own eyes lifted and locked with Mollie's—"were a vivid violet hue."

Lips parted, Mollie stared at him. A cloud passed behind her own violet eyes and she said in a voice hardly above a whisper, "Professor, you just described my mother."

Nodding, he confirmed it. "Yes, child, I'm speaking

of the young, beautiful Sarah Hunt. Your dear deceased mother."

"Did . . . did she love you?"

He smiled wistfully. "I thought she did. And perhaps she thought so as well until she met a big, handsome, red-haired army lieutenant at a summertime ball."

"Papa?"

"Yes, your papa." His narrow shoulders lifted in an almost imperceptible shrug. "I introduced them. I met Cord my first year at the university and had tried for years to get him to come to Texas for a visit. I wanted my best friend to meet my sweetheart." He paused, chuckled softly, and shook his head. "He never came; he was always too busy. Your papa was a devil with the ladies. The prettiest always flocked to Cord. He couldn't get away from them.

"But, after he joined the army he was sent to Fort Griffin. One summer weekend he came to Marshall with a detail of soldiers to transport lumber back to the fort. He rode out to the plantation late Saturday evening and learned I had attended a dance. He came looking for me."

Eyes wide, Mollie said softly, "And he found my mother?"

"Yes. I knew the minute their eyes met that I had lost her."

Her heart filled with compassion, Mollie laid a hand atop his, and said, "I'm sure my mother never meant to hurt you."

"Of course she didn't; nor your papa. We are not always responsible for whom we choose to love. They couldn't help falling in love any more than I could help continuing to love Sarah." Pensively, he added, "The poet said, 'I must love her that loves me not.'"

"Is that why you left Texas? Why you never came back?"

"I thought it best for everyone."

"Oh, Professor," Mollie said, tears gathering in her eyes, "I never knew. I'm sorry, so sorry."

His hand turned over and enclosed hers. "Don't be, child. It was a long time ago and long since healed."

"But you must have—"

"It's very late, dear. Time you were in bed. You've had a busy day."

"Yes, I . . . I'll go up." She rose to her feet, her eyes fixed on the kind man who had spent all his life in love with a woman he could never have—her own mother. Impulsively, Mollie leaned down, threw her arms around his neck, and kissed his cheek. "I love you, Professor. I love you almost as much as I loved Papa and Mama."

"And I love you as if you were my own daughter. Good night, child."

Teeth clenched, muttering oaths beneath his breath, Lew rode away from the Manzanita Avenue mansion and Mollie. As he rode he slapped the long reins against his mount's flanks and cursed the blond temptress responsible for his deep frustration.

A man could only stand so much, and he had just about reached his boiling point. His nerves were stretched and frayed. His entire body was tense with unspent sexual energy. He willed himself to relax, commanded his muscles to be still.

But even with desert winds whipping against his face and cooling his burning skin, his blood surged, rushed, and scalded through his veins.

He wanted this woman.

He wanted her with a white-hot desire that had

nothing to do with required seduction. Try as he might to find her repugnant, it was impossible. It did no good to constantly remind himself who she was. Not when her sweet, warm lips were moving beneath his and her soft arms were around his neck.

Lew drew in a long, deep gulp of the clean night air.

No. He didn't really want *her,* for Christ's sake! He wanted a woman. It was as simple as that. He had been spending all his nights holding hands, behaving like a gentleman, keeping his desire in check when what he needed was a few satisfying hours in bed with a beautiful, passionate woman. Any woman.

Lew started grinning.

Out of the blue Mary Beth McCalister's highly appealing invitation came back to him. It had been on the fringes of his mind all evening. The erotic images she had evoked of chilled champagne and fur coverlets and bare bodies had brought on this aching arousal. Not Mollie. Mollie's parted lips on his bare belly had only stirred the passion sparked by the beautiful Mary Beth with her provocative promises of melting ice on heated flesh.

That was it. He wanted the daring divorcée. And he could have her within the hour and the devil take the hindermost! It would be worth the risk. Besides, who'd ever know? It was past two in the morning, and the McCalister mansion was on a secluded spread three miles south of town.

He pulled up, wheeled the stallion around in a tight semicircle, then urged the big steed into a ground-eating gallop. Laughing in the wind, Lew raced straight toward Mary Beth and ecstasy.

The long, hot days of summer continued to slide lazily by as July's end approached. With each passing day, Mollie became more confident of Lew's growing affection for her.

So did the professor.

He had seen Lew put to a test most men would not have passed. The invitation to share Mary Beth McCalister's bed. The professor knew what had happened the night of the dance. He had heard Mary Beth proposition Lew, and he knew, as well, that Lew had almost succumbed to temptation.

The report he had received the next morning had been clear and concise. After bringing Mollie home, Lew had not headed to the Willard ranch, but out to the McCalister mansion.

The journey was never completed.

Lew had ridden to a rise within sight of Mary Beth's home. There he had pulled up, sat in his saddle unmoving for a good fifteen minutes, staring at the well-lighted house. Then he had turned away and ridden home. After hearing the news, the professor was convinced that Lew was either a man who possessed superhuman willpower or else he was in love.

He felt only a little guilty about having Lew followed. Sarah's child was in his care and he meant to protect her. He had to be sure Lew Taylor was trustworthy, sincere in his feelings for Mollie, would not break her trusting heart.

Now, as he sat behind his desk above the bank on this hot July morning, the professor was completely comfortable with the idea of leaving Mollie behind when he went to California.

Lew would take good care of her.

He sighed with satisfaction, rose from his chair, and crossed to a window fronting onto Main Street. He raised the shade, looked down on the street, and began to smile.

A tall, slim boy was leisurely escorting a small, lovely girl toward the plaza. John Distant Star and Margarita Rios were holding hands and laughing, their high spirits unhampered by the wilting July heat.

Mollie's remarks came back to him as he watched the happy youngsters go by. *"Isn't it grand, Professor? Already John and Margarita are inseparable, and John's completely over his schoolboy crush on me. He's so good and sweet; I want him to be as happy as I am."*

The professor was still smiling when he returned to his chair. Shrugging out of his buff-colored suit coat, he untied his brown cravat and loosened his tight shirt collar. He leaned back in his chair and closed his eyes.

All was well with his world.

Lew was in love with Mollie. John Distant Star and Margarita Rios had discovered each other, thanks to Mollie. Next week he could leave for California without worrying about any of them.

All was well.

24

At nine A.M. on Sunday, August fourth, the professor loaded his luggage into the stage boot, shook hands with Lew, then swept Mollie into his arms.

Against her ear, he said, "I'll miss you, child. I hate leaving you alone."

She kissed his cheek and whispered, "I'm not alone. I have Lew."

He nodded as the stage driver called out, "All aboard."

The last one to board, the professor finally swung up into the coach, closed the door, and immediately felt the wheels begin turning beneath him.

Leaning out the window, he waved long and hard, watching as the tall, imposing man and pretty blond girl at his side grew smaller and smaller. In minutes all he could make out was the brilliant rose hue of Mollie's new dress and her gleaming golden hair.

He pulled his head inside, realizing with surprise that a mysterious lump had formed in his throat. He berated himself for his foolish sentimentality. He was behaving like a nervous new parent leaving his baby girl for the first time.

He sighed, smiled, leaned back and laced his fingers together in his lap. There was no cause for worry. Mollie would be fine. Just fine.

Lew would take care of her.

Mollie and Lew went directly from the stage station to the First Methodist Church. Mary Beth McCalister, seated directly across the aisle, kept casting wistful glances at Lew throughout the service. Nodding to Mary Beth, Mollie possessively wrapped her hand around Lew's arm and smiled smugly, thinking that the bold divorcée was a beautiful, flirtatious spider who hadn't managed to draw Lew into her snaring web. Thank heaven.

Mollie glanced up at Lew's handsome face and felt a shiver of exhilaration rush through her. This was going to be such a lovely day. And night. For weeks she and Lew had planned this day—a day that would be theirs and theirs alone.

After church they were to have lunch at the Nueva Sol. Then, in the hottest part of the afternoon, she would rest at the Manzanita Avenue mansion while Lew relaxed out at the Willard ranch. At sundown he would return to town and they would share a romantic candlelight dinner prepared by Louise. After dinner came the best part. A moonlight ride up into Cholla Canyon, a blanket spread on the grass, and . . . and . . .

Mollie felt herself flushing as she realized that she was sitting in church thinking about kissing Lew while from the pulpit the preacher was shouting out his fiery sermon about the wages of sin being everlasting punishment in a lake of fire and brimstone.

Impassioned, the red-faced minister slammed a beefy fist down on the podium and thundered, "Brothers and sisters, yield not to temptation! The lust of the flesh can send your souls to eternal damnation! Don't let that evil old Satan ever get ahold of you!"

Satan won't get ahold of me, Mollie thought irreverently, *unless he happens to have blue eyes and black hair.*

"You're not supposed to smile in church," Lew leaned close and whispered, a teasing gleam in his summer blue eyes.

Mollie's playful response was, "Are you Satan, Lew?"

At six that afternoon Mollie awakened with a start from a deep slumber. She bolted up, trembling. Her silk chemise was drenched with perspiration, and damp hair clung to her face and neck. Lunging anxiously from the bed, she raced across the room to throw open the double doors to the balcony, instantly flooding the room with afternoon sunlight.

She stood there in the doorway, her heart pounding, breath short, fighting the illogical fear that gripped her. Shivering in the fierce August heat, she hugged herself and tried to blot out the too-real nightmare that had awakened her.

The dream had begun beautifully.

It was her wedding day and she was dressed in a shimmering white gown. She was walking down the aisle to Lew. He waited there, tall and handsome, his hand held out to her.

Eager to reach him, she tried to hurry, to rush to his arms. But her feet had grown very heavy. She could hardly lift them. Her billowing wedding gown and long train weighed her down. Her progress was so slow she became frightened that Lew would grow impatient. Terrified that he might leave, she tried harder to reach him.

Finally she did, and he was so glad that she had come to him, he swept her up into his arms, mindless of the preacher and the wedding guests. But as his lips descended to hers, he changed into someone else. Someone bigger and stockier and not handsome at all. He no longer had beautiful blue eyes and midnight black hair. He had eyes of slate gray and dark brown hair.

And a beard. A thick, bushy, ill-kept beard that scratched her face and suffocated her.

The Kid!

Mollie, trembling now in the brilliant sunlight, felt terror rising up to choke her. She hadn't thought of the Kid in months. Why was she dreaming of him now? What did it mean? Had he learned where she was? Was he coming after her?

No. No, she told herself. That was impossible. It had been more than a year since that day down in Mexico when she had stabbed him. In all that time he hadn't come for her; he wasn't coming for her. She had killed him. He was dead.

The Kid was dead.

Commanding her tensed muscles to relax, Mollie walked into her dressing room, stripping off her perspiration-soaked underwear as she went.

It had been a terrible nightmare, nothing more. A bad, bad dream. She was in no danger.

In the deserted bunkhouse at the Willard ranch on that hot Sunday afternoon, Lew lay on his narrow bed, wide awake, staring at the ceiling. A sheen of perspiration covered his bare chest and long arms, but he hardly noticed the heat.

His troubled thoughts in a turmoil, he was strongly considering calling off his plans. It would be the easiest thing to do. He could leave Maya—alone—tonight. Never show up at the Manzanita Avenue mansion. Let Mollie wonder what had happened to him. Ride back to New Mexico and leave her in the professor's care. Just let the whole thing pass. Let it go.

No! Damn it, no!

If not for that fact that he had "let it go" when his father was murdered, Teresa and Dan Nighthorse would be alive today. Lew hardened his heart. He would *not* let it go this time. If this girl was Mollie Rogers—and he was going to find out tonight—then she would damned well pay for her part in the crimes. He would force her to tell him what had happened to her father, and if Rogers *was* still alive, he would pay, too.

Lew's mind was made up. He would proceed with his plans. He'd take Mollie directly to Denver, turn her over to the Pinks, and he didn't care if she rotted in prison for the rest of her life.

Feeling oddly cold despite the rivulets of sweat trickling down his bare belly, Lew rose from the bunk. He went to the piñon chest where he kept his personal possessions. He was alone in the bunkhouse, so he unlocked the chest, pushed aside some shirts and underwear, drew out a half-blackened gold cross, gazed at it fondly, and put it around his neck.

He reached back into the chest and took out a fading yellow wanted poster. He studied—as he had a hundred times—the likeness of a girl with pale, unruly hair sticking up in short spiky locks all over her head.

Lew stared at the poster and told himself that the beautiful young woman he was taking on a moonlight ride to Cholla Canyon couldn't possibly be this girl. He would find no telltale butterfly birthmark on Fontaine Gayerre's creamy flesh. *Please, God, no.*

Lew put the handbill back under the shirts, exhaled heavily, and withdrew another article.

A pair of shiny handcuffs.

"Could a hungry bronc-rider get a bite to eat here, miss?" Lew teased when Mollie opened the front door at twilight.

He could, she thought guiltily, get just about anything he wanted when he stood there smiling at her, all scrubbed and handsome in a starched white shirt and a pair of snug-fitting dark trousers.

"I don't know," she said coyly, tilting her head to one side, "I'll have to think—"

The sentence was never finished. Seeing that they were alone, Lew pulled her to him and kissed her. When their lips separated, he said, "Thanks for wearing the dress, sweetheart."

"You're very welcome," Mollie said, wondering why this particular dress was his favorite. She had many that were prettier. There was nothing special about this yellow-and-white flowered muslin with its low, round, off-the-shoulder bodice. The back *did* dip daringly low into a wide V beneath which four pearl buttons secured the tight bodice. Maybe that's why he liked it. She hated wearing it because it buttoned in back, making it difficult to get dressed alone. But Lew had asked her to wear it, and she wanted to please him.

Mollie led Lew into the high-ceilinged dining room, which was lighted only by white candles in a silver candelabrum. Fine bone china and sterling silver cutlery rested on a tablecloth of pale yellow damask. Mexican poppies mixed with pinkish red blossoms from the beaver tail cactus floated in a huge, water-filled crystal bowl.

It was elegant, it was formal, it was impressive.

But the two place settings had been laid out at opposite ends of the long dining table. Lew pulled out a high-backed chair for Mollie. When she was seated and he had pushed the chair back in place, he cupped her bare shoulders with warm hands, leaned down, and said, "Did you really suppose I'd allow you to sit this far from me?"

Charmed, Mollie pressed her cheek to his hand. "Louise insisted that this was the way a table should be set . . . said it was proper."

"Proper, perhaps, but I prefer intimate."

He walked to the far end of the table, picked up serviette, dinner plate, silverware, and crystal. Balancing it all atop his palm as though he were a waiter, he came back, placed the dishes on the table close to hers, and drew up a chair.

He sat down, took Mollie's hand in his, and said, "Now isn't this better? Intimate as opposed to proper?"

A quick tingle of excitement rushed through her, and she had the distinct impression that he was referring to more than the table arrangements. The aura of power emanating from him was unusually potent on this hot August evening, and Mollie, looking into those fathomless blue eyes gleaming in the candle's glow, felt light-headed and nervous. His warm lips pressed kisses to her fingertips as he waited for an answer.

To break the spell, she pressed her palm down on the serving bell and immediately a young Mexican servant entered, carrying bowls of consommé.

From the clear steaming soup to the rich coconut pie, the meal was superb. But Lew had to force himself to eat. His mouth was dry and his stomach was queasy. As he sat there in the candlelit dining room of the Manzanita Avenue mansion, he felt like Judas Iscariot sharing with this beautiful, unsuspecting woman her last supper.

Mollie was not hungry either, but for a different reason. She was too excited to eat. All her senses told her that this was to be an unforgettable night. She was uncertain about exactly what was going to happen. But she knew—beyond a doubt—that she loved this man so completely that if he wanted her to be "intimate as opposed to proper," she could no more say no than she could keep the sun from rising in the morning.

Mollie watched Lew lounging easily back in his chair, enjoying a second cup of coffee. So compelling, so masterful, so much the center of her world. It was hard to believe what had happened to her since meeting him. All her life she had been so headstrong, in command at all times, never knuckling under to anyone or anything. She had never let anybody get one up on her or tell her what to do. She'd done no one's bidding. Had brashly called the shots, thought for herself, and feared nor favored no man.

Now she was a stranger to herself. She had only to gaze into Lew's beautiful blue eyes and she was ready to surrender her will to his. Mollie Rogers no longer existed. In her place was a woman so in love with a man that she would, this very night, become his in every way if he wanted her.

Intimate, as opposed to proper.

The prospect caused the blood to race through her veins and her face to heat and flood with color.

As though he had read her thoughts, Lew took the napkin from his knees, folded it, laid it alongside his plate, and said, "It's awfully warm inside tonight." Mollie nodded anxiously. "Let's go for that moonlight ride." He rose and drew her to her feet.

They said their good-nights to Louise Emerson. Lew complimented Louise on the outstanding meal, and Louise warned him to have Fontaine back at a decent hour. Then they were alone in the front foyer and Mollie said, "I'll run upstairs and grab a shawl while you harness the team to the brougham."

"I've a better idea," he said, tracing her collarbone with his little finger. "Let's leave the carriage here and ride tandem on my stallion."

Whispering, she said, "But I thought we were going to take a blanket and—"

"We are. It's tied behind the cantle and there's wine in my saddlebags." He flashed her a devastating smile and said, "Come with me, sweetheart?"

"As far as you want to take me."

25

The ride across the moonlit Sonoran Desert was exhilarating, exciting, wonderful. Lew held Mollie across the saddle in front of him, his arm wrapped securely around her. They were atop the powerful bay stallion that had once thrown Lew. The big steed raced across the forbidding land, whipping around giant saguaro cactus rising thirty to forty feet above the desert floor, dwarfing the prickly pear and organ-pipe cactus at their base.

In minutes the fleet-footed stallion, snorting and blowing with exertion, had reached the eroded buttes and volcanic rock near Cholla Canyon. Mollie, flushed with anticipation and happiness, lay back in the strong arm supporting her, trusting this magnificent man and this magnificent horse to transport her safely into the longed-for seclusion of the steep-sided canyon.

Lew was silent. His intense gaze was on the tricky terrain before them. Her head resting over his heart, Mollie could feel its heavy beating beneath her cheek. She studied his handsome face, the moonlight causing some features to stand out in high relief, leaving the rest in shadow.

There was about him, more than ever on this hot

summer night, a potent magnetism, an aura of impervious determination that intoxicated her. Lying in his arms, she felt at once safe and in peril. Despite the heat and hardness of his lean body pressed so close to hers, she was strangely chilled. Her eyes never leaving his hard-planed face, she recognized her emotions for what they were.

She was half-afraid of this dark, godlike creature. The power he held over her was absolute. She knew that now—knew as he masterfully reined the big mount toward the concealed mouth of Cholla Canyon, his beautiful eyes flashing in the moonlight, that she was his to do with as he pleased.

Traces of the indomitable will that had been so much a part of her rose to refute such an appalling admission. She had never been afraid of anyone. She was *not* afraid of Lew.

Her silent denials vanished as quickly as they had come. She sighed and snuggled closer to Lew's broad chest. She had no desire to fight the dominance of this rugged, virile male. She understood, finally, how it was between a man and a woman. Knew now why her gentle mother had always yielded so willingly to the authority of her father. Mollie realized, with absolutely no regret, that she longed to surrender her will, her body, her very soul to this dark, silent man whose strong arms enclosed her.

Mollie closed her eyes, inhaled deeply, and smiled.

Lew, teeth clenched, nerves raw, neck-reined the big bay through the undergrowth into the canyon's narrow mouth. He stole occasional glances at the beautiful woman snuggling trustingly in his arms and felt a painful squeezing of his heart.

He had told himself that this night's work would be a snap. A moonlight ride, a few swallows of wine, a few heated kisses, an easy seduction, and . . . the truth. He would finally know her true identity. This woman was either Fontaine Gayerre, in which case he would make patient, gentle love to her, or she was Mollie Rogers. As the moment of truth drew nearer, it no longer seemed quite so simple and easy.

Lew gloomily turned the stallion into the darkened canyon, feeling as if he were riding to his doom. But he never considered turning the big horse around. On he rode, not pulling up until they were a mile inside the canyon. There he drew rein beside a gurgling stream that flowed through a grassy meadow.

Lew swung down off the horse and reached for Mollie. He lifted her from the saddle, lowered her to the ground. Then stood, unmoving, his hands on her waist, the moon at his back. For what seemed to Mollie like an eternity, he stared fixedly at her. She felt that same tantalizing mixture of fear and excitement that had come and gone all evening. She couldn't see Lew's face, but she could make out a tenseness in his shadowed features that was puzzling.

"Lew?" she said softly, lifting a hand to his cheek.

He said nothing, just pulled her to him and kissed her with an urgency that took her breath away. He held her so tightly, so forcefully, forgetting his superior strength, that she felt as if he would surely squeeze the life from her. Abruptly the fierce embrace ended and he almost flung her from him.

"I'm sorry," he said coldly and Mollie, bewildered, stood speechless watching him unstrap the blanket and toss the saddlebags over his shoulder.

She laid a hand on his back and said, "Is something wrong, Lew?"

He turned, and his face was struck fully by the moonlight. Any hint of strangeness was gone, and he was smiling that devilish smile she found so appealing.

"No, sweetheart, nothing's wrong." He reached out, took her hand. "I just couldn't wait one more minute to kiss you."

Flattered, she smiled and said, "Follow me. Cholla is my special canyon. I know just the right place to spread the blanket."

The spot she chose was on the smooth gassy bank a few short feet from the rushing stream. A full, white moon bathed the meadow with a silvery light and a gentle night breeze cooled and sweetened the air. A few short minutes in the cold canyon stream and the wine was cooled and ready for sipping.

Seated on the spread blanket, Mollie laughed with delight when Lew withdrew from his saddlebags two long-stemmed crystal glasses. She smiled approvingly as he splashed the chilled wine into the glasses and handed one to her.

She touched her glass to his and said shyly, "To the happiest night of our lives."

Lew said nothing, only nodded, and she caught a flicker of unease pass over his face before he drank thirstily. She sipped her own chilled wine and was relieved when—setting his glass aside—he turned about and sank gracefully down onto his back, placing his head in her lap.

Her fingers toying with the raven black curls that fell onto his high forehead, Mollie heard him say, "The first time I saw you was in this canyon."

"You saw me here? I don't remember that."

"You didn't know. You were wading, and I watched from up on the cliff. You never knew I was there, and I never knew it was you until now. It was you, wasn't it?"

"Yes, yes it was," she said. "Why didn't you make your presence known?"

"Afraid I would frighten you. I was trail-dirty and had a bushy beard that—"

"I hate beards," she passionately interrupted, caught herself, and amended, "Well, not all beards. My papa's beard was . . . I don't much like beards."

Lew hooked an arm around her back and turned his face in. "You looked so cute that morning with your boots and stockings off. I wanted to ride down and play, wade with you." He pressed his lips to her trim midriff and Mollie felt the heat through the delicate fabric of her dress.

For a time he was silent and so was Mollie. Content, immensely enjoying the night, the privacy, and him, she continued to sip her wine. Eager to share, she tipped the glass up over his mouth and laughed when a few drops of the wine dribbled down his chin. When her glass was empty, Lew poured her another.

Mollie felt herself becoming slightly light-headed. But she didn't mind. It was a warm, fuzzy, pleasant feeling. She took another long, cool drink and then set the glass aside, sighing contentedly. She couldn't remember ever being quite so happy as she was at this minute.

"Kiss me, Fontaine," Lew said, looking up at her, his muscular arm tightening around her waist. She leaned down as he lifted his head. Their lips met and blended in a warm, sweet kiss that left her cheeks flushed. Lew lay back down and his hand began to move caressingly over her back. "God, you're beautiful," he said. "Don't you have any flaws, sweetheart?"

"What do you mean?" She drew a shallow breath when the lean fingers that were roaming so enticingly over her back snagged a puffed sleeve and tugged until it slipped down her arm, leaving her shoulder bare.

"I mean you're exquisite, perfect. Are you perfect all over?"

Mollie blushed in the moonlight. "I . . . I don't know."

Lew slowly eased himself up until he was seated facing her, his arm braced across her, palm spread on the ground. His unblinking gaze on the pale swell of her breasts, he languidly pushed down the other puffed sleeve. His voice low, soft, he said, "I'll bet your body is sheer unadulterated splendor. No imperfections of any kind."

Mollie's heart stood still for a minute when he slowly bent his dark head and kissed her in the warm, shadowy spot between her breasts. And as he kissed her, he urged the slipping bodice of her yellow-and-white dress even lower, exposing her throat, her pale shoulders, and the swelling tops of her breasts. Only the shy pink nipples that were rapidly growing taut remained concealed.

"I told you once that I would kiss you right here," he said, his lips moving stirringly against her tingling flesh, his face pressed into the valley between her perfumed breasts. One of his hands cupped a bare shoulder, the other settled on her waist.

"You . . . must . . . stop . . . , Lew." Mollie murmured, but she didn't sound convincing, even to herself.

She didn't really want him to stop. She wanted him to keep on kissing her just the way he was kissing her. It felt wonderful and she loved it and she hoped he would never, ever stop. She sat there in the moonlight leaning back on stiffened arms, enjoying to the fullest Lew's heated lips moving so seductively on flesh no other had ever seen or touched.

When at last he raised his dark head and their eyes met, Mollie drew a shallow breath and trembled. But she sighed when he pulled her into his embrace, urging her head back against his supporting arm and bending to her.

His lips lowering to hers, he said, "Baby, you're so sweet, so perfect."

His kisses were tender, gentle, devastatingly persuasive. Enthralled, Mollie leaned back in his arms and shivered from the exquisite pleasure he seemed so intent on giving to her. She knew that she had aroused a fierce passion in him, and having all that leashed power beneath her hands sent shock waves of delight through her.

It was absolutely glorious to have his blazing hot lips tasting hers sweetly, patiently. Tonight they had all the time in the world, and she could lie here in his arms savoring his kisses for as long as she pleased.

Sensitive to her wish that he take it slow and easy, Lew continued to kiss her lightly, warmly, his mouth paying sweet homage to hers. His lips teased, tasted, adored until he heard her sighs grow louder and she began to press her slender body closer to his. At once he could feel her diamond-hard nipples through the fabric of his shirt.

He groaned and deepened the kiss, his tongue sliding into her mouth to mate with hers. Instinctively, Mollie sucked at his tongue, and their caresses changed swiftly into deep, probing kisses of such force and urgency that they shifted frantically, trying to get closer together, their pressing bodies as hungry as their burning lips.

Lew's hand impatiently moved to the swell of Mollie's breasts, and his callused thumb went to a hardened nipple to circle it through the covering fabric of her dress. An involuntary tremor swept through Mollie, and Lew immediately lifted his head to look at her. Her face was tilted up to his and the moonlight was kissing her just as he'd been kissing her.

She was beauty unblemished.

All that a man ever dreamed of in a woman was here in the moonlight before him. Trembling, he eased her up with him until they were kneeling facing each other. He kissed her open lips again, then, looking directly into her flashing violet eyes, he caught the frilly edge of her plunging bodice between two fingers and slowly lowered it until her bare left breast spilled out, pale and luminous in the moonlight.

Her eyes never wavering from his, Mollie helplessly emitted a little gasp of wonder when his warm hand closed gently over the naked breast and he again bent and kissed her, drinking from her open lips as though his thirst for her would never be quenched. When his mouth finally left hers and his lips slipped down over her chin to her throat, Mollie threw her head back. She stared straight up at the moon and exhaled deeply as his masterful, marvelous mouth moved unerringly down her throat and over the swell of her breast to the aching nipple he'd uncovered.

But her head bowed to gaze down at him when his hot, plucking lips enclosed that pulsing point of sensation and tugged provocatively, drawing on her eagerly, sending messages throughout her tingling body the kind of which it had never before received.

"Lew," she whispered breathlessly, "oh, Lew."

"Mmm," he murmured, his lips never fully releasing her throbbing nipple.

His mouth hotly enclosing her breast, he sucked vigorously on the erect nipple until Mollie's slender back was arched stiffly and her hands were anxiously gripping his dark moving head. Weak with desire, she eagerly pressed herself to his dazzling mouth and wondered why—when it was her nipple he kissed—there was a deep throbbing in her lower belly that was part pain, part pleasure. It was if she could feel the incredible heat of his lips and mouth between her legs.

Lew gave her nipple one final sucking kiss and, with an economy of motion, gently took her arm and turned her about so that he was kneeling behind her. Mollie, knowing his intent, sagged willingly back against him, a foolish smile on her face. Her dress opened down the back; he was going to take it off. And she was going to let him.

Lew's arms went around Mollie. His hand warmly cupped her bared breast. His gentle fingers caressed the wet nipple while he pressed kisses to the side of her neck and murmured the foolish, forbidden words of passion no woman can resist.

"You're mine, sweetheart, all mine. I want you, baby. I want you so badly I can't stand it any longer. I've never wanted a woman as much as I want you. You're so sweet, so incredibly beautiful, I want to kiss you all over. Let me, baby. Let me undress you and hold you naked in my arms." His fiery lips nibbled at the curve of her neck and shoulder, thrilling her, igniting her. "We have all night, sweetheart. Let me make love to you." His lips slid up, his tongue touched the pulse beneath her ear. "I want to kiss your toes and the dimples behind your knees." Mollie shuddered against him. "I do, baby. I want to kiss you until there's no spot left on your beautiful body unkissed."

On fire, swept away on a rising tide of passion, Mollie longed to have him kiss all the places he promised. She could only whisper his name and hope he knew she meant yes. Yes, yes, yes.

Lew's hands went to the buttons at the back of her dress. His heart pounding, fingers shaking, he released the first of the four buttons from its tiny buttonhole. Wildly aroused by this highly desirable woman, Lew prayed silently that the beautiful blond temptress kneeling before him, allowing him to undress her, was really Fontaine Gayerre. Nothing would make him happier. The fragrance of her hair, the soft skin beneath his trembling hands, the sweet, sweet kisses—all combined to make the blood beat and rush through his body. The words he'd whispered were true. He desired her as he had never desired another woman. He yearned to do just as he promised—to undress her totally and then kiss her warm bare body until she was begging him to take her.

The second button came undone.

Lew was now so hot for her he only hoped he could be gentle. He wasn't sure he could. He didn't want to frighten her. If she really was Fontaine Gayerre, then he felt sure she was a virgin. If that were the case, he would have to go slowly and keep his raging passion in check.

The third button was released.

Lew was breathing through his mouth now as his heart thumped so violently against his chest it was painful. But not as painful as the throbbing tumescence straining the fabric of his tight trousers. His swollen groin ached with his urgent need, and he knew that in this willing girl lay sweet release.

Button number four slipped through its buttonhole.

Every nerve and muscle in his body tensed, Lew slowly pushed the opened dress apart. His stiffened fingers curling down inside the elastic waistband of her silky underwear, he dragged the lace-trimmed pantalets down below her waist.

A soft groan of despair broke from his tight lips.

There at the top of one creamy buttock—a perfectly shaped butterfly. His throat closed. He felt sick. His vision blurred.

Foolishly, he said, "What is this, sweetheart? Did you hurt yourself?"

Mollie's soft laughter told him of his folly. "No, silly. That's my birthmark. A butterfly. No one's ever seen it but you. Well, my mama and papa."

Lew stared at the damning birthmark. Disbelief gave way to bitter disappointment, then to anger, and finally to cold wrath. He touched the wine-colored imperfection and felt his fury mount with the realization that he still wanted her. At least his body wanted hers, needed hers, craved what she could give him. Teeth clamped down tight, a muscle spasming in his jaw, Lew Hatton knelt there in the moonlight behind the half-dressed Mollie battling with himself.

He was tempted to go ahead and strip her clothes away. To push her over onto the blanket and quickly take her for his own base pleasure. What difference would it make? Why not wait until after he'd spent himself in her to tell her he knew who she was?

Lew shook his head, disgusted with himself. He couldn't do it. Even he wasn't that big of a bastard.

"Lew," Mollie said nervously over her shoulder, "you're not . . . repulsed by my birthmark, are you? You still think I'm pretty, don't you?"

"Yes," he said, his voice oddly distant, "I still think you're pretty."

"I want to be pretty for you, Lew."

He made no reply. His hands moved up to cup her shoulders, then slipped down her arms. He covered her hands with his own. Trusting him completely, Mollie simply sighed when he drew her arms behind her and held both her hands in one of his.

Lew reached into his saddlebags.

The steel handcuffs gleamed in the moonlight. Lew bit his bottom lip until it bled.

The sound reverberated throughout the steep-sided canyon when he swiftly snapped the handcuffs around her fragile wrists, saying, "Sorry, Mollie."

26

His bloodshot blue eyes were half-shut with fatigue. He pulled his stiff-brimmed Stetson lower against the sun's punishing glare. His head ached dully, and the center of his back—between his shoulder blades—felt as though a sharp knife were sticking out of it. His chambray shirt was soaked with sweat and covered with grime and the potent scent of his own unwashed body was strong in his nostrils.

He rubbed gingerly at the beard-stubbled jaw that was still uncomfortably sore after three days. Then he looked back over his shoulder at the fiercely belligerent woman responsible for the pain. She was mounted on a dun stallion, her cuffed hands resting on the saddle horn. She was far too stubborn to wear a hat, so her fair face was badly sunburned and her lips were chapped and cracked. Her unkempt blond hair lay in perspiration-dampened tangles around her neck and shoulders. She was half-asleep in the saddle, her head bowed with weariness.

But it slowly raised as she sensed him looking back at her. Her chin jutted pugnaciously when their gazes clashed and in her violet eyes hatred blazed.

A chill of uneasiness shot up Lew's spine as he turned back around. His own eyes shuttering with hostility, he resisted the impulse to grind his teeth. He had unthinkingly done so a time or two in the past three days and he'd paid dearly. It had caused his sore jaw to throb violently, had sent waves of pain up through his cheekbone to his ear.

Lew shook his head tiredly.

He had to hand it to the woman; she was just as wild and mean and hard to handle as had been reported. A good thing he'd had the cuffs that night, he reflected dryly, recalling the bitter struggle that had ensued when he had clasped the steel bracelets on her wrists in Cholla Canyon.

It had taken her a moment to realize what had happened. That moment had seemed a lifetime to Lew. When the handcuffs had snapped into place, he had held his breath and waited, while Mollie, not fully aware of what was happening, slowly turned to look over her shoulder at him, an expression of bewilderment on her face.

"You!" she said finally and before he could respond, she shot to her feet and whirled around, understanding and anger flashing in her eyes. "It's you!" she shrieked. "The bounty hunter!"

Still on his knees, Lew nodded resolutely. "I'm taking you to Denver, Miss Rogers." He started to rise.

That's when she got him. "You're taking me nowhere, you bastard!" she shouted and kicked him full in the face.

The toe of her dainty kid slipper, with the full weight of her body behind it, caught him on the left cheek, just above the jawbone. The blow stunned him and knocked him over backward.

Mollie wasted no time. She ran, heading straight for

the tethered stallion, cursing the handcuffs and the long, cumbersome skirts threatening to trip her.

The grazing horse lifted his head and shook it up and down when she came crashing through the undergrowth. Desperate to be up on his back and gone, Mollie rushed toward the stallion. She was less than six feet away—ready to lunge up into the saddle—when Lew caught up with her.

She screamed her outrage and fought him when his arms came around her from behind.

"No!" she hissed, furious, "Let me go! Damn you, let me go!" She kicked at him and tossed her head from side to side, wincing in pain when he jerked her back against him, catching her cuffed hands between their pressing bodies.

"You're only making it hard on yourself, Mollie," Lew said flatly. "You know I won't let go, so you may as well stop fighting me."

"You unscrupulous bastard!" she shrieked, chafing against the strong arms that encircled her, helpless as she'd never been in her life. "You despicable, deceitful charlatan!"

She managed to jab a sharp elbow into his ribs. Lew winced and loosened his grip slightly. Mollie immediately twisted around and managed to sink her teeth into his left shoulder. He yelped in pain and automatically released her. She spun the rest of the way around until she was facing him. Then she swiftly brought her knee up, slamming it forcefully into his groin. He groaned and paled, but managed to grab her skirts as she wheeled away. It threw her off balance and she crashed to the ground at his feet. Bent over with agony, muttering oaths, Lew clung tenaciously to the billowing skirts and sank to his knees beside her.

Mollie struggled and fought him for what seemed an eternity. They were both breathing hard from exertion, each determined to subdue and conquer the other. At a definite disadvantage, Mollie, with so much more to lose than Lew, fought wildly, kicking and biting and wrestling as though her life depended on it.

Lew, his jaw and ribs and groin hurting badly, stayed with her, letting her beat herself. Hardened outlaw though she was, he couldn't bring himself to rough her up. Cuffing a female had been distasteful enough. Striking her was out of the question, as foreign to his nature as surrendering was to hers.

So he allowed her to pummel him as best she could. He ducked the most vicious blows from her flailing feet and carefully avoided her sharp teeth.

He knew that she was tiring when, tears of frustration slipping down her hot cheeks, she threatened hollowly, "You'll never reach Denver and the authorities! You hear me? Never!" Her breasts were rising and falling from the strenuous exercise and from the sobs she could no longer hold back. "I'll escape if it's the last thing I do, bounty chaser! You're right, I am the last of the Rogers Renegades, and nobody will ever take me in. Not marshal or deputy or sheriff." She spat contemptuously on the ground. "And certainly not some mercenary bounty hunter who pretended to be . . . who cruelly led me to believe . . . who . . . who . . ." Out of breath, out of hope, she struggled back up onto her knees. Then sank back onto her heels, blinking back her tears, her slender body jerking and trembling.

Lew, crouching close, watched her warily, expecting the unexpected. Naked to the waist, she looked haughty and proud kneeling there with her head held high, her blond tangled hair falling into her face. One yellow Mexican poppy remained pinned above her right ear. Another blossom, slightly crushed, clung to her left breast. Shiny with perspiration, the bare breast quivered involuntarily when she felt his eyes touch her.

"I'll help you get dressed," he said, and gently pushed the fallen bodice up to cover her nakedness.

Her eyes closed, and she refused to speak or to look at him. Ever watchful, he maneuvered himself around behind her and began pulling the dress together in back. His jaw hardened when his eyes again fell on the damning butterfly birthmark.

"I've money," he heard her say finally in a tired voice. "You can have it all. The price on my head can't be nearly as much as I have. Take me back to Maya and I'll give you the gold. Lots of gold."

Lew finished buttoning her dress. He pulled the puffed sleeves up over her shoulders, then dropped his hands away. Coldly, he said, "There's not enough gold in this world."

Baffled, Mollie's anger rose anew and she hissed, "Then what the devil is this all about if not for money? Why the hell have you—"

"Let's go," he cut her off, reached out, took her arm, and drew her to her feet.

He shoved her toward the stallion, his face as hard as stone. Mollie could tell by the rigid set of his jaw and the punishing fingers gripping her arm that it was futile to argue or question him. She stared at him, angry and mystified. This couldn't be happening. It just couldn't. The kind, handsome man she thought she was in love with, a cold-blooded bounty hunter? And why wouldn't he listen when she offered him the gold?

Confused and heartsick, Mollie turned her thoughts to the professor. What would he do when he learned that Lew had taken her? If no one else in the whole wide world cared about her, the professor did. This would never have happened if he had been in Maya. The professor would never have allowed some revenge-seeking bounty hunter to get his hands on her.

Poor, dear Professor Dixon. Lew had fooled him too. She knew what the professor would do as soon as he learned she was missing. He would come after her! That thought gave her comfort for only a minute before she considered what might happen if the professor found them. He would try to kill Lew, she knew he would, but the professor was no gunfighter. He was a gentle, refined man more at home with a book in his hand than a gun.

Mollie shuddered.

Lew could easily kill the professor if they went up against each other. She couldn't let that happen. She wouldn't. But there was only one way she could keep the professor from following them.

"I'll come with you willingly," she said, half startling Lew. "But please, can't we go by the mansion so that I can get a few of my things?"

Lew lifted her atop the bay stallion, then swung up behind her. "I'll take you there, but I'll be watching you every minute. If you have any notions of slipping away from me, forget them."

At the Manzanita Avenue mansion the pair tiptoed quietly up the stairs. Louise Emerson, sound asleep in a room at the back of the house, never knew they were on the premises.

Inside Mollie's room Lew unlocked the handcuffs with the whispered warning, "Don't try anything foolish."

Mollie shot him a scathing look which he ignored. He leaned against the door frame while she changed her clothes behind a dressing screen. His eyes never left her. When she stepped out from behind the screen, Fontaine Gayerre was gone forever.

A defiant Mollie Rogers stood before him in a pair of tight buckskin trousers, loose-fitting shirt, and tall boots. The transformation was remarkable. Not just the change in costume, but the tilt of her determined chin, the unfamiliar stance, the murderous look in her eyes.

Staring at her, Lew felt the hair on the back of his neck rise. Her appearance and manner were so unlike the beautiful young woman he had courted all summer. It was easy to picture this insolent, trousered woman with a gun on her hip and larceny in her heart.

"I'll just throw a few things in my saddlebags," she coolly informed him and headed for her dressing room.

Pushing away from the door, he said, "I'll come with you."

"I'm hiding no firearms, bounty hunter," she said icily.

He didn't reply, but followed her into the dressing room where row upon row of colorful feminine frocks hung above dozens of pairs of shoes. Already she looked out of place here. Yet Mollie, changed irrevocably by the happy time she had spent in the professor's home, automatically snatched up silky underwear, lavender-scented soap, and a silver hairbrush. She crammed the articles into her red leather saddlebags.

She hurried back into the bedroom. Lew was right behind her. From her vanity she picked up an ivory-handled mirror, a bottle of French perfume, and some expensive skin cream. Then she grabbed a couple of her favorite books and some lilac-hued notepaper and pencils from her writing desk.

"That's it, outlaw," said Lew.

Mollie nodded, but reached for the fancy velvet sewing box—a gift from the professor—with its colored thread and needles and pin cushion and silver thimble and sharp embroidery scissors.

"Now!" Lew ordered, taking her arm.

Mollie thrust the bulging saddlebags at him and returned to the desk. Taking a feathered quill from its inkwell, she hurriedly wrote notes to both the professor and Louise Emerson. She sealed the professor's message. Louise's she merely folded and laid atop her big four-poster—the first place Louise would look in the morning.

Mollie hated the lies she told them in the notes, but she had no choice. She was far too fond of the professor to risk his being shot. This way was best. The note would keep the professor from coming after her.

Mollie crossed to where Lew waited impatiently. She paused there, turned, and looked back on the decidedly feminine room where Fontaine Gayerre had been so happy—where she had spent so many pleasant hours daydreaming about a tall, handsome, black-haired broncbuster.

Mollie felt the abominable lump rise to her throat, but refused to give in to self-pity or fear or to any more foolish tears. Fontaine might have done so. Mollie Rogers would not.

"It's a long way to Denver, outlaw." Lew's hand was cupping the back of her neck.

Swallowing with difficulty, she looked up at him, and said, "You'll never get me there, bounty chaser." She jerked free of his hold and told him, "You've known only Fontaine Gayerre. Meet Mollie Rogers!"

Now, three days later, Lew knew what she had meant. The sullen, sunburned woman riding behind him was nothing at all like the sweet-tempered, lovely Fontaine Gayerre. Every hour, every mile had been pure torture. Mollie had already tried a half dozen times to escape. Each time he had caught her it had taken a little more out of him. She could fight like a wildcat and cuss like a trail boss and he found himself having to constantly curb the strong impulse to slug her, which was what she deserved. She couldn't be trusted for a minute, and he was bone-tired from watching her every move and sleeping with one eye open.

Lew rubbed his burning eyes and looked at the salmon-colored cliffs looming in the near distance ahead. They were starting to climb out of the valley. Tonight they could camp on the banks of the Santa Maria and head on up into the Weaver Mountains come morning. In three or four days they would reach Prescott.

Lew smiled at the prospect.

Cherry Sellers was in Prescott. Big, warmhearted Cherry. He could stop in and stay with Cherry for a night. Have a home cooked meal. Take a bath in a real bathtub. And get a good night's sleep while Cherry, ever a nocturnal creature from all the years she had spent at the Red Slipper, kept an eye on Mollie.

In silence they rode on, each lost in his own thoughts while the sun westered to their left.

Mollie, watching the dark, broad-shouldered rider through half-closed eyes, silently conceded that he was harder to handle than any man she had ever known. He didn't let down his guard for a minute. In the three days they had been riding north, she had failed to escape him, despite several serious attempts.

The maddening man seemed to be constantly poised and alert for trouble, his lean, lithe body ready to spring into action in a heartbeat, like a deadly predator. It was as if he was able to sense when she was thinking about trying something. And when she had made those failed attempts to escape, he had pursued her like a demon out of hell.

Mollie cringed recalling the mad gallop across the hot desert sands that first afternoon when she had thought Lew was dozing in the saddle. Seizing the opportunity, she had wheeled her mount about and dug her heels into his belly, spurring him on. But in a matter of seconds Lew had caught up with her, reached out, grabbed the bridle and brought her horse to a plunging halt.

Angry, she had struck out at him, lost her balance, and fallen to the ground. Before she could scramble to her feet, he was off his horse and to her. She hit at him frantically, screaming at him and doing her best to hurt him. Remaining irritatingly composed, he had calmly climbed atop her, deaf to her sputters of outrage. He had pinned her to the ground with the weight of his body, catching her wrists and easily forcing them up over her head. And then he simply looked down at her from icy blue eyes while she struggled futilely and cursed him hotly, detesting the forced intimacy of his hard, heavy body pressing down on hers. When finally she could no longer move a muscle and went limp beneath him, she felt his lean body relax. He moved off her, stood up, reached down, hauled her to her feet, and snapped the handcuffs back on her.

Trapped and furious, she had said, "Why don't you save us both a lot of trouble, bounty hunter? Why don't you cut my head off and take it back to Denver in a sack? That's how it's done, isn't it? You turn in my head and collect the reward."

Holding her by her shirt collar, Lew looked down at her and whistled through his teeth. "You sure have a vivid imagination, outlaw."

"Do I?" She tried to shrug free of his grasp. Failed. "Isn't that how it's done? The sneaky bounty hunter takes in the head of the captured outlaw, dumps it out on the table, and collects his blood money."

"You've a pretty head, outlaw. I'll let you keep it."

"No!" she shouted at him. "Don't you call me pretty. Never again, you hear me, you repulsive, unprincipled impostor."

A dark eyebrow lifted. "I an impostor? And what are you, outlaw? You unstrapped your gun belt, put on a petticoat, and pretended to be a prim young lady."

"You go to hell!"

"Baby, we're on the way."

That had been but one of several similar incidents, and Mollie had to admit that it was not going to be as easy to elude this cold, heartless man as she had first supposed. He was as hard and ungiving as she. And he was every bit as determined, as crafty, as smart.

Or was he? An idea occurred and began to take hold. What if she played her hand differently? What if she stopped being so cross and peevish and behaved more like Fontaine Gayerre? What if she pretended that she was ready for a truce? Convinced him that she would cause him no more trouble? Hope renewed, Mollie could barely suppress a wicked grin.

By sunset they had climbed out of the wide valley. When the shimmering river came into view, Lew pulled up on his mount.

"We'll camp here, outlaw." He turned in the saddle, waiting calmly to hear the snarled protests of his unfailingly disagreeable companion.

Mollie smiled at him and said sweetly, "Looks like a fine place to me, Lew."

27

Lew threw a long leg over his horse and dropped to the ground. He walked directly to Mollie and plucked her out of the saddle. Setting her on her feet, he said skeptically, "I'll bet Eve smiled like that at poor old Adam when she handed him the apple."

Mollie, resolved to win his confidence, bit back a hateful retort, and said, "You've every reason to distrust me, but—"

"You can say that again."

Fighting to keep her composure, she continued as if he hadn't spoken. "You've every reason to distrust me, Lew, but the truth is I am really quite weary and I know that you are too. I'll give you no more trouble. Honest."

"Honest?" he repeated cynically. "Outlaws don't know the meaning of the word."

Mollie lost her temper. "And you do? Hah! You, Taylor, are without a doubt the most dishonest person I have ever known. You came to Maya pretending to be a hardworking cowboy when all the time you were . . . you were . . . Every man who ever rode with the Rogers Renegades had more scruples than you!"

"Really?" he said coolly. "Even your outlaw lover?"

"My lover?" Mollie frowned.

"Too general? Let me correct myself. I meant your favorite lover, the Texas Kid. I realize the Kid was not your only one." His expressive blue eyes clouded with disgust.

Mollie's first impulse was to defend herself, but she didn't. All at once she had a great compulsion to shock the presumptuous bounty hunter who had callously pretended to care for her. With a naughty smile, she said, "Granted, the Kid was one of many, but he was by far the best. As a lover he has no equal, and I still shiver when—"

"Shut up!" Lew grabbed her by her leather belt and jerked her roughly to him. "Damn you, shut your mouth! I don't want to hear it." He instinctively ground his teeth and immediately winced with pain.

Mollie laughed in his angry face. "Why, I do believe that I've upset you, Taylor. Your face is beet red. Perhaps you'd better go down to the river and cool off."

Abruptly Lew released her and stepped back. His self-possession rapidly returning, he began to leisurely unbutton his shirt. "A splendid idea, outlaw," he said, took off the soiled shirt, wadded it, and blotted the perspiration from his naked torso. "You coming?"

"With you?" She was horrified.

"Don't you need a bath?"

Mollie could think of nothing she needed—or wanted—more. They'd not had a bath in three long days. She was miserably hot and dirty and the clear, cool river looked so inviting.

"I have no intention of bathing with you!" she snapped.

Lew lifted bare shoulders in a shrug. "Then you won't mind waiting on the bank for me."

Mollie felt her heartbeat accelerate. With Taylor

naked in the water, it would be child's play to steal his clothes and the horses. She would ride away and leave him stranded.

Purposely making her face and her tone expressionless, she said, "I'll wait."

"Good." He smiled easily and reached into his pants pocket for the handcuffs key. It was all Mollie could do to keep from laughing out loud. He was going to take off her handcuffs, the fool! When the steel bracelets came open, she felt almost dizzy with delight. Lew nodded to a tall cottonwood at water's edge. "Sit there, please."

Congenial, Mollie quickly complied, taking a seat beside the tree. But she hissed like a cat when Lew crouched down beside her and drew her slender arms around the cottonwood's narrow trunk.

"You are not going to . . . you wouldn't!" She was incredulous.

But he would. And he did. He cuffed her to the tree while she kicked and cursed him.

Rising, Lew smiled down at her. "As soon as I've had my bath, you can take one, outlaw."

"You big, bullying son of a bitch! You'll pay for this! Better watch your back, bounty hunter. Better stay awake every minute day and night because I . . ."

Mollie raved on, threatening him, livid that once again he had raised her hopes, then dashed them. Lew paid her no attention. Unruffled, he stood with his back to her, calmly undressing in the gathering twilight. When he stepped out of his trousers, Mollie blinked and faltered in her heated diatribe. Surely he did not intend to . . .

She gasped when Lew casually pulled off his cotton underwear and stood there in the dying sunlight as naked as the day he was born. Mollie squeezed her eyes shut, but then couldn't resist peeking. He continued to stand there unmoving as though he had forgotten her presence.

Incensed, but fascinated, Mollie opened her eyes fully and stared. She had never before seen a naked man, and she was naturally curious. So she took a good look. His tall, powerful male form, unadorned, was quite magnificent, she grudgingly conceded. His skin was very dark, a deep golden bronze. All over. Including those parts of his body that were usually covered with clothing.

His broad, gleaming shoulders had the appearance of having been chiseled from stone. His back was long, smooth, and deeply clefted. His hips were slim, his tight buttocks lean and hard. His legs were long and well-muscled. He was, whatever else he might be, a splendid specimen of manhood, so incredibly beautiful that the mere sight of him made her forget for a moment just how much she hated him. Awestruck, she gazed at him, wondering how it would feel to let her hands travel the full length of this superbly built male animal.

Her starving lungs filled with air and she exhaled with relief when finally he dove gracefully into the water. With the unsettling sight of him no longer clouding her judgment, her animosity returned. Her jaw hardening, she wondered why he had undressed in front of her. And why had he left his clothes almost within her reach. He had done it purposely to annoy her. To mock her. To tempt her.

The key to the handcuffs was in his pants pocket. He meant for her to futilely try to reach for the trousers. The cruel bastard! It amused him to toy with her. Well, she'd be damned if she'd give him the satisfaction.

Eyes narrowed, she looked and saw his dark head far

out in the river. She looked back at the trousers. They were no more than four feet from her. She looked again at Lew.

If she could just slide her arms down the tree trunk a bit, she could stretch her long legs out and catch the pants on her boot toe. Mollie immediately began scooting down, dropping her arms along the tree's trunk, maneuvering herself into a reclining position. The tip of her tongue caught between her teeth in concentration, she worked furiously as the sun disappeared completely.

She labored with single-minded determination, contorting her body, ignoring the pain of the cuffs cutting into her wrists and the tree's bark scratching her arms. She made several unsuccessful passes at the trousers with her right foot. Patiently, she continued while crickets croaked and other night creatures took up the chorus.

She almost sobbed with joy when she managed to snag the elusive breeches with her boot's toe. Trembling with excitement, she very slowly, very carefully flexed her toes back and forth until the pants were securely snared. Stifling a shout of victory, she gingerly lifted her foot, bending her knee ever so slowly and drawing the trousers toward her. Her heart pounded. She felt giddy. Escape was within reach.

Mollie screamed when the pants were yanked from her foot and Lew, standing directly above, dripping water, said in a low, slow voice, "Thanks, outlaw. You shouldn't have. I could have stooped and picked up my pants."

She continued to scream at the top of her lungs while Lew unhurriedly pulled the trousers on and buttoned them. He ambled away then and when he returned, he was smoking a cigar. Ignoring her curses and threats, he sat down on an overturned log close to Mollie and calmly smoked, his low-lidded eyes on the placid river.

When finally she quieted, he turned to look at her. "Would you like a bath now?" Mollie glared at him. "You're dirty, outlaw. Either take a bath or I give you one."

Mollie knew he meant it. "I'll take a bath," she said softly, "but only if you turn your back and promise not to look."

Lew flicked his cigar away, rose, reached down into his pants pocket and produced the key she had tried so hard to get. He sank to his heels before her, unlocked her handcuffs, took them off, and shoved them into his back pocket.

"I'll promise nothing, outlaw," he said, "but let me assure you that I've no great interest in seeing you unclothed. So strip and get into the water." He sat down beside her, leaned back against the tree.

Mollie shot to her feet, thinking that he had to be the most contemptible man it had ever been her misfortune to meet. He was cold-hearted, mean, and downright insulting. While she would most certainly never dream of allowing him to see her undressed, she couldn't help but be offended that he would have no desire to see her naked. She had sure been curious about him.

His indifference was an unspoken challenge. Her back to Lew, Mollie began to smile She unbuttoned her white shirt and let it slide slowly down her slender arms and fall to the ground at her feet. Bending from the waist, she took off her left boot and dropped it. Then the right. She drew in a deep breath and unbuttoned her buckskin pants.

While the last faint tinges of pink and purple lingered in the west, she slithered out of the trousers, taking her good sweet time, making a provocative ritual of it. And all the while she was wondering if the silent man behind her even bothered to watch.

His blue eyes narrowed with anger *and* interest, Lew didn't miss a single seductive movement. His heart thudding in his chest, he watched helplessly, wishing it were not too late to get up and walk away.

But it was. If he fled, she'd know she had affected him. Besides, he couldn't have left if he tried. Mesmerized, he stared unblinkingly as she stood there in her shiny satin chemise and nothing else. And he hoped she would immediately dash into the water so he could get his breath.

She did not. Instead she lifted a hand and languidly peeled a narrow satin strap down over her shoulder. Now Lew prayed that either she would stop or he would be struck blind. But she didn't stop and he didn't go blind. She undressed right down to her silky skin and he never took his eyes off her.

Naked she stood in the lingering light, tall and slim and delicate, the sun's afterglow bathing her bare beautiful body a pinkish gold. Lew ground his teeth but never felt the pain in his injured jaw.

Her exquisite back tapered symmetrically to a very narrow waist, which in turn gave way to flaring hips and an appealingly firm, rounded bottom and gorgeous legs, long, slender, and shapely.

Mollie stood there for what seemed forever. Finally giving up, conceding that the sight of her unclothed disturbed him not at all, she walked down to the water and jumped in. Feeling oddly disappointed and hurt, she moved swiftly out into the cool, deep river, swimming with sure, long strokes. It was not until she had been in the water for several minutes that it occurred to her that she'd left her clothes at Lew's feet. The realization filled her with dread. It was one thing to stand with her bare backside to him, quite another to face him naked. Even if he wasn't interested.

Mollie waited for Lew to get up and move away. But he didn't. He remained where he was, back against the tree, knees bent and wide apart, arms resting atop them. She was growing chilled and tired. She longed to get out, dress, and eat supper. She swam toward the bank, stopping to tread water when she was close.

"Taylor, I'm ready to get out," she called to him.

"Good. I'm getting hungry." He didn't move a muscle.

"My clothes?"

"Right where you stepped out of them."

"I know very well where they are," she snapped, her irritation mounting. "Will you kindly bring them to me."

Lew crossed his arms over his chest. "Come and get them."

"Oh! I should have expected as much from you! I'll stay in the damned river all night before I come out with you sitting there!"

"Suit yourself, outlaw."

Long minutes passed. Mollie grew angrier and angrier. Cold, exhausted, she was trapped. He'd stay there forever just to spite her. Well, what difference did it make? She had aroused absolutely no interest when she undressed before him. To hell with him!

Mollie swam to shore, climbed out and headed toward Lew, her bravado slipping as she neared him. Teeth chattering, she used her hands to try and cover herself. Her face turning crimson, she felt as if she might die of embarrassment. But he never so much as lifted a dark eyebrow. He lazily lit a fresh cigar, the brief flame of the sulfur match illuminating his indifferent face. Languidly he smoked, the cheroot's tip glowing hot as he drew deeply on it.

Well, if he didn't care, neither did she! Mollie dropped her hands to her sides, threw back her shoulders, and walked directly toward him.

Squinting in the half light, Lew watched her, but it was too dark for her to see the tortured expression that came into his eyes. Everything about him suggested complete repose, a negligent attitude, totally uncaring and uninterested.

That's the message Mollie received, and it hurt. It also made her angry. So when she reached her clothes, she didn't pick them up. She stepped right over them and stopped directly in front of him.

She stood so close he could have easily reached out and touched her. So close that her firm, high breasts—their rosy crests puckered from the cold—jutted provocatively above him. She was so close the golden triangle of curls between her pale thighs, beaded with water and dripping tiny rivulets down her long legs, was exactly at his eye level. So close, he could see a tiny mole on the inside of her right thigh.

It was a Mexican standoff.

Mollie was determined to get a rise out of this unfeeling, bloodless man. Lew was just as determined that this ruthless renegade woman would not get under his skin. The clash of wills was almost tangible in the still night air.

Lew was only human and standing before him, seeming somehow nakeder than naked, was a shameless bitch who was so breathtakingly beautiful he itched to yank her to him and bury his face in her bare, flat belly.

But he'd die a celibate monk before he'd let her know it.

Mollie, feeling Lew's eyes glide hotly over her body was touched by their heat and seized with the insane desire to feel the heartless bastard's warm lips touch her as well.

But she would have cut out her tongue before she would have admitted it.

Finally Mollie knew that she was the undisputed victor when Lew's eyes closed and ordered irritably, "Put on your goddamned clothes, outlaw."

28

The thrill of triumph was fleeting.

Before Mollie could pick up her clothes, Lew had risen to stand uncomfortably close. His eyes met hers squarely, but she couldn't read the expression in them any more than she could read the set of his mouth. He loomed tall and menacing before her. The threat he exuded and the black stubble of beard covering his lower face was reminiscent of another time, another man.

Wishing she hadn't behaved so foolishly, Mollie trembled. Here she stood, naked and vulnerable, before a vengeful bounty hunter who had no more regard for her than the Texas Kid. And the Kid had tried to rape her.

Lew shifted and Mollie winced.

Bending from the waist, Lew picked up her clothes and handed them to her. "I'll lay out our meal in the main dining hall while my lady attends to her toilette," he said, smiling easily again, his teeth flashing starkly white against the black beard.

Mollie's unease quickly changed to irritation. She snatched her clothes from him and held them before her. Looking pointedly at his unshaven face, she said acidly, "Indeed? Why not eat your meal on all fours like the other animals?" She turned and walked away.

Moments later, dressed and hungry, Mollie sat down before the small campfire Lew had built. Inhaling deeply of the sweet-scented smoke from the ocotillo wood, she waited eagerly for supper, foolishly hoping that the evening's menu might be different from the past three days.

It wasn't.

"Dinner is served," said Lew and held out a tin plate with the usual jerked beef, stale bread, and cold beans.

Sighing, Mollie dispiritedly took the plate. She looked at the unappetizing fare, made a face, and felt her empty stomach rebel. She impulsively flung the plate away. It sailed through the air, losing its contents in flight.

"Ah, too bad," said Lew. "You were expecting quail in aspic with champagne?"

Then he grinned, took up his own plate and began to eat heartily, sighing and rolling his eyes as though he had never tasted anything quite so tempting.

Mollie wanted to strangle him.

The next day she again wanted to strangle him as they rode across parched arroyos and long-dry washes under a broiling afternoon sun. The blazing heat of the lowland summer had spread to encompass the high desert. She was miserable and thirsty and her face was painfully burned. Hot gusts of wind stung her eyes and chapped her lips. Squinting, she looked at the dark man riding alongside her.

His face, throat, and forearms gleamed with perspiration, yet he didn't appear to be the least bit hot. He rode slouched in the saddle, relaxed and comfortable. Apparently Lew Taylor was like the resilient saguaro cactus—impervious to wind and sun alike. Damn him for not suffering!

Abruptly Lew's squint-eyed gaze swung around to her. "Want to stop and make camp, outlaw?"

"What would make you think that?"

A sardonic gleam came into his blue eyes and he grinned. "You look like you can hardly stay in the saddle."

"I can outride you any day, bounty hunter," she said, squaring her tired shoulders. "Don't forget who I am."

His smiled vanished. "There's no danger of my ever forgetting who you are, outlaw," he said, and Mollie saw the ridging of his jaw as he turned his attention back on the trail ahead. He took off his hat, wiped his forehead on his shirtsleeve, and replaced the Stetson, pulling the brim low over his eyes. "If you're not tired we'll push on until sundown. I'd like to make Prescott in a couple of days."

It was the first mention he had made of Prescott. Mollie immediately felt her pulse quicken. In busy Prescott she might get the chance to escape. People in the West hated bounty hunters more than they hated outlaws. Maybe she could persuade someone to help her elude her cruel captor.

Keeping her voice well modulated, she said, "Are you planning to stop off in Prescott?"

He nodded almost imperceptibly. "A good friend of mine lives in Prescott. I thought we might take a couple of days to rest and replenish our supplies before heading up into the rough country."

Mollie could hardly conceal her excitement. A couple of days! Anything could happen in a couple of days. Her thoughts racing ahead, she tried to imagine what Lew Taylor's friend would be like. Cold and heartless like him? Or a kinder, more understanding man who—appalled by Lew's plans for her—might become her ally?

Mollie no longer felt tired. She could ride until sundown. She could ride forever now that Prescott was her goal.

Forty-eight hours later Mollie and Lew topped a gentle rise and saw, spread out below, the community of Prescott. The bustling little town, resting in a vast bowl of gray volcanic rock and surrounded by tall green pines, looked good to them both. They rode forward, skirted the large army settlement of Whipple Barracks, and headed for town.

The square was surrounded by false-fronted buildings. They rode past Bates's Dry Goods store, Clem's Barbershop, an assay office, and a couple of hotels. And down past the stage office, a string of rowdy saloons stretched down Gurley Street.

Following Lew's lead, Mollie turned her mount after passing the governor's log mansion. They rode in silence up dusty Walpi Street. Six blocks from the square, nestled among huge gray boulders at the town's edge, a freshly painted white frame house with bright red shutters was set apart from its neighbors.

"This is it," said Lew, pulling up.

The first thing Mollie noticed was that all the window shades were drawn although it was not yet five in the afternoon. How odd. While Lew tethered the horses to the hitching rail at the edge of a small, well-tended yard, Mollie stared at the house, wondering at the eccentricity of the man who lived there. Then she told herself she was being foolish. The drawn shades obviously meant that the gentleman was not at home. She was sure she had guessed correctly when Lew, not bothering to knock, led her inside.

Blinking, Mollie looked curiously around. Her eyes grew wide and her mouth rounded into an O. Everything was red. Everything. Wine red rugs on the floor. Rose red wallpaper. Blood red velvet settee and wing chairs. Dark red damask window curtains. Even the miniature Italian-style fireplace was of pinkish red marble.

The reds blurred as Lew took her arm and guided her through the sitting room, down a darkened hallway, and to a spacious bedroom. A red bedroom. In the open doorway he released her.

Speechless, her eyes adjusting to the shadowy light, Mollie stared, thunderstruck, as Lew crossed the room to a huge four-poster bed hung with red silk. On that canopied bed, a female lay sleeping on sheets of shimmering red satin. The slumbering woman wore a revealing scarlet lace nightgown that barely concealed a voluptuous body. Riotous locks of flaming red hair spilled across the red pillows and around milky white shoulders. A sleeping mask of red velvet covered the woman's eyes.

Mollie blinked in shock when Lew unceremoniously took a seat on the bed, leaned down and kissed the sleeping woman squarely on the mouth. Mollie's hand lifted to her own mouth as confusion, anger, and jealousy overwhelmed her.

She fully expected the sleeping woman to scream and lash out in fear at the impertinent intruder. The woman in red did nothing of the kind. Instead she smiled dreamily and said in a sleep-heavy voice, "One more, darling. I'm not quite certain."

Lew kissed her again.

Bare fleshy arms then went around his neck and hands with long red painted nails twined in his dark hair. Mollie watched, appalled, as they kissed.

Finally Lew lifted his head and the woman licked her wet, red lips, laughed huskily, and said, "Lew!" She snatched off the red sleeping mask, flung it to the floor and sat up, eagerly wrapping her arms around his neck. "You irresistible devil, I'd know that sulky, sexy mouth anywhere!" She embraced him warmly, then pulled back a little, saying, "Let me look at you, darlin'." She smiled into his eyes, then shook her head, and sighed. "My God, you're so damn handsome it's sinful. Ain't no man alive supposed to be so downright pretty. What do you say? Let's turn old Clint's picture to the wall and you climb in bed with me." She hugged him again.

Mollie didn't realize that she was frowning so fiercely until the red-haired woman, catching sight of her over Lew's shoulder, abruptly pushed him away, and said, "Damn, Lew, I didn't realize you had your little sweetheart with you." Beckoning to Mollie, she said, "Stop your frowning and come on over here, honey. There's no call for the jealousy I see in your pretty eyes. Why, Lew and me, we're just old friends. I was teasing about that bed stuff. Come on over here."

Mollie didn't budge. Unreasonably angry, she said, "I am *not* his little sweetheart and never was!" She turned to storm out.

"Hold on, outlaw!" Lew was off the bed and across the room with the swiftness of a cat. He caught her and, holding her by the belt, said over his shoulder, "Cherry, we'll be in the kitchen. Come on out and I'll introduce you two."

Three hours later Mollie, fresh from a bath in Cherry's big zinc tub, sat at the table in the red-walled dining room. Despite the abundance of good food spread out before her, she sullenly picked at her plate, her appetite missing. Twenty-four hours earlier she would have walked over broken glass for this meal of thick, juicy steak, pan-fried potatoes, string beans, buttered carrots, fresh baked bread and creamy butter, tea with ice chunks, and hot peach cobbler.

But now she was tempted by none of it. She had not recovered from the shock and disappointment of learning that Lew's friend was not some kind, understanding man who might help her escape. The friend was a painted woman who lived in an all-red house and was obviously so crazy about Lew she would do anything for him.

Mollie could tell by the way that Cherry looked at her that Lew had told the redhead everything. Not that Cherry's glances held any censure. What they held was pity, and that burned Mollie up. The idea of a woman who made no bones about the fact that she had once been an Albuquerque prostitute feeling sorry for her, Mollie Louise Rogers, was highly insulting.

Mollie pushed her plate away and folded her hands in her lap. Lew and Cherry, seated across from each other, ate and drank and laughed with great zest. They had been laughing all evening, and it was getting on Mollie's nerves.

She pushed back her chair and rose. "May the prisoner please retire to her cell?" she asked hatefully, looking at Lew.

Lew slowly chewed a mouthful of food, swallowed,

wiped his lips with a brilliant red napkin, and said, "What do you think, Cherry? Mollie in the guest room, me in your bed?" As he spoke, he looked only at Mollie.

"Why, sure," Cherry said, rising. She seductively smoothed the tight-fitting scarlet dress over her generous hips, picked up a coal-oil lamp, and motioned for Mollie to follow her. "You look mighty tired, honey," she said as she ushered Mollie into a small, neat bedroom. She placed the lamp on a bedside table. "And your face, it's all sunburned. Why don't I get you some nice cream for—"

"I have my own," Mollie said sharply.

Cherry shrugged and turned back the bed covers. "Honey, all you need is sleep to put you right as rain. You'll feel better tomorrow. Good night." She smiled, turned, and left the room.

Mollie was angry and frustrated, but she also was so weary she could hardly hold her eyes open. She undressed quickly, blew out the lamp, and got into the soft, clean bed that, mercifully, was not red but snowy white. Too exhausted to even think about escape, Mollie was asleep the minute her head hit the pillow.

Much later she awoke with a start. Unsure where she was, she sat up and looked anxiously around. Somewhere in the house a clock struck three. It all came back. Prescott. Cherry. The red rooms. She heard faint laughter and turned her head to listen.

It was Lew. He was laughing again. Or still. She wasn't sure which. Since his reunion with Cherry he had laughed more than in all the time she had known him. She wondered just what Cherry was saying—or doing—that so amused him at three in the morning. Mollie got out of bed, tiptoed across the darkened room, and eased the door open.

". . . and remember when Clint came in and found us?" It was Cherry's husky voice.

"Jesus, do I!" came Lew's laughing reply.

Mollie stepped out into the hall and inched her way toward Cherry's bedroom. The bedroom door stood open wide. Guiltily, Mollie peeked inside. The room was empty. Relieved, Mollie exhaled. She moved on to the sitting room and found it equally empty. But a rectangle of light shone from the open dining room door and through it came loud feminine laughter and the sound of water splashing.

Unable to stop herself, Mollie inched her way closer. She stopped a few feet shy of the open door. Concealed in darkness, she cautiously peered inside. And almost choked. Biting back a gasp of horror, she took in the whole shocking scene in an instant.

The supper dishes were still on the red-clothed dining table. And there was something else on the sturdy table as well. The long zinc tub she had bathed in earlier was, of all places, on top of the table. And in the tub was Lew Taylor, his broad bare shoulders and brown knees sticking up out of rich white suds. In his mouth was a lighted cigar and in his soapy right hand a bottle of whiskey.

That wasn't the worst of it.

On her knees atop the table and directly beside the tub, a laughing Cherry, garbed in a feather-trimmed crimson dressing gown open to her waist, was merrily scrubbing Lew's back with a long-handled red brush.

It was sickening to watch.

But Mollie couldn't turn away. It was just too ludicrous to be believed. A grown man was sitting in a tub that had been lifted up atop the dining table while a scantily clad woman laughingly bathed him. Was this the way lovers behaved? Would it be enjoyable to do what they were doing?

Disgusted with them and with herself, Mollie felt her face flush. She turned to leave just as Cherry, moving the brush to Lew's soapy chest, said, "Lew, honey, that sunburned bandit's a real beauty. You been sleeping with her on the trail?"

He was quick to answer. "Hell, Cherry, I'm not that hard up."

Cherry giggled. "Lew, don't say that around me unless you mean it."

"Say what?"

"Hard and up in the same sentence, honey."

They both howled with laughter and Mollie clenched her fists, wishing to high heaven she could drown them both in the bath water. When they'd quieted, Lew took another long pull on the whiskey bottle and started reminiscing again. "Remember the night Clint and I rode our horses into the Shy Violet Saloon?"

Throaty laughter from Cherry, then: "And you ordered buckets of beer for the beasts and Clint shot down the chandelier when the barkeep refused to serve 'em!"

Shaking her head in disgust, Mollie slipped silently away. Back in bed she lay awake thinking about what she had heard and seen. There was no doubt in her mind that the playful pair would soon stumble into Cherry's red bedroom and make love. She told herself she didn't care that Lew Taylor would hold and kiss and do all the things to Cherry that he had done to her. And more. It didn't matter. Not at all. They deserved each other. They were two of a kind.

She only wished that she were not too bone-tired to slip away while the amorous, asinine pair were caught up in their indecent fun. She promised herself she would escape before leaving Prescott. It was going to be easier than she had thought. Much easier. If the foolish couple had that much fun in the dining room she could well imagine how lost in each other they'd be once they retired to Cherry's red bedroom.

The thought made Mollie see red.

29

The next time Mollie awakened, bright sunlight streamed in the small bedroom's east windows. She got out of bed and looked for her discarded pants and shirt. They were nowhere to be found.

Making a face, she picked up the robe that had been tossed across the foot of the bed. Bright red. Rolling her eyes heavenward, Mollie slipped her arms into the sleeves of the gaudy red wrapper and tied the sash tightly.

She pushed sleep-tousled hair from her eyes. Her hair was badly tangled and needed brushing, but she had learned that it irritated Lew when she refused to brush her hair, so she didn't touch it. She had even considered, on a couple of occasions, cutting it short the way she'd worn it in her renegade days. But she couldn't quite bring herself to do something that drastic.

Holding the red robe's lapels together, Mollie quietly tiptoed by Cherry's big red bedroom. The door was open a crack. She glanced inside. It was very dim in the large red room; the heavy red curtains were closed. Mollie squinted toward the scarlet-hung four-poster. She saw a dark head on the red satin pillow before she turned away, not wanting to see more. If she continued to look, she was certain she'd see a flaming red head beside the dark one. And she would know that beneath the rumpled scarlet sheets bare brown muscular limbs were entwined with soft white ones.

Mollie fought the distaste threatening to choke her. She reminded herself that this was exactly what she wanted. It was her chance. With the shameless pair hung over and exhausted from lovemaking, they would sleep the sleep of the dead. And while they were passed out in their drunken stupor, she could—as soon as she could find her damned pants—flee.

Mollie returned to the guest room and again searched frantically for clothes. Any clothes. There were none. She shook her head in frustration. She didn't dare risk going into Cherry's room to take something of hers.

Mollie hurried into the red sitting room and looked around. A red fringed scarf draped over the grand piano was a possibility. She remembered the red tablecloth and sailed into the dining room. She skidded to a stop in the doorway. The red damask tablecloth was gone, and so was the zinc tub. The long mahogany table was polished to a high gleam and smelled faintly of lemon seed oil.

But in her mind's eye Mollie could still clearly see the tub atop the table with a naked Lew in it, laughing and frolicking with the red-robed Cherry.

"Animals," she muttered under her breath, then turned her head quickly as she caught the scent of freshly brewed coffee.

Following the aroma, she pushed open the swinging door between the dining room and kitchen.

"Well, good morning," said a smiling, cheerful Cherry. "What can I fix you for breakfast?"

Mollie stared at the beaming, full-figured woman who wore a fresh, cool summer dress of red-and-white striped cotton.

"I'm not hungry. If I could just have my clothes—"

"Sure you're hungry. Why, you hardly touched your supper last night." Cherry wiped her hands on her red organdy apron and poured Mollie a cup of hot coffee. "I washed your clothes and hung them out. In this heat, they'll be dry in an hour."

Bested, Mollie nodded and dropped down onto a straight-backed chair. Cherry turned back to the cook stove, saying, "I'll whip you up some of my special scrambled eggs. My Clint always said there were two things I was the best in the world at and one of them was scrambling eggs." She laughed merrily at her own joke, then began talking fondly of her late husband who had, one long-ago night, come with his best friends, Lew and Dan Nighthorse, to the Albuquerque bordello where she entertained gentlemen callers.

"All of 'em were young and lusty and lookin' for a good time," she said, reminiscing.

"And you gave them *all* a good time?" Mollie felt sick.

Cracking eggs into a pottery bowl, Cherry laughed. "I didn't want to play favorites, but Lew being the handsomest of the three, I naturally—"

"Took him first," Mollie cut in.

"No, let me finish." Cherry brought the bowl of eggs to the table and sat down. Beating briskly, she said, "They flipped a twenty-dollar gold piece, and Clint Sellers won." She burst out laughing and added, "He won a lot more. He won my heart. And he fell for me too. Denounced his family, gave up a big inheritance for me."

Not knowing what to say, Mollie said, "He must have loved you very much."

"Almost as much as I loved him," Cherry said, then sighed. "Five years ago my Clint was shot dead by a man who showed up in Prescott, a customer from the old days. Clint never was one to let anybody insult his wife." She rose, went back to the stove.

"Wasn't Clint jealous of Lew?" Mollie asked.

"There was not a jealous bone in Clint's body," came a low, deep voice from the doorway.

Both women looked around. Lew stood there leaning a muscular shoulder against the door frame. He was shirtless and shoeless and his dark hair was disheveled, his heavy-lidded eyes bloodshot. But the beard was gone—shaved off sometime during the night, Mollie assumed. His handsome face, all shadowed hollows and sculpted planes, wore a distinct look of displeasure.

"No, there really wasn't," Cherry agreed with him. Then she walked straight to Lew, spread her hands on his bare chest, and said, "But he sure as hell should have been jealous." Over her shoulder to Mollie, "I've always been crazy about this good-looking scamp."

Lew gently pushed Cherry away and came to the table. His cold blue eyes slid over Mollie as he sat down.

Cherry hurried to pour his coffee. "Mollie, why don't you slice some fresh honeydew while I cook the eggs."

"All right," Mollie said, eager to put some distance between herself and the scowling, bare-chested man at the table.

His head aching from too much whiskey, Lew silently drank his coffee and tried to keep his eyes off Mollie. Without success. His narrowed gaze followed her as she moved about the kitchen, seemingly oblivious to his presence.

"Set this in the window, Mollie," Cherry said.

Lew's half-shut eyes were riveted to Mollie as she crossed the room, stopped, leaned over and set the freshly baked cherry pie on the sill. She then turned around, yawned and stretched.

Lew stared.

She looked exceptionally cute standing there, backlit by the morning sun, her golden hair igniting in the light. The ridiculous red robe she wore was too large. It drooped off her slender shoulders and hid her bare feet. She looked like a child. Young and sweet. Warm and sleepy. And innocent.

And that irritated the hell out of Lew. Where were her pants and boots? He wanted them back on her so she'd look like what she was—a lawless bandit. A hard woman who had held up stages and trains and banks and then celebrated the heists by sharing the Texas Kid's bed.

Mollie became aware of Lew's disapproving looks. Feeling suddenly self-conscious, she tugged her robe's sash tighter and pulled the lapels together. Then she quickly reminded herself that he was the one who had been drunk and naked and behaving disgracefully. So she dropped her hands away, lifted her chin, and met his gaze, defiance flashing in her violet eyes.

"Lewton, damn you, answer me!" Cherry's good-natured scolding finally got his attention.

"I'm sorry. What did you say, honey?"

Cherry shook her head. "Have you gone deaf as a stone?"

"She asked three times what you want for breakfast," Mollie coolly informed him, starting to smile.

"Coffee's fine," he muttered. "Nothing more."

"All right, but you know that you're on your own for the rest of the day," said Cherry, bringing Mollie's plate to the table. "Sit down here, Mollie, and eat your eggs while they're hot."

Lew remained uncommunicative throughout the meal. Cherry chattered gaily. Mollie listened politely. After the dishes had been cleared away, Cherry took off her red apron. "Time for my beauty sleep," she announced, stifling a yawn. "I'll see you two later." And she disappeared.

Puzzled, Mollie said, "She's already going back to bed? Didn't she just get up?"

Lew's answer was a shuttered look and a curt reminder that this was Cherry's house and she could sleep any time she chose. Sullenly he drank his coffee. Mollie fidgeted, longing to ask questions, not daring to do so.

Finally, Lew looked at her. "What? What is it?"

"Nothing. Not a thing, but—"

"Spit it out."

"Well . . . it's just . . . that woman." She wrinkled her nose. "You have a lot of nerve bringing me to the home of a common prostitute."

Lew set his coffee cup down. "There's not a thing common about Cherry. And she's the one to whom I owe an apology."

"I beg your pardon?"

He leaned up to the table. "I've brought an uncommon criminal into her home."

Mollie glared at him. "Well, if she's offended, it's only because I'm a woman. I'm sure she's 'entertained' more than one outlaw."

"Could be. I never asked."

"Mmm. Too busy enjoying her charms yourself, I imagine." She thoughtfully scratched her chin with a forefinger. "Tell me, does she still charge or is it free to you now?"

Lew never answered. He rose, circled the table, took hold of Mollie's arm, and yanked her up out of the chair. "Put on some clothes and brush that damned hair."

Mollie got dressed. But she didn't brush her hair. Restless, she ambled around the house, looking at Cherry's treasures, thinking that the woman had abominable taste. She made the mistake of saying so to Lew. He set her straight in record time, indicating, in less-than-gentle language, that she was not to say another unkind word about Cherry Sellers.

Unrepentant, but keeping her opinions to herself, Mollie chose one of Cherry's dime novels from a stack and flung herself down on the red velvet settee to read. And to plan her escape. Lew, unusually edgy, moodily watched Mollie, determined to not let her out of his sight.

As the day dragged on, he decided they'd leave come morning. The sooner he got this beautiful bandit to Denver the better.

At shortly after five that afternoon, Cherry, rested and in high spirits, joined them. "I've a marvelous idea," she said, smiling broadly. "We'll make a night of it!" Ignoring the fierce shaking of Lew's dark head, she continued enthusiastically, "We'll get all gussied up and go out on the town! Drink champagne and play roulette and dance. What do you say?" She plopped down on the arm of Lew's chair and ruffled his hair.

"Honey, you know we can't do that." His voice, when he spoke to Cherry, was soft and kind. "I have to go get supplies, and I want you to watch Mollie for me. We're leaving bright and early tomorrow."

"Oh, Lewton, don't be an old meanie," trilled Cherry. "You know how lonely I get. The only time I ever have any fun is when you come through. Don't I deserve a good time once in a blue moon?" Pouting, she twined locks of his hair around her fingers.

Lew sighed. "Sure you do, honey, and any other time I'd—"

"Please, Lew, please. I haven't danced in ages."

He inclined his head toward Mollie. "You're forgetting something, darlin'. I can't let her out of my sight for a second."

"I know that," Cherry said. "She'll go with us, of course."

He snorted. "Like that?" He looked pointedly at Mollie's tight buckskins, man's shirt, scuffed boots, and tangled hair.

Mollie shot him a wilting look.

"Tell you what," said Cherry, "you go on to town and get your supplies. I'll fix Mollie up. I'll find her something to wear and do her hair. And you can wear those evening clothes you left here that time we went to the opening of the Cibola Hotel."

Lew finally gave in, and Mollie could hardly hide her excitement. A night on the town with the liquor flowing freely was just the edge she needed. The pleasant scenario flashed through her mind: Lew and Cherry, drunk on champagne and passed out in Cherry's red bedroom while she rode away into the night!

"Come on, Mollie," Cherry immediately took her to the red bedroom and began bringing out gaudy gowns and holding them up to Mollie's slender frame. "This is the one!" Cherry finally said, choosing a shimmering silk evening gown of flaming scarlet.

"I don't think so, Cherry," Mollie said. "It's not—"

"It's perfect. Or will be as soon as I do a bit of alteration. Slip it on while I get the pins. A tuck here and there and you'll be absolutely stunning."

"Thanks for letting me wear it," said Mollie, resolved to be congenial.

"Glad to, honey. Now, you go wash your hair while I alter the dress." She winked at Mollie.

The two women spent the next couple of hours preparing for a gala evening on the town. Cherry chattered companionably as they worked while Mollie listened, asking an occasional question. The talkative Cherry told more than she was asked. She spoke at length about Lew, the complicated man she so adored. She regaled Mollie with tales of their shared escapades and when, finally, she spoke of the beautiful, aristocratic Spanish fiancée whom Lew had worshiped, Mollie felt a pang of jealousy slam through her.

Sarcastically, she said, "I should think that a high-born young lady would prefer someone with a bit more class and character than a bounty hunter."

Cherry's needle stopped flashing. "Mollie, Lew is one of the richest ranchers in the New Mexico Territory. This bounty hunting business didn't begin until two years ago when his beautiful fiancée died."

"Died? How did she . . . ? What happened?"

Cherry shrugged. "I've never learned the full story. All I know is that Lew became a bitter man after the girl's death. And he's been determined to bring in all the . . . the . . ."

"Rogers Renegades?"

Nodding, Cherry said, "Sorry, honey. It's unlike Lew to mistreat a woman, and I told him last night that I thought he should let you go. Why, you're nothing but a child, and I'm sure you didn't do anything bad."

"I robbed banks and trains," Mollie confessed honestly. "I make no apologies for it. I rode with my papa."

"Far be it from me to judge."

"What I can't understand," said Mollie thoughtfully, "is how my robbing a few banks has anything to do with Lew. The Renegades never touched a New Mexico bank. If he is a rich New Mexico rancher, why is he so dead set on bringing me in? What did I ever do to him?"

A compassionate woman, Cherry said, "I honestly don't know, honey. Lew's a closemouthed man. Plays them close to the vest and reveals little." She brightened then and said, "If I were you, I'd use some powerful ammunition against old Lewton. See if I couldn't change his mind."

"Ammunition? I'm not allowed guns or bullets, so—"

"No!" squealed Cherry. "I mean your beauty. Lew's never been immune to a beautiful woman. Make him desire you."

Mollie exhaled. "Lew desire an outlaw?"

"You're a woman first, dearie."

30

Lew was alone in the red sitting room. A drink in hand, he stood before the cold fireplace. His blue eyes widened, then narrowed when, just as the clock struck nine, Mollie joined him. For a long moment he stared at her in speechless fury.

Her borrowed red dress fit her like a second skin and was cut daringly low. The skirt was tight down to her knees where it flared so she could walk. Her golden hair had been dressed into shimmering curls atop her head. A red velvet bow was pinned above her left ear.

"Jesus Christ!" he said finally, his long fingers tightening on the whiskey glass. "You're not going out like that, are you?"

"She most certainly is!" Cherry said, sweeping into the room in a cloud of French perfume and a gown of fragile red lace. She stepped up and put her arm around Mollie's narrow waist. "Doesn't she look beautiful?"

"She looks like a—" Lew caught himself, shot Cherry an apologetic glance. "She looks naked." He downed the rest of his drink and stood flexing his fingers around the empty glass.

Cherry came to him, took the glass, and set it aside.

"Lewton, you old hypocrite. You've seen me wear that very gown and told me how much you liked it." Ignoring the stormy look in his eyes, she said, "Come on, let's go have a good time."

The trio headed for the bright lights of Prescott. Lew wanted to make the evening an enjoyable one for Cherry. So he forced himself to be congenial and charming. He ordered the finest champagne at the Yavapai Hotel dining room and smiled easily when Mollie, always up for a new experience, drank down the bubbly with relish and eagerly nodded yes when he offered to pour her another.

Mollie didn't realize that she was feeling the effects of the wine. She supposed that her hot face and fast-beating heart were because she would be a free woman in just a few hours. So she continued to drink freely of the sparkling champagne, feeling incredibly carefree and happy. She never noticed that dozens of men were casting heated looks at her.

She promised herself she would do nothing to annoy Lew. She didn't want him cutting the evening short and insisting they return home before he had gotten good and drunk. She went out of her way to be agreeable. It wasn't that difficult.

Mollie thought it exciting to roam down Whiskey Row, stopping in at all the rowdy fun places along the way. She was alarmed by the noise, the crowds, the flirtations, and the brawls. But she was enchanted with the gambling, the music, and the dancing. And with the protective solicitousness of the darkly handsome man at her side who, more than once, placed a possessive hand on her arm or shoulder or waist.

She played faro—Lew taught her how. She drank

more chilled champagne. She laughed at Lew's jokes. She flirted with him, just as Cherry flirted, and took turns in his arms on the dance floor. She blinked foggily when—as she was waiting at the table while Lew and Cherry danced—a tall, richly tailored gentleman slipped down into the chair beside her, put a hand on her bare back, leaned close, and said, "Darlin', you're the prettiest thing I've seen." His gaze dropped to her cleavage and his hand covetously cupped her bare shoulder. "I'll give you a fifty-dollar gold piece if you'll come upstairs and take off that pretty red dress."

Mollie opened her mouth but never got the chance to answer.

A lean brown hand shot out like a striking serpent, gripped the man's collar, and jerked him up out of his chair.

Standing face-to-face with the startled man, a fierce-looking Lew said in a voice that was deadly cold, "What did you say to the young lady?"

"Since when are whores considered ladies?" said the man.

Lew slammed a hard fist into the man's mouth, and the entire saloon seemed to explode. Mollie, standing now, watched wide-eyed as fights broke out and furniture flew and bottles broke and the piano player struck up a loud rendition of "Little Brown Jug."

Mollie saw Cherry—squealing at the top of her lungs—leap onto the back of a big, bearlike man who was coming at Lew from behind. Mollie clapped her hands. Carefully pouring herself one more glass of champagne, she stood there amidst the pandemonium and calmly drank it down. Then she picked up the empty bottle just as a big, bald miner picked her up.

She brought the bottle crashing down on his smooth pate. As he was going down she felt another man's arms come around her waist and snatch her away from the miner.

She screamed, raised the bottle, and heard that unmistakable voice say, "It's Lew, Mollie. You're safe." She went limp against him and he swung her easily up into his arms. Shouting, "Cherry, let's get out of here," he strode toward the door with Cherry right behind him.

Mollie was never quite sure how the three of them managed to get through the brawling crowd and out the swinging doors, but they did. And they laughed all the way home, reliving the good time they'd had. Mollie, intoxicated for the first time in her life, forgot completely about her plan to escape. She forgot something else as well—how much she hated Lew.

Skipping along the street beside him, Mollie clung to his arm and admired his classic profile etched against the night sky. She felt exquisite little shivers of delight from being so close to such a handsome, compelling man.

Lew felt good too. Better than he had felt in months. The strenuous exercise of the fistfight had been exactly what he had needed. Building frustrations and mounting tensions had been greatly eased by the physical release afforded by the brawl. He felt wonderfully liberated for the first time in weeks. His coiled muscles had relaxed. His mind was unburdened. His soul cleansed.

When the laughing trio reached Cherry's house, Mollie's head was still spinning. She stumbled on the front steps. For the second time that night Lew swiftly swept her up into his arms. Mollie giggled as he walked through the front door carrying her high against his chest.

In a chivalrous mood, Lew said to Cherry, "I'll put her to bed."

"No," Mollie protested, laughing and kicking her feet. "I'm not the least bit sleepy. Is there more champagne?"

"You've had enough," Lew said and carried her directly to the guest room.

He lowered her to the edge of the bed and Mollie, still laughing, promptly tumbled over backward. Leaving the lamp unlighted, Lew drew her up and sat down beside her. With deft, sure fingers he unhooked the tight scarlet dress and peeled the sleeves down her limp arms. When the red dress lay around her waist, Lew rose to his feet, bringing Mollie up with him.

"Mollie, put your hands on my shoulders," he commanded.

"Want to dance again?" she asked and, humming happily, locked her hands behind his head.

Ignoring the question, Lew eased the tight dress down over her hips, then released it and allowed it to fall to the floor. Her head thrown back, Mollie swayed to him, pressing her chemise-clad body to the hard length of his.

His hands at her waist, Lew set her back, and said, "Get in bed, outlaw."

Nodding agreeably, Mollie sank down on the bed and again fell over backward. Lew turned her about so that she was lying with her head on the pillows. He straightened, looked at her stretched out on the bed, and smiled down at her.

"We forgot your shoes," he said softly and sat down beside her.

Giggling, Mollie lifted her feet. Lew removed the borrowed red kid slippers.

"What about the stockings?" Mollie slurred the words.

Lew swallowed hard. He removed a coquettish red garter from above her left knee before peeling off the silky stocking. Perspiration dotted his forehead by the time the stockings were laid aside and Mollie's long shapely legs were bare.

He felt his heart kick against his ribs when she said sleepily, "Kiss me good night, Lew."

"Don't be silly," he said, starting to rise.

She caught his jacket sleeve. "We've been silly all night and it's been such fun." She looked up at him with teasing violet eyes. "It would be silly not to be silly now. Kiss me, Silly. Silly-kiss me."

"Then will you go to sleep?"

Her fingers toying with a button at the center of his chest, she said, "If you'll make the kiss silly."

Removing her hand from his shirtfront, Lew leaned down and turned his face so that his lips were perpendicular to hers. He kissed her quickly and said, "That silly enough?"

"Now it's my turn to give you a silly kiss," was her reply. "Come here." She grabbed his lapels, pulled his face down to hers. She kissed—not his lips—but the appealing cleft in his chin, putting out the tip of her tongue to lick the tiny indentation.

Lew made a face and wiped his chin while she laughed. "Now you again," she said.

He grinned and kissed her small, well-shaped nose. She laughed and kissed his left eyebrow. He kissed her right earlobe. She kissed his damp temple. He kissed her spiky eyelashes. They kissed and kissed until they ran out of places to silly-kiss and, laughing, stopped and looked at each other.

Their gazes locked, their laughter died. Slowly, surely, Lew's dark head descended as Mollie's lifted from the pillow. Their mouths touched and met, but the silly kisses had ceased. Mollie's soft warm lips parted beneath Lew's, and she sighed when his tongue slid into her mouth. He kissed her deeply, probingly, his lips hot on hers.

As they kissed, Mollie wrapped her arms around him and drew him down to her, her fingertips gliding over the fine fabric of the evening jacket stretching across his back. When at last his burning lips left hers and he raised his dark head, Lew stared down at her with an intensity that was electrifying. Pure animal desire gleamed from his humid blue eyes and a vein throbbed on his tanned brow.

His sultry gaze holding hers, Lew's fingers went to the black silk cravat at his throat. He impatiently jerked it loose and anxiously unbuttoned his shirt. Her eyes never leaving his passion-hardened face, Mollie eagerly slipped her hand inside the opened shirt. Her nails raked through the crisp hair on his hard muscled chest. He shuddered and slowly bent to her.

But as he leaned down the gold cross he wore fell forward and hung suspended. Swinging back and forth, it presented an insurmountable barrier between them. The cross reminded him painfully of who he was and who she was and why they were here together.

Lew's lips hovered inches about Mollie's. She waited breathlessly for the caress that never came. Slowly, he straightened, his eyes now gone cold. Buttoning his shirt he rose and crossed the room.

At the door he said over his shoulder, "Get some sleep, outlaw."

31

"She doesn't look or act like a dangerous desperado," Cherry said to Lew when he returned to the sitting room.

"And you don't look or act like a respectable young widow, but you are."

Cherry laughed. "That's true, that's true." She patted the settee beside her. "Still, Mollie's just a girl. Young, impressionable, an innocent."

"Innocent? Christ, how can you make such a ridiculous statement?" He sank down on the sofa beside her.

"Is it? I don't think so." Cherry waved a red-nailed hand. "All right, so she rode with the Renegades on a few holdups. She loved her father very much, so she naturally supposed that whatever daddy did couldn't be bad."

"She didn't just ride with daddy. She rode, ate, and slept with eight violent bandits." Lew's jaw hardened. "Likely as not, they passed her around like an Indian peace pipe."

Cherry laid a hand on his shoulder. "I'd bet my finest pair of red garters against it." Lew rolled his eyes, started to speak. She stopped him. "Whether you know it or not, my friend, you have become involved with our little blond bandit."

"Jesus, what a foolish—"

"Hear me out, Lew. Because you are a man, you can't see the situation logically the way I can. Women can tell a lot about another woman, see things men can't see. Any woman can fool a man, but she can't fool another woman."

"If there's a point to be made here, I wish you'd make it."

"Mollie allows you to *think* she slept with the Kid. I don't believe she's ever slept with anyone but her dolly."

Lew's cold blue eyes flickered. "What woman in her right mind would want the world to think that she—"

"Not the world, Lewton. You. She wants you to think it."

"Should I ask why?"

Cherry shrugged. "To hurt you."

"Hurt me?" His eyes turned flinty hard. "There's no one left who can hurt me. You know that."

"Mmm. I believe you, so . . . why not let her go?"

Lew shook his head. "No. I am taking Mollie Rogers to Denver and then I am going after her father. When I bring him in, it will finally be over. Not before."

"I see," said Cherry. "Then what?"

It was Lew's turn to shrug. "I haven't thought that far ahead. Go on living, I suppose. Same as everybody else." He smiled at her, his mood finally softening.

Cherry smiled back and lifted a hand to his face. Allowing her fingertips to travel down his smoothly shaven jaw, she said wistfully, "Reckon we made a mistake all those years ago when we promised old Clint we'd never get into the sack together?"

Lew grinned, took her hand, and kissed it. "Could be.

Think we should just forget that promise?" He knew her answer.

Cherry patted his chest affectionately. "Don't think I'm not tempted, Lew, but . . . no. We loved Clint too much to go back on our word."

"In that case, I'm awfully tired, honey. Think I'll get some sleep." He squeezed her hand and rose.

"Lew."

"Yes?"

"Remember, things are not *always* what they appear to be."

"Mostly they are, darlin'."

"Not really. Take the way Mollie perceives the relationship between you and me, for instance. We could never convince her that we're not lovers. Why, right now she's lying in there wide awake, thinking we're in bed together."

"What Mollie thinks is of little interest to me. Night, now."

In Cherry's red bedroom, Lew stripped to the skin and crawled into bed. But he didn't sleep. An arm folded beneath his head, he stared at the scarlet canopy above him and absently twisted the gold chain on his neck.

His thoughts, for once, were not on the beautiful dark-haired Spanish girl to whom he had given the chain and cross. Nor were they on the voluptuous red-head in whose bed he now lay. He closed his eyes and saw only Mollie. Mollie wearing nothing but her lacy chemise. Mollie tipsy from too much champagne. Mollie laughing giddily. Mollie eagerly opening her soft, warm lips under his own.

A painful heaviness pressed down on Lew's bare

chest as he saw with vivid clarity a saucy red garter encircling a long, silken leg. The frilly feminine garter was out of place on Mollie's knee, but powerfully provocative. The recollection brought instant arousal. Lew felt his groin swell and his heart begin to pound.

Anger mixing with desire, he impatiently threw back the covers and swung his bare feet to the lush red carpet.

"I just need a woman. Any woman," he muttered to himself. "And right out there in the sitting room is more woman than Mollie Rogers will ever be."

Lew reached for his trousers, paused, and left them where they lay. It was no good. He didn't want Cherry Sellers. Wouldn't take her to bed even if he could persuade her to forget their vow to Clint.

He wanted Mollie.

That realization disgusted him, but his body remained rigid with his need. He stalked to the window, his throbbing, thrusting tumescence mocking him, infuriating him, frightening him. Like it or not, the unlikely temptress held a measure of power over him. If not over his mind, at least over his body.

"Damn you, outlaw," he said through thinned lips as he stood at the open window clutching the heavy red curtain.

Cursing his weakness and the woman responsible for it, he stayed there until the night air cooled his scalding blood and the physical evidence of his desire finally disappeared. Sighing heavily, Lew returned to the bed, took a cigar from the bedside table, and lighted it with shaking hands. He puffed and blew out the smoke, cautioning himself about the days ahead. He'd have to be on guard at all times. Couldn't allow himself to think of Mollie as anything other than one of the gang of notorious bandits responsible for the deaths of those he most loved.

It would be easier once they were back on the trail. Then Mollie would be in her trousers and her hair would be a tangled mess and her face all sunburned.

And no more long, bare legs and flirtatious red garters.

Mollie lay awake in the moonlight long after Lew had left her. When it seemed an eternity had gone by and the effects of the champagne had worn off and the house was totally silent, Mollie rose. She pulled on her buckskins, shirt, and boots, and grabbed up her red saddlebags. Cautiously, she opened the bedroom door. All was quiet.

She drew a shallow breath and glanced toward Cherry's room. The door was shut. Certain that Lew and Cherry were together on the other side of that closed door, Mollie refused to let herself consider what they were probably doing. Telling herself she didn't care, she hurried to the living room.

And stopped short.

Cherry was curled up on the red velvet settee, reading. Her eyes lifted to meet Mollie's.

Lowering her book, she wagged her head back and forth. "I can't let you do that, Mollie."

Shoulders slumping, Mollie said, "Please, Cherry. Pretend you didn't know, didn't see me leave. Tell Lew I must have slipped out the bedroom window and—"

"I wish I could, honest I do. But I promised Lew, and I keep my promises."

Her face screwed up in a frown, Mollie pleaded her case. "I'll die in prison, I will. Do you want that?"

"No, I don't." Cherry smiled then and it was an almost motherly smile. Softly she said, "But I'm not worried about that happening. You see, I know Lew better than you. You'll never make it to Denver. Mark my words. Now go back to bed and get some rest, honey."

Mollie's thick lashes lowered in defeat, then lifted questioningly. "Why aren't you in bed?"

"Honey, there's two things I never do. And one of them is go to bed before the sun rises." She laughed.

"And the other?"

"Go to bed with Lew."

Mollie's mouth fell open. She quickly closed it, shrugged, and said, "I'm sure I don't care whether you go to bed with him or not."

A well-arched red eyebrow lifted. "And I'm just as sure that you do."

With morning the first hint of an early autumn chilled the crisp dawn air. Mollie and Lew, preparing to depart, said little to each other, though their eyes met often. It was not lost on Cherry.

When she kissed Lew good-bye, her eyes filled with tears, and she whispered in his ear, "Honey, people ought to not live in the past."

Embracing her, he said, "Look who's talking."

Cherry sighed, released him, hurried back toward the house, turned, and called out, "Lew, honey, wait one minute. Mollie, come here, please. I have something I meant to give you."

Mollie, already mounted, looked to Lew for permission. He nodded. She slid out of the saddle and went back up the front walk as the sun's first pink rays seeped over the rugged mountain peaks.

Cherry met her on the front porch. She took Mollie's hand and pressed into it the red satin garter she had loaned Mollie last night. The garter that Lew had so expertly peeled down Mollie's left leg.

"You never know when a red garter will come in handy," Cherry said, winking at Mollie. "Put it in your pocket, honey. Then some night when Lew is in a congenial mood and the two of you are sitting around the campfire and it's almost bedtime . . . You strip right down to your underwear and slip on the red garter." Before Mollie could say anything, Cherry impulsively hugged her tightly. Into Mollie's ear she whispered, "Hell, honey, he's just a man. Make him want you."

Mollie snorted. "Make Lew Taylor want me? Not likely!"

Cherry pulled back and looked at her. "Taylor? Mollie, Lew's name is Hatton. Lew Hatton."

The chill had long since left the dry air and the August sun was high and hot overhead as Lew and Mollie rode in sullen silence across the flat Chino Valley. Lew's eyes were unflickering in their concentration on the trail ahead. Mollie's were fixed with anger.

Hatton! The name kept ringing in her head. Hatton. Hatton. Hatton.

Now it all made sense. Lew was William Hatton's son, and William Hatton was the Yankee colonel her papa's men had killed in the last days of the war. Rather, William Hatton was the man that the Kid had killed and in so doing changed all their lives forever. William Hatton's death was the reason they'd had to leave their Texas home. The reason her mother had died on the trail. The reason her papa had started drinking. The reason the Rogers Renegades were born.

Mollie cast a glance at Lew's hard face and felt her

anger grow. She had lost far more than he had, and he was determined she would lose still more—her freedom. Damn him! It was unfair and she wouldn't let it happen. One way or another, she would escape.

The sun suddenly went behind a cloud and the stark high desert darkened as though catching Mollie's mood. Her eyes riveted to Lew, she thought grimly that no one would ever have recognized this cold, uninterested man slouched in the saddle as the same one who—less than twenty-four hours ago—had bought her champagne and taught her to gamble and danced seductively with her and got into a fistfight to defend her honor. And then later had gently undressed her and laughed and teased and kissed her in a moonlit bedroom.

The heartless bastard! The unprincipled son of a bitch!

"Something on your mind, outlaw?" Lew turned and caught her staring at him, a murderous look in her flashing violet eyes.

"Plenty," she said and ranged her mount alongside his. "Why in blazes—after you trapped me—didn't you tell me that your name is really Hatton?"

He shrugged. "Slipped my mind."

Mollie gritted her teeth. "Nothing has *ever* slipped your mind, bounty hunter. You're a cold, calculating impostor with a big stone for a heart and ice water for blood in your veins. Yet, it's still hard for me to believe that any man—even one as unscrupulous as you— would make me pay for your father's death all those years ago. Good Lord, I was a fifteen-year-old girl living with my mother on our Texas plantation."

"Outlaw, this has nothing to do with my father's death."

"Then what is it? What have I done to—"

He cut her off. "Guess it's slipped your mind."

32

The pair were mute throughout supper.

Lew was firmly resolved to keep Mollie at arm's length. Mollie was just as determined to never again let her defenses down. Lew read the growing hatred in Mollie's expressive eyes but was unmoved. If anything, he was glad to see it. A spiteful, disheveled Mollie Rogers in buckskins and boots was far easier to resist than the sweet-smelling, red-gartered girl he had foolishly kissed back in Prescott.

Crouching on his heels, Lew tossed the dregs from his coffee cup into the dying campfire, then got to his feet. "Bedtime," he announced, his gaze touching Mollie where she sat across the fire, her arms wrapped around her bent knees.

Mollie didn't answer, but rose and followed him to a spot near the banks of the Big Chino Wash where he had stacked their gear. Lew picked up their two blankets, tossed the brown one to her, and waited while she wrapped herself in it and lay down. He spun the red-and-blue Indian blanket around his shoulders and stretched out near—but not too near—Mollie.

He exhaled heavily, closed his tired eyes, and was

lightly dozing almost immediately. Mollie, getting comfortable, hunched her shoulders and drew the coarse brown blanket up around her ears and face. She inhaled deeply and caught a hint of Lew's unique scent. She sniffed the blanket. It smelled of him, that tantalizing scent that always clung to him. A provocative mixture of tobacco and leather and clean, sunwarmed flesh. Annoyed, she threw off the offensive cover and sat up.

"You have my blanket," she said irritably.

Blinking, Lew came instantly awake. "What are you talking about?"

"I want my blanket, damn you. This one's yours. You have mine and I want it!"

"You can have both if you'll quiet down and go to sleep."

"I don't want both. I want mine."

Wondering what the hell difference it made which blanket she had, Lew sat up, passed her the red-and-blue blanket and took the brown one.

Glaring at him, Mollie swept the cover around her shoulders and warned, "Never take my blanket again, bounty hunter."

The disagreement over the blanket was not to be their only one. They clashed over which route they would take north and over the choice of campsites along the way and over how often they would stop to rest and over when and what they would eat.

And over his unkempt black beard and her tangled blond hair.

With each passing mile and hour, the pair grew more

hostile toward one another. Physically, each had become what the other found most offensive.

To a woman who shuddered at the thought of a big, bearded, dangerous-looking man, Lew was both menacing and repugnant. His hard biceps strained the tight sleeves of his sweat-stained shirt, his shaggy raven hair curled down over his collar, and his beard was as thick and black as the darkest midnight.

To a man who had never taken a second glance at a woman who wasn't well-groomed and delicate and endlessly feminine, Mollie was both annoying and disgusting. In her buckskin pants and man's shirt she looked like a slim boy. Her face was sunburned and streaked with dirt and her hair was either flying in tangled disarray or carelessly knotted atop her head.

The two spent a lot of time casting disapproving looks at each other, allowing their expressions to speak volumes. But it was Mollie who first put it into words. It happened one hot afternoon when Lew reined his mount in a bit too close and inadvertently brushed her leg with his own.

She glared at him and said hotly, "Hatton, you are exactly the kind of man I find repulsive."

Eyeing her dusty buckskins, sweat-soaked shirt, and stringy hair, he replied, "And you, outlaw, are just the kind of woman I find revolting."

They argued for a while about who was the most offensive. But moments later they were silent as they rode single file, angling around a steep cliff on their way down into the wide, flat Dead Horse Canyon. They were almost down when Mollie abruptly pulled up on her mount and called out to Lew. His squinty-eyed gaze followed her pointing finger.

On the canyon floor, a couple of miles away, a detail of mounted men cantered in their direction. Guidons fluttered in the light breeze, and the dust of the ponies spiraled against the cloudless Arizona sky. Even at this distance Lew could make out the civilian clothing and the dark skin of the Apache Scouts Corps of the U.S. Army. Two dozen soldiers in military blues rode with the scouts.

Lew knew what it meant. The Apaches were off the reservation again and causing trouble somewhere in the vicinity.

Mollie, watching the strange contingent move steadily forward, felt her pulse quicken. Since leaving Prescott, they had seen no one. She'd had no opportunity to escape. Perhaps here was her chance. She quickly lifted her eyes to the sun. It was on its westerly drop.

Kneeing her horse to urge it on down the trail, she said as casually as possible, "I'm awfully hungry. Are you?"

"A little." Lew's horse whickered, picking up the scent of the approaching scouts' mounts. "Maybe they'll invite us to supper."

She nodded, then asked, "What are those savages doing with the soldiers?"

"They're Apache scouts hired by the army to track down renegade Indians."

Before she could reply, a slim, uniformed soldier broke ranks and galloped forward to meet them. He brought his stallion to a halt a few yards away, raised a gloved hand, and snapped off a crisp military salute. He introduced himself and graciously invited them to join the garrison of the Fifth Cavalry, United States Army, for the evening meal.

"My sister and I would be honored, Captain Jackson," said Lew and Mollie's head snapped around. He silenced her with a look and introduced her as Miss Mollie Hatton.

The detachment quickly and efficiently set up camp at the base of the seven thousand–foot Casner Mountain. At sundown an appetizing meal was served and Mollie found herself seated between Lew and a young, curly-haired lieutenant who couldn't take his eyes off her.

Lew talked quietly with the commanding officer on his left, but kept an ear tuned to Mollie's conversation with the obviously smitten lieutenant. He couldn't recall her ever being quite so talkative and attentive. Casting cool, cynical glances her way, Lew noted with amusement the way she smiled flirtatiously at the young soldier. She looked up at the boy with wide violet eyes, listening to him speak as though he were the most fascinating man she had ever met.

Mollie shot Lew a sideways glance when he rose to his feet and shook hands with an officer who had just joined them. But the curly-haired lieutenant quickly brought her attention back to him.

"I sure wish you and I could take a stroll in the moonlight, Miss Hatton," he said, then blushed to the roots of his hair and swallowed nervously, his Adam's apple bobbing up and down.

Sweetly, Mollie said, "My big brother is very protective, but perhaps we could take a short walk."

"I can't, Miss Hatton. I'm not a free man."

"You're not?"

"No. I'm to stand first guard with the picketed horses. I don't get off watch until two A.M."

"I see," she said and smiled, plans for the unsuspecting lieutenant rapidly forming in her head. "And exactly where, Ben, are the horses picketed?"

He inclined his head. "About two hundred yards west of here, around the base of the mountain."

Mollie smiled enigmatically. "Some other time then, Ben."

"Yes, Miss Hatton," he said, crestfallen that such an unexpected opportunity had to be passed up in the line of duty.

Much later that night, Mollie, wide awake and tingling with anticipation, lay beside the sleeping Lew on a grassy slope up the mountain and apart from the soldiers. Patiently she waited for the soldiers' conversations and occasional laughter to die away. Finally a nighttime hush fell over the camp and the fires burned low. Mollie turned her head and looked at Lew. He lay on his back, eyes closed. She leaned close and whispered his name. No response. His head turned slightly and he licked his lips, but his eyes remained closed in slumber. The gold chain he wore gleamed on his tan throat and Mollie momentarily wondered—as she had many times before—what was on the chain.

Her curiosity passed immediately. She had work to do. She eased herself up into a sitting position. When Lew still didn't move, she threw off the blanket, picked up her sheepskin jacket, and shot to her feet. Her eyes on the sleeping Lew, Mollie backed away, her heart hammering in her chest. When there was twenty yards between them, she turned and hurried off into the night.

She shoved her arms into the sheepskin jacket and, walking briskly, skirted the camp. She picked her way around the mountain slope, scrambling over scattered boulders and ducking beneath the stiff-limbed juniper and piñon pines, at times losing the bright moonlight as she trudged through the dense forest.

She was out of breath when she finally spotted the long line of picketed horses and the lone soldier standing guard. Mollie paused, looked about, stooped and picked up a smooth rock. She weighed it in her hand. Satisfied, she shoved it into her jacket pocket and ambled nonchalantly down the incline.

"Halt!" said Lieutenant Benjamin J. Atwood, raising his rifle.

"Ben, it's me," Mollie lifted her hands and fanned out her long blond hair. "Mollie Hatton."

"Mollie?" he said, slowly lowering the rifle.

"Yes, Ben. I couldn't sleep. I kept thinking about you." She quickly crossed the space between them. "Have you been thinking about me?" She stepped up close to him.

"Ah . . . I . . . I've thought of nothing else," said the soldier truthfully. "You're just the prettiest girl I ever did see."

With cool authority, Mollie took the rifle from the lieutenant. He was so entranced he made no attempt to stop her.

"You won't need this weapon while I'm here, will you?" she said, then walked over and leaned the rifle against the trunk of a towering Ponderosa pine. "Unless," she came back to him, reached up and toyed with a brass button on his uniform blouse, "you're afraid of me. Are you, Ben?"

Lieutenant Benjamin Atwood swallowed hard, but lifted his hands to gently cup her upturned face. "No, Mollie. Are you afraid of me?"

"Should I be?"

"No." His thumbs skimmed over her cheeks when he added, "But I sure would like to kiss you."

"Then why don't you?" Mollie swayed closer.

His lips trembled as they descended to hers. Their mouths met. The kiss lasted for only a few seconds. Mollie could hardly hide her frustration. She needed more time. She went up on tiptoes, put her arms around the lieutenant's neck, and said, "Oh, Ben, Ben, kiss me again."

Ben kissed her again, his soft, dry lips moving enthusiastically on hers. Mollie responded, but as she kissed the eager youth the insane thought flashed through her mind that Lieutenant Benjamin J. Atwood sure didn't know how to kiss like Lew Hatton. Nonetheless she sighed as though swept away by his caress.

It worked wonders on the amorous lieutenant. Desire and confidence swiftly rising, he became more aggressive. He closed his eyes and opened his mouth and touched Mollie's lips with his tongue. Mollie feigned a swooning reaction to his boldness. Allowing the trembling lieutenant to draw her closer as he deepened the kiss, Mollie slipped a hand into her jacket pocket and her fingers closed around the heavy stone.

Lieutenant Atwood took his lips from hers just as she pulled the rock out of her pocket. "Oh, Ben, Ben," she murmured breathlessly and pulled his mouth back down to hers.

Ben put everything he had into that kiss. He wrapped his long arms tightly around Mollie and held her against his tall, shaking body and kissed her with all the passion he felt. He was totally lost in the kiss as Mollie slowly raised the rock, lifting it up, up directly over his head.

But just as she started to bring the rock crashing down, strong fingers wrapped themselves firmly around her wrist and stayed her hand. Mollie screamed, but no more than a muffled groan escaped her lips trapped beneath the lieutenant's. The startled soldier quickly lifted his head, a puzzled expression on his face.

Mollie was just as confused as he. She looked up at the restraining fingers clasping her wrist and automatically took a step backward, bumping into a man's hard chest.

"Lieutenant Atwood," came that low familiar voice from over her head, "did that kiss make you see stars?"

Flustered, the lieutenant stammered, "N-n-no, sir."

"Well, you were about to, my boy," Lew said, roughly jerking Mollie's hand down to her side and shaking the stone loose.

The lieutenant stood at attention, baffled and uneasy. "Sir?"

"See stars, son. See stars." Lew grinned suddenly and said, "At ease, Lieutenant." He pulled Mollie around in front of him and held her there, his hands clamped firmly down atop her shoulders. He said into her ear, "Little sister, I believe you owe Lieutenant Atwood an apology."

Mollie tossed her head angrily and tried to pull free of his grasp. Lew smiled at the dumbfounded soldier and said, "She's a playful little thing, and her manners are abominable, I'm afraid." To Mollie, "Say good night, now." Mollie snorted indignantly. Lew shrugged and said to the young man, "What did I tell you?"

Apologizing for her, Lew ushered the angry Mollie back to where she belonged. When they reached their campsite they stood facing each other. Mollie's eyes flashed with fury. Lew's were as cold as ice.

He said in a deceptively calm voice, "Why don't you pick on somebody your own size?"

"I beg your pardon," she snapped.

"You took advantage of a naive boy. You were going to bash the poor kid's head while he reeled from your kisses. That wouldn't work on a man."

"Oh, yes it would," she said smugly, hands going to her hips.

Lew immediately bent and picked up a rock. He took her hand, placed the heavy stone in it.

"What's the idea . . . ?" she began.

The sentence was never finished. With a swiftness that caught Mollie off guard, Lew grabbed her by the shirt front and pulled her roughly against him. His mouth came down on hers in an audacious kiss that was so hot and forceful she was as shocked as she was angry. No sweet preliminaries. No teasing and testing. No tender persuasion or gentlemanly consideration.

His muscular arm quickly went around her waist, and he pressed her head back against his supporting shoulder. Long, tanned fingers closed around her delicate throat to hold her still. He kissed her probingly, hungrily, as though he would draw the very breath from her body.

Mollie squirmed and tried to voice her outrage, but the sound never left her throat. Lew's hot, questing lips remained on hers, and his sleek tongue delved deeply into the warm darkness of her mouth in a prolonged kiss that was invasive, demanding, brazen. And incredibly thrilling in its raw, unleashed passion.

Mollie, reeling from the onslaught to her senses, finally remembered the rock in her hand. The rock that he had given her, so cocksure was he. So arrogantly certain that she wouldn't use it on him. Mollie raised her hand. She was ready and eager to bring the rock crashing down directly atop his thick skull.

But just as she got it poised above his bent head, Lew sighed softly, coaxingly sucked her tongue into his mouth, shifted ever so slightly, and with a spread hand cupping her bottom, urged her pelvis up to his.

His black soft beard tickling her flushed cheeks, Mollie fought for breath and for equilibrium. Straining against him, she was dazzled by the taste of him and assailed with the masculine scent of him. The lean, hard body pressed so intimately to hers radiated a fierce animal heat that seemed to burn right through her clothes and singe her tingling flesh.

The rock she held above Lew's head was becoming very heavy.

Lew again shifted and the new position pressed her right breast flush against his heart. She could feel its heavy beating throbbing through her as if it were her own. And somehow he managed to pull his shirttail free of his trousers, found her free hand, and drew it between their pressing bodies. Skillfully he guided her hand down his chest and tucked her trembling fingertips inside the waistband of his pants. Mollie was immediately curious and awed and frightened. Her curled fingers were brushing against a hard, hot belly that seemed to be beating as forcefully as his heart.

She was tempted to slide her fingers on further down inside his tight breeches. She knew that she should yank her hand up out of his trousers at once. She was unable to do either. Mollie allowed her other hand—the one holding the heavy rock—to fall limply to her side.

While Lew's burning lips continued to set her mouth afire and his tight belly beckoned her to explore all that forbidden virility just inches below her fingertips, Mollie released the rock. It dropped to the dirt with a thud.

The instant it hit the ground, Lew tore his lips from hers and lifted his head. Mollie's eyes opened in stunned surprise to see him smiling down at her. Her heart plummeted as he moved back a half step and let his accusing gaze slide down to the tenacious fingers still curled inside his pants.

His smile was derisive when he said, "As I told you, it doesn't work on a man."

Mollie, although hurt and furious, knew that the last laugh was hers. Leisurely releasing her hold on his trousers, she put out the tip of her tongue and licked her full bottom lip. Then, resting her hands on her hips, she smiled seductively at him and pointedly lowered her accusing gaze to his straining, swollen groin.

"Oh, yes it does."

33

A high, piercing scream brought Lew crashing through the undergrowth. Realizing that he had forgotten to pick up his rifle, he reached the edge of a sundappled clearing and saw Mollie. Bare to the waist, her arms crossed over her breasts, she was surrounded by a circle of silent, leering Apaches.

All were mounted, save one tall, broad-shouldered Indian in breechcloth and moccasins who stood directly in front of the terrified Mollie. Lew's keen gaze flicked to the giant's coppery face and immediately he felt his tight lungs fill with air, his pounding heart slow. He exhaled and grinned broadly.

"Chief Red Sunset," he called out companionably.

Every eye turned on him as he came forward, his hands raised in the air. He walked directly toward to the tall Apache. The chief squinted at the approaching white man and began shaking his head.

"Singing Boy," he boomed, his deep, loud voice coming from down inside his massive chest.

His fierce face broke into an almost boyish grin, and Mollie, trembling violently, watched in disbelief as the big, muscular Indian swallowed Lew up in an affectionate bear hug. As soon as the chief released him, Lew stepped over to Mollie, put his arms around her, and drew her into his protective embrace.

Continuing to smile and nod to the tall chief, he whispered to Mollie, "It's all right. All right. Do exactly as I tell you."

She nodded, unable to speak, and turned gratefully into his shielding chest. Trembling, she pressed her face into the curve of his neck and shoulder while the restless, scowling Apaches muttered among themselves.

"Quien es?" asked the Apache chief.

"Mi querida," Lew told the Indian. Then quickly to Mollie, "Unbutton my shirt."

She anxiously obeyed while Lew's hands remained resting possessively on her bare back. His body was pressed close against hers, concealing her nakedness from a dozen sets of curious black eyes. He spoke to the chief in Spanish and although Mollie understood little, she knew that he was talking about her. She winced when she felt callused fingers sweep over her trembling back and pull down the waistband of her buckskins.

"Marca de nacimiento," Lew calmly explained and Mollie realized it was her birthmark that so intrigued the giant Indian.

"Mariposa," said the Apache chief, his blunt fingers tracing the top edge of the birthmark. *"Es mariposa."*

"Yes," said Lew, "a butterfly. A perfect butterfly."

His shirt now unbuttoned, Lew took it off and whirled it around Mollie's slender shoulders. He handled the quick exchange with an economy of motion that managed to preserve Mollie's modesty. As soon as her arms were in the sleeves, he deftly buttoned the shirt.

Then he drew her around to his side and said, "Mollie, shake hands with Chief Red Sunset, one of the bravest and noblest Apache chiefs ever to ride the Arizona Territory."

Mollie obediently put out her hand. Chief Red Sunset eagerly took her hand and shook it firmly. His black eyes were on her tumbled golden hair and there was an expression of awe in their glittery depths. He said something to Lew.

"*Sí*, Chief." To her, "He wants to touch your hair."

Mollie gazed up at the tall, near-naked savage and wisely smiled. She shook her head about so that the tangled locks fell forward. Leaning close to Lew, she fanned her hair out on her palm and then fought the urge to scream as the fierce-looking Indian took a shiny lock between his thumb and forefinger and rubbed it. Muttering unintelligible words, he toyed with the lock of hair, his black eyes glazed.

"That's enough, Chief," Lew finally said.

Chief Red Sunset reluctantly released the hair. Lew drew Mollie directly in front of him. He wrapped his arms around her and locked his wrists just below her breasts. She had no choice but to stand there against him as he talked and laughed and carried on with the savages as all the others dismounted and crowded around. They all stared unblinkingly at her and Mollie was reminded of a pack of hungry wolves.

So she didn't bridle at Lew's familiarity or try to resist his embrace. Instead, her still-trembling hands came up to clutch at Lew's tanned forearms and she pressed her head back against his shoulder. She was grateful that he held her. She doubted that her own watery knees would support her.

Mollie stood there listening, understanding enough to know that Lew was inquiring about the chief's younger sister. The chief informed him that the sister, now the wife of Gilberto Lopez, lived happily with her husband down in Magdalena, Mexico, and that happy pair had many fine sons.

Lew shook his head, exclaiming, "Little Desert Flower a mother! I don't believe it."

Mollie wondered how Lew came to know these Apaches. He even knew that this imposing chief had a little sister named Desert Flower. She gave silent thanks that he *did* know the savages. But for his perfectly timed intervention she might well have been raped and killed.

Mollie shivered, recalling how quickly and unexpectedly it had all happened.

She and Lew had left the Fifth U.S. Cavalry at daybreak. Apparently Lieutenant Atwood held no grudges, because he had kissed her hand and said he hoped they would meet again. Captain Jackson had then warned Lew to be careful of renegade Apaches. Said they were off the reservation again, causing trouble.

The mention of Apaches had made Mollie's blood run cold. Before the soldiers had ridden out of sight, she'd said, "Is it worth risking your scalp to take me in, bounty hunter?"

"Outlaw, if we meet up with any savages, you just kiss 'em and I'll see to it you have an ample supply of rocks."

Annoyed that he never took her seriously, she had retorted, "You arrogant fool, your head is as hard as a rock!"

He grinned. "True. And when you're around—as you pointed out last night—my head's not all that's hard."

She shot him a wilting look and said, "And not an ounce of brains in either!"

She kicked her horse into a gallop and was incensed to hear deep laughter echoing after her. She would never understand the maddening, paradoxical Lew Hatton. She would have thought he would want to forget last night's embarrassing incident, would be mortified should it ever be mentioned. Yet he had brought it up and was laughing about it. Obviously he was totally insensitive.

His insensitivity was still plaguing her when, riding across the vast Verde Valley around four that afternoon, Lew had said, "I'm so sleepy I'm about to fall out of the saddle. Suppose I could trust you for half an hour while I nap?"

Hot and tired, Mollie asked, "Is there water nearby?"

Lew pointed. "I'm certain that stand of trees means water. Want a bath?"

"I'll only bathe if you're asleep."

He grinned. "And I'll only sleep if you're bathing."

So he did.

And she did.

Or at least that had been her intention. While he had stretched out under a shade-giving evergreen and immediately fallen to dozing, Mollie had sauntered around a gentle curve of the stream and came upon a small sun-warmed clearing. Smiling, she hurried down to the inviting water. At the stream's edge, she sighed and eagerly peeled off her hot shirt. Then just as quickly she lifted her soiled chemise over her head.

Her hands were at the waistband of her buckskins when a twig snapped close by. She swallowed nervously and cast a curious glance over her shoulder. She saw nothing, but was sure Lew was spying on her.

Not turning around, she said angrily, "You get out of here this minute, bounty hunter!"

A horse snorted then, and Mollie felt the hair rise on her nape. When she stooped to grab her clothes, an Indian brought his big moccasin down on top of them. Mollie gasped and looked up into a fierce coppery face.

That's when she had started screaming. The rest was a blur. She was surrounded by at least a dozen mounted braves while the one who had put his foot on her clothes calmly stalked her. As the giant savage bore steadily down on her, Mollie saw, from the corner of her eye, Lew running swiftly toward them.

She had never been as glad to see anybody in her life. Then, when to her shocked surprise, Lew had smiled and spoke to the menacing redskin, she had known in an instant that she was safe.

Now, the danger past, Mollie was already starting to chafe at the bit. She wanted out of Lew's encircling arms. She didn't appreciate the intimate way he held her. Didn't like the feel of his broad chest pressing against her back. Was incensed by the constant contact of his hard thighs against her bottom.

She wasn't certain what Lew had told the Apaches about her, but she had the distinct impression that they looked on her as the squaw of "Singing Boy."

Hoping Lew would soon bid them good day and the Indians would ride away, Mollie's head snapped around when Lew told her, "The chief and his braves want us to spend the night with them. I told them we'd be most honored."

As irritated as she was, Mollie wasn't foolish enough to put up a fuss. She merely nodded and smiled. And as night fell, she found herself seated before a campfire over which freshly killed elk roasted on a spit. When the meat was cooked, Chief Red Sunset drew from his breechcloth a sharp hunting knife, sliced off a large hunk of the roasted elk, and placed it on Mollie's tin plate. The chief stood waiting. Mollie looked to Lew.

"He wants you to taste it, see if it suits," Lew prompted.

Mollie took a bite of the succulent roasted meat, chewed, and then nodded appreciatively. She hadn't tasted anything that good since they'd left Prescott. Looking directly at the expectant chief, she asked Lew to tell him the meat was delicious. Chief Red Sunset's face broke into a grin, and his black eyes crinkled with pleasure.

Much laughing and whiskey-drinking accompanied the meal. Mollie noticed that Lew turned up the bottle almost as often as his Apache friends. Setting her plate aside, she yawned sleepily and asked Lew if she could go on to bed.

"Sure," he said, turning to the chief, who was speaking. Mollie could tell by the expression on the chief's coppery face that he was saying something about her. Smiling easily, Lew told her, "Chief Red Sunset wishes to see Sunshine Hair's birthmark again."

"Chief Red Sunset can go to blazes!" Mollie snapped, starting to rise.

"You'll go to blazes if you don't behave," warned Lew, pulling her to him.

He turned her so that her back was to the chief and lifted her shirttail while Mollie fumed. Again she felt those blunt, callused fingers on her flesh and wanted to shout her objections. But Lew's level gaze, holding hers, made her think better of it. She sighed with relief when finally the chief withdrew his exploring hand. Lew immediately drew her to her feet and ushered her to the edge of the firelight, where their blankets were stored.

"See you shortly," he said and left her.

Mollie watched him walk back to the fire, take the proffered whiskey bottle, and turn it up to his lips. By the time she had lain down and pulled her red-and-blue blanket up over her shoulders, music had begun. One of the braves, who was half-Mexican, half-Apache, had a battered guitar. He strummed it with talented fingers and after shouts and pleas from the Indians, a lone voice began to sing along. A deep, unmistakable voice.

It quickly became evident why the Apaches called Lew "Singing Boy." His rich, pleasing baritone carried on the thin night air as he sang in romantic Spanish. Mollie lay awake listening, her heart fluttering crazily. She turned onto her side, rested her face in her hands, and stared across the distance at Lew. He sat cross-legged staring into the fire as he sang, a dreamy, trance-like expression on his handsome face.

A tightness suddenly pressed down on Mollie's chest, and she wondered who he was thinking of as he sang of true love and endless desire. Of the Spanish girl who had died? Was he still heartbroken over her death? So heartbroken he would never love again?

Blinking, Mollie realized that tears were stinging her

eyes. She felt more lonely than she'd felt since her papa died. This handsome man had come into her life as if he had stepped out of her sweetest dreams, and from that first moment she had been his for the taking. What a hopeless fool she had been. What a hopeless fool she still was.

Fool. Fool. Fool.

She repeated the word over and over before finally falling asleep. Later she came wide awake when Lew lifted the blanket and crawled in next to her.

"How dare you! What are you doing?" she hissed, raising up onto her elbows.

"I assured the chief we share a hot blanket," said Lew, chuckling, as he pulled her back down.

"I don't give a damn what you told—"

"You'd better," he cut her off, slurring his words a little, "unless you'd like to share his blanket."

Mollie turned over to look at him. "I have no intention of sharing anybody's blanket, and you can just get up this minute!"

She pushed on his bare chest.

Lew caught her hands. "Listen to me. The chief and his braves believe that you are *my* woman. I told them you are. Because you are mine, they haven't touched you. Need I say more?"

"Do you honestly expect me to believe that?"

"Believe anything you like, but you're sleeping here with me, under this blanket, in my arms, all night long. Savvy?"

For a long uncertain moment Mollie stared into Lew's flashing eyes. Then quietly she turned over, showing her back to him. "I don't like this one bit, bounty hunter."

"Too bad, outlaw."

She was silent for a moment, then asked, "Would the chief actually rape me if he didn't think that you and I—"

"The chief first. Then all his braves."

Mollie shuddered involuntarily and she didn't attempt to pull away when Lew's arms tightened around her and he drew her back against him. She whispered, "Surely they won't harm me if—"

Lew laughed drunkenly. "Harm Singing Boy's woman? Never." He sighed heavily. "The chief wants you, though. He's fascinated with your light hair and your birthmark. Said he'd never had a squaw with a *mariposa* birthmark. Asked me what it's like." Again Lew laughed. "That birthmark sure gets you in trouble. If not for it, I wouldn't have—"

"Hatton," Mollie interrupted angrily.

"Hmm?"

"Kiss my butterfly!"

"I'd like to, honey," he slurred, his breath warm on the back of her neck, "I sure would."

"Oh!"

Mollie awakened with a start early the next morning. Her eyes opened to see Chief Red Sunset's broad ugly face. He was squatted there above them, totally silent, grinning down at her. Her heart thumping beneath her ribs, Mollie anxiously snuggled back against the slumbering Lew.

"Lew," she said softly, "wake up. Lew."

Lew slowly roused. "Hmm?" he murmured, pressing his face into her hair. "Time to get up already?"

"Enjuh?" said the Apache chief, and Lew's eyes

came open. *"Enjuh?"* the chief said again, speaking to Lew, but looking at Mollie.

Lew grinned and hugged Mollie tightly. *"Sí. Enjuh. Muy enjuh."*

That seemed to please the chief because he threw back his head and laughed heartily, then rose and walked away repeating, *"Enjuh. Muy enjuh."*

Mollie immediately threw off Lew's arms and sat up. "What does *enjuh* mean?"

Lew yawned and unselfconsciously rubbed his bare chest. "Good."

Puzzled, Mollie stared down at him. "Good? You told him something was good? What?" She waited for an answer, noticing the gold chain winking on his neck, wishing that the memento it supported hadn't fallen down over his shoulder so she could see what it was.

"You," said Lew.

Mollie blinked. "I beg your pardon."

"The chief wanted to know if you were good last night. I assured him that you were."

"Good Lord, he doesn't think we . . . he actually believes that you and I . . . with all of them right over there and . . . that is the most . . . the most . . ."

"Uncivilized?"

"Exactly!"

Smiling, Lew sat up. "They're savages, remember."

"And you are too, Lew Hatton."

"No, outlaw, I'm not. If I were," his gaze swung to her face, "then I would know if you really are *enjuh*."

Mollie flushed hotly and shot to her feet. Lew rose beside her and said, "You've played it smart so far. Don't ruin it now. They'll be leaving within the hour."

Exactly one hour later Mollie and Lew stood in the

rapidly heating sun saying good-bye to the smiling Chief Red Sunset while his mounted braves waited patiently. The chief's affection for Lew was evident, and although she couldn't understand what he said, she nodded, smiled, and thanked him for everything.

The chief bobbed his head happily and pointed from Lew to Mollie and back again and, his black eyes sparkling as though he knew a secret, he said, *"Solo un idioma, el idioma del amor."*

Mollie looked at Lew and could have sworn he flushed beneath his tan. Clasping the chief's outstretched hand, he shook his head and said, *"Sí. Sí."*

The tall chief backed away, still gesturing and beaming while Lew put an arm around Mollie and both waved until the Apaches, mounted on their mustangs, had thundered out of sight.

"What was that the chief said about understanding the language?" Mollie asked, turning to Lew.

"He said that for you and me there is . . . ," he paused, his lids lowering, his voice dropping, *". . . solo un idioma, el idioma del amor."*

"What does it mean?"

" 'Only one language, the language of love.' "

34

"Ride into town and fan out. Drink in the saloons. Buy whiskey for the patrons. Visit the brothels. Question the girls. Don't come back until you can tell me if she's in Maya."

The big, bearded man drew a long black cigar from his shirt pocket, stuck it into his mouth, and waited until one of his minions anxiously lighted it. Then he said, "If she is no longer there, find out where she went. And with whom."

The half dozen Mexican bandits nodded eagerly, impatient to get to their task. One, the mean-eyed man with the droopy mustache who, due to his fondness for knife fighting was called Cuchillo, looked at their leader and said, "*Sí, jefe.* You wish Cuchillo to bring you a woman to help pass the time till you find your *chica*?"

The Texas Kid thoughtfully puffed on his cigar. His gaze slowly swept the nightlit city of Maya below. "No. I will save myself for her. In a matter of hours she'll be in my arms." An evil grin stretched his thin lips when he added, "My beloved deserves all my passion."

"*Sí. Sí.*" Cuchillo said and laughed heartily. Then: "Tell us again, *jefe*, exactly what we are to do when we find her."

"You do nothing. Nothing. You watch her every move. Follow her. Find out where she is living and then wait until you are sure she is in bed sound asleep."

"And then?" Cuchillo twirled the end of his mustache.

"Come tell me. I'll go after her." The Kid took the cigar from his mouth. A string of spittle momentarily linked it to his lips. "I know how to persuade my fiery little sweetheart to hand over the gold and come with me." His gray eyes became demonic. "Now go!"

The riders galloped down the rocky plateau toward Maya. The Kid, staying behind, watched until they were swallowed up in the darkness of the hot August night. He then unsaddled his dun-colored stallion, pulled a bottle from his saddlebags, and made himself comfortable.

While he waited, he drank of the whiskey and daydreamed of the passion-filled nights ahead with his golden-haired spitfire. It would take a while to break her properly, but it would be worth the trouble. He smiled, took another long pull from the bottle, and shuddered with anticipation. In just a few short hours she would be in his arms.

But several hours passed and the Texas Kid, out of whiskey, out of patience, paced back and forth, swearing under his breath, his anger and frustration growing steadily.

Dawn was beginning to streak the eastern sky when he heard the sound of hoofbeats. He stopped his restless pacing and watched as six riders thundered up the incline. Cuchillo dismounted first and came running to him.

"I am sorry, *jefe*. Your *querida*, she not there. She go."
The Kid grabbed Cuchillo. His face inches from the

nervous Mexican's, he said, "What the hell do you mean?"

"Is like I say. She go away from Maya." Cuchillo quickly told the angered Kid that the woman they were trailing had left Maya with a man she was to marry. The couple had headed to New Mexico a good ten days ago.

"You're lying!" snarled the red-faced Kid.

"No, is true. Is talk of the town. Everybody say beautiful blond *señorita* and handsome broncbuster are much in love, mean to marry."

For relaying this information, Cuchillo got a hard slap across his face. His eyes flickered and his initial instinct was to draw the knife tucked into the waistband of his trousers.

"Don't try it," warned his boss. Then looking directly into the bleeding Mexican's angry eyes, he addressed them all. "Do not unsaddle. We leave at once for New Mexico."

A collective groan went up from the tired men. But they immediately fell silent when the Kid drew one of his ivory-handled Colts, cocked it, and waved it at them.

"Mollie Rogers is mine," he said. "She will marry me. Even if it means we ride nonstop until we capture them! *Comprende?*"

"*Sí, sí.*" murmured the men, fearing for their lives.

"Prepare to depart!" said the Kid, reholstering his pistol. Swiftly he saddled his dun stallion and swung up onto its back. He placed his wide-brimmed sombrero on his head, drew the string tight beneath his chin and, focusing on the northeast, absently tugged at his lobeless left ear. Then, digging his sharp-roweled spurs into his mount's sides, the Texas Kid rode after Mollie Rogers.

Mollie didn't understand him.

She couldn't figure out why, after they'd said good-bye to the Apaches, Lew was so pointedly distant and uncommunicative. Or why his face was set in a permanent scowl and why he went out of his way to treat her coldly.

Lew saw the hurt and puzzled expression in Mollie's eyes, but he didn't care. He was in a bad mood himself and didn't feel like talking or even being civil. He was unreasonably annoyed that the Apache chief had said, as though his word were gospel, that he could see the great affection "Singing Boy" had for "Sunshine Hair." The chief had said that it was "like a slow-burning fire that had started in the soul and was growing, growing until one day it would consume him. "She is your destiny," the chief had told him. "She has been your destiny from the beginning. A destiny you cannot deny."

Lew had laughed it off. The sentimental chief had thought he saw something between Mollie and him that simply wasn't there. Not there at all.

But the words kept ringing in Lew's ears, making him uneasy, edgy. The chief's parting words—only one language, the language of love—had really bothered him. He wondered now, was it because they were too close to the mark.

No!

Damn it to hell, no!

The Indians were a bunch of romantic dreamers for all their wildness and savagery. Reading hidden meaning into every innocent gesture, for pete's sake. Mollie meant nothing to him.

Lew gritted his teeth and glanced at Mollie as she asked another of her endless questions. He wondered, irritably, if she ever shut her mouth.

Mollie fell silent and wondered why he was frowning so furiously. All day he had said less than a dozen words, although she had tried to be pleasant and draw him out. A naturally curious person, she wondered about his friendship with the Apaches. So she asked him about it.

Had he known the chief for a long time? Had he once lived among the Apaches? Had he had his own Apache squaw? Had he ridden into their camp alone? If not, who was with him?

But she got only grunts to the questions she posed, and she'd had just about enough of his insufferable rudeness. She was growing angry, and when they stopped to rest at midafternoon, she let him know it.

"See here, bounty hunter," she stepped up to him, her hands on her hips, "I'm getting bored with all this mystery."

"What mystery?"

Mollie glared at him. "Every damned thing about you is a mystery. Just what the hell were you doing with a bunch of savages? Did you live with them and . . . Oh, never mind. I don't care about any of that. I just want to know what I am doing here. Why are you taking me to Denver? You admitted that it wasn't because of your father's death. So what is it? What's this all about? What did I ever do to you? I have a right to know why I'm being persecuted. You are taking me to the gallows and I don't even know the reason. I would have given you the gold, but you refused it. Why? Why are you . . . ?"

"Why?" he hotly interrupted and she saw his jaw

tighten as his eyes flashed blue fire. He stepped closer to her and yanked his white shirt open down his dark chest. A small gold cross, resting amidst the crisp black hair, gleamed in the alpine sunshine. He lifted the cross. "This. This is *why*. Ever see it before?" He raised it up close to her face. "Can you read the inscription? It says, '*Mi tesoro.*' But then you already knew that, didn't you?"

Mollie swallowed hard. She *had* seen the cross before. The Kid had worn it around his neck. More than once she had seen him sliding the cross up and down the chain, caressing it in a strangely obscene way while smiling wickedly. She had never known where it came from—never asked—but when she thought back on it now, she didn't recall it being around his neck when she'd stabbed him in the Mexican hotel room.

"I . . . I don't know where . . ."

"You know exactly where the cross came from," he said accusingly.

He could tell by the expression in her eyes that she recognized the cross. He released it, allowing it to fall back onto his chest. He started to turn away. She grabbed his arm.

"All right, all right, I have seen the cross, but I . . ."

"Where?"

"Ah . . . it . . . it was . . ."

"Around your lover's neck? He took it from my helpless Teresa after he had brutally raped her! From that day I have been determined to bring all of you in. And I will too. As soon as I get you to Denver, I'm going after your old man." Lew paused, fighting for control, his bared chest heaving with emotion. "Mystery cleared up now?"

Shocked and horrified, Mollie stared at him, shaking her head. "I honestly don't know . . ."

"No?" his tone was deadly cold. "Let me refresh your faulty memory. The Texas Kid, leading the Rogers Renegades, held up a stage outside Bernalillo, New Mexico, more than two years ago. Teresa Castillo was on that stage. The Kid shot and killed Dan Nighthorse, the man I had sent along to guard Teresa, a man who was like a brother to me. After he'd killed Dan, the Kid raped my fiancée, Teresa. Come back to you now?" His eyes were narrowed slits of fury. "My most bitter regret is that the law got to the Kid before I could."

"But that's not—"

"I'll get your father, so help me God."

"No . . . no, my papa is—"

"Your papa's like the rest of them and so are you. The fact that you're a woman changes nothing."

"I tell you I never—"

"Tell me anything you please, but you're wasting your breath. You just admitted you've seen the cross and we both know where." He leaned menacingly close, and said, "How many hot desert nights did this cross rest on your naked breasts while the Kid pumped into you?"

"No!" Mollie exclaimed, horrified. "No, no, I never—"

"Save it, I'm not buying. Teresa Castillo is dead! An innocent girl who never harmed anyone was killed by your lover, and all I have is you and this cross." His eyes reflected contempt. "The cross has more value to me than you."

Hurt, confused, on the verge of tears, Mollie shouted angrily, "No!" Then she impulsively reached out and jerked on the chain until it snapped. "To hell with you and your precious cross!" Before he could stop her, she

flung the cross as far as she could, not thinking or caring what the consequences would be. "There!" she
screamed up into his stunned face. "It's gone and you'll
never find it. Gone like the dead girl it belonged to!
Gone like the past you insist on living in! Gone, damn
you, gone!" Hot tears streamed down her cheeks.

It took a minute for it to sink in on Lew. His hand
kept frantically patting his chest, feeling for the missing
cross, while his face changed from shock to anger to
rage. He reached out, grabbed her roughly by the upper
arms, and yanked her to him.

"I'll kill you," he said through clenched teeth.

"Go ahead, I'm tired of living anyhow," she sobbed.

"I'll kill you," he repeated, his hands cutting into the
flesh of her upper arms, an enlarged vein pulsing on his
forehead.

"What are you waiting for?" she taunted.

For a long, tense moment Mollie thought he actually
would kill her. She had never seen a man struggle so
desperately to keep from committing an act of violence.
He *wanted* to kill her.

It was written on his hard, chiseled features, was
there in his dangerously wild eyes. Mollie waited for
him to lift his hands, wrap them around her neck and
soundly snap it.

She stood there resigned, looking up at him, her
vision blurred with tears. She knew she was in danger,
but felt no fear. If he killed her, it would almost be a
welcome release from a world that no longer held any
joy for her.

"Goddamn you," he said finally. "I can't kill you. I
can't do it."

Disgusted with himself, he shoved her away from

him. Mollie lost her footing and fell, sprawling spread-eagled before him. He stepped right over her and went in search of the cross, swearing under his breath.

He ordered her to help him look for the cross.

She refused.

He stayed on his hands and knees for the rest of the afternoon, searching in vain for the small gold cross that was the last remaining link to his lost Teresa. At sundown he gave up and found, to his surprise, that he no longer felt anything other than extreme physical weariness. His rage was gone, sweated out of him along with his energy. Strangely, his mind seemed cleared, less burdened than it had in ages. He realized that all he wanted was a good meal, a bath, and a night's sleep.

Lew headed straight for the rushing brook, feeling pleasantly exhausted, both mentally and physically. He stripped and stepped into the frothy stream. The shock of the icy water made his tired muscles tingle and jump and he winced as he lowered his overheated, sweat-slick body into the cold, mountain-fed rapids. When he emerged and began dressing, his teeth were chattering, and goose bumps covered his arms and legs.

Lew walked back to where Mollie sat, sullen and silent, against a giant boulder. He glanced at her and almost felt sorry for her. He wanted to tell her he was no longer angry, but the minute she saw him, she shot to her feet and started past him. He stopped her.

"Where are you going?"

"To take a bath," she said, refusing to look at him.

"No." He quickly explained, "The water's too cold."

"I don't care."

"I said no. You'll catch a cold."

"*You* bathed in it."

"I was hot and tired."

"So am I, and I'm taking a bath."

"The sun's going down. You'll freeze."

"I'll chance it."

"I'm telling you, you'll catch a cold."

"I'm going." She took a couple of steps.

"Please," he said, "come back here. You'll get a cold!"

"Would you really care?"

"Yes. I want to get over the mountains before the weather turns. If you catch cold it might slow us down."

"My, my, your concern for my health is most touching." She turned and walked away.

"Outlaw," he called after her, "I forbid you to get in that water!"

"Bounty hunter, I'm taking a bath and that's final!"

"Damn it, you are going to catch a cold!"

35

"*Ah-choo!*"

"You've caught a cold."

"I have not. I . . . I . . . ah . . . ah . . . ah-choo!"

"Yes, you have."

"No. No, I haven't. It's just . . . it's . . . aaah . . . aaah-choo!"

"You should have known better."

"Ah-choo! Very fun . . . fun . . . fun . . . ah . . . ah . . . ah-choo!"

"I knew you should never have bathed in that cold water."

"Ah-choo! Ah-choo! That's right. Rub it in."

"Think maybe we'd better spend the day here and let you get some rest?" Mollie smiled at the sneezing man.

"Certainly not," Lew glared at her. "I'm fine, thank you very much. Wipe that supercilious grin off your face or I'll . . . I'll . . . aah . . . aah . . . ah-choo!"

It was early morning.

Mollie had awakened to the sound of Lew's furious sneezing. She couldn't help but be amused. After all his stern warnings for her to stay out of the frigid water, it was he who had caught cold. His eyes and nose were already red, and he looked miserable. She could have told him he shouldn't have gone into the freezing water while he was so overheated, but it would have done no good. He was as hardheaded as she.

She looked at him now and saw a slight tremor rush through his lean body. Almost feeling sorry for him, she said, "I mean it—why don't we stay here for a while? You look like you could use some rest."

"Ah-choo! We are going. Get your horse saddled. Ah-choo!"

"You're the boss, boss."

"Do me a favor, will you? Ah-choo! Keep your little witticisms to yourself. Ah-choo!"

"Anything you say."

Without further delay they broke camp and rode away. By noon they had left the lush, flat Verde Valley behind and had reached the mouth of the gigantic, steep-walled Oak Creek Canyon.

In the lead, Lew, still sneezing constantly, coaxed his horse up the rocky twists and turns while Mollie gaped up in amazement at the vermilion-hued canyon with its sandstone walls soaring thousands of feet above.

As far as she could see were pink and red and gold sandstone spires and chiseled walls and towering cliffs. And a roaring creek tumbling down past them as they climbed. As they rode farther up into the vast, colorful canyon, Mollie was delighted to find many crystal pools and eddies, and she laughed aloud when schools of golden trout flashed in the morning sunshine.

Lew was not as enchanted. His head ached and his nose ran and his eyes watered. And he was chilled, although the canyon temperature was pleasantly warm.

By nightfall, when they'd climbed far up into the

broad canyon and had chosen a wide, flat, scooped-out cradle of sandstone for the night's camp, Lew was a sick man. It was more than a head cold. His chest hurt and he was running a fever. But he said nothing to Mollie about his condition, and he shot her an angry look when she inquired about it.

Mollie suspected that he was really quite sick when he unstrapped his gun belt, dropped it to the ground, and lay down beside the small campfire without mentioning supper. Mollie fell to her knees beside him.

"You're sick," she said gently.

His eyelids drooped as he looked at her. "A little. Be okay tomorrow." His eyes closed.

"Want something to eat?"

His teeth had begun to chatter. "I'm . . . not . . . hungry."

"Then why don't you take your blanket, move in under the rock ledge, and get some rest."

"I . . . will . . . in a . . . minute." In seconds he was sound asleep.

Mollie remained on her knees, looking at him. His gun belt and gun lay six feet from him. His rifle leaned against a rock wall. Both guns were well out of his reach. She felt a great rush of excitement. If ever there was an opportunity to get away from him, it was now.

She looked at the handsome sleeping face, pale beneath his tan, and hardened her heart. This seemingly helpless man was taking her to the authorities, uncaring that she would waste away in some federal prison for the rest of her days.

Mollie slowly rose to her feet.

She turned, picked up Lew's discarded gun belt and strapped it around her hips. Then she went for the rifle, but decided against taking it. She was an excellent shot. The Colt was all she needed.

Hurrying now, anxious to be gone, she rushed to fill her red saddlebags with food. She snatched up the water-filled canteen, grabbed her red-and-blue blanket and rain slicker, and rolled both up in a canvas tarp.

Lew's sick eyes slowly opened. "Going somewhere?"

Mollie stopped short. Then squared her shoulders and continued her preparation, determined she'd not let anything he said, or the sight of him sick and trembling, change her mind.

"Yes, I'm leaving, bounty hunter. Don't try and stop me. If you do, I'll have to shoot you."

"Why don't you wait until morning? It's too dangerous to ride back down the steep trail in darkness."

"You think I'll fall for that?" She looped the reins over her saddled mount's neck and climbed on his back.

"Be careful, Mollie," Lew said, sounding almost as if he meant it.

"Same to you, Hatton."

Mollie rode away into the gathering dusk. Cautiously, carefully she guided the surefooted stallion back down the steep, treacherous trail as an early-rising moon sailed over the canyon's rim to light her way.

Mollie could hardly believe that she was a free woman at last! Her jailer had been left behind, weak and powerless. By the time he was able to ride after her, she'd be long gone. No dank, musty jail cell for her. Not for Mollie Rogers! She would ride all the way back to Mexico if need be. Where she went really didn't matter, so long as it was far, far away from Lew Hatton.

The temperature inside the canyon had quickly

cooled with the falling of night. It was, Mollie realized, downright cold. She reached behind her, unstrapped the heavy sheepskin jacket, and put it on. As she turned the fleecy collar up around her chilled ears, she wondered if Lew would be too weak and sick to get up and put on his jacket. Would he be able to move into the warmth and shelter of the sandstone cave? Or would he lie there in the cold, exposed and freezing?

Mollie firmly shook her head. Who cared? Let the bastard freeze to death!

Horse and rider dropped lower and lower along the narrow serpentine path. They traveled farther and farther from the chilled, sick man lying under the moon and stars. And closer and closer to Mollie's longed-for freedom. The steady, rhythmic sound of the horse's hooves striking the hard sandstone became the only sound as night deepened. Mollie, lulled by the echo, let her head drop forward. She dozed.

The rumble of distant thunder awakened her. She looked straight up, searching for a moon that had gone behind the clouds. A flash of summer lightning streaked across the sky, crashing to its target somewhere back inside the canyon. The first raindrops were huge but sporadic, plopping and hissing against the jutting spires and steep canyon walls.

Within minutes it was a full-fledged summer rainstorm, and Mollie, reining her mount to halt, anxiously unstrapped the heavy tarp from behind the cantle. She drew out her rain slicker, put it on, and wondered if it was raining on Lew. The prospect sent a sharp pain through her heart.

In her mind's eye she saw Lew, sick and feverish, lying there alone, unprotected, unable to move to shelter, the cold rain pounding down on him, saturating his clothes and chilling his fevered skin.

"Dear God, what have I done?" Mollie wailed aloud. And losing no time, she reined the big steed around in a tight semicircle. "Lew, oh Lew," she murmured, and dug her heels into the stallion's sides.

Unconcerned for her own safety, Mollie urged the horse into a swift gallop, anxious to get back to the only man she would ever love. And she *did* love him. She admitted it to herself as the frightening and very real possibility of his death stared her squarely in the face. She had to get back to him. She had to save him! His life meant more than her own. She loved him, had loved him from that first meeting at the Emporium, would love him forever. She could fight it no longer. She loved him and hated herself for so selfishly putting his life in peril.

The rain continued and grew heavier. It came in sheets so blinding that Mollie could scarcely see a foot before her face. But the well-trained horse kept climbing steadily up the wet, slippery trail, his powerful lungs straining with the effort.

Finally, after what seemed an eternity to Mollie, she reached the high canyon camp with its long-dead fire where she'd left the dangerously sick Lew. She bounded out of the saddle, dashed the water from her eyes, and ran to the deathly still figure on the soaked ground. He was lying just as she had left him.

Heart pounding painfully, she fell to her knees beside him, cupped his wet cheeks in her hands and bent to him, pressing her chilled face to his hot, wet one.

"My darling," she said, sobbing now, and fondly, foolishly kissed his closed eyes, his wet mouth, his beard-stubbled jaw, murmuring, "I've come back, Lew. I've come back. I'll save you, I will, I promise, my precious darling."

With reserves of strength she didn't know she possessed, Mollie struggled to get the sick, unconscious man moved in beneath the overhang of rock and into the dry sandstone enclosure. Talking to him the whole time in low, soothing tones, she pushed him up into a sitting position, moved around behind him, locked her arms over his chest, and dragged him through the falling rain to the dry, warm room of rock.

Once inside, she hurriedly went about undressing him. She didn't stop until she had peeled away the sopping-wet clothes right down to his wet, feverish skin. Faced with this life-or-death situation, she did not consider her modesty—or his. She was concerned only with making him warm and safe. When she had quickly but thoroughly dried him off—from the thick, soaked hair of his head down to his cold bare feet—she dashed back out into the rain and pulled down the rolled-up tarp from behind her saddle.

Back inside the dry rock room, Mollie took from the tarp her dry red-and-blue blanket. She spread it on the flat rock floor directly beside Lew, then rolled him over onto it. She managed to get him turned onto his back on the blanket and she pulled the blanket up around him, tucking it in under his shoulders.

Absently patting his chest, she said, "My darling, I'll be right back. I'll make you well, I will."

Again she raced out into the rainstorm, led both horses up under the protective rock ledge at the cave's mouth, quickly unsaddled them, and went back to her patient, unhooking her long rain slicker as she came.

Beneath the slicker, her sheepskin jacket was perfectly dry, as was her shirt. Only her boots and buckskin pants were sopping wet. Mollie shed them where she stood, hunched out of the warm jacket, and went to Lew. She swept the blanket apart and put her jacket on him backward, laboring to get his long arms pulled through the sleeves.

"There," she said, pleased, and her eyes were drawn down his long, lean body to his hair-dusted right leg.

She laid a hand on the network of wide zigzag scars that reached from thigh to shin. Frowning, she let her fingers run the length of the badly scarred leg. Then she anxiously drew the blanket back around him, covering him.

Her journey ended, her tasks completed, Mollie sat there on her heels, out of breath, watching Lew. Despite the heavy jacket and warm blanket, his lean body was still racked with deep, wrenching chills. He didn't respond when she spoke his name. He coughed and choked when she dribbled water from the canteen onto his burning lips.

Mollie put her hand over her mouth to stifle a sob of despair. She too, trembled, but her shaking was from fear. Fear and guilt. She had left him sick and alone and he was going to die because of her!

"No," she sobbed, the denial tearing from her tight throat like the wail of an animal. "No, no."

Shaking almost as violently as Lew, Mollie swept one side of the blanket aside and crawled into it with him, hurriedly drawing it back up over the both of them.

"Please, my love, don't leave me," she whispered, snuggling close, draping an arm across his chest and a knee across his thighs. "Speak to me, darling. Open your eyes, Lew."

Hugging him fiercely, determined to transfer her body heat to him, Mollie lay awake holding him close through the longest night of her life. Caressing him, kissing him, talking quietly to him, she lovingly coaxed him to live.

The rain finally stopped. Daylight was close. Lew, struggling to shake off the last weak chains of unconsciousness, had the sensation of being smothered. Coming slowly out of the fog, he became aware of warm, soft lips covering his own. A mouth, dewy and gentle, was pressing his, over and over again. Kisses. Someone was kissing him. Someone he could not see, could only feel.

Mollie, unaware he was emerging from the fevered coma that enveloped him, was leaning over Lew's face, kissing him when suddenly his eyelids fluttered, lifted, and his questioning blue eyes were staring into hers.

Tears filling her eyes, Mollie said softly, "Oh, thank God. Lew, Lew." And she kissed him again, right on the mouth.

"Where are my pants?" was his raspy reply.

"You won't be needing your pants for a while," Mollie told him, then blushed hotly realizing that her bare legs were entwined with his beneath the blanket, "but perhaps I'd better get back into mine."

36

He couldn't do it.

Lew knew he couldn't take Mollie in. She had come back and he knew that their volatile relationship was forever changed. Even before her return last night he had begun to suffer great twinges of doubt about taking her to Denver. Now he knew he couldn't do it. How could a man take a woman like her to prison? Especially one who had saved his life.

For Mollie, everything had, overnight, become simple. She loved Lew Hatton. And she intended to cherish the short time she had left with him. For her the days would be golden, precious. From morning until night she would be allowed to look on his classic profile, hear his deep, slow voice, touch him as she tenderly nursed him back to health.

Guiltily, she found herself almost wishing that he would remain weak and helpless for a time. It was so sweet and enjoyable to minister to him. To feed him and rub his aching legs and watch over him while he slept.

But in only a few short days, Lew was almost completely well. Still, life remained sweet. Unhurriedly they rode further into the giant canyon, Mollie insisting that they stop at noon, warning Lew he was not to overdo. He should rest all afternoon. Lew agreed and they made camp in a splendid expanse of grassy meadow beside a wide, clear stream. At the meadow's edge, a deep, narrow crevice wound back inside the canyon.

"Be a good place to sleep tonight," Lew observed, exploring the crevice, and Mollie, nodding, helped place their belongings inside the dim, concealed corridor.

After the noon meal, Mollie said, "Now you are to take a nap and no back talk. Savvy?"

He grinned boyishly. "Savvy."

"And toss me your clothes."

"You don't aim to steal them, do you?"

"I aim to wash them."

It was a gloriously beautiful day in the canyon. Clear, bright, with a touch of fall in the thin, dry air. While Lew slept, Mollie, humming happily, washed their clothes and spread them out in the sun to dry. Then she bathed and shampooed her long, tangled hair.

When Lew awakened, his fresh pants and shirt lay beside him. He yawned lazily, dressed, and went in search of Mollie. He found her seated astride a fallen pine tree. She held a long-handled brush in her hand. Her hair, obviously freshly washed, gleamed like spun gold in the brilliant Arizona sunshine. Mollie sensed his presence, turned, and smiled at him, and Lew felt his heart skip a beat.

"Sleep well?" she asked sweetly and drew the brush through her long, clean hair.

Lew didn't answer. Staring helplessly, he came to her, stood close beside her. Softly he asked, "May I?"

"Certainly," she replied and handed him the brush.

Gripping it tightly, Lew threw a long leg over the

fallen tree trunk and straddled it directly behind her. Mesmerized, he brushed her golden hair while she told him of the summer-fat deer she had seen, about a couple of hawks that had winged lazily overhead while she had dried their laundry, and of the wildflowers she had picked in the meadow.

Lew listened, but didn't hear a thing she said. When finally she reached up, caught the brush, turned, and said, "My hair is nicer now, isn't it?"

"Beautiful."

"Yours is shaggy. It needs cutting." She smiled. "May I?"

He shrugged. "Why not?"

Mollie got out her embroidery scissors and ordered Lew to remove his freshly laundered shirt. Then she went right to work on him, snipping away, while Lew, seated astride the tree trunk, held her long-handled mirror up before his bearded face, watching skeptically.

But soon he was smiling. Then laughing. He was totally charmed by Mollie's determination to give him a good haircut. Her incredible violet eyes were narrowed in concentration, and the tip of her tongue was caught between her even white teeth. The scent and sight of her lustrous locks made it hard to worry too much about his own hair.

When Mollie was finished and Lew saw in the mirror that despite her best effort, she had somehow gotten the hair above his left ear much shorter than the right, he pretended dismay.

Scowling darkly, he said, "Mollie, you're the worst barber I've ever had."

At his scolding, her lovely face screwed up into a frown and she said, "I'm so sorry, Lew. I never meant to—"

"Ah, honey, I was teasing you," he said, playfully grabbing her wrist, afraid he had really hurt her feelings. Laughing good-naturedly, he said, "It's a fine haircut. Thank you."

"You're welcome," Mollie said, shaken by his use of an endearment and wondering if he realized that he had called her *honey*.

"Tell you what," he said, still holding her fragile wrist. "My haircut looks so good"—his hand left her wrist, went to his face—"I believe I'll shave."

It was Mollie's turn to laugh. "Want me to do it for you?"

He lithely eased himself up off the log. "I think not."

And they both laughed.

Lew, smoothly shaven, his full strength rapidly returning, caught trout for their supper. They leisurely ate the evening meal as the sun disappeared. Seated across a blazing campfire from each other, they talked companionably as they'd never talked before. Mollie, resolved not to be bothersome, asked Lew no questions, but quietly, willingly answered his, not stopping to wonder why he was asking.

She told Lew about her relationship with Professor Dixon. She revealed how the professor had taken her in and given her a home when she had none, telling everyone that she was his niece. She talked about her days as a young girl in Texas. She told of their leaving Texas after her papa was accused of killing Lew's father, of her mother's death on the trail, of robbing banks and trains and living in leased haciendas in Mexico.

She said truthfully, "I never thought about the robberies being wrong. My papa was the leader of the Renegades. I thought my papa hung the moon, so I figured whatever he did was all right."

Lew found her admission touching. It was just as Cherry had told him. Mollie had adored her father and had blindly approved of anything he did.

Lew, puffing on a fresh cigar, said, "I understand. I felt much the same way about my father."

And then he began to talk. He told Mollie of his big New Mexico *rancho*. Of his brother, Dan Nighthorse. Of the two of them living among the Apaches. Of going off to war.

Forgetting herself, Mollie asked, "That where you were badly wounded?" Lew lifted his eyes to meet hers. "I . . . ah . . . I mean . . . well, when you were so sick I saw the scars on your leg and I assumed that you were hurt in the war."

Yes, he told her, he was wounded in the war, but it wasn't nearly as bad as it looked. He quickly changed the subject. They continued to talk easily, leaving some things unsaid, some questions unasked, as a big harvest moon rose high above them and the dry night air cooled.

At last Mollie rose, stretched, and said, "I think I'll go to bed."

Lew nodded, stayed where he was. She stood unmoving, looking at him from across the fire. Their eyes met and held. She smiled and slowly circled the campfire. She stopped beside him, reached out, and laid her soft fingertips on his smoothly shaven cheek. Her touch sent a quick rush of feeling through him.

Looking straight into his eyes, Mollie said, "If it matters, I've not been the Kid's, nor any man's."

She turned and walked away.

Lew's riveted gaze followed her as she unhurriedly walked across the moonlit meadow and disappeared in the darkness of the towering canyon walls. Slowly, he turned back to gaze into the fire. For a long, silent time he stared at the dying flames, his thoughts on the desirable, golden-haired woman who had just announced that she had been no man's.

He couldn't deny the rush of joy her unexpected declaration had caused. Foolish though it might be, he believed her. And hard as he tried to convince himself that it made no difference to him, it did. He felt almost lighthearted knowing that the vile animal who had raped Teresa Castillo had never laid a hand on the beautiful Mollie Rogers.

His lips curving into a smile, he recalled Cherry's saying that she was certain Mollie had never known a man. That Mollie had allowed him to believe the opposite in order to hurt him. And it had hurt. He realized that now. If it hadn't, then why was he so relieved?

Lew's mood was confusing to him. He was buoyant, yet pensive. Impulsive, but reflective. But he decided, right then and there, to begin treating Mollie differently. He would show her some respect. He had always desired her, and now he wanted her more than ever. But he would protect her, even from himself. He would go inside that dark canyon crevice where she slept, lie down close beside her, and watch over her through the night.

If she were untouched, then it was her right and her decision to choose the lucky man who would be her first lover. Maybe he would take her home to Santa Fe instead of Denver. Take care of her. See to it that she once more lived as the polished young lady he had met in Maya. He would buy her pretty dresses and send her on the grand tour of Europe and perhaps have a hand in picking suitable beaus.

Lew slowly rose to his feet.

He told himself that he would be an older brother to Mollie, just as he had been to Dan Nighthorse. He would look out for her, take up for her, pick up where the professor had left off.

With those noble intentions firmly in mind, Lew yawned and unhurriedly headed to the canyon crevice. His heart stopped beating when, reaching the chosen spot inside where they were to spend the night, he found little sister was missing.

Lew rushed back outside, stopped, looked frantically around. He spotted something in the distance, in the moonlight, beside a bend in the rushing mountain stream. He crossed the grassy meadow in long quick strides, the sound of the roaring waters competing with the violent beating of his heart.

Then he saw her.

Mollie lay stretched out atop her carefully spread red-and-blue Indian blanket. His blanket, the brown one, was spread over her, covering her.

Reaching her, he said nothing. For a long, tense moment he stood above, looking down at her, his knees weak, his feelings of brotherly protectiveness rapidly vanishing.

When he could speak, he smiled at her, crouched down on his heels beside her, and gently teased, "You have my blanket."

Mollie sighed softly, moved her arms out from under the stiff brown blanket, raised them up over her head in a powerfully provocative gesture, and smiled back at him.

"If it belongs to you," she said, "why don't you take it?"

"Mollie," he murmured as his shaking hand went to the blanket's top edge. His smoldering blue eyes holding hers, he slowly peeled the brown blanket down her slender body until it rested well below her bare feet. A slow grin came to his lips when he saw the saucy red garter just above her left knee. The grin quickly faded and he anxiously inhaled.

The garter was all Mollie wore.

37

Lew stayed there crouched on his heels, not touching Mollie, shamelessly admiring the pale feminine beauty stretched out before him. The bright moonlight made her flawless skin appear to be the color and texture of fine cultured pearls. Her bare, slender body was as unblemished as her exquisitely lovely face.

She was as near to perfect as any woman God had ever created. Her throat was long and swanlike, her shoulders delicate. Her breasts, even as she lay flat, rose seductively in twin peaks of loveliness, the soft firm mounds of luminous flesh tipped with large satiny nipples that tempted him to taste.

Her stomach, so flat it was almost concave, was visibly trembling, and he vowed silently to kiss that flat, warm belly until it trembled no more. Between her pale thighs, an alluring triangle of thick golden curls shone silvery in the moonlight. A gentle canyon breeze lightly ruffled those pale angel curls and sent a shiver of ecstasy up his spine.

If Lew delighted in brazenly examining the lovely naked Mollie, Mollie just as brashly enjoyed his admiration. Feeling the heat and the pressure of his hot eyes keenly inspecting her, she stretched and sighed and knew she was pleasing him. His smoldering gaze lingered on her swelling breasts, her trembling stomach, her tensed thighs.

So intense was his heated gaze, it was as though his hands were on her, caressing, stroking, adoring. Mollie felt the blood scalding through her veins, and she marveled that such incredible heat could be generated between a man and a woman who were not even touching. Ignorant to the ways of love, Mollie was quickly learning that there was much more to lovemaking than she had suspected. They were making love now. Doing wonderfully exciting things to each other.

This wanton exhibition of her nude body and Lew's lusty examination of it was, she happily realized, a form of lovemaking, one she found fantastically exciting. So much so she hoped that Lew wouldn't touch her for a long time, but would continue to caress her with his burning blue eyes.

But only if that's what he wanted too. Like a naive, naked nymphet, Mollie lay there like a willing sacrifice before her great God of Love. She relied totally on his wisdom and skill to guide her and teach her. Trusting him completely, she was certain that he would be the patient, yet fiery, lover of her girlish dreams.

And he was.

Entrusted with the offered gift of her beautiful untouched body as well as her equally innocent heart, Lew manfully fought the blinding desire that was testing his willpower to the limit. The hot blood was beating in his ears, and every muscle in his body was tensed and coiled. His already painfully aroused body was demanding that he behave the hungered animal. The blood-filled erection straining against his tight trousers ordered him to strip off his clothes and hurriedly bury himself deep within the soft, warm waiting flesh that would afford immediate release.

That he didn't do so was Lew's first unspoken admission that this beautiful naked girl meant more to him than a hot receptive body on a cool moonlit night. The fact that her pleasure meant more to him than his own startled and frightened Lew. While he'd always tried to be a caring lover—even with the most jaded of females—he had never before so wanted to please a woman.

Lew trembled.

He felt like a young, inexperienced boy, terrified of making a mistake. Of not measuring up. Of handling the seduction all wrong. Of bumbling it so badly Mollie would end up in tears, her expectations of beautiful lovemaking forever spoiled.

His eyes still locked on her, Lew unbuttoned his shirt, reached up behind his head, peeled it off, and dropped it to the grass. He went down on one knee and laid a warm, gentle hand on Mollie's thigh. He stuck two fingers underneath the flirtatious red garter, leaned over and bent his head to her bare trembling belly.

He pressed a kiss to the pale quivering flesh, laid his burning cheek against the silky skin, and murmured, "Mollie, are you sure you want this?"

Mollie's hands came to his dark head. Her nervous fingers entwining in his thick raven hair, she looked straight up at the man in the moon and said honestly, "It's what I have wanted from the first day you walked into the Maya Emporium." She lowered her gaze to his bent head and whispered, "Make love to me, Lew. Please."

Lew kissed a delicate hipbone, then lifted his head.

"Ah, sweetheart," he said and lithely stretched out beside her, resting his weight on an elbow. His face just above hers, he looked into her shining eyes and told her, "I don't want to hurt you, Mollie." His fingertips touched her feverish cheek. He brushed his lips to hers. "We'll go slowly, I promise you."

"I'm not afraid," she said and her hand went to his bare chest.

Then the kisses began. Slow, languid kisses of exploration. Mouths nibbling and nuzzling. Lips playing and plucking. Lew teased Mollie with long but undemanding caresses, carefully fanning the fires within her, skillfully guiding her along the lovely path toward total ecstasy.

Her lips combined with his, Mollie suddenly shifted. She turned to lie on her side facing Lew. Like him, she supported her weight on an elbow. Lips to lips, tongue to tongue, they lay there facing each other in the moonlight, kissing and kissing, each kiss growing hotter, longer, deeper.

Lew's arms went around Mollie. He pulled her to him, rolled over onto his back and settled her atop him, his lips never leaving hers. When finally Mollie breathlessly raised her head, her bare legs were tangled with his trousered ones and her breasts were resting on his bare chest. His hands swept slowly over her tingling body, the long, tapered fingers spreading fire in their path.

Lew lifted his head to kiss her again, but Mollie stopped him, saying, "Please, please." She laid her cheek to his. "Just hold me for a minute."

"Sure, baby, sure," he murmured, allowing her to lie

there on him while she struggled to accustom herself to the new sensations washing over her.

Innately sensual, she squirmed sweetly atop him, erotically rubbing her taut nipples against his naked chest while she began brushing eager kisses to his throat, his jaw, his temples. Lew moved his hands from her waist, placed them unthreateningly on her flaring hips. Leaving them there for a minute, he slid his spread fingers up over the swell of her bottom and, after again pausing, down to cup the firm twin cheeks. Gripping her gently, he urged her closer to him and at the same time he flexed his buttocks and thrust his pelvis up and forward. Her unclothed groin met his clothed one, and he heard her sharp intake of breath. With a minimum of effort he managed to get her long, slender legs outside his, and then it was Mollie who obligingly shifted, drawing her knees up so that she was seated astride him, her pale thighs and the heat between now fully open to him.

Cautiously Mollie lifted her head to look at Lew.

"Kiss me, sweetheart," he softly commanded and she quickly bent to him.

It was a long, deep kiss of unrestrained passion and when finally their lips separated, Mollie, with only the slightest guidance from Lew's hands on her bare buttocks, began the age-old movements of lovemaking. Burning hot for this marvelous man, she unconsciously began grinding her hips, pressing her fevered body down on his in rhythmic, circular motions that made Lew groan with raging desire.

He allowed her to continue experimenting, watching the changing emotions march across her beautiful face, permitting her to become fully aware of exactly what she was doing to him. Wantonly, wildly, Mollie pressed her throbbing flesh to that awesome hardness restrained by the fabric of his tight pants. Soon she made small, pleading sounds low in her throat.

Lew agilely rolled up into a sitting position and kissed her, thrusting his tongue deep into her mouth. Finally, he tore his lips from hers, put his hands under her arms, and lifted her up so that she was kneeling astride him. He bent his dark head and his heated lips went to her breast. Mollie gasped, then moaned when she felt the hard, aching crest warmly enclosed in his loving mouth. Lew wrapped his long arms around her and sucked on her breast while Mollie threw back her head and panted, gripping his wide shoulders with sharp-nailed fingers.

They stayed that way for a long, lovely time. Then, giving her left nipple one last loving lick, Lew shifted and began kissing her right breast. And as he closed his eyes and sucked on her breast, he moved his hand around between their bodies, slipping it quickly between her parted legs. While his teeth gently nipped at her hard wet nipple, his gentle, practiced fingers sought the ultrasensitive nubbin of flesh protected by the downy silvered curls between her spread thighs. With fore and middle fingertips he touched her, and Mollie quivered and whimpered and gripped his bare shoulders more tightly, her nails cutting into his flesh.

Lew's fingers were instantly wet with the silky fire of passion flowing freely from her and he knew there was no need to wait any longer. Still, he did. For a sweet, highly pleasurable time for them both, he continued to kiss Mollie's pinkened breasts while he tenderly touched and toyed with her, circling, caressing, giving her a glimpse of joy to come.

Touching her this way—and having her respond like

this—Lew felt as though his heart would explode with happiness, his body with longing. The delightful thought skipped through his mind that his adorable Mollie was going to be as much of an adventuress at lovemaking as she was at everything else.

She was indeed untouched, but there was nothing of the reluctant, fearful virgin about her. She was as hot as he. If his stroking fingers were brazen upon her, she was just as brazen in her response. She pressed eagerly against his stroking fingers, giving herself to him, offering him all that she had, insistent on taking all the joy he could provide.

Mollie knelt there in the high desert moonlight glorying in the wonder of full-blown passion. Never in her wildest dreams had she imagined anything half this wicked and wonderful. No wonder women constantly whispered and gossiped about marriage and making love! She wondered, as she felt Lew's moving fingers set her on fire, how she had waited this long to experience such incredible pleasure.

Mollie's nervous hands went to Lew's dark moving head and she sighed and smiled and moaned and willingly surrendered to blazing desire. She loved the feel of Lew's warm, wet mouth on her breasts, sucking, biting, licking. And even more wonderful was the touch of his fingers stroking her there between her legs where she was so unbelievably hot. She loved it that he was so intimately caressing the slick, burning flesh that had never been exposed to anyone before.

Mollie felt the flames blaze out of control when Lew took his mouth from her breast, lifted his head and looked directly into her eyes while he continued to stroke her.

His sultry gaze holding hers, he caressed and coaxed and cupped her, murmuring, "Tell me if it feels good, baby."

"Oh, it does, it does," she said breathlessly, her eyes closing.

"Look at me, sweetheart. Let me see the ecstasy in your eyes."

Mollie breathlessly obeyed. She looked directly into his eyes, but soon became so hot and restless, she started tossing her head and murmuring, "Lew . . . Lew . . . I . . . I . . ."

"I know, baby, I know," he said, and took his hand from her and gently laid her down on the blanket. He leaned over her, kissed her mouth, and said, "I want to love you, Mollie. Really love you."

"Yes, oh yes," she whispered, ready and eager.

Lew rose to his feet and swiftly undressed. Naked, he continued to stand there above Mollie in the day-bright moonlight, allowing her to get a good look at his fully aroused male body. She didn't disappoint. She stared up at him, her wide eyes riveted to his horizontal-thrusting tumescence. He caught his breath when she abruptly rolled up to sitting position, rose to her knees, and unabashedly reached for him.

"God, honey," gasped Lew and, before she could touch him, sank to his knees before her.

"But you touched me," she said, her fingers poised above the rigid masculine flesh. "Now I want to touch you. Let me?"

"Y-yes . . . all right," he managed, his voice husky, and he took her hand and guided it to him, shuddering when her fingertips brushed him.

Her wide eyes locked on him, Mollie wrapped her

fingers around his awesome erection and made a little gasp of shocked delight when it involuntarily jerked in her grasp. Having no idea just how much she was affecting Lew, she examined him curiously, amazed by the heat and power she held in her hand.

Determined to indulge her every charming whim, Lew knelt there in the bright moonlight, trembling, while the marveling Mollie caressed him with soft, small hands. Gritting his teeth, he submitted, hoping against hope that he could continue to hold himself in check until she tired of this sweet torture. At last Mollie's eyes lifted to meet his and her hand left his genitals.

She raised her arms up around his neck and said, "I love you, Lew Hatton. I love you and I want to do everything with you that a woman can do with the man she loves."

Then she leaned to him and kissed him as she had never kissed him before. When that long kiss ended, they were no longer kneeling. They were lying on the blanket, their heated, naked bodies pressing close together. And when Lew, sprinkling a few quick kisses over her throat and shoulders and breasts, moved between her legs, Mollie realized that she couldn't wait one second longer to have him inside her.

"Darling . . . please," she whispered.

"Yes, sweetheart," he crooned.

And then, looking into her beautiful violet eyes, he took her with a swift, sure thrust of his hard male flesh. Mollie cried out in startled pain.

"Ah, sweet baby," Lew murmured comfortingly and lay completely still within her, kissing her, soothing her, patiently waiting until the pain subsided and pleasure began to take its place.

Then he slowly, expertly loved her. And as he did so, he murmured sweet words of love that Mollie knew she would remember for as long as she lived. Making love with this magnificent man was all and more than she could have hoped for, dreamed of, imagined. So wonderful was this physical joining of their bare heated bodies, Mollie was certain that this was all there was to lovemaking.

Until her orgasm began.

"Lew?" Mollie's eyes widened in surprise, "I . . . I. . . ."

"Yes, sweetheart, it's all right. All right. Let it come, baby. I've got you. I love you, Mollie. I love you."

Mollie felt as if her body were no longer her own. She had no command or control over it. It writhed and bucked against her lover, her pelvis surging up in a frightening, wonderful, intimate dance of joy. And as she bucked wildly against him, Mollie cried out in fear and wonder as her rapidly escalating ecstasy became a fierce explosion of rapture.

Lew, watching Mollie's beautiful face contort with her buffeting orgasm, waited until he was sure she had gotten it all out. Then he sought his own release. Changing his pace, plunging deeply, he let go. Pumping and pouring the hot liquid into her, he finally groaned with deep satisfaction. Totally sated, he tiredly collapsed atop her.

Mollie, not sure of exactly what had happened to him, asked fearfully, "Lew, are you all right?"

Too exhausted and happy to move, he said, "Baby, I've never been *more* all right in my life." His dark head then shot up and he looked at her worriedly. "Jesus, are you? Did I hurt you, Mollie?"

Tears stinging her eyes, Mollie smiled and pushed

back a damp lock of hair from his forehead. Too emotional to speak, she shook her head no and possessively clasped him back to her breasts thinking how much it was going to hurt her when they reached Denver and he left her.

More, so much more, now that she knew about ecstasy.

38

Mollie closed her eyes, hugged Lew fiercely, and pushed aside troublesome thoughts of the future. There was no future. There was only now. This minute. This hour of happiness and fulfillment and she was going to enjoy and savor it. Inhaling deeply, she stroked Lew's long, smooth back and smiled dreamily when he nuzzled the curve of her neck and shoulder.

"I think," he said, rolling over, bringing her with him, "we'd better go into the canyon where it's warmer." He raised his hands to capture the long, silvery hair the winds were tossing about Mollie's face.

"But it's so magical here," she protested, reluctant to leave their moonlit bed of bliss.

"So it is," he said, his lips curved in a half smile. "But we'll make it magical inside as well. I'll build a fire. We'll heat some water and clean up a little."

Mollie said teasingly, "No more baths in icy streams?"

Lew turned his head to the side, playfully bit her shoulder, and said with mock gruffness, "Woman, don't make fun of your man."

Mollie laughed with delight. She liked the sound of

that. She *was* his woman. And he was her man. At least for now. She said softly, earnestly, "I am your woman, Lew. Teach me how to please you. I'll do anything for you. With you."

Lew sighed with satisfaction. "Sweetheart, you do please me. Can't you tell?"

"I'm so new in the ways of love. I want to learn all there is to learn, to do all the things with you that . . . that your other women have done. Will you show me?"

Charmed by her frank approach to all aspects of life, Lew laughed and gave her bare bottom a possessive slap. "Consider it done, baby."

The wind continued to rise, whipping through the canyon, chilling them both. With Mollie in his arms and their blankets and clothes in her arms, Lew crossed the wide meadow while Mollie's long blond hair blew into his face, occasionally blinding him. Both were laughing. Both were freezing. Both were happy. After several near-falls, Lew stumbled into the pitch black canyon crevice with his giggling burden intact.

Inside he stopped, kissed Mollie, and laughed because a strand of her hair had caught between their lips. Both sputtered and spit and tried the kiss again, this time with complete success.

Then slowly Lew lowered Mollie to her feet and said, "Stay right where you are, sweetheart."

He fished inside the pocket of his discarded pants and found some matches. He struck one on the boulder beside his head and held it high. Its tiny flame illuminating a small portion of the narrow canyon, he led Mollie around the many twists and turns of jutting rock where the moonlight never reached.

In seconds they stepped into the wider area where

they would sleep. Short minutes later Lew had a fire going, its orange glow the only light in the inky blackness enveloping the canyon.

Soon, Mollie, standing naked before the fire, felt her face flush and blamed it on her closeness to the flames. But it wasn't really the fire. Lew was kneeling directly before her, repeatedly dipping a cloth into heated water and carefully, gently bathing her. He left no part of her untouched, from her crimson face to her curling toes. When he had cleansed her completely, he solicitously wrapped a blanket around her bare shoulders and sat her down by the fire.

Then Mollie watched, transfixed, while Lew unselfconsciously washed himself. She never took her eyes off him. His lean, naked body, licked by the flickering firelight, was powerfully beautiful to the woman who loved him. The play of muscles in his back and shoulders. The sheen of moisture on his dark chest and arms. The firmness of his tight, smooth buttocks and tempered steel of his hard thighs. The profusion of dense raven hair around that most male part of his splendid anatomy. Every inch of him was masculine perfection, and Mollie was almost sorry when his sponge bath ended and he tossed the damp cloth aside.

Turning, he asked, "Hungry, baby?"

"No."

"Thirsty?"

"No."

"Sleepy?"

"A little."

"Me, too." He grinned and came to her as Mollie rose and looked around. Puzzled, he said, "Lose something?"

She nodded and started past him. "My clothes. I folded them and left . . ."

"Sweetheart," he caught her arm, drew her to him, "You won't be sleeping in your clothes this night."

"I won't?"

Shaking his head, he pushed the blanket from her shoulders, allowed it to drop to the canyon floor. "Ever sleep naked?"

"Never."

"It's very comfortable."

Mollie smiled and put her arms around his neck. "Then naked it is."

They quickly stretched out in the firelight, Lew on his back with a long arm around Mollie. She snuggled against him, sighing, stretching, listening to his deep, sure voice as he—at her request—spun ghost stories. Mollie loved it. She loved lying naked in the darkness with her fearless lover while he made up spooky tales to scare her so that she'd cling tightly to him.

The last thing Mollie remembered was pressing close against Lew's hard, warm body and his being halfway through a scary story about a half man, half beast. A huge, frightening predator who hunted those who had lost a personal item which he in turn had found. With something of his victim's in hand, the monster ruthlessly stalked his unsuspecting prey and . . .

Mollie was fast asleep.

"Mollie?" Lew's voice was a low, soft whisper. "Honey?" No answer.

He smiled, kissed her temple and sighed. He considered getting up to put more wood on the fire. Then yawned and decided against it. He didn't want to disturb the slumbering Mollie. He would keep her warm.

He pulled the blanket up around her shoulders and drew her closer. Soon he, too, was fast asleep.

The fire had gone out. It was totally black in the canyon when Mollie awakened, panicky from a terrifying nightmare. A horrible dream in which a big half man, half beast was bearing down on them. The huge being was bearded, ugly, grotesque. He held in his hand something that belonged to them, but she couldn't make out what it was.

Chilled and trembling, Mollie realized that Lew's protective arms were no longer around her. His back was to her. He had turned in his sleep as though he no longer wanted her close. She felt alone and afraid. It was too dark in the canyon. Dark and cold and claustrophobic. Too cut off from the world.

In the distance a night bird made a strange, unearthly sound and Mollie shuddered.

Overwhelmed with a feeling of uneasiness, she felt as though the cliffs of the narrow canyon were beginning to lean. She felt as if they were going to fall in and swallow her up. The night silence was deafening, and Mollie longed for the daylight, still hours away.

The nightmare continued to nag and Mollie, seeing the huge hairy being whether her eyes were open or closed, tried desperately to make out what it was he carried. It was something that glittered and shone brightly and . . . and . . .

"No!" Mollie screamed and bolted upright.

"Sweetheart?" Lew came instantly awake. "What is it?"

Mollie couldn't see Lew in the thick darkness, could only feel his hand on her arm. She sobbed, "I'm afraid!

I had a dream and . . . and . . ." She stopped, shook her head.

"And what, baby?" he urged, drawing her into his embrace, gently rocking her.

"I . . . I don't remember."

"That's good, then. It's already forgotten, the way bad dreams ought to be."

"Yes," she murmured, wishing that it really was forgotten. Wondering why she dreamed of the Kid. Hoping it had no meaning.

"It's my fault," Lew said, turning her so that she was draped across his lap and leaning back in his arms. "It was stupid of me to tell all those spooky stories. I'm sorry."

Mollie pressed her cheek to his warm solid chest. "You don't believe dreams come true, do you, Lew?"

"Only good ones," he said. "Sometimes they come true."

"Have you ever had one come true?"

"Yes, I have. I dreamed that a beautiful, golden-haired, gloriously naked girl was alone with me in a dark canyon."

Mollie lifted her head, saw his eyes flashing in the darkness. "And what did you do? You and this naked girl?"

"We made love until the sun came up."

Lew kissed Mollie until she became warm and pliant in his arms, then he made slow, sweet love to her.

The nightmare was forgotten.

When the first faint glimmer of light made its tenacious way down into the narrow passages and rocky overhangs of Oak Creek Canyon, an indulgent Lew and an inquisitive Mollie were still making love.

Lew now lay stretched out on his stomach with his cheek resting on his folded arms. Mollie was astride his hips, her hands clutching his ribs. She was bending to him, pressing kisses to his long, smooth, deeply clefted back. The reason? He had done so to her earlier. He'd had her lie on her stomach and he'd straddled her and kissed her bare, tingling backside for a long, lovely time, giving the butterfly birthmark an inordinate amount of attention, before turning her over and making love to her.

It had been incredibly pleasurable for Mollie, so after they had rested and talked and dozed, she asked Lew if she could do to him what he had done to her. His answer was a kiss and a quick turn onto his stomach.

So she sat astride him now, kissing him just as he had kissed her. She trailed wet, warm caresses over his shoulder blades, down his arms, across his waist. And just as she had when he did this to her, Lew sighed and squirmed and tensed.

Still, Mollie was at a loss when, asking that she rise to her knees for a second, Lew turned over to lie on his back.

Mollie's eyes immediately went to his rigid masculinity and she heard him say, "Well, aren't you going to do to me what I did to you?"

Her eyes sought his. "But that was different. You could put . . . I can't do the same . . . we'll have to change places." She started to slide off him.

He stopped her, his hands swiftly gripping her narrow waist. "No, sweetheart, we don't. You can make love to me like this."

"I can?" She looked doubtful.

"You will," he told her. "Raise up on your knees again, honey." Still skeptical, Mollie obeyed. Lew took her hand, placed it on his pulsing erection, and with his long, brown fingers covering hers, helped her guide his hard flesh up into her waiting warmth. Mollie, violet eyes wide, held her breath as cautiously, inch by careful inch, she slowly impaled herself on the hard, throbbing heat of him.

"Lewwww," she gasped, awed, excited.

She was afraid to move, afraid she would hurt him, afraid she would hurt herself. But not for long. Soon passion and Lew led her and Mollie began to accommodate Lew's slow driving thrusts with lazy rolls of her hips, gyrating, squeezing, loving him. Reality slipped away, and Mollie eagerly rode her lover in the dawn light, the motion of her hips increasing their rhythm, her bare breasts swaying with her movements. Her wild, untamed hair falling into her face, she tossed her head and clung to Lew's ribs as she looked steadily into his eyes and loved him good.

Lew put his hands under her arms and urged her down to him. He lifted his head and captured a hard-tipped nipple with his mouth. He sucked vigorously while Mollie continued to grind and roll and buck against him in an increasingly frantic climb toward orgasmic ecstasy. When he had kissed and licked both breasts until they were pinkened and tender from his caresses, Mollie pulled away and sat back up. She arched her throat, let her head fall back and—so inflamed she thought she would explode—felt the first violent contractions beginning.

"Lew . . . Lew . . . it . . . it's happening," she said excitedly, as once again the brand-new, frightening, fabulous sensations of searing sexual climax claimed her.

Lew stayed with her, pumping into her, gripping and guiding her hips, until both were caught up in that magical moment of carnal euphoria. Mollie screamed out her wrenching release. Lew groaned his. And when it was passed, Mollie collapsed on him as tiny tremors still jolted through her body and her heart beat double time.

Her flushed cheek rested on Lew's heaving chest and his body was still a part of hers when he said, "Any doubts left about that particular position for making love?"

Mollie sighed blissfully. "None. It's my absolute favorite."

Lew chuckled. "Sweetheart, you can't say that until you've tried them all."

"You mean there's more?"

"Many more. We've only just begun."

Happily Mollie smiled, kissed Lew's damp chest, and said, "Just let me catch my breath."

39

◇

  Saddle leather squeaked and horses' hooves kicked up dust as the riders began their long climb into Oak Creek Canyon.

In the lead, a big, bearded man glanced irritably up at the leaden sky and cursed. The air was heavy with rain and clouds blotted out the sun, making the crimson cliffs look dark and slippery. Thunder rumbled and lightning streaked across the heavens.

Shortly, great sheets of water cascaded down from an angry sky as the sudden summer storm unleashed its full fury. The drenched riders complained bitterly, protesting that to ride on in the blinding rain was foolish and unnecessary.

Their bearded leader pulled up on his mount, turned in the saddle, and drew an ivory-handled revolver, aiming it at the man nearest him.

"You want to die, *amigo?*" said the Texas Kid.

"No, *jefe.*"

"Then you, Cuchillo," the Kid waved the revolver, "and the rest of you had better stop your bellyaching. We are riding on, rain or no rain. Any man who's opposed can damn well stay right here." He grinned then, his teeth white against his wet, dark beard. "Forever."

They rode on and no one dared complain, despite the lashing rains that made traversing the narrow, winding canyon trail extremely dangerous.

The heavy rains continued throughout the morning, washing silt over the canyon's steep sides, sending rivers of water coursing down the treacherous path, and filling streams to overflowing.

And, up in a lush, green meadow, uncovering a gold cross and chain.

The cloudburst didn't bother Lew and Mollie. They played in the rain like a couple of kids, laughing and squealing, unconcerned about getting their clothes wet because they wore no clothes.

After the leisurely dawn loving, Lew had asked Mollie if she would like him to show her a very special place farther back inside the canyon. A place where the entrance was so narrow a horse could not pass through.

"Should I get dressed?" she asked.

"You won't need clothes where we're going."

Curious, Mollie clung to his hand while Lew led her deeper into the canyon crevice. The walls grew closer and taller. The two of them soon had to move single file, so tight was the trail. And even then they had to duck and turn to the side and climb over fallen rock and squeeze through tight places. At last Lew stopped and Mollie blinked when thick steam rose up to envelop them.

Lew, carefully pulling her around in front of him, asked, "Can you see it?"

Mollie squinted.

Through the rolling mists she saw that the canyon had widened dramatically and that they stood at the edge of a huge rocky room whose floor was a calm, clear pool. There was no path around it. The red cliffs on all sides were so tall and steep it would be impossible to edge along their faces.

"This is absolutely beautiful," Mollie said, amazed, "and so concealed. How did you know it was here?"

"Dan Nighthorse and Clint Sellers and I used to swim here when we lived among the Apaches." Lew pointed to the pool's center. "How deep do you suppose it is?"

Mollie could see the bottom. Every tumbled boulder was visible. "Mmm, two, three feet."

Lew chuckled. "Twenty."

"You're teasing me."

"No. I'll show you."

With that he stepped around her and dove into the water. His gracefully arched body parted the surface of the limpid pool and went beneath. Mollie leaned forward and watched him swim about under water. She could see him so clearly he appeared to be under glass. Lew flipped onto his back, remaining submerged, opened his eyes and looked up at her. He picked up a rock and lifted it to show her that he was on the bottom.

When he dropped the pebble and made beckoning gestures with his hands, Mollie laughed. Then she took a deep breath and dove into the cold, clear pool, keeping her eyes wide open. She reached out to Lew. He took her hand and pulled her down to him. It was a strange sensation. She sat on Lew's lap twenty feet under water and could see the tall sides of the canyon above, the changing sky, the first drops of rain peppering the smooth surface over their heads.

She turned to look at Lew. He smiled and tapped his

lips with a forefinger, inviting her to kiss him. Mollie gripped his dark hair, leaned to him, and pressed her lips to his. But foolishly forgetting, both opened their mouths to deepen the kiss, and water poured in.

They shot to the surface, sputtering and coughing. Then, treading water, they tried the kiss again, this time achieving their goal. They kissed anxiously, their wet lips combined in a quickly heating kiss. The heavy rains began as they kissed there in the pool. When the prolonged kiss ended, they broke apart, turned their faces up to the sky, and laughed.

They stayed in the water and played in the pounding downpour as the sky darkened ominously and thunder rumbled through the canyon. They'd momentarily lose each other in the thick swirling mists and blinding rain, then find one another and kiss and hug as though they'd actually been lost. It was during one of those pleasurable reunions that Lew noticed Mollie's bottom lip was trembling.

"Ah, baby, you're freezing," he murmured, pressing her to him. "Let's go."

Back at camp they chose a nice, dry place beneath a jutting overhang and Mollie lazily stretched out while Lew built a fire. When the flames were shooting high and generating welcome heat, he came to Mollie and stood there above her, his intense blue gaze sliding slowly over her naked body.

Smiling finally, he said, "I believe you have something of mine."

Puzzled, Mollie glanced at the blanket beneath her. It was her own red-and-blue one. "What?"

In a low-timbred voice, Lew said, "My heart."

For a long, uncertain minute Mollie stared at him.

Afraid he was teasing her, she asked cautiously, "You mean it?"

Lew fell to his knees, stretched out beside her, took her hand, and placed it over his heart. "I do mean it, sweetheart. My heart belongs to you. I love you, Mollie. I love you."

Mollie's violet eyes widened as her own heart raced with wild happiness. But she said, "That is impossible. You can't really love me, Lew. You know of my past, and I—"

"Everyone has a past; we're planning our future." He leaned down and brushed a kiss to her parted lips. When he lifted his head, his steady gaze held hers. "Our future is together in New Mexico. Marry me, Mollie. Be my first and last wife."

"Your wife?" she repeated, dumbstruck.

"Yes. Just as soon as we reach Santa Fe. That is, if you'll have me."

"Oh, Lew!" She wrapped her arms around his neck and drew him down to her. "Yes, yes, yes," she declared while tears of happiness filled her eyes. "I want to marry you! There's nothing I want more than to be your wife."

"You mean it?" he teased.

"You know I do."

"Then kiss me and promise me you'll be content to spend the rest of your days with me."

Mollie gave him the kiss and the promise. Then, contented and tired from their long night of loving, they lay sheltered from the driving rains, talking quietly of their bright future together and speaking frankly about their pasts.

Mollie told him, finally, that her papa was dead and that was the reason she had come to live with Professor Dixon, an old friend of both her parents.

Listening, Lew said, "I felt awful about taking you away from the professor. He's a good man and he must be worried sick."

Mollie smiled mischievously. "I doubt it. I left him a letter telling him that we had eloped to New Mexico."

Lew grinned. "I'm marrying a fortune-teller."

"No, silly, I . . . I . . ."

Mollie stopped speaking. At the mention of a fortune-teller, her visit to the turbaned prophet on Maya's carnival night came flooding back. *"I see two weddings,"* the crystal gazer had said, *"two weddings, two men."* Mollie's eyes clouded and Lew felt a shiver rush through her slender body.

"Sweetheart, what is it?" he asked.

"Nothing. Nothing. Really," Mollie lied and buried her face in Lew's shoulder, closing her eyes tightly.

A cold sense of foreboding swept over her.

The Kid was alive. She knew he was. But she didn't dare let Lew know. He believed that the Kid was dead, and she would never tell him differently. She loved Lew with all her heart and couldn't bear the thought of losing him. She pressed closer to Lew, feeling safe in his strong arms. Maybe the Kid *was* dead. Maybe she had killed him.

Snuggling close, she said, "Tell me about Teresa."

Lew's voice was low and calm as he spoke of the Spanish girl he had once loved. He told Mollie everything and when he finally fell silent, Mollie, fighting her jealousy, said gently, "I am so sorry. I know that no one can ever take Teresa's place, but I will try to make you happy."

"Listen to me, sweetheart," Lew captured her chin in his hand, turned her face up to his, "I have never been as happy as I am here and now with you. The past is dead, mine and yours, and there's no room in my heart for anyone but you. I love you, Mollie, more than I've ever loved anyone." All his love in his eyes, he kissed her with exquisite tenderness.

Mollie sighed, lay back down on his chest, and hugged him tightly as he mused aloud. "Your father's dead. The Kid is dead. All the others have been brought in. It's finally over." His arms tightened around her. "I have the last of the Rogers Renegades right here in my arms."

"Yes, you do," Mollie was quick to agree and her thoughts turned dreamily to the wonder of how perfectly her body fit against his. "What do you plan to do with the last of the breed?" She blew gently on the crisp black hair of his chest and felt that sweet ache inside beginning anew.

"I plan to take you prisoner. Jail you forever in my house and in my heart," Lew said and yawned.

"I see. How will you go about keeping the prisoner in line?" Mollie asked with a smile in her voice.

"I could always get out the handcuffs again and cuff you to me."

Laughing softly, Mollie lifted her head. "I've a much better idea of how you can bind me to you." Her eyes twinkled with naughty mischief.

"Woman," he said, grinning, "you are becoming a wanton." Quickly he changed their positions and Mollie, giggling, found herself flat on her back with Lew above her. "A beautiful, brazen wanton," he murmured as his lips and his hands and the weight of his body brought her wave after wave of pleasure.

"Lew."

"Hmm?"

"Will you make a me a promise?"

"Try me, sweetheart."

Mollie smiled. "When we get to your New Mexico

ranch, will you let me give you a bath in a tub on top of the dining table?"

Lew's head shot up. His blue eyes held a pained expression. "Jesus, honey, you didn't see . . . oh, God almighty . . . Mollie, I never . . . we never . . . Cherry and I were just—"

"It doesn't matter," Mollie said, still smiling.

"Yes, it does. Sweetheart, I was very drunk that night in Prescott. I hardly remember what happened, but I'll tell you what *didn't* happen. I never—"

"Shhhh!" She lifted her fingers to his lips.

Lew swept her hand away. "I know how it must have looked, but I swear to you I didn't sleep with Cherry Sellers. I have never been to bed with Cherry, no matter what you—"

"I know that."

"You do? How?"

Mollie sighed and shrugged. "Never mind. I just know. Can we take a bath atop your dining table? It looked like such fun."

Shaking his head with relief, Lew said, "We can bathe there every night if you'd like. Anything you want."

"Anything?"

"No questions asked."

She framed his handsome face in her hands. "Make love to me now, here, where we can hear and smell the rain."

"Ah, baby, baby."

While the rains lashed the rocky canyon a few feet from them, Lew and Mollie kissed and clung together, letting passion slowly, surely ignite.

"Lew," Mollie said dreamily, looking into his smoldering blue eyes, "is this real? Are we really lying here naked in this rocky, rainy canyon or is it only a dream?"

He said, *"All that we see or seem is but a dream within a dream."*

Mollie smiled. "Poe?"

"Could be. Damned if I know. I love you, Mollie."

"I'm glad," she said, almost shouting now to be heard above the falling rain. "So glad."

They made fierce love, challenging the storm. Then they slept peacefully in each other's arms while the downpour continued. When, hours later, they awakened, the clouds had rolled away and a bright summer sun was shining.

Unhurriedly they dressed and broke camp.

They rode on up into the winding canyon. Lew had a spot in mind, a place he knew Mollie would like. The sun was starting its descent when they reached their destination.

"Lew!" Mollie shouted, pulling up on her mount and looking all around.

They were in a wide corridor of rock where there was nothing green in sight. No trees, no grass, no vegetation of any kind. Only rock. The entire floor was rock. Sheet upon sheet of smooth, flat, shiny rock. One side of the canyon corridor's floor was bone-dry. But on the other side, slow-moving water spilled over the giant rocks, its depth mere inches.

"Nice?" Lew asked.

"Unbelievable. Unlike any place I've ever seen."

"Want to stay the night here?"

"No. I want to stay the rest of my life here."

He grinned and went about unsaddling the horses. "Honey, I'll gather the firewood," he told her. "You see what we have to eat."

"Mmm," Mollie answered, her gaze sweeping over the vast world of rock.

Lew left her there, returning less than a half hour later. He rounded a bend in the canyon, saw Mollie, stopped abruptly, and stood stock-still, staring. She hadn't seen to their supper. She had taken off all her clothes and she sat now, splendidly nude, upon a huge flat sheet of rock in the shallow, crystal water.

Lew dropped the firewood. His eyes never leaving the beautiful untamed creature on the rocks, he swiftly stripped down to his skin. Mollie slowly turned her head, saw him, and smiled seductively. His heart thundered in his chest as he started toward her.

She sat there, leaning back, her weight supported on stiff arms, her long legs stretched out before her. Her face was tilted up to the sun, and her loose hair tumbled down her back.

Lew reached her.

"I thought you were hungry," he said, standing between her and the sun.

Mollie's violet gaze languidly climbed up his bare, brown body to his face. "I decided I was thirsty. I came out to get a drink."

Lew dropped down beside her. "I'm thirsty myself."

Mollie cupped her hand into the shallow water beside her hip, brought it up to his lips. "Then drink."

Lew sipped the water from her palm, looked into her eyes, shuddered, and kissed her. An aggressive, intrusive kiss. As they kissed, Mollie put her arms around his neck and, bringing him down with her, leaned all the way back until she was reclining on the satin-smooth rock in the shallow water.

Lew raised his head to look at her. Her hair swirled around her head in an oversized fan of gleaming gold and her breasts were pointing proudly to the sun, their crests tight little rosettes of sweetness. He felt his breath grow short, felt his growing erection.

"I'm still thirsty," he said, scooped up a handful of water and let it spill from his palm into the hollow of Mollie's throat. He bent his head and captured the water with his mouth as it trickled down her chest.

Mollie's breath grew short too. "Still thirsty?" she asked huskily.

He nodded, his silky black hair tickling her chin. She scooped up more water and dribbled it onto her taut, left nipple. Lew licked away the diamond droplets and stayed to suck on the passion-hardened center as Mollie's eyes closed in building rapture. He lazily spilled some water over her right nipple and his lips moved to it while Mollie's fingers curled into his hair to press him closer.

Mollie lay there stretched out on her bed of rock in the shallow, placid water while Lew's warm mouth enclosed her aching nipple and his hard, heavy cock pressed insistently against her bare hip. She was suddenly very grateful for the cooling water flowing around her. If not for it she would surely have burst into flame.

Her eyes opening and closing with pleasure, she watched Lew's lips leave her tingling nipple. He put out the tip of his tongue and licked a circle around the passion-darkened bud, then dragged his teeth across it and said hoarsely, "I'm still thirsty."

He cupped more water in his hand, poured it into her navel, and looked at her face, his blue eyes burning with desire.

"Drink," Mollie whispered breathlessly. "Drink, my love."

Lew bent to her. Mollie's stomach quivered when his

hot, wet lips covered the small indentation and rolled the beads of water up onto his tongue. He stayed to probe the navel for any residue of moisture and to place dozens of plucking kisses around its circumference. Mollie luxuriated in the delicious joy, but felt that she would surely explode from the excitement surging through her heated, yearning body.

Finally Lew raised his head. With quick, fluid grace, he parted her legs and moved between, sliding down on his stomach until his face was above her flat belly. Mollie tensed when he cupped more water into his palm and moved his hand directly over the blond triangle between her pale, parted thighs. Their gazes locked as Lew slowly spread his fingers and allowed the cool water to spill down into the golden curls.

"Still thirsty," he said, as the water beaded, then trickled down through the dense golden triangle to the hot, slick flesh beneath and Lew's gentle fingers urged the springy coils aside so the water could find and follow its natural path. "Let me, baby," he whispered. "Let me drink my fill."

Mollie couldn't answer. Her throat wouldn't work. It was far too tight, too dry. Her heart beat fiercely and she felt she couldn't get a breath. Her arms, her legs, they wouldn't move. As if in a dream, she lay there totally still and helpless with this daring, dark-skinned god lying between her parted thighs, his handsome face slowly, surely lowering to her.

"Soooo thirsty," Lew murmured as his hands went beneath her and Mollie anxiously exhaled when his strong fingers cupped her buttocks and he gently lifted her to him.

"Lewwww," his name came out in a startled gasp as

this magnificent man she loved bent to her and pressed his dark hot face into the dampened golden curls.

Mollie's entire body spasmed when he nuzzled and kissed her in that spot where she was throbbing and blazing hot. Her back arched up out of the shallow water and her eyes closed when his mouth found and enclosed that pulsing, aching source of all her sensual joy.

Lew's face sank deeper into her. His eyes wide open, he stroked her lovingly with his tongue while Mollie moaned and called his name and tossed her head as jolt after jolt of incredible sensation shook her to the core. The shocking pleasure was so intense it swept away all logical thought. Mollie felt herself being lifted into a wild new kingdom of exquisite ecstasy. Time did not exist there, space did not exist there, the whole troubled world did not exist there.

Only incredible splendor.

40

"Mollie, my love," he mused aloud, *"you'll* never be free of me." His grin was evil, his gray eyes demonic, as he lifted the cross he had found to his bearded face and pressed his thin lips to it. Looking up then, the Texas Kid said, "They're not far ahead. They camped here in the past two or three days. We'll ride out of the canyon, head due east and overtake them." He put the cross in his breast pocket. "Remember, when we find them, nobody is to touch Mollie. Understand?"

His men nodded.

"Kill him if you get the chance, but don't risk firing if there's any danger of hitting her." He grinned and scratched his bearded chin. "She'll get her punishment, but I'll be the one doling it out. *Comprende?*"

Again his men nodded.

"Then let's go get her," said the Kid, and climbed back on his horse. He slapped the reins across his gelding's neck as tingling excitement filled his chest. In a matter of hours—days at most—his little blond wildcat would be back in his arms.

And he would never let her go.

Mollie and Lew had quit the canyon and were riding through the colorful Goldmine Mountains of the towering San Francisco Range as the sun began to wester. Lew explained to Mollie that they would ride to Flagstaff Spring and stay the night at a brand-new hotel an enterprising Easterner had recently built there.

There they would purchase supplies, buy a couple of fresh horses from an area rancher, enjoy a fancy meal, and sleep in an honest-to-God bed. After a good night's rest, they would head east and, hopefully, make it down out of the mountains before the snows came.

Lengthening shadows stole down the sides of the timbered mountains when Lew, pointing, said, "There it is, honey. The Hotel Mountainaire."

Two hundred feet below, a huge, three-story brick building was the only structure in the wide, high valley. It looked out of place amidst the towering pines and fragrant cedars. Rising grandly toward the cloudless Arizona sky, the big hotel was a pleasing sight to Mollie. Her first thought on seeing it was, *Tonight I'll sleep in a comfortable bed with Lew. Such luxury.*

When Lew led Mollie into the hotel's lobby, she admired the many-prismed chandelier suspended from the three-story-high ceiling. She looked around. To one side of the darkly paneled lobby, a pair of louvered swinging doors opened into a saloon. Directly opposite the saloon entrance, a matching pair of doors was the entrance to a general store.

Mollie paused beside a tall wing chair of smooth wine leather while Lew walked to the back of the lobby and rang the bell for service. She couldn't hear what

Lew was saying, but she saw the puzzled look on the desk clerk's thin face give way to disdain as he threw his hands in the air as if giving up.

Seemingly undaunted, Lew continued to talk softly, smiling as he spoke. Straining to hear, Mollie wondered with dismay if the hotel was full. Disappointment swamped her at the prospect.

The conversation between Lew and desk clerk continued and, his smile growing broader, Lew pulled out a roll of paper bills, peeled off several, and laid them on the counter. The clerk looked at the money, then at Lew, and finally nodded his head. Lew signed the guest register and Mollie breathed a great sigh of relief.

"We have the fanciest suite in the Mountainaire," Lew said when he came to her, took her arm.

"Wonderful. Let's go right up and—"

"Not just yet. We need those supplies."

"Lew, let's do that tomorrow. I'm tired and hungry."

"I know, but the room's not quite ready."

Mollie sighed wearily. "How long before . . . ?"

"Not long." He propelled her to the general store's slatted doors and urged her inside.

A portly woman looked up and smiled warmly. "Anything special you folks need? We have just about everything."

Her mind on the evening meal and the comfortable room awaiting them, Mollie leaned on the counter while Lew chose warm clothes, fur covers, canned goods, rope and candles. When the counter was stacked high with his choices, he told the proprietress he would be back come morning to pay and pick up the merchandise.

Back out in the lobby, Lew said, "Let's go play a quick hand of—"

Mollie irritably interrupted, "Lew, I am starving. Let's go to the dining room for dinner."

"Ah, Mollie, just one hand of faro." His voice was soft, persuasive. "Remember how much you liked the game in Prescott?"

She pursed her lips, but allowed him to usher her into the saloon and gambling hall. He directed her to a faro table where a tall, rawboned dealer nodded and went to work as soon as she was seated.

Mollie felt a mild flutter of excitement similar to that on the night she had gambled in Prescott. In a few short minutes she was winning and having such a good time she had forgotten about dinner.

Standing behind her, his bootheel hooked over the bottom rung of her chair, Lew said, after a half hour had passed, "That's it, sweetheart. Let's go."

"Oh, must we?" She protested. "I'm winning, and—"

"You can play again after dinner if you like."

"Very well, but don't forget you said so."

"I won't forget," he said, smiling enigmatically and adding mysteriously, "but you may."

When he headed for the stairs, Mollie said, "Aren't we going to the dining room?"

"I think not," he said and winked at her.

"What's going on here?" Mollie asked as they climbed the carpeted stairs. "There's a devilish gleam in your eyes like you know something I don't. What is it?"

Lew shrugged, smiled. "You're imagining things."

On the second floor, at the end of the corridor, Lew stopped before a massive door, put a key in the lock, and said, "I believe, Miss Rogers, you'll approve of your accommodations."

He opened the door, and Mollie swept inside. She

was midway through the spacious sitting room when she stopped short and her hands flew up to her cheeks as she squealed, "Lew Hatton! I don't believe it! I do not believe it!"

Across the silk-walled room, below a quartet of two-story high windows with the heavy drapes thrown open to the star-filled night, sat a large dining table. A red linen cloth covered the table's surface and fell to the plush carpet. Upon the cloth covered table, two dozen tall, red candles in silver candelabrum cast soft, honeyed light on sparkling crystal, fine porcelain, and Georgian silver.

And on an oversized bathtub with steam rising from its soapy depths. The tub was atop the table.

Loving the look on her face, Lew said, "What are you waiting for?"

Mollie turned to him, her cheeks hot, her eyes flashing with excitement and surprise. "I never expected . . . I didn't actually mean . . ."

"Didn't you?" He stepped closer, his heavy-lidded gaze becoming blatantly sexual. He unbuckled his gun belt and laid it aside. "Got cold feet? Change your mind?"

Lew opened his shirt down his dark chest and reached for Mollie. He deftly unbuttoned hers, pushed it down her arms and off, then lifted her chemise up over her head. Holding the flimsy satin undergarment in his hand, he drew her to him, tilted her face up to his, and kissed her.

He said, "Aren't you going to give me a bath like you promised? Or must I find myself another woman?"

Mollie's hands went to his belt buckle as she said, "You'll *never* need another woman." She whipped the belt out of his trousers, whirled it around his waist, and drew him closer. "Never. You hear me, Hatton?"

"I hear you, sweetheart."

"I, and no other, will do everything for you and to you," Mollie told him, feeling his body's response to her nearness. Experiencing a delicious sense of power, she said, "I am indeed going to bathe you, my love."

She slipped a hand between them and began unbuttoning his snug trousers while Lew, enjoying her assertiveness to the fullest, let his arms fall to his sides and stood there gladly allowing her to undress him.

"You're mighty good at this," he teased when she managed to get his boots off and then swiftly peeled his trousers down his hips. "Sure you haven't had practice?"

Mollie smiled. "I'm good at anything I enjoy."

And she was.

And so while Lew, lounging in the suds-filled tub atop the table, groaned and sighed and smoked a cigar and sipped champagne, Mollie, as naked as he, her hair pinned atop her head, knelt on the elegantly laid dining table and laughed and sang and drew a soapy sponge over his dark chest, bending to give him sweet kisses and to drink champagne from his mouth.

It was a lovely, wicked, dreamlike episode. The two of them playing like naughty children there atop the table in the candlelit suite while outside beyond the tall glass windows a million stars filled the chilly night and across the room a blazing fire in the marble fireplace warmed their private, intimate world.

At Lew's urging, Mollie soon joined him in the tub. He leaned lazily back against the headrest while Mollie sat between his long, bent legs and leaned lazily back against him.

"This is really decadent," she said, trailing soapy water down her throat.

"That, sweet, is what makes it so enjoyable."

When the water cooled, they reluctantly left the tub and dried themselves before the fire. Then, wearing only large white towels, they returned to the dining table to enjoy a late supper.

The towel knotted atop his hip, Lew sat down in a tall backed chair and pulled Mollie onto his lap. "What is there to eat?" he asked, nuzzling her neck. "Anything good?"

"Plenty," she said and recited the many choices.

It was a long, leisurely meal. They sampled some of everything and washed it all down with champagne. Mollie was munching on smoked almonds when Lew said, "What do you say we move this little celebration to the bed?"

Mollie snatched up a bunch of grapes from a silver bowl. "Let's take the champagne with us."

"By all means," said Lew. "And anything else you want."

"I want you."

In the bedroom Lew set the champagne on a night table, took Mollie's half-eaten bunch of grapes and laid them aside. He loosened the towel knotted above her breasts and pulled it open. For a moment he stood there, framing her with the towel, admiring her. Then he released the towel, drew her up on tiptoe and bent to kiss her. Her lips quickly parting beneath his, Mollie tasted the wine and tobacco on his mouth and relished it.

While he kissed her, Mollie unknotted the towel on Lew's hip and shoved it to the floor. Then she pressed her body to his and he lifted his head. Wordlessly, he picked her up and carried her to the high, white-sheeted bed. He joined her there and they oohed and aaahed and sighed and moaned over the almost-forgotten comfort of a clean, soft bed. Then they lay, silent and content, in the middle of that big, comfortable bed while the fire warmed them and a wonderful sense of well-being enveloped them, lulling them, nudging them toward slumber.

But they were too much in love to go to sleep. They couldn't get enough of each other, and as badly as they needed rest, they couldn't waste these precious hours in this luxurious room in this cozy bed doing something so mundane as sleeping.

They talked quietly, punctuating each sentence with kisses to eyes, ears, and lips. Lew, lying flat on his back, smiled lazily when Mollie, on her stomach beside him, dabbed her little finger into a glass of champagne and skimmed it across his bottom lip.

Teasingly, she said, "Lord, I'm thirsty."

She bent and kissed his mouth. Lew's heartbeat speeded. Vividly, he recalled where the foolish game of thirst had led when they had played it back in the canyon. The recollection made his breath grow short. He lost it completely when Mollie tipped the fluted glass and dribbled a little of the wine directly onto his right nipple. He groaned when she lowered her face and licked it dry, the tip of her tongue dabbing sweetly, her small white teeth nipping gently.

Mollie set the glass aside. She place her hands on his ribcage and leaned over him. Like a kitten lapping cream, she flicked her tongue rhythmically while Lew, his chest heaving, his fully formed erection surging inches from her face, clutched at the sheet beneath him and wondered just how far she would go with the game.

Brushing Lew's prominent hipbone with her lips, Mollie sat up and reached for the champagne. Looking straight into Lew's hot, tortured eyes, she dipped all five fingers into the bubbly wine, set the glass aside, and lowered her hand to him. Lew watched, transfixed, as her wine-wet fingers skimmed down his aching erection.

Mollie studied the heavy, rigid maleness, now glistening with wine. A wild, hungered expression came into her violet eyes. She said softly, "Thirsty. Soooo thirsty."

All the breath left his body, and Lew's belly contracted as she slowly bent to him. He felt her soft, searching lips and he shuddered in ecstasy. His hands went to her bent head. He meant to pull her up, but just as he was about to, Mollie put out her tongue and licked him. Lew's eyes closed and his lean fingers tangled in her hair.

Awed by the fierce power beneath her lips, Mollie licked her slow, tantalizing way from the very base all the way up to the pulsing tip. She paused for only a second, then opened her mouth and slid it over the hot, velvet smoothness. Gently sucking the wine from it, she wondered if Lew was feeling the same wild pleasure he had given to her when he'd kissed her like this in the rock canyon.

So she lifted her head and asked him. "Darling, does that feel good?"

His eyes restlessly opened and Lew looked down at the beautiful golden-haired goddess lying between his spread legs with her soft hands cupping him and her full, red lips wet with wine.

"It's heaven," he said huskily, wishing that she would never stop, knowing that she had better stop.

She didn't.

Mollie smiled dreamily and bent back to him. Bolder now, she put out her tongue and sanguinely stroked him while Lew, inhaling raggedly, felt his passion intensify to the point where it was a mixture of pain and pleasure. How quickly she had learned, this sensual shameless temptress he adored. Already she was teasing him unmercifully, licking him languidly, then pausing to make him wait and strain and beg for more.

When her lips moved up the length of him and she again enclosed the throbbing tip, Lew's fingers tightened in her hair and for one heart-stopping minute he allowed her to draw him deeply inside the warm, wet promise of her loving mouth. Then gritting his teeth in both agony and ecstasy, he anxiously pulled her head up.

"I thought you liked it," Mollie murmured as he swiftly turned her onto her back.

"I do," he said, "too much."

"Then why . . . ?"

"Because," he said hoarsely, "I want to be inside you."

Mollie liked his answer. Her hands skimmed his tanned shoulders. "That's what I want, too."

"Do you, sweetheart?"

"Oh, yes," she breathed, aching to be filled with him, longing to have all that hot power buried deep inside her.

Mollie trembled when she felt Lew's lean fingers touch her there where she burned for him. Gently, exquisitely, he caressed her, readying her for his loving. And when those practiced fingers slid easily, effortlessly in the wetness flowing from her, Lew moved his hand to her hip.

"Look at me, Mollie," he said, his voice low, caressing. "Open your eyes and look at me, sweetheart."

Mollie sighed and let her eyes flutter open. His handsome face, hardened with passion, was just above her own. She looked at him as he took her hand in his, drew it down to him.

His heavy-lidded gaze holding hers, he said, "You want me inside you, put me there."

Mollie didn't hesitate. She wrapped eager fingers around his hard, heavy flesh and deftly guided him into her soft wet heat. Both gasped with pleasure as he slid painlessly in and Mollie let her hand move up his belly to his chest as Lew slowly, carefully inched into her.

For an incredibly erotic moment they lay there completely still, looking into each other's eyes, their straining, joined bodies poised and in place for a feverish, frenzied dance of untamed passion.

And then the dance started.

Lew began the slow sensual surging of his slim hips, languidly thrusting, almost withdrawing, then thrusting once more. Mollie immediately found his easy, indolent rhythm and moved with him, her arms looped around his neck, her knees bent. They stayed like that for a time, sighing, loving, moving lazily.

Finally Lew's hands went beneath Mollie to lift her to him as he changed the tempo minutely, but still keeping to a leisurely, erotic pace. With patience and expertise, he made love to Mollie, taking her higher and higher, leading her up the rising steps of passion and through the varying stages of changing rhythms until their hearts were pounding like jungle drums and they were bucking and thrusting like two sleek animals, their bodies slick with perspiration, their quest for the ultimate totally uninhibited.

"Yes . . . yes . . ." Mollie exulted as her release began. "It's so good, so good. . . . Don't stop, please don't stop. Oh, yes, like that, like that . . ."

"Like this, sweetheart?" Lew asked, holding back his own joy, giving it all to her, feeling the tight, sweet squeezing of her body on his as her forceful climax began.

"Yes! Yes! Oooh . . . oooh. . . . Lew! Lewwww!" Her nails dug into his shoulders and she cried out and looked up at him with widened eyes as the frightening wonder claimed her.

"Baby . . . oh, God, baby . . ." he groaned and joined her in paradise.

41

◈

"You ready?"

"Ready for what?"

"I thought you wanted to play faro after supper," Lew teased.

"Very funny," she said, too exhausted to hit him.

Lew chuckled and asked, "Which do you like best? Gambling or lovemaking?"

Mollie yawned, sighed. "I'd like a bit more of each before I make a decision."

Enchanted, Lew laughed heartily and admitted, "Sweetheart, if you do more of either tonight, I'm afraid it will have to be gambling. You've worn me out."

Mollie let her hand slide down his chest to his belly. "Yes, I can see that. Still, I think I'll stay right here for a while. Maybe you'll get your second wind."

"Don't count on it," he said, drew a deep, relaxed breath, and gave no reply when Mollie asked him a question.

She eased up onto her elbow and softly spoke his name. No answer. Lew was sound asleep. Reluctant to release her hold on bliss, Mollie tried very hard to stay awake. She didn't want to sleep. She wanted to lie and look at her beautiful lover forever. But a hard day in the saddle and the relaxation that comes with total gratification changed her plans. She was almost instantly asleep.

When Mollie awakened, bright sunlight streamed in through the tall windows. She slowly turned her head on the pillow and saw a pair of hypnotic blue eyes looking at her. Without a word, Lew kissed her and made slow, sweet love to her.

An hour later, when they left their high mountain haven, the sun was almost at its zenith. The day was bright and cool, the air pleasantly crisp. Autumn had arrived in the high country with its colorful banners proudly raised—the flaming red of the maples and gold of the willows and aspen. The tallest of the majestic San Francisco peaks wore a cloak of snow, while lacy patches of ice covered some of the shadier spots on the ground.

Heading east, Lew and Mollie rode through the splendidly remote, rugged country where the only sounds were the hoarse croaking of a raven and the wind stirring the pines. A feeling of welcome isolation filled Mollie as they rode through the cool uplands. It was easy to pretend that she and Lew were the only two people on earth.

The day was perfect.

Life was perfect.

But minutes later, the quiet, sunny solitude changed. The bright blue sky darkened and the air grew cold as the sun disappeared. The wind changed from a gentle sigh to a mournful wail, then howled forcefully through the trees. A lone eagle glided through the sky and circled high above.

Mollie shuddered involuntarily as a sense of foreboding washed over her.

The rains began, coming in quick, angry sheets of water and Lew, shouting to be heard, told her they would take cover and wait out the rainstorm. They hurriedly dismounted under the sheltering branches of a giant ponderosa pine and Lew, his mood still buoyant, laughed, pulled Mollie close, and said, "Don't look so serious. This won't last long. Just a quick mountain thunderstorm." He looked into her eyes, saw the anxiety there. "What is it, sweetheart?"

Telling herself she was being foolish, that the worrisome premonition nagging at her meant nothing, Mollie smiled. "Not a thing."

"Sure?"

"Sure."

Lew relaxed then, leaned back against the tree trunk and hugged Mollie to him. She turned up her face, eager for his kiss. When his lips closed over hers, she kissed him passionately, anxiously, as though she might never kiss him again. While Lew's response was warm, Mollie's was white-hot.

She tore at his buttons, pushed his shirt apart, and kissed his bared chest, murmuring, "Love me, Lew. Love me."

"Sure, baby. I'll get the fur robe and toss it on—"

"No," Mollie's tone was almost frantic.

She pulled his head down and kissed him again. Her mouth on his was ravenous. The almost savage kiss combined with the aggressive undulation of her hips against his brought on immediate arousal.

Lew's heart hammered. He moved his booted feet apart and filled his hands with her soft, rounded bottom.

He gripped her firmly and drew her up on her toes and into him, pressing her groin to the strong, uncontrollable pulsing of his own.

They finally broke apart, panted for breath, and began tearing off their clothes. Naked, they sank to the ground and Lew rolled over onto Mollie. She could feel the hard length of him pressing against her quivering belly and she wanted him more than ever.

"Take me," she urged breathlessly, on fire, hurting.

Lew's hand slipped between her legs. She was already hot and wet and ready. His own blood up, he took her quickly with a deep, hard thrust that made them both gasp and tremble.

Mollie arched her back to receive him fully, greedy for all of him. Her restless hands trailed down his back to the smooth, tanned flesh of his buttocks.

Her fingers splayed and, gripping him, she drew him to her, eagerly accepting each deep thrust, longing to keep him inside her forever. Fiercely, she loved him, enveloping him in the torrid heat of her unleashed sexuality.

She was a living, searing flame of passion that engulfed him until Lew, too, was raging out of control. He made love to her with an urgency that bordered on violence. Faster and faster he moved, accelerating his deep, driving thrusts, increasing his strokes until he was pounding uncontrollably into her.

It was exactly what Mollie wanted.

Her pelvis rose up to accept each brutal, probing plunge, her body zealously accepting the powerful pain-pleasure, needing it, demanding it. Savagely she bucked against him, primitive in her passion, barbaric in her senseless desire to possess him completely.

Mollie felt her orgasm beginning and cried out in anguished protest. "No! No!"

She didn't want it to come yet. She didn't want this wild loving to end. Ever. She would hold back! She'd not let it happen. She would keep Lew loving her like this for all eternity.

Mollie gritted her teeth and started to moan helplessly as she felt herself slipping over the edge. Powerless against the tremendous shocks of joy jolting through her, she looked up into Lew's hot, pleading eyes and surrendered to the inevitable. She let herself go and Lew let himself go. Together they attained a frightening level of satisfaction, reaching a pinnacle of pleasure that far surpassed any they'd climbed to before.

It shook them both to their very souls and after it ended, Mollie realized that she was crying when Lew, murmuring endearments, kissed the tears from her eyes. He held her until she calmed, assuring her that he was hers and would always be hers.

After dozens of soothing kisses and professions of undying love, Lew said gently, "Sweetheart, the rain has stopped."

Mollie smiled, kissed his shoulder, and rose from their bed of damp pine needles. She stretched lazily, then walked naked out into the clearing. The sky overhead was clear blue, the sun bright and hot.

Lew came to her. He stepped up behind her, slipped his arms around her waist, and drew her back against him.

Mollie leaned her head on his shoulder, covered his hands with hers, and said, almost shyly, "My primal burst of passion must have shocked you."

"It delighted me."

"I know, but you must wonder . . . I . . . have you ever experienced an irrational fear that something bad was going to happen?"

"Everybody has, I suppose. Doesn't mean a thing." His protective arms tightened around her. "The worst thing that's going to happen to you has already happened."

"It has? What?"

"Me."

Mollie laughed and closed her eyes for a second. When she opened them, she saw it.

A wide, colorful rainbow arcing across the azure sky.

Later that same afternoon they stood, fully dressed now, on a jutting ledge of rock high above Diablo Canyon, holding hands and watching the spectacular sunset. From their vantage point they could see, in all directions, astounding vistas and desert ranges.

"Sunset Crater," Lew said, pointing north. "And Humphreys Peak just west of the crater."

Mollie was still gazing at the twelve thousand foot mountain peak when Lew turned her around to face east. "The Little Colorado River," he indicated a curving ribbon of water. "Bet there's snow on the banks."

"So early?" Mollie looked up at him.

Lew nodded. "Look there, honey, to the south. The Mongollon Rim. Further down the Santa Cantalinas, the Pinalenos, and the Chiricahuas."

Mollie shook her head. "I wonder if . . . ?"

"Yes. If we strain real hard, we can see the deserts around Maya." He glanced at her. "No, look a little more to the west." Again he pointed.

Mollie followed his pointing finger, squinted, and finally saw the flat, arid desert in the distance. "Yes!" she exclaimed. "I do see it. Is that really it, Lew? Is Maya out there in the—"

"You mean you can't see the town?"

She lifted a hand to shade her eyes. "Well, no, I—"

"No? Why, there's the Maya Emporium and the—"

"Where? I still can't—"

"The Nueva Sol and the new Methodist church and . . . and . . . Well, I'll be damned!"

"What? What is it? Tell me!" Mollie's voice had risen an octave and she was squinting hard.

"There comes the professor down the steps of the Manzanita Avenue mansion and I believe . . . yes, he's waving at us and—"

"Ooooh! Lew Hatton, you devil!" she shrieked, "you're teasing me!" She whirled around and began beating furiously on his chest and calling him names.

At that moment a small band of riders topped a gentle ridge not fifty yards from them. Mollie's back was to the intruders and Lew, making faces, pretending that she was hurting him, was looking only at Mollie, playfully fending off her blows and yelping loudly. Neither saw or heard the riders.

The Kid's gray eyes narrowed as he calmly pulled an ivory-handled .44 from its holster and urged his gelding down the slope.

"A lover's spat?" he asked coldly and pulled the trigger.

The bullet caught Lew in the left shoulder and for a stunned second, both he and Mollie stared, dumbfounded, at the bright blossom of blood that appeared on his soft chamois shirt.

Then Mollie screamed and whirled about as Lew looked over her head to the semicircle of mounted men. All had guns drawn and pointed at him. He knew it was suicide to draw his own.

"Get behind me," Lew calmly ordered, but Mollie refused to budge.

"Kid," she murmured, disbelieving.

"Get your hands above your head, Taylor," the Kid ordered, his steely gaze on Lew. Then his attention swung to Mollie. He grinned evilly and said, "Hello, darlin'. You planing to give this broke broncbuster my gold and marry—"

"You've got it all wrong, Kid," Mollie interrupted. "He's no broncbuster, and his name's not Taylor. He's Lew Hatton."

"Hatton?" The Kid's eyes went back to Lew.

"Yes, Hatton. William Hatton's only son," she said. "And besides that, he's the bounty hunter that brought in all our men. He took me against my will. I swear it, Kid."

Lew couldn't believe his eyes or his ears. He was face-to-face with the Texas Kid after believing for years that the man was dead. And he was listening to the woman he loved betray him to the Kid while he stood here as impotent and helpless as a newborn infant.

The Kid said to Mollie, "Get his gun, darlin'."

Mollie immediately obeyed. She stuck the gun in Lew's ribs while she said, "Kid, thank God you've finally come for me."

The Texas Kid grinned like a shy schoolboy. "I'm not too late, am I, Mollie? He hasn't . . . hurt you or anything?" He swung down off his horse and started toward her.

Lew forcefully shoved Mollie away from him. "Kid, let's you and I settle this—"

"No!" Mollie screamed and flung herself at Lew. "Shut up, bounty hunter! You have no say in this!" She again poked the revolver in his ribs, managing as she did so, to stand between him and the Kid.

The big, bearded Kid beamed with pride. "Step away from him now, honey. I'll kill the son of a bitch right where he stands."

"No," Mollie said, thinking fast, stalling for time. "Let's have some fun with him first. Cover him for me, Kid."

The Kid's eyes glittered with anticipation of just what kind of torture she had in mind for Hatton. Pointing both ivory-handled pistols at Lew, he ordered Lew to keep his hands held high or else have his head blown off.

Mollie shoved Lew's revolver into the waistband of her breeches, slipped the bandanna from her throat and raised it to Lew's lips.

"Mollie," Lew said, "what the hell are—"

"Shut your mouth, bounty hunter," said the Kid and cocked his pistols.

Mollie said nothing. She glanced briefly into Lew's eyes, shoved the silk bandanna between his lips and dashed around in back of him to tie it, expertly gagging him so that he could no longer speak. Dusting her hands together, she sauntered back around in front of him.

The Kid roared with laughter, then announced proudly to his men, "There, by God, is a woman! And she's *my* woman." Wiping his thin, drooling lips on the back of his hand, he said to Mollie, "Now tell the bastard, honey. Tell him what you're going to do to him."

"I will, but first . . . You're not still angry, are you, Kid? I have the gold stashed in a safe place. I hid it from Hatton."

"Mollie, darlin', you know I can't stay mad at you. You ready to stop fighting and marry me?"

"Yes," Mollie replied. "I've always wanted to get married in that little Catholic church in San Carlos and—"

"No, honey, we can't. We're still wanted in Arizona. We'll go back to Mexico and—"

"San Carlos is a sleepy little place, Kid. Besides, the man who's caused us all the trouble is right here." She inclined her head.

The Kid shoved one pistol back into the holster, scratched his lobeless ear, and said affectionately, "You're still a mighty bossy little thing." His bearded face broke into a wide grin and he added, "Hell, if it'll make you happy, we'll get married in San Carlos."

"At the Catholic church on the town square? With a priest and flowers and me in a long white lace dress?"

The Kid's heavy eyebrows shot up. "My Mollie in a dress?"

"A long lace dress. I want everything to be proper and nice, Kid. A wedding day we'll never forget."

Throughout the exchange, Lew's eyes were wild, his heart about to explode in his chest. In a matter of seconds everything had changed. All he had believed to be real was not. Mollie had lied to him all this time. She had known all along that the Kid was alive, but she had let him believe that the Kid was dead. Had all the rest been lies as well? God in heaven, how could he have allowed this to happen? He should have been more alert, should have been looking over his shoulder all along. Should never have trusted Mollie Rogers.

Mollie continued to stand directly in front of Lew and all at once he realized that she was purposely shielding him from the seven raised guns. His wild thoughts of doubt departed and he knew exactly what she was doing. She was saving him! She was sacrificing herself for him. Jesus God, she was going to give herself to the Kid in exchange for his life. She would be at the Kid's mercy, and the Kid had no mercy!

". . . and kill him so we can get on our way," the Kid was saying.

"I've a much better idea," Mollie said. "Let's leave him here to die."

"You mean not shoot him again?" The Kid was skeptical. "I don't much like the idea of—"

"Don't you see," Mollie cut in, "it would be far greater punishment. If you shoot him, it's over in seconds. But leave him alone out here and it could take days for him to die."

The Kid started grinning. "We'll shoot the horses and take all the food."

Mollie swallowed hard. "Sure. Leave the wounded bastard afoot. See how far he gets."

"Mollie, my own, no wonder I've missed you. Let's get the hell out of here. I'm anxious to get to San Carlos and the padre."

"Soon as I say good-bye to the bounty hunter." She winked at the Kid, turned, stepped up close to Lew's face, and said loudly, "*Adios,* vermin. You're on your own." Then quickly she mouthed the words, "I love you, my darling."

While Lew gagged, unable to speak past the bandanna, his eyes spoke volumes. Mollie pivoted and walked straight to the Kid. Laughing, the Kid gestured with his ivory-handled pistol and at once the air was filled with gunfire as the men turned their guns on Lew's horses.

Holstering his own gun, the Kid lifted Mollie up onto his prancing gelding, swung up behind her, put his arms around her, and dug his big-roweled spurs into the horse's flanks. Away they thundered, his men right on their heels and Mollie, playing her role to the end, never even looked back.

Lew was a wild man. Tearing the bandanna from his mouth, he ran after the departing gang, shouting for them to come back. To let Mollie go. To take him instead.

He ran and ran and was still running long after they had left him behind. He was winded and his side ached and blood streamed down his left arm, and still he ran, blinking furiously, trying to keep Mollie in sight.

Lew continued to run in a foolish, futile attempt to save her. Panting heavily, tears of frustration stinging his eyes, he stumbled and staggered and finally crashed to the ground. A groan of despair and pain erupted from his lips.

He was back up at once, running again. Blindly, wearily he dashed through the undergrowth and tripped on a fallen log. He rose, staggered, faltered, and sank to his knees. Howling like a wounded animal, he crawled on his hands and knees until he was unable even to do that.

He collapsed on his belly, tried to get up. His heated lungs labored feebly, painfully, and sweat poured into his burning eyes. Weak from exertion and loss of blood, Lew felt the dreaded darkness dragging him under. Manfully he fought against it, willing himself to stay conscious, telling himself he couldn't let Mollie down. He had to save her, he had to.

With superhuman effort he got to his feet one more time. But the rise was too rapid. The whole world spun dizzily out of control and the earth came up to meet him.

42

Mollie was hardly aware that she was atop a galloping horse, tightly enclosed in the Kid's muscular arms. Only vaguely conscious of her cheek being crushed to his chest, of his repellent scent and maniacal laughter. She had not yet considered what horrors were in store for her in the days and nights ahead. She hadn't given a thought to her promise to marry this evil man she despised and feared.

There was only one thing on her mind. Only one man on her mind.

Lew.

Had she saved him or only managed to prolong his agony? How far was it back to Flagstaff Spring? Could he walk that distance? Could he even walk? Was he so badly wounded that he would die without a doctor? Was he lying unconscious with the cold night closing in?

Oh, dear God, please let him live! Don't let him die because of me. His life is all that matters. Nothing else. Please, God, let him live. Let him live. Let him live. Those words became a litany, desperately repeated over and over in her mind.

"I've never seen you so quiet, darlin'." The Kid's

voice broke into her reverie and Mollie, looking up at him, realized that they were no longer riding.

She was now on the ground, but didn't remember how she got there. The Kid stood before her, tall and menacing, a dangerous light shining in his eyes.

"I'm very tired," Mollie said, and unconsciously took a step back. He followed.

"Sure you are, honey." He laid a possessive hand on her shoulder. "The boys are building a fire. As soon as we've had supper, we'll both get some rest." Moving closer, he added with a sly grin, "Together."

Mollie shuddered.

"It's grown cold," she said, hurriedly turning away. Hugging herself, she walked over to the campfire and dropped to her knees before its warmth. Again the Kid followed and sat down beside her. Throughout the evening meal his eyes were riveted on Mollie, a slightly satanic stare that chilled her very soul. When he set his empty plate aside and took hers, she stiffened.

But to her relief, he didn't make a move when he said, "Go on. Bedtime. Get some rest."

Like a reprieved prisoner, she felt a great weight momentarily lifted from her tired shoulders. "Yes, I . . . thanks."

Mollie rose and, without looking at the Kid or the six Mexicans around the fire, turned and walked away.

Low talking and laughter accompanied her and when she heard the Kid confidently brag, "Yes, isn't she. And it all belongs to me," she clenched her fists and told herself she would figure some way out of all this horror. Seconds later, he made a statement that brought catcalls and laughter from his men. "All of you stay where you are for the next hour. *Comprende?*"

Mollie's heart stood still as the Kid came up close behind her. In agony she waited until he caught her roughly to him. He crushed her against his powerful body and forced her head back over his arm.

Fear and disgust spurring her, Mollie shoved on his chest. And when his big hand swept across the curve of her breast, she snarled, "Don't!"

The Kid laughed. "Why, honey, in a few days we'll be married and—"

"I know, and you promised you would wait."

"I did? I don't remember making any such promise. All I said was—"

"You said it would be a proper wedding with the church and the priest and all." She glared at him and squirmed within his arms, hunching her shoulders in a vain attempt to shield herself from his unwanted touch.

"I know, but why can't we—"

"No! Absolutely not!" She said it as forcefully as she could and wrenched herself free. "The very idea! Out here in the wilds and your men within hearing distance! I refuse, do you hear me? Keep your hands off me until we get to San Carlos where we can be alone!" Her violent eyes glittered and the attitude of her slender body as she took up an arrogant, hands-on-hips stance, belied her anxiety.

Excited by her nearness and charmed by her indomitable spirit, the Kid grinned and said, "Honey, no woman's ever talked to me the way you do." He pulled her back to him, leaned down and rubbed his bearded face against hers, almost suffocating her. "I'll wait if you insist, but it's not going to be easy." He set her back a little.

"I know," she replied, forcing herself to finally smile at him. "It won't be easy for me either." She swallowed and continued, "but think what a wedding night we'll have." She lowered her lashes flirtatiously.

The Kid trembled. "Darlin'," he said, that satanic light back in his eyes, "it *will* be memorable, I promise you that. We'll make love for hours. I'll do things to you that—"

"I know," she cut him off, not wanting to hear more. "Now, please, I need sleep." She rudely pushed him away.

The Kid fought the strong desire to ignore her wishes and go ahead and take her right then and there. But Mollie, showing him her back, crawled in between the blankets. The Kid stretched out beside her, so close his breathing was loud and offensive in her ears and his body heat assaulted her.

But Mollie was thinking only of Lew. Sick with worry, she thought about him through that long sleepless night. A night filled with a kind of agony she'd never before experienced.

In and out of consciousness throughout the long, chilly night, Lew wasn't sure if the riders were real or only an illusion when, at daybreak, they appeared on the south rim.

But when he saw Chief Red Sunset's classic profile against the dawn sky, Lew, staggering to his feet, waved madly with his good arm.

"Singing Boy," boomed the chief, dismounting, coming to Lew. "Are you badly hurt? Where is Sunshine Hair?" he asked in Spanish.

While the chief unstrapped his medicine bundle from his belt and went about removing the bullet from Lew's left shoulder, Lew told him what had happened.

Chafing under the chief's slow, thorough ministrations, Lew said he had to leave at once for San Carlos. The chief's braves—a dozen of them—stood listening and shaking their heads.

His black eyes fierce, Chief Red Sunset said, "We, too, are hunting the Texas Kid. We were told he was headed east."

"He was," Lew said, pushing the chief's hands away, impatient to be off. "He was coming after us. Now he's turned back south. When they reach San Carlos, Sunshine Hair will become his wife. I must go at once."

Staying Lew with one big hand, the chief lifted his other and motioned to one of his companions. The slim man came forward, crouched down on his heels, and Lew saw that he was not Apache, but Mexican.

"Gilberto Lopez," Chief Red Sunset introduced him. "The husband of my sister, Desert Flower."

"When we find them," said the unsmiling Mexican without preamble, "I want the Kid." His dark eyes were even more fierce than the chief's.

The chief explained. "The Kid and his men rode into Magdalena, Mexico, and took Desert Flower from the street. For five days they held her." Teeth clenching, his eyes closed.

"She's not . . . ?" Lew began.

"She lives," said Gilberto Lopez simply. "But the gringo dog who used her will not!"

"Agreed," said Lew, adjusting the newly tied sling on his left arm. "I'll kill him as soon as Sunshine Hair is safe."

"No!" said Gilberto passionately, "The Texas Kid is mine!"

"Let me have him first for a few minutes, *amigo,*"

said Lew. The Mexican nodded. "*Sí.* But I want him alive, *comprende*?"

"*Comprende.* Let's ride."

The church bells tolled.

Straight-up noon in San Carlos. Mollie's wedding day. Outside the white adobe mission, past the plaza on the town's outskirts, the Kid's men, lounging lazily in the hot Arizona sun, stood guard. Inside the mission, the nervous bridegroom waited at the altar with the Mexican padre.

When the bells stopped ringing, Mollie, pale and beautiful in a long flowing gown of snowy white lace, took the longest walk of her life. Down the aisle to the waiting arms of the Texas Kid.

Mollie moved forward in a daze of despair, unshed tears shining in her sad violet eyes, her heart breaking. Praying that a merciful God would strike her dead, she reached the altar and shuddered when the Kid leaned close and kissed her cheek.

The little, black-robed padre cleared his throat, lifted his Bible, and began to speak. While his voice rose and fell and candles flickered in their holders and incense sweetened the still air, Mollie met her inevitable doom.

"Do you, Mollie Louise Rogers, take this man to be your lawful wedded husband?" asked the padre.

"I . . ." she drew a shallow, painful breath, "I . . . do."

The Kid beamed when the padre turned to him. In a voice sure and strong, he repeated his vows, promising to "love and cherish this woman until death do us part."

The ceremony was almost ended. The groom, eager to get his hands on his bride, was only half listening when the padre said, "Do any here object to this union? If so, speak now or forever hold your peace."

"I object," came a cold, determined voice from the back of the church and three startled people turned quickly to see a lone man—silhouetted against the fierce sunlight—standing in the open church door, his left arm in a sling, his booted feet apart.

"Holy Mary . . ." uttered the padre and dropped his bible.

"What the goddamned hell?" blurted the stunned Kid.

"Lew," breathed Mollie, as the Maya fortune-teller's prediction flashed through her mind: *two men, two weddings, and on the same day.* "Lew," she shouted as the Kid, reality dawning, swiftly drew his guns.

Mollie lunged at the Kid, knocking one Colt from his hand just as it cleared the holster. It clattered to the floor, discharging as it struck stone. Quickly the Kid fired the other, missing Lew by inches. Lew calmly drew, took quick aim, and squeezed the trigger, shooting the Kid's smoking gun from his hand. The Kid yelped in pain and terror.

"Step away from him, Mollie," Lew said evenly, his finger caressing the raised revolver's trigger.

"Mollie! My gun. Toss it to me," shouted the Kid, his eyes on the tall man now striding determinedly down the aisle. Under his breath, the Kid muttered, "Where the hell are my raiders?" Then frantically, "My gun, damn you, Mollie. Hurry!"

Mollie swooped down, snatched up the pistol and, trembling with emotion, gripped it with both hands, raised it, and pointed it straight at the Kid.

"Don't do it, sweetheart," Lew cautioned in that soft, low voice, his eyes riveted to the Kid. "You and the padre go on into the vestry. But see that the padre doesn't leave, Mollie. We'll need him."

"Yes! Yes, Lew," Mollie said, laughing and crying at once. "Yes, my darling, yes."

"Yes?" echoed the Kid dumbly, his eyes nervously darting back and forth between Lew and Mollie. "Shoot the bastard, Mollie! What are you waiting for?" There was a growing edge of panic in his voice. "Mollie, honey, help me. Hatton's going to kill me!"

But Mollie was already leading the frightened padre toward the back door as Lew slowly, surely advanced on the terrified Kid.

"Look here, Hatton," the Kid said, lifting his hands high, "can't we settle this? The girl doesn't mean anything to me. You want her? Take her and I'll—"

"It's you I want, Kid." Lew moved closer, his face hard, his eyes murderous.

"Me?" The Kid's voice had lifted an octave. "I . . . I haven't done anything. I haven't touched her. Ask her, just ask her." He smiled nervously, hopefully.

"This goes back to before Mollie."

The Kid swallowed hard. "I tell you, Hatton, I haven't done anything! Not a thing. Surely you can't hold your old man's death against me." He laughed uneasily and shook his head. "After all, it was war. You must have killed a few men yourself back then. Hell, we all did, on both sides." He again swallowed convulsively as Lew's cold stare went to his lobeless ear. The Kid's fingers automatically went to that ear.

"Let's step outside, Kid," said Lew, his icy stare returning to the Kid's fear-paled face.

"Hatton, this can be settled right here. There's—"

"No, it can't. I will not desecrate this holy place with the blood of a rapist and murderer."

At the word *rapist,* the Kid's jaw went slack and he began to shake.

"Move it," Lew commanded, and the petrified Kid reluctantly walked up the aisle.

Which woman? Which rape? His troubled mind raced as he reached the open church door and stepped, blinking, out into the sunlight. Expectantly, he looked around, searching the small plaza, the empty street.

"Lose something?" asked Lew, his voice as calm and cold as ever. "If it's your boys you're hunting, you won't find them."

The Kid's head whipped around. "They'll kill you, Hatton! All I have to do is give the command." He wanted to believe that it was true. Hoped it was true. Surely, any second now one of his men would put a well-aimed bullet through Hatton's heart.

"Ever spend any time around the Apache?" asked Lew, conversationally. "Nobody quieter than an Apache. He can sneak right up on a man and slit his throat before you could blink your eyes."

The Kid felt a terrible sinking feeling in the pit of his gut. But he tried to sound confident when he said, "Hasn't been any Apaches around here for—"

"You're wrong, Kid. Dead wrong. There's an even dozen Apaches in San Carlos right now, entertaining your boys."

"You're bluffing, Hatton," said the Kid, fighting his paralyzing terror.

"Am I? Call them. Invite them to join us."

The Kid swallowed twice and shouted anxiously, "Cuchillo! José! Roberto!" He continued to call to his absent men, his voice echoing through the quiet street. Louder and Louder he shouted, near tears, pleading, begging for help.

No answer.

"You won't get away with it," the Kid said, trying a different tack. "The marshal will—"

"—thank me for cleaning up his town. Eight to five says you've been bragging ever since you got here how the law's afraid to bother you."

The Kid stumbled and almost fell. It was true. From the minute they had ridden into San Carlos, he'd had his men put out the word that anybody—including the marshal and his deputy—who gave them any trouble would end up in the cemetery beside the old mission.

"It's you and me, Kid," taunted Lew. "Stop walking when you reach that stand of cottonwoods just beyond the cemetery."

"Goddamn it, Hatton, what is it?" The Kid glanced over his shoulder. "The price on my head? You looking for money?" They reached the stand of cottonwoods. "I got plenty. Gold. Enough gold to make you rich. Let's go to the—"

"That's far enough," Lew said as the Kid stepped beneath a tall cottonwood. "Turn around."

The Kid spun around. "Tell me what you want from me!"

"Your life," said Lew, a muscle clenching tightly in his tanned jaw. "I figure I owe you four shots, Kid." He raised his gun, took aim, pulled the trigger. The Kid screamed with fear and pain when the bullet grazed his collarbone and glanced off. "That one," drawled Lew, unmoved, "was for the bullet you put in my left shoulder."

Tears filling his eyes as he clutched at his bloody shirt-front, the Kid sputtered, "Okay! Okay! We're even."

"Not quite."

"Jesus God, you're crazy," ranted the Kid, turning to run, sobbing like a baby now.

A second shot rang out. The Kid fell to the ground as the bullet pierced his right thigh just above the knee. Lew resolutely advanced on him.

Standing over the wounded Kid, Lew said levelly, "That one was for my father, William Hatton. You shot him in the back three months after the war had ended. He was unarmed."

"Please, please," whimpered the Kid. "I'm sorry, I'm sorry."

"Are you? Are you sorry about Dan Nighthorse as well? Stand up."

Blubbering, his big body jerking uncontrollably, the Kid struggled up, favoring his wounded right leg and wiping his nose on the back of his hand. "I . . . I don't know what you're talking about. I never . . ."

A bullet shattered his ribs and exited his back, causing the words to die instantly on his lips.

"Let me refresh your memory. You murdered my brother while holding up a stage in Bernalillo, New Mexico a few years back. Remember? A half-breed riding shotgun behind the stage?"

"It wasn't my fault!" the Kid frantically pleaded his case. "I never meant to—"

Cutting him off, Lew said, "Know what Dan Nighthorse was guarding, Kid?"

Tears streaming down his bearded face, sweat and blood staining his clothes, the Kid, realizing that he was not yet mortally wounded, cried, "Please! You've paid me back for everything! Now let me go!"

"I asked you a question. Do you know what my brother was guarding that day?"

Babbling foolishly, the Kid said, "Gold, but I—"

"Something far more precious than gold. An innocent young woman. Teresa Castillo." Lew paused, then added, *"Mi tesoro."*

"Oh . . . m-my G . . . no, God, no!" the Kid stuttered as the indelible sight of the beautiful young Spanish girl's tear-stained face as he raped her flashed before his eyes. "No! I never—"

"Lower your trousers, Kid," said Lew, his voice still soft, calm.

The Kid screeched like a banshee and violently shook his head, hysteria overtaking him. "No, no, no!" he wailed, "you've got it wrong. It wasn't rape at all. She made me do it! She wanted it and I—"

"Let's see what she wanted, Kid. Skin 'em down."

"Holy God!" wept the Kid, as his trembling, bloodied fingers went to the buttons of his pants. Bawling like a baby, he dropped his trousers to the ground and stood, trembling like a leaf in the wind with his big hands protectively closed over his naked groin.

"Hands on your head, Kid," ordered Lew. Sobs ripped from the Kid's aching throat, but he obeyed. Lew aimed his pistol downward.

"You wouldn't!" screamed the horrified Kid.

"Yes, I would."

For a long, tense moment Lew trembled almost as violently as the man standing before him. Perspiration dotted his upper lip. His trigger finger was slippery with sweat. His heart pounded heavily in his chest.

He cocked the hammer.

"Raise 'em high, *amigo*," came a Spanish-accented voice from just behind Lew and Lew felt the steel barrel of a gun poking his back. Lew raised his good right hand. The gun was taken from his fingers and a voice he recognized as Gilberto Perez's said, "He is mine now. Your bride awaits you."

Lew turned, nodded, and holstered the revolver Perez handed back to him. The Kid, blinking back tears, attempting to make out which one of his men had come to help, gurgled gratefully. "Thank God, thank God." Slobbering, his nose running, he bent to pick up his pants, saying, "Shoot Hatton! Shoot the bastard!"

"Kid, meet Gilberto Perez," Lew said evenly, "I believe you know Gilberto's wife. Petra Perez."

The Kid dropped the pants, straightened, looked into the mean black eyes fastened on him and sobbed, "Noooo!"

Gilberto Perez swiftly drew a knife from the waist-band of his black charro pants. The knife's long blade flashed in the brilliant sunshine and the Texas Kid, choking with fear, grabbed his crotch and fell to his knees, realizing that a horror far worse than death was in store for him.

"He's all yours, *amigo*," Lew said to Gilberto Perez, turned, and walked away.

"Padre, you came here to perform a wedding ceremony. Please continue," said Lew minutes later, as he stood in the mission before the confused priest with a smiling, relieved Mollie at his side.

"Yes, Father," said Mollie, happily. "This is the only man I ever meant to marry." She laid a gentle hand on Lew's bandaged shoulder.

The puzzled padre shook his head, sighed, raised his Bible, and began again, "Do you, Mollie Louise

Rogers. . . ." And within five minutes, he said with a note of relief in his tone, "I now pronounce you man and wife. You may kiss—"

Lew swept Mollie into his good right arm and kissed her long and lovingly. Then, laughing like two carefree children, they hurried up the aisle and outside to the big white steed tethered there. The beaming groom set the blushing bride atop the pawing stallion and swung up behind her.

The newlyweds rode away in the noonday sun with Mollie saying, "I love you, Lew. Soooo much."

"I love you, sweetheart. And there's not even a hotel in San Carlos," Lew lamented as the horse cantered down the dusty street.

"Since when have we needed a hotel?" asked his bride, kissing his handsome, suntanned face and laughing.

Lew laughed too. "I thought now that you're a respectable married lady you would—"

"You thought no such thing." She glanced at the makeshift sling supporting his wounded left arm. "Is your shoulder all right? Can you . . . ah . . . ?"

"Make love to my beautiful bride? Try me, baby."

"Oh, I intend to. Let's see . . . there's an abandoned gambling hall on the river, two miles south of San Carlos."

"I don't know." He glanced at her, grinned. "You might insist on playing faro all afternoon."

She hugged him happily. "No, but the dice table's still in place. Big solid table. Soft green felt covering it. Make a perfect bed."

"God, I love you, Mollie Rogers Hatton."

"Then hurry."

Lew kicked the stallion into a gallop.

FOR THE FINEST IN
WESTERN HISTORICAL ROMANCE

HONEYSUCKLE DeVINE by Susan Macias

To collect her inheritance, Laura Cannon needs to join Jesse Travers's cattle drive—and become his wife. The match is only temporary, but long days on the trail lead to nights filled with fiery passion.

TEXAS LONESOME by Alice Duncan

In 1890s San Francisco, Emily von Plotz gives advice to the lovelorn in her weekly newspaper column. A reader who calls himself "Texas Lonesome" seems to be the man for her, but wealthy rancher Will Tate is more than willing to show her who the real expert is in matters of the heart.

THE BRIDE WORE SPURS by Sharon Ihle

Arriving in Wyoming as a mail-order bride, Kathleen O'Carroll is shocked to learn that her would-be husband, John Winterhawke, hasn't actually ordered her. Kathleen is determined to win over the fiercely handsome half-Indian, and claim his wild heart on her own terms.